A Deadly Reunion

Jordan Logue

Jordan Logue

Disclaimer

This is a work of fiction. Some of the things in this story happened. There was a War Between the States. Immaculate Conception Church was sacked by Union Soldiers. I don't know what, if anything, was stolen. The United Confederate Veterans did hold a reunion in Jacksonville in 1914. I don't know if anyone was murdered or got sick with dysentery. I use these historical events as a framework to tell a story that is entirely fiction.

Dedication

This is dedicated to orphans, veterans, priests, nuns and detectives everywhere.

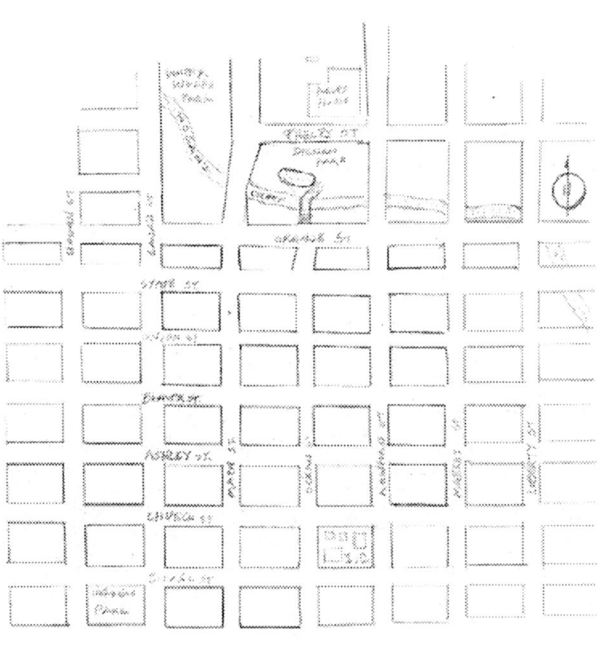

March 28, 1863.

Jacksonville, Florida

Captain Thomas W. Higginson, in command of the 1st South Carolina Loyal Volunteers, a group of black soldiers recruited to fight for the Union, had been put in charge of all Union occupation forces in Jacksonville, Florida. As he was finishing his coffee in the riverfront warehouse that he had converted into his headquarters, four Union boats pulled up to the wharves. Higginson assumed they were carrying enough troops that they could maintain their current hold on the city and push south along the river and westward inland, to rid the state of Confederate forces and recruit more freed blacks to join the Union cause. Instead, it conveyed orders quite to the contrary: "Abandon all East Florida operations and the occupation of Jacksonville. All men are to board the steamer Boston for immediate transport to operations in the port of Charleston, S.C. Any Union equipment and provisions that cannot be secured aboard Union vessels for removal must be destroyed."

Word of this had already made its way out, as the troops were setting fire to anything they could on their way to the docks. "Why?" Higginson wondered. A few bands of Confederate guerrillas were causing some annoyance, and a small number of regulars were encamped eight miles to the west. With a little effort, they could all be repulsed and the entire state claimed for the Union. But it made no difference. He knew better than to question orders. He said to his lieutenants, "Give the orders. Get the men to the docks and begin boarding. Then set fire to the building." There was nothing of any value. Just piles of random items that they had looted from somewhere in Jacksonville. He could think of no particular reason to salvage much. The Connecticut Rifles were the last Union detachment to stárt toward the riverfront. They tried setting fire to every building they passed. Several of them would check inside first, to see what portable and pocket-sized valuables might be purloined.

Sergeant Bryant and his ragtag Confederate picket force had been camped in a dense thicket along the upper reaches of McCoys Creek. It was a volunteer militia raised by him after he was separated from his regulars, and they had nothing that would pass for uniforms, and precious little ammunition left. His network of spies and informants got word of the evacuation to him shortly after Higginson had received the orders himself. They quickly boarded their makeshift barges and began poling their way downstream. As the western edge of town came into view, Jake Souder, one of his informants who convincingly played the dual roles of town drunk and harmless village idiot, appeared on the bank.

"They settin' fire to everything. They's a-lootin' stores and churches and taking all they can carry."

"Where's Delwyn?"

"They been hiding up along Longbranch Creek. He be a-coming in from the north."

Bryant split the company into groups of two and three and sent them into town to see what was happening. "Try to stay out of sight. If they's a-leaving, leave 'em go. We can't match their firepower, so let's just concentrate on gettin' the town back and the fires under control. I'll get word out to Camp Finegan."

Alden James and two others managed to find their way into town and sneaked up the back stairs of an abandoned rooming house on Ocean Street. They watched as a few Union soldiers broke windows and kicked in doors, trying to start fires. If any of them had been just a little less drunk than they were, they might have had more success. He saw one man come out the side door of the Immaculate Conception Catholic Church with an armful of assorted religious items — candlesticks, crosses, prayer books and rosary beads. He spread out a linen altar cloth, bundled everything up in it and tied that to a six-foot-long staff with a gold crucifix at its top, and headed down the street like an old hobo with his belongings swinging from a pole over his shoulder.

Another man emerged, trying to catch up to him. He was drunk on altar wine and fully dressed out in priestly vestments over his uniform. He called to his compatriot. “Hey! Bring me some of that hardtack and let me see if I can turn it into something we can eat. Now that would be a goddam miracle!” The two whooped with laughter, then a third appeared dressed in the black cassock and white surplice of an altar boy and carrying a case of sacramental wine. James was not a Catholic, but even a born-again Southern Baptist like him could barely observe this devilry without weeping. Sergeant Bryant found them and watched from the window, too.

“James! You and Coffey and Townsend follow that bunch and try to recover those items. Shouldn’t be too hard. They seem pretty drunk. Just try to roll them and get the stuff back, don’t waste a bullet on them unless you have to. I’m going to set up temporary headquarters right here. Let me know what happens and bring back whatever you can recover."

The three Confederate soldiers cut through alleyways behind the smoldering, abandoned buildings until they got a block ahead of the drunken looters. James stood in the doorway of what had once been a tavern and rooming house. As he saw the three men stumbling down the middle of the street, he said, "Hey, you guys going to keep drinking that grape juice or do you want some real whiskey? I got six or seven bottles of good stuff in here that somebody left. We can't carry it all. Come and get some." As proof of his claim, he held up a couple of glass bottles — bottles he and his buddies had urinated in and corked. The three Union men were suspicious, but the temptation of real whiskey got the better of them. They stepped into the abandoned tavern. The man wearing the priest's vestments was clearly the leader. He was also considerably drunker than the other two.

"Lemme see that!" he barked at James. He sniffed at it, then held it up high, as though inspecting it for impurities. George Townsend was standing on the second step of the staircase, so the Yankee looked up, right into his eyes for a couple of seconds before his head was shattered by the heavy oak newel post that Townsend had removed from the banister. Weldon Beauchamp, of the 96th Connecticut Rifles, would not wake for several days. But he would never forget the last two faces he saw before he blacked out — George Townsend and Alden James. The other two Yankee soldiers dropped the loot they were carrying and ran before they could suffer the same fate.

Coffey, Townsend and James inspected the bundles that the men had taken from the church and found an assortment of fancy religious items. Several gold crosses, candlestick holders, little gold plates, rosaries made of gold chains and precious gems, assorted rings and trinkets that none of them could identify. When they pulled back the vestments that the ringleader was wearing, they found a gold chalice, encrusted with diamonds, rubies and emeralds, strapped under his belt.

Private Coffey took the leadership role. "Well, it looks to me like the only things worth keeping are these crosses, them beads and rings, and that fancy drinking cup. Towney, you take the rings and beads, I'll take the crosses, and Alden, you take that goblet. The rest of it we'll bundle back up and take to the sergeant. Tell him this was all we could find. Take the robes offa him, too, and we'll throw them in with the rest of the stuff."

"I don't want that thing," Alden James protested. "I don't want any of this stuff. I want nothing to do with any of it!" James stared at the chalice. It was beautiful and frightening at the same time. Bright, gleaming gold, mounted with jewels, and colorful enamel. Around the base, rectangular diamonds alternated with square-cut sapphires. On the bowl, red rubies, shaped as droplets of blood, surrounded by tiny diamonds, dripped from the rim. On each compass point of the bowl, six large diamonds formed a cross, a circle of green emeralds creating a halo where the two axes crossed.

"Oh, hell, James, you scared of this stuff, are ya? Listen, we all got to be together in this. This stuff was already stole, so you ain't really doing nothing wrong. Take it home with you as a souvenir. Everybody's got war loot that they's a-bringin' home with them. We just hit the jackpot is all. That thing looks valuable. If you fall on hard times down the road sometime, you can pry some of them rubies and diamonds offa there and sell them for some real money. Now don't you let your conscience get in the way of me and him harvesting some battle bounty."

They bundled up the remaining items and returned to the rooming house where the sergeant had set up his temporary headquarters. James had taken the chalice and wrapped it up in some old rags and stowed it in his knapsack.

Chapter 1

"All right, all right. Everybody get back to your seats and let's get some work done." Council President Jimmie Calton called the meeting to order, banging a gavel several times. The Jacksonville City Council had disposed of all the usual business on their agenda for the first meeting in January, 1914. They were taking a break before tackling the special agenda, which entailed reviewing the work of the various committees planning the 1914 Confederate Veterans Reunion that would be held in May. During the refreshment break, Charles Davidson, Commander of the R.E. Lee Camp, United Confederate Veterans, had given councilmembers large ceramic coffee mugs, with their names and the official Camp badge on them. They were all quite proud to sip coffee from such magnificent mugs.

The Council Chamber was filled with sound of shuffling feet and quiet talk as people made their way back to their seats. As Council President, Calton held an important seat in the complicated municipal morass under which Jacksonville struggled toward progress. And he used it well to his advantage. He could have moved right into the business of the agenda, but like most politicians, he viewed any gathering of people as an assembly of his adoring public, anxious to hear his every word, and he would not disappoint them. He spoke softly, with a natural drawl, slightly nasal and a little high-pitched.

"Just to let everybody know, this is the first in a series of meetings, the purpose of which is to prepare for the Confederate Veterans Reunion which will take place in May of this year." He clipped the middle syllable out of *veterans* — *vet'rans.* "And just so's you don't go thinking this is just a bunch of bake sales and ladies' teas, this reunion is a big deal. We have had us a clutch of committees and volunteers working on this for months, and now we begin the process of them reporting to us so that we can take whatever official acts as may be necessary to keep this thing moving along." He did the same thing with *necessary* — it came out *necess'ry*. He had perfected the politician's persona — that of a non-politician. He spoke loud enough to be heard, but soft enough that you had to stop and pay attention if you were going to hear him. This persona clashed with his natural look. His thin, almost wispy mustache contrasted rather unpleasantly with his pasty white complexion, causing him to look like an adolescent boy trying to grow facial hair before his hormones were quite ready to cooperate. Cheeks that turned apple pink upon the slightest physical exertion made it appear that he was forever at the end of a fraying rope of frustration. Aware that this was no look for a leader, Jimmie's wife, who had spent some time in the theater in New York, had concocted a foundation that he could apply to his face that gave just the slightest hint of tan, and hid the embarrassing pinking of his cheeks. Clipping and waxing the flimsy growth on his upper lip gave the impression of a mustache. It was a great deal of work to maintain the fiction of handsome leadership. An unexpected rainstorm could cause a veritable mudslide on his visage. An afternoon roll in the sheets with a prostitute called for complete facial reconstruction before he could re-enter polite society.

"And, let me say what an honor I think it is that the United

Confederate Veterans has chosen Jacksonville as the site for their 24th annual reunion. We all know that Florida was one of the earliest states to enter an ordinance of secession, and hosting the reunion is our way of honoring those brave men who answered the call to fight for our independence. It will also be nice to follow a winter full of Yankees with a springtime of courtly Southerners.

"Over the next several weeks, we will hear from various committees presenting their plans to us. Some of these may require that we appropriate some funds, pass some temporary ordinances, or expedite a project here and there. Now, the State Legislature has very generously appropriated some funds to help us with some of the expenses of this upcoming event, and we have to come up with an equal share. We can meet that share with cold hard cash or — my preference — we meet as much of it as we can with in-kind services. That takes a right talented bit of bookkeeping, but I think we got enough pencil-sharpeners and paper-pushers on the city payroll to meet the challenge. The Board of Trade is raising some money and we can count that, but the rest of it is all our responsibility.

"Our distinguished mayor has submitted to us a list of expenditures that he wants to make." He held up several sheets of paper, grasped by the corner as if there were something contemptible about the pages themselves. "We will give it due consideration, but he has to be reminded every now and then of the proper roles and responsibilities. The mayor and commissioners spend their days dreaming up ways to spend money, but it is left to us, the Council, to appropriate the funds. And that means that we have to take it from hard-working men. Not something to which I give lightweight consideration." He emphasized the 'I' as if he were the only soul on Earth concerned with the earnings of hard-working people. "With all that in mind, I call upon the Honorable Commissioner Tad Ferguson, the city Finance Commissioner, who also chairs the reunion steering committee for the city, to give us a report. Thank you for coming, Commissioner Ferguson. It is not often that we get commissioners willing to come to the Council in a spirit of cooperation such as this. Commissioner?"

Tad Ferguson was a large man, generally round in every dimension. Most politicians had a trademark look that their constituency associated with them. It might be a certain kind of feather in the hat band, or special cufflinks that stood out, a boutonnière always present in the lapel. Ferguson did not need to create a trademark; he was born with one — excessive sweat. Always and heavily. Regardless of the weather or any other external factor, his face constantly streamed sweat. To hide the underarm stains on his shirts, he always wore a coat, which made him sweat more. But his biggest onus as a politician was sweaty hands. He kept a tiny satin pillow, filled with a mixture of cornstarch, talcum powder and pine rosin, in his coat pocket. He always stuck his right hand in there to dry it immediately before shaking hands with anybody.

"Thank you, Mr. Council President." Ferguson spoke fast. Not fast like he was impatient, but fast like he was afraid people would stop paying attention to what he was saying before he finished saying it. "Speaking just for myself, I am absolutely delighted to be working with the Council and the various committees planning this event. I hope we can find more events like this that can bring out the cooperative nature in us all. Let me first report to you on the efforts of the visitors committee. We estimate that the number of actual veterans who will attend the reunion to be somewhere in the neighborhood of between 5,000 and 8,000." He slowed down and repeated the words 5,000 and 8,000 to make sure the impact of the numbers was realized. "We expect that many of these may be accompanied by family members and guests. We have encouraged them to do that and stay on a few extra days and make a holiday of it. Some folks may not understand that this is not only the Confederate Veterans Reunion, but simultaneous with it is the annual meeting of affiliated organizations, the Sons of Confederate Veterans, the United Daughters of the Confederacy, and the Confederate Memorial Association. So the total number of visitors could be around 8,000 to 12,000 people. The visitors committee has a quite impressive list of families who will open their homes to provide bed and board for some of these veterans, since the projected attendance will no doubt exceed the amount of hotel lodgings that are available. I would like to personally thank all of these kind people and hope that the Council will see fit to present each family who volunteers with a Certificate of Appreciation." *Here-heres* and *harrumphs* briefly filled the air. "A great many of the old veterans will travel with their individual camps in their home towns and set up camp here. I have worked with the Recreation Department to dedicate all of Springfield Park, the Waterworks Park and Dignan Park for the camping and other reunion activities. I had one of the draftsmen in the engineer's office draw y'all a map of the parks and where the mess tent will go, the medical tent, the different camping areas and the latrines and so forth. It's all there in the materials in front of you."

"Mr. Ferguson," Council President Calton addressed the speaker, "is there a way that you can tally up those rooms in private homes and find an average cost for lodgings and count that as an in-kind service to meet our state match?"

"I can do all the 'rithmetic you want, Mr. President, but trying to qualify that as an in-kind expenditure on the part of the city may be a stretch, sir."

"Fair enough, sir. Just thought I would inquire. Proceed."

"Our second biggest concerns are the safety and health of our visitors. I will say that the State Board of Health has offered its full cooperation, inspecting for proper drainage and sanitary facilities, and they are welcome so long as they don't start demanding things of us that are unreasonable, and I don't think they will. The state wants this to be successful just as much as we do. Now, speaking of the safety of our visitors, I would like to ask Police Chief Luther Wilson to address some issues for you." Ferguson sat down and the police chief rose and approached the speaker's podium. A handsome and imposing figure, clean-shaven and well-groomed, he had the booming voice of a revival preacher, tempered with the demeanor of a college professor. His long, wavy brown hair touched the collar of his starched white shirt, over which he wore his best dress blue uniform, bedecked with polished brass buttons and gold braid for the occasion. Jimmie Calton wondered if the city had made the right decision in hiring Luther Wilson a year ago. His thoughts wandered, *"College-educated, brief military career, then a short time as a railroad detective. From a good South Carolina family whose money came from the textile industry. Spent some time in the business. A smart man, no doubt, but does all that make him the right police chief?"* But he was Mayor Langen's choice. The mayor had explained that the city was growing and needed someone who could manage the challenges of a growing metropolitan police department, not just someone who would schedule men to cover shifts. Wilson seemed to be the right man for that, but Calton had his occasional doubts. The chief stood at the podium, his hands clasped behind his back. He looked first one way, then slowly to the other. When everyone had endured complete silence for nearly a minute, he began.

"Pickpockets, con-men and prostitutes. Moonshiners, petty thieves and two-bit burglars. That, gentlemen, is what we can expect to flood this city, side-by-side with our veterans. Looking to enrich themselves and take advantage of these brave, aging war heroes, who fought for our cause more than 50 years ago. To keep such pestilence in check, I estimate that I will need at least 10 extra men on duty during the whole event, and another eight in reserve, trained and ready to go if the situation demands it. I can draw upon my supernumerary force for this purpose, as they meet all the necessary requirements. I will need to deploy these men for several days prior to the start of the event, and keep them on for the entire three-day duration. Depending on how many visitors choose to stay on a bit, I may need them for three or four days after the reunion. So at least five days, maybe up to 10. I will pay them eight dollars a day. Most of you know your times tables well enough to calculate that out. Now, if these extra men perform as they have been trained, I suspect that the jail will be at or over its normal capacity, and I may need another $5 or $10 to buy grits, flour and salt pork to feed the extra prisoners. Depending on how much we have to use the reserve men, this is likely to cost us a couple of thousand dollars."

The chief stood there and allowed the moment of silence to punctuate his message before he returned to his seat and Ferguson rose to speak again. "A couple of thousand dollars is surely not too much to provide the kind of police protection needed for so important an event as this, now, is it, gentlemen? And there are other safety issues as well. The parks will become not only campgrounds, but focal points of many of the activities. I will rely on the State Board of Health, as I said before, to assure that drainage and sanitation issues are addressed. But there will be other fire and safety regulations that must be rigorously enforced. There is a high probability of accidents. Not only with automobiles, carts and wagons, but all those men and their campfires, well, the scene could turn ugly. I don't know that our fire protection system has been examined with a critical eye since it was modernized right after the big fire in nineteen and one. So I am asking for the authorization to spend up to $500 to inventory and assess the readiness and capability of our fire suppression assets."

"Does this mean you going to pay your cousin $200 to go out and count the fire plugs again?" Councilman Willie Doss spoke without waiting to be recognized by the chair. Willie was one of the more vocal and less-refined members of the Council, often interrupting with points of order that could not be found in any parliamentary handbook. Calton had worked hard to get Willie elected to the Council, mistakenly thinking that the yokel was just the right balance between stupid and gullible to be an easily controlled part of his team. But Willie turned out to be so stupid that he didn't even know his own mind. It was Calton's cross to bear, but not for long. He would put Willie's stupidity on public display often enough that replacing him in the next election would be easy.

"That is an integral part of an inventory of fire suppression assets, sir," responded Ferguson. "But if you want us to leave your district out of the count, we can oblige. It appears you don't care what burns on the Eastside, anyway." He was referring to a recent mysterious fire that had destroyed a warehouse that was in competition with one of Doss' financial supporters.

"Now, don't you go telling lies that you don't know is true," said Willie.

"That don't even make sense, Willie," said the commissioner.

"All right, you two, save your battles for another time. I would like to get through with this," said Calton. "Now, if you're finished, we can move on to hear from some others. Gentlemen, I have asked Hank Clark to attend our meeting today. Hank is not a member of any of these committees, but he is Commissioner of Roads and Bridges for the city and, as such, probably has some expertise that is not bestowed upon the many knowledgeable folks who are volunteering their time to serve on these various committees. Hank, would you please shower us with your wisdom and knowledge?" Several folks stifled chuckles, some more successfully than others.

The evolution of municipal government had reached a point that it allowed for as much theater as governance. The Charter called for a City Council with members elected from nine districts. The council was the legislative body which set the tax rates throughout the city, adopted the annual budget, and saw to other legislative duties, such as making certain unsavory behavior illegal and prescribing appropriate punishment for those who transgressed. There was also a City Commission comprising five members, elected citywide, to serve in executive capacities over departments of the city government. It was hard to say which of the two bodies lent itself more easily than the other to corruption, but both seemed adept at finding ways to lighten the public treasury. The problem was that councilmembers needed cooperative commissioners if their schemes of personal enrichment were to be fruitful. Commissioners needed councilmembers to mind their own business if they wished to prosper. If everybody had to have a share, then each share was inevitably smaller, creating a natural friction between the individual members of the two bodies. As long as the public perceived them as always feuding with one another, they would never think that any of them were getting away with much. Politicians in Jacksonville relied heavily on this perception.

"Thank you, Mr. President and members of the council." Hank Clark was an aloof but likable man. He did not go around smiling, shaking hands and slapping backs. He was pleasant, just not overtly so. Clark had correctly surmised that voters would tolerate a level of political shenanigans almost everywhere but in the area of roads, bridges and sewers. Keeping roads smooth and shit flowing downstream was important, and Hank Clark acted important. He always spoke directly and matter-of-factly about what he can do, and had done, rather than bemoan what he could not do. "I have been invited here to tell you some things that I am going to be doing to prepare for the reunion. I have no mind of asking you for any funds. I am quite capable of squeezing some extra work out of my folks, and some of the companies that do business with the city, such that I can absorb some of these expenses in the budget that y'all have already approved." As he spoke, he occasionally looked down at some papers in his hand, but he never made eye contact with anyone on the dais. He looked over their heads, to the side, or down, but never directly at them.

"Point of order, Mr. President?" Willie Doss interrupted again. "Just because he has the money in his department don't mean he can just go and spend it any ol' how he wants. We approved that budget based on the line items of things that was in it, and he can't go spending it on something that we did not approve. Am I right?"

"Aww, pipe down, Willie," said Jimmie Calton. "These are somewhat special circumstances, and I recall we were a might stingy this year on budgets. Let's hear what he has to say before we go jumping all in his business. Proceed, Commissioner Clark."

"Thank you, sir. Gentlemen, this upcoming event is going to put a stress upon our roads and bridges unlike what we ordinarily experience. Oh, I know we get an extra 10,000 or 20,000 people in here every winter in the way of Yankee tourists, but this is going to be a little different. They will all be here at one time, unlike the Yankees who flutter in and out like snowbirds all winter long. Fortunately, the Road and Bridges Department, under my leadership, has always kept the roads and bridges in tip-top shape. Nevertheless,

I have taken it upon myself to conduct an inspection of the bridges that I think may be at some risk of failure.

"Since most of the activity will be concentrated around Dignan Park and Springfield Park, and the waterworks, I have focused my attentions on the roads that cross Hogans Creek. As I am sure you gentlemen know, these parks do double duty. They are not only recreational in nature, but allow us to do some very effective flood control using the creek's own flood plain. Over the years, through some very sophisticated public works projects, we have dredged and channelized the creek, and built concrete embankments to keep it from flooding. However, we all know that nature will have her way when she wants to, and the parks on either side of the creek are a way of giving relief when the embankment structures are overwhelmed. Now, just after the creek passes under Main Street, the topography and elevation change. In a mild rainstorm, the floodwaters that the creek cannot handle are discharged into the pond there. The island in the middle of that pond is the spoil from the dredging the creek to keep it flowing, an improvement made back during the yellow fever days. The parks themselves are not my responsibility. They come under the domain of our honorable mayor, but the roads and bridges are mine.

"I can offer assurances that the roads through the park and the bridges over the creek will be in good repair for the reunion. What I cannot guarantee is any cooperation from the weather. If we get a hard rain just before or during the reunion, the entire area will be unusable for the reunion due to flooding."

"Well, now, wait a minute." It was Councilman Doss again. "It seems to me that for as long as I can recollect, we been talking about getting that park to where it don't flood."

"That may be, sir. But talk does not stop flooding. My job is to keep the bridges in good repair. Whether the creek floods or not, my bridges will hold."

"But we have gotten money from the State Lands Improvement Fund, and I think our friends in Washington have even contributed some."

"Councilman, if you have received money for an improvement project, it is your job to approve the project and appropriate the funds. The parks come under the mayor, and those floodwaters go under my bridges. Perhaps the councilman needs to study the organizational charts a bit more closely."

"Mr. President! We cannot allow such impertinent testimony from a commissioner!" Voices were being raised, and the specter of an assault titillated the audience.

"You're both right," responded the council president with enough diplomacy to calm nerves. "Commissioner Clark, I must caution you against any personal remarks aimed at any individual member of the Council. On the other hand, Councilman Doss, this is not the time to go flying off the handle about flood control projects. That is an issue to take up with the mayor. Now, Commissioner Clark, you may continue with your report, and please do so hastily." Calton left the room briefly so he could check his face in his compact's mirror. His intervention between Willie Doss and the commissioners had caused some exertion and he wanted to make sure that his face was holding up to the pressure.

"Yessir. Thank you. Main Street has always, and will continue to bear most of the traffic load. This bridge is in excellent shape as borne out by a recent inspection by the state road department, and engineers the city hired. To the west of Main Street, we have bridges at Laura Street, Pearl Street and Broad Street. In addition, there are several pedestrian bridges throughout the park. Then, there are smaller bridges at Sixth Street and Eighth Street. The Laura Street bridge was rebuilt after the fire 13 years ago and is in good shape, but detailed inspections of all bridges will be done. Moving to the east of Main, we have Hubbard Street, Market Street and Liberty Street. From my understanding, this section of the park is where most of the camping activities will be concentrated; thus, I expect a lot of traffic. So our highest priority will be to inspect these bridges from underneath and whatever repairs or reinforcements are needed will be made from a barge below the bridge. I have hired Butch Warren, one of the most respected bridge engineers around, to undertake this. Butch is very familiar with all of these bridges, having served as supervising consultant on all of them. He and his crew will be up and down Hogan's Creek on a narrow barge, tending to all this work right up to the start of the reunion. All of this will be done at minimal cost to the city, and if there is any significant expense, I have a reserve fund that I can use — and Willie, you got nothing to say about how I use my reserve funds."

"What about the pedestrian bridges?" asked the president.

"There are several pedestrian bridges that cross Hogan's Creek. In Dignan Park, there are two pedestrian bridges out to the island in the center of the pond. These pedestrian bridges, gentlemen, are part of the recreation department's responsibility. I will inspect and service these bridges, but then y'all will have to transfer funds to my department from the recreation department."

"Can't the parks commissioner go and hire his own bridge inspector?" asked the curious Councilman Doss.

"That would be inadvisable, Councilman. I have the best bridge engineer around under contract to me. It would make much more sense to add it to my contract than to have another city department start all over negotiating a deal. Besides, you don't want too many different companies doing these inspections. You lose consistency in standards. But that is up to you."

"Well, thank you, Commissioner Clark," said Calton. "I am sure we are all grateful for your expertise and your dedication. We'll make sure the funds get to the right place. And if there are other expenses, we would like an accounting of them, so we can show it as part of the in-kind match to the state."

"If there is any expense, I will share that information with you." As if to demonstrate that the Roads and Bridges Commissioner is far too important to listen to City Council business, much less mere citizens committee reports, Hank Clark left Council Chambers without so much as a handshake or a backslap, those two most important physical functions of a politician. He made only one stop — to chat briefly with Finance Commissioner Tad Ferguson, who handed him a small, thick envelope and whispered, "Here's a little something for you to add to your stamp collection, Hank."

"Now, gentlemen, I believe that we now have the privilege of hearing from Miss Dolly Tanner, the current social secretary of the local United Daughters of the Confederacy. Miz Tanner."

All nine of the men on the city council stood and smiled at Dolly Tanner, stunning beauty and great-granddaughter of Colonel Miles Tanner, who commanded the Jacksonville Light Infantry Brigade and took credit for forcing the lice-ridden Yankee vermin from Jacksonville several times. Whether or not he actually did was a bit of historical trivia that no one bothered to investigate and confirm.

"Thank you, Mister Jimmie. And thank all of you for allowing the Daughters to play a role in this wonderful reunion. We are going to move our Annual Confederate Ball from the fall to the spring this year, so that it will coincide with this event. As you know, the Ball raises money for some important causes that the Daughters support, such as the Soldiers and Sailors Home, and maintenance of several of the memorials around town. I think I can safely say that outside of the tourist season, it is one of the most important and anticipated annual events we have here in Jacksonville. This year, it will not be a fundraiser, but rather an opportunity to honor our brave, old veterans. The ball will be held on Tuesday evening, the night before the official start of the reunion, in the auditorium of the Shrine Temple, and all Confederate veterans will be admitted at no charge. And not only that, but they will be able to choose from among Jacksonville's most beautiful young ladies for a dance. We intend to send these men back to their tents or rooms tired, and happy, and proud of the South." The here-heres, and harrumphs were augmented by a number of huzzahs and good shows, and nearly drowned out by applause and desk-pounding.

"I have a question of Miz Tanner if I may, Mr. President." Willie

Doss spoke up again, startling the other members by asking to be recognized before blurting out his usual nonsense.

"The Chair commends Mr. Doss for seeking recognition before speaking and gleefully grants him the floor for a question. Please proceed, sir."

"Now, Miz Tanner, putting on a fancy ball like you and the ladies is doing is certainly outside of my bailiwick, but I just have to ask why you would schedule it on the first night of the reunion? Wouldn't it be more in the tradition of such events to close the reunion with the fancy ball?"

"Well, thank you for that question, Mr. Doss. It is simply a matter of, uh, well, certain considerations that are important. As I explained, we have a bevy of lovely young ladies who have volunteered to be dance partners for any old veteran who would like. But these old men will have been sleeping in tents for three or four nights by the end of the reunion, and who knows what kind of hygiene and cleanliness practices they might be keeping. Our girls would prefer to dance with them sooner rather than later." She wrinkled her nose and gave a devilish grin all at the same time.

"Oh, yes. Well, I guess that makes good sense," said Willie as he looked back and forth across the dais in an attempt to judge the reactions of the other councilmember. Encountering expressions that revealed nothing, he said, "Thank you, Miz Tanner." After a moment of awkward silence, the company gently rumbled with a chorus of muffled laughter and snorts.

Jimmie Calton banged his gavel a few times to try to quiet down the small crowd in the Council Chambers. "Miz Tanner, thank you and the other Daughters for your valiant efforts. We have the greatest confidence that the ball will be a wonderful event, and you keep track of your expenses so we can submit them to the state. And if any of us can do anything to help, please let us know. Now, then, I think we have somebody from the R.E. Lee Camp of the United Confederate Veterans. Commander Davidson? The floor is yours, sir."

Charles Davidson, in full uniform, approached the speaker's podium, striding with the military bearing that befit a commander. Jimmie Calton barked "Atten-shun!" and all of the city councilmembers rose to attention and saluted as the commander reached the podium. Commander Davidson smiled and said, "Thank you, gentlemen, as you were." And they all sat back down. "The R.E. Lee Camp of the United Confederate Veterans is the host chapter for this year's reunion, gentlemen."

"Excuse me, Commander," interrupted Jimmie Calton.

"Yes, sir, Mr. President?"

"Before you begin, I just want to thank you from the bottom of my heart for this wonderful coffee mug you have presented to me and the other councilmembers here this morning. It will make my morning coffee ever so much more pleasant. And I think I speak for all of us here in saying that."

"Here, here."

"Indeed."

"Wonderful coffee mugs."

The interruption threw Commander Davidson off a little bit from his memorized script, but he soldiered on. "It is our privilege to present those to you. I'm glad you like them. Now, like I was saying, the R.E. Lee Camp of the United Confederate Veterans is the host chapter for this year's reunion, and let me say what an honor it is. First, I want to take just a moment to dispel some thoughts about our organization. Most folks know this, but I want to say it here for purposes of getting it in the public record. The United Confederate Veterans is an organization that is patterned on military lines and commanded from a headquarters through a system of military ranks. But we are not a military organization. We have a constitution that defines the social, literary, historical and benevolent purposes for which we exist. You should not expect any kind of an uprising from this gathering. And if there was one, given the average age of the veterans, it would be quelled with very little bother. I would reckon that the dance class at Miss Buckland's Arts Academy would have little trouble restoring order." He was briefly interrupted by polite laughter.

"But in all seriousness, gentlemen, I want to express our appreciation for all the hard work that has gone into this. And as far as attendance — it's always very difficult to predict. Eight years ago in Little Rock, they prepared for 25,000 and 106,000 showed up. I don't expect that will happen here, but one must always prepare. We've communicated with all the Camp Commanders, and for those who will be camping, certain areas have been assigned in Dignan Park. Most of the official business to be conducted concerning the United Confederate Veterans will be held in committees and plenary sessions at the Kirby Smith Camp Auditorium, which is a temporary structure that will be erected the week prior to the opening ceremonies. The auditorium has a wooden floor, a skeleton of heart pine lumber and walls of canvas. This has been used for several years and has served us well. Schematic diagrams and construction guidance have been in the hands of the city building inspector for a couple of weeks now, and I think he has some suggestions, but will allow it to be used. It will be erected on the grounds of the waterworks at First and Laura streets.

"The full schedule of activities is not yet complete, but when it is finalized, we shall certainly provide that to you. I can tell you that we have several very entertaining events planned that will be open to the public. As always, we have the bugling contest and the Rebel Yell contest. Several Camps have formed choirs and marching bands, and you'll get to see most of them in the opening day parade. And, of course, we are most grateful to Miz Dolly Tanner and the Daughters for their plans for the Confederate Ball. I can assure you that a lot of old men will be very grateful for the effort as well. Thank you, gentlemen."

The councilmembers again stood at attention as Commander Davidson returned to his seat. "All right, fellas, you've heard the reports. All the actions necessary — as far as appropriations, authorizations, resolutions and whatnot — are included in that big stack of material in front of you. I am open to a motion to approve," said Calton.

"Don't you think we ought to read through some of this?" asked Willie Doss, rummaging through several pages of official-looking documents.

"What for, Willie? You just heard it all explained."

"Well, it just seems like we ought to take the time to read it before we vote."

"Go ahead and read it, Willie. We'll all wait. Just let me know when you're done and everybody can get about their business."

Councilman Doss acquired an uncomfortable look on his face — he had not expected he'd be put on the spot. He donned a pair of spectacles and thumbed through the three-inch-thick stack of papers very quickly, pausing occasionally to study something in detail for three or four seconds, or to make his fellow legislators believe he was perusing the material thoroughly. Finally, he said, "Everything appears in good order, Mr. President. I move approval."

"Councilman Doss enthusiastically moves approval," said the council president. "Do I have a second?"

"Second," boomed an unidentified voice from somewhere on the dais.

"It has been moved by Mr. Doss and seconded. Anybody agin it? Seeing no objection, this here measure is passed and we are adjourned."

Chapter 2

Chief Luther Wilson had summoned the top brass of the Jacksonville Police Department to a meeting in his office. The top brass, consisting of two captains and four lieutenants, who kept the patrol shifts going, and guarded the prisoners in the city jail. Four detectives reported directly to the chief. He would meet with them later. Everybody in the police department had been a little nervous when Luther Wilson was hired to take the position of police chief, a little more than a year earlier. Bringing in an outsider for the top job surprised most folks, and they didn't know what to expect. And although he was decidedly a different personality than they had been accustomed to, they soon figured him out and accepted him as, if not one of their own, one they could well tolerate.

"Men, this is going to be a very delicate balancing act for us. There are going to be a lot of people, no doubt. I have authorization to bring in reserves, but we are going to have to be very diplomatic. These veterans deserve respect. Of that there is no doubt. However, we can't let them think Jacksonville is a lawless outpost where they can carry on drinking and chasing whores to their hearts' content. If any of them are well enough and well off enough to get down to Ward Street and take advantage of the offerings, that's their business. But I will not have ladies of ill repute immodestly dressed, prancing freely around Dignan Park. We will keep a high visibility of uniformed men on hand and, if necessary, we can bring in some Pinkerton Men to work undercover."

"Hire a Pinkerton Man to catch a whore? That ought to be fun to watch," one of his lieutenants sneered.

"Be careful of your remarks, Floyd. The Pinkerton organization is not one to be scoffed at. The other thing we need to watch for is moonshine liquor. I don't want to be the one denying an old war veteran a well-deserved drink of whiskey, but one of the benefits of this event is the economic boost to our merchants. If the old guys are drinking untaxed whiskey, that's a lot of money that we don't get. Plus, God only knows what kind of poison you get from some of these old 'shiners. We must all be on the lookout for that. So, instruct your men to be vigilant.

"Now, Captain, I want you to check all 86 emergency telephones and whatever emergency lights we still have in use and make sure everything is working. And I bet somebody will want to use our Cadillac in the opening parade. Make sure it's polished up and looking sharp. I don't know who's going to drive it, much less ride in it, but I want it to look good. Understood?"

"What about you, Chief? Don't you want to drive it?" asked another lieutenant. It was a poorly kept secret that Chief Wilson was not enamored of automobiles in general.

"That machine goes entirely too fast for my comfort. If the mayor insists that I drive him or some other dignitary in the parade, I might accommodate him. A parade is sort of a self-regulating mechanism as to speed. But you know that Cadillac automobile was a gift to the police department from the local dealer, and I won't have it looking shabby.

"Now, I have corresponded with various city officials in Birmingham where they held the last such reunion. One of the big problems they had was with counterfeit goods."

"What kind of counterfeit goods, Chief?"

"The United Confederate Veterans authorizes certain companies to manufacture memorabilia such as ribbons, pins, ashtrays — hell, anything you can think of. The Veterans make a little something on the sale of each one. Some folks found profit in counterfeiting the souvenirs, undercutting the price and not paying their tribute. It means very little to me who makes or who sells trinkets, but we promised to help enforce these rules, so just keep your eyes peeled. Now, I think that covers everything I know about so far, so you gentlemen may return to your duties. Captain, send Harriet in here with some coffee for me."

The officers left and Harriet, the chief's secretary, came in clutching a large ceramic mug of coffee and put it carefully on the desk. "Thank you, Harriett. Would you be so kind as to go get the detective squad for me?" As Harriet went on her way, Wilson poured half the coffee into the moldy soil of a flower pot by the window. Sprouting precariously from that perch was an indeterminate plant clinging tentatively to life, apparently suffering from frequent doses of stronger coffee than was horticulturally appropriate. The chief pulled an amber bottle from the bottom drawer of his desk and augmented what was left of the coffee with a rich, dark rum. Moments later and none the wiser, four men — dressed as well as men can on a salary of $65 a month — came in and seated themselves in a semicircle before his desk.

Lambert Van Poole was the clear leader, not just by virtue of his seniority but, by the sheer force of his personality. He was the one to whom they all looked for guidance on the rare occasion that it was needed for something other than how to cultivate a new merchant who has not yet learned the courtesies that are customarily extended to policemen. Well-groomed and aging quite handsomely, he might easily have been mistaken for a successful lawyer or a banker. He dressed meticulously, often as not choosing the more modern look of a straight tie rather than a bow tie, and always topping his ensemble with a pale-blue felt fedora. His graying temples and tan complexion enhanced the hat's contrast.

Like many others, Van Poole was a policeman by default. As a youngster, he experienced his family torn apart in the aftermath of the War of Northern Aggression. His mother had run off and left his father, who was quickly swindled out of a very successful building business by Reconstruction authorities. The mortgage on the family home fell into arrears and their domicile was auctioned off to a Yankee. Arlen Van Poole drank himself to death; his young son found him beneath the back steps of the rooming house where they were living. The police came to investigate the death, and the sergeant talked Lambert into volunteering for nighttime patrol duty. Before he knew it, the young man had a paid position which suited him well, as a means to save money so that he could return to college and finish his education. Forty years later, he was still investigating murders and chasing con men at the train station.

He had now been a detective longer than most of the men in his office had been on the force. He was one of the first men to be appointed detective in 1899, when the city authorized the police chief to make such appointments. Prior to that, when detecting was needed, it was usually done by private detectives, hired by banks or other aggrieved parties to catch criminals who eluded the local police. Lambert Van Poole, however, proved that policemen could solve crimes just as well, if not better than, anybody from the Pinkerton Agency.

When Luther Wilson came to Jacksonville to be chief of police, he found in Detective Van Poole what he considered a kindred spirit. Idiosyncratic, but in an endearing, rather than annoying, sort of way. Very thorough and diligent in his work, well-mannered and courteous. Van Poole was older than Wilson by several years, but the detective was considered by many to be a man in the prime of his life. Wilson enjoyed Van Poole's company and this was generally reciprocated, though not without some hesitance, awkward as it was to split his loyalties between the men he worked with day to day and a new-in-town police chief.

As the men sat down, Van Poole retrieved a small, black, leather-bound notebook from his coat pocket, opened it and thumbed through until he found a blank page. Then, he patted through all his pockets and found his pen. He carefully unscrewed the cap, perched it on the end of the pen barrel and began to write. The dry, sharp nib of the pen made scratching sounds, but left no mark as he tried to inscribe the date across the top of the page. He gently shook the pen up and down, trying to coax the ink toward the tip. More scribbling produced more noise, but nothing else. He manipulated the lever on the barrel of the pen, returned the nib to the paper and produced a blue ink spot that grew to twice the size of a silver dollar and penetrated several pages, exhausting the ink supply, leaving the nib dry again. He closed the pen, reached into his coat pocket again, and produced a reliable back-up. A pencil, the point of which was worn down to a useless nub. He took out a small jackknife and sharpened the lead. Finally, he was ready, unaware that all gathered there were staring at him, awaiting his comfort so they could proceed.

"Are you quite ready, Van Poole?" asked the chief.

"Yes, sir. Go ahead. I just want to be able to take good notes," said Van Poole, with little trace of apology.

"You and your notebook, Van Poole. We often wonder what sort of secrets might be among your pages, do we not, men?"

"No secrets, Chief. Just facts, a few observations. Things one ought to know of the criminal element, like you are no doubt about to share with us." Van Poole held the notebook up high, like a preacher brandishing his Bible at a camp meeting.

"Facts and observations. The truth is very useful, indeed," said the Chief.

"I like to know the truth before I decide how usefully it may serve me."

"Well, I was just explaining to the patrol commanders about some things for which we must exercise vigilance during the veterans' reunion. I don't need to tell you men what we will be dealing with. You know, Earl," he peered at Earl White, an overweight detective about 40, "there may be times when you just have to smile, tell a fellow to watch himself a little and then keep on going. Not everything you see has to result in a free trip to jail."

"But, Chief, the law is the law," protested the rotund Earl, who had once arrested the lawyer son of a prominent judge for riding his bicycle on a wooden sidewalk on the side of the courthouse. "The

Municipal Code clearly says that if a sidewalk is made of wood or otherwise paved, and raised above the level of the street, it shall be reserved for the use of pedestrians only." The young attorney had been hurrying to a court hearing and crossed the wooden walkway on his bicycle instead of dismounting in the street and walking the bicycle to the rack. Clearly an intentional violation of the law which could not be tolerated. Not by Earl White, anyway.

"Yes, and discretion is the better part of valor. Or whatever Shakespeare said. You're lucky you still have a job. I suggest you acquire some tolerance."

"Yessir," the chastised detective muttered, not convincing anyone of his sincerity.

"Now, as I was telling the other fellows, I have been in contact with several other cities that have hosted this event. We can expect the usual brouhaha and folderol, but I have heard of a particular con that we need to watch for. The con men walk up to some fellow who has just arrived in town, obviously on his way to the reunion. Most of these old guys are wearing some sort of insignia of the outfit they were in during the war. These slick-talkers know all the insignias, what state they're from and so forth. They go up to the old war horse and say 'Hey, you in the whatever unit — maybe it's Smoking Guns of Augusta. My good friend was a Smoking Gun. Maybe you knew him? Joe Smith is his name. He's fallen on real hard times and can't raise the money to get here for the reunion. Tearing him up that he ain't gonna make it this year. He's never missed a reunion yet. Could you come up with 50 cents or something to help us get him here? He already has a reservation on tomorrow morning's train, he's just waitin' for me to wire him the fare.' Then they pull him aside and start talking real low, you know, like, 'He says he still has some old brass buttons and belt buckles and such that he took off some dead Union soldiers, and that he can get a better price for them here than he can in Augusta. I'm thinkin' whatever scratch you can give toward his fare you'll get back double by tomorrow afternoon.' Of course, the codgers fall for it every time. So two of you are going to be at the train depot and you better keep your eyes and ears open. Also, I want you to help the uniformed men keep an eye on the campgrounds and keep the whores out. They can carry on their business on Ward Street, but not in Dignan Park. There's likely to be kids around there."

"Hell, Chief, some of those kids is probably getting a cut of the action," chortled Detective Bobby Flowers.

"Detective Flowers, if you know of any such behavior, why don't I see a case file and some activity reports? If you can't keep the whores where they belong, then maybe you should be down there with them!" No one knew what the nature of this admonishment was supposed to be, but it did silence the braggart. "Now, what would you fellows think of us bringing in some, uh, Pinkerton Agents? Just to help out some? We could well be outnumbered by all manner of thieves and fast-talkers and a little bit of help might be in order. You know, they could work undercover, do some of the dirty work."

"Pinkerton? For heaven's sake, Chief! Why do we need those men here? You don't think we can handle a trainload of con men?" sputtered Van Poole.

"I'm just thinking some extra hands around would be helpful, is all."

"Chief, with all due respect, I am surprised by this talk of Pinkerton Men. If it is purely a matter of manpower, why don't you suit up more of the reserves, and put some of the patrol officers in plainclothes as a temporary assignment during the reunion? It would be good experience for some of them," Van Poole stated a bit smugly. The four detectives stared at the chief for an answer through an uncomfortable moment of silence; his expression began to show anger.

"The truth is I don't want any Pinkerton Agents here. The mayor's cousin in Atlanta has been appointed manager of Pinkerton's Southeastern district and he wants to make a good first impression. We're getting five Pinkerton Agents whether we want them or not, so we may as well make good use of them."

"Well, for heaven's sake, Chief, have them work the train station for those con games you just been talking about. They seem entirely too enthusiastic to put out here chasing whores. That kind of dandy duty should be left to men with local experience," said another detective. His declaration was so overly strong that one would not be faulted for questioning his motives.

"Quite right," said Chief Wilson. "Very observant of you. Then we all agree, Pinkerton Men stay at the train station and perhaps hotel lobbies, on the lookout for pickpockets, con men, and the like. All agreed?" The detectives all nodded as one. Having their opinions considered as anything other than insubordination was a new experience, and most had not quite gotten used to it. Van Poole's notebook inscription: *Pickpockets, con-men and prostitutes.*

Chapter 3

"Why in heaven's name we have to be doing this so early on Saturday morning, I cannot understand. For heaven's sake, Mr. Warren, the sun ain't even up yet." Bert Lewis, dressed in his sweat-stained work clothes and a vest at least two sizes too small, poled the small barge up under the bridge where Market Street crossed Hogan's Creek right in the middle of Dignan Park. "It's so dark under here, I can't hardly see a thing." The oil lamp on a pole affixed to the front of the barge gave precious little light.

"Shut up and push us up a little more and over to the right. That's good right there," snarled Butch Warren. Two more mismatched characters could never be than Bert Lewis and Butch Warren. "You know what would happen if we did this in broad daylight? We'd have the nosiest bunch of folks trying to tell us everything we're doin' wrong. You ought to know that. Men on a barge working under a bridge draws a bigger audience than a boxing match. And everybody would want to know what's in these crates. There is a good, deep, dry spot up here where the road decking clears the bank before it comes back to grade level. We should be able to fit everything up in there, then we'll cover it with some canvas and lumber and no one will be able to see a thing, even if they come nosing about down here. When the sun gets a might higher, by the time a crowd starts to gather, they'll see us hauling lumber and nails and sandbags and such down under there — we just tell them we're shoring up the supports and crossbeams. A perfectly logical explanation for being under a bridge on a construction barge. Then, in a couple of days, when this place is crawling with veterans who desperately want some whiskey, well, it's already here. Nothing left to do but take two greenbacks a bottle for it. Is that enough to get you to stop carrying on about having to get up early for once in your sorry life?"

"I reckon. But if it's such a good idea, how come everybody else ain't doing it?"

"Because not everybody is able to come up with good ideas such as this. And furthermore, I know all the right people and got the details of the whole deal worked out. Some folks think of me as nothing more than a troll. That's what they call me up in Brunswick, because I'm always working up under a bridge. Truth is, I'm a businessman with wide-ranging interests. Underneath these old canvas coveralls, I'm wearing a starched collar and tie. I can walk into any bank in this town and negotiate a business deal. I have prepared all of the construction documents and supervised the work on bridges throughout the Southeast. I go in and out of City Hall like it's mine. I know how to put together a business deal. Get the right folks involved and make sure everybody gets treated right. See, I have one friend who's in charge of all these bridges. I have another friend who has a wagonload of bootleg whiskey that he'd like to be rid of. So, I figured a few thousand Confederate veterans ought to be able to make short work of a wagonload of whiskey. We just need a way to get it to them. So, I negotiated a rate for this space under the bridge, I negotiated a price for the whiskey. Men who want a drink can buy a drink, men who have whiskey to sell can make money. That, my friend, is how the world of business works. And I am assured that the police will most likely be very sympathetic to the old veterans who have earned the right to a bottle of liquor, taxes paid or not.

"Every bridge that crosses this creek now has a stash of whiskey up under it. They're going to have state inspectors all over the place looking for moonshine whiskey, and we already got our whiskey in the park. Anybody, anywhere in this whole camp needs a bottle of whiskey, we can accommodate them with a short walk. Nobody else in town is going to have the advantage that we do. And that's why I am successful. I get the right people working with me. I look out for them and they look out for me. We need to be thinking about our distribution network, though."

"Our what?" asked Bert.

"Distribution. We need some trustworthy men spread throughout the park who can slip down under the bridges and get the whiskey out for quick delivery. You don't want to be running back and forth the length of two or three miles selling whiskey, do you? Neither do I. So we need some men we can depend on to handle that for us."

Just as the two moonshiners started to load their crates of still whiskey up under the bridge, a third voice, one they had not anticipated, joined in the conversation. "Maybe you ought to let me help you with distribution." Twelve-year-old Tommy Whitehead, just waking up, threw off his wool blanket and rose to his knees in the dry space where the criminals had intended to store the 'shine.

"Tommy Whitehead! You little juvenile delinquent. What in hell are you doing down here under a bridge?"

Tommy Whitehead was indeed well-known in certain quarters of Jacksonville. His father was a petty thief, his mother a popular prostitute, and he had brothers and sisters who seemed to come and go with the seasons. The family had never really settled in any one particular place, but floated from camp to shanty. Occasionally, some of the children were enrolled in school, but they could never bear the rigor of it for more than a few days, and went back to hunting, fishing, foraging, and stealing. No family member got along particularly well with any other family member so, when Tommy's daddy said they had to pull up stakes and move because he took an advance on his first week's pay from a sawmill and had no intention of showing up to earn it, Tommy decided to stay put instead, setting up homestead underneath Market Street in Dignan Park. Butch Warren had encountered Tommy in the past, as he often loitered around construction sites, offering to run errands for the workers. If somebody gave him a nickel to get them a sandwich, Tommy took the nickel and was not seen again for a few days. He always had some wild story, like some colored boys beat him up and took the nickel, or the coin fell from his pocket and rolled under a street car. When he was offered real work, like hauling brick or moving a stack of lumber, he'd disappear even faster. He was a troublemaker, but a small-time one, and Butch figured he could handle him.

"I live here. And if you goin' to store whiskey in my bedroom, you goin' to have to pay me some rent."

"I have already paid rent on this space, so that makes you the trespasser. Now you get on home and get ready for school."

"This is my home. And I ain't been to school since way last year." Tommy was slipping on a pair of worn leather shoes, the insides lined with heavy paper.

"You seem to excel at bringing trouble with you wherever you go. Such trouble as you're likely to attract, we do not need."

"You going to turn me over to the police? I'll tell 'em about your whiskey stash. They might give me a medal or a reward or something. Or maybe you could give me a reward for keeping it secret?"

"Well, make yourself useful and help us stow these crates and then we'll talk about compensation."

Little Tommy was small and limber enough to get the wooden crates stored way up under the bridge, so that the canvas and lumber were hardly necessary to conceal the existence of the contraband. There was still enough room to stretch out at night. He carefully stacked them so that there was no danger of them toppling over and falling into Hogans Creek. "There you go, Mr. Warren. Won't nobody but us know what's down here now. And since I sleep here every night, I can keep a watch on them for ya."

"Well, I like the way you think, but we may have to see to some alternative sleeping arrangements for you during the reunion. I won't be having you down here with this stuff. You'll be selling it right out from under me. I have a good mind to take you right to the nearest policeman I find and tell him you're out playing hooky."

"I'll tell 'em about your whiskey!"

"Oh, and you think they're going to believe a little troublemaking ragamuffin over a respected road and bridge engineer like me?"

"I didn't know you was a engineer," mumbled Bert Lewis.

"Shut up, Bert. They'll make short work of a little snot like you, they will. Send you off to that reform school and we'll never hear from you again. That's what I aim to do." Butch kept trying to scare Tommy, but was not succeeding.

"Aw, hell, an old man like you can't even catch me. I'll be out of here in a split. Run up the street and tug on a policeman's shirttail and get him to chasing me. And you know where I'm a-running to? Right here. Of course, then we'd have to offer to cut him in on the deal, too. And you know what happens then? All your profit margin goes a-trickling down a drain."

Butch was trying to figure how to respond to this pint-sized threat when his less-educated compatriot asked the obvious question. "How do you sleep down here? Don't it get snakes and rats in here come nighttime?"

"I just pee a line around the edges of my territory. The scent keeps the rats away. No rats to eat, the snakes won't come slithering around. I guess I could try sprinkling some of that moonshine around and see how that works. Maybe I could sell it as snake repellent, since it probably ain't even drinkable whiskey."

"Now, just what would a little kid like you know about whiskey?"

"I know I can help you sell it. You just cut me in for 10 cents a bottle. That's the same as two nickels a bottle, the way I figure it. Right?" In Tommy Whitehead's world, the nickel was the basic unit of currency.

"You get your scrawny little ass in this boat and let's get out of here. We can talk about nickels and such someplace where it may be easier to breathe."

Tommy pulled on an old cloth cap that flopped a little toward the front bill. His hair was listless, matted and flat, suffering a deficiency of both nutrients and shampoo. He scampered down the bank and jumped onto the barge, causing it to sway. "Be careful, damn yer little hide. You're liable to sink us," snarled Butch.

"Flat barge like this can't hardly sink. Any numbskull knows that."

"What do you know about barges?"

"I know enough. You know ol' Weasel Jones? He's got these little barges with whores on them. They come up here under the bridge at night and them things gets to rocking and swaying a lot more than what happens with just me jumping on one. And they never sink."

"Oh, is that a fact?"

"Yeah, that's a fact. And he pays me a nickel to make scary noises if they stay too long. I've scared some nasty ol' men right into the water, but the barges never sink." No more was spoken as they poled the barge back downstream and came to a dock and a small building just before the creek emptied into the St. Johns River east of Downtown. The two men moored the barge to the dock and took the youngster into the building with them. A wood fire was burning in an old stove, just enough to keep a pot of coffee hot, and each man poured himself a cup. "What? Your new business partner don't even get the offer of a cup of coffee?" asked Tommy, feigning offense.

"Welcome to the headquarters of this little operation. If you want coffee, you get it your own damn self. And, if you're going to be a partner in this operation, you're going to have to pull some of the weight." Butch Warren sat at a makeshift desk formed by empty shipping crates and random scraps of wood. The building was filled with stacks of lumber, piles of sandbags and crates of whiskey. He pulled a set of ledgers out from behind a loose board in the wall. "Now, listen here to me. I got a record of every damn bottle of liquor we put up there in the park. Here's the deal: You make yourself scarce during the day. Bert and I still have a considerable amount of legitimate work to do up under those bridges. You're lucky the one you sleep under hasn't already caved in and crushed your sorry little ass. We're going to have crates of whiskey stuck up under each bridge, and maybe a few other places. But I'm keeping a record of every bottle. And I will be checking on them every day while we're working. Every bottle missing is going to come right out of your ass, you understand? If the counts all work out, and nothing gets stolen, I'll grant you a commission of two cents for every bottle you sell. We settle up every day during the reunion. And if one single damn word of this gets out, you get fed to an alligator. If he'll even waste his time trying to eat yer scrawny little ass. Got it?"

"I'd prefer to get a nickel for every bottle you're a-storing down there. That's what seems fair to me. I mean, you cramping up my dwelling space."

"You are an enterprising little turd, aren't you? That's not your dwelling space anymore. You sleep here in this shack from now through the end of the reunion. Then I don't care what you do. Now, what do you do with yourself during the day? Surely you don't spend the whole day skulking around under that bridge. I can't have you hanging around. You'll attract too much attention."

"Oh, I keep myself busy. I do some fishing. Sometimes I'll run messages for some of the men at the train station. If I get too hungry, I walk down Bay Street and wait for the whistle on the peanut wagon to blow. Then I steal a handful of hot roasted peanuts from that dumb ol' blind nigger right when he's dumping them out of the roaster and putting them in bags." He giggled thinking about his larcenous behavior.

"Well, ain't you just proud of yourself, stealing peanuts from an ol' blind nigger?"

"Aw, hell, a kid's got to eat, you know?" Tommy started with his self-pitiful act that served him so well during the winter months, when the rich Yankees were all too anxious to give aid to a poor little waif, the likes of which they'd deny existed in their sophisticated Northern cities. "Sometimes I'll go two or three days on nothing but a handful of them stole peanuts. I have gotten lucky enough to find some oysters that somebody couldn't finish, thrown out in the alley behind Finley's, but you can't count on that every day. So, I mostly wander around trying to find a way to get something to eat. You don't know what it's like going to bed hungry every night under that bridge."

Butch Warren stood and fished four dimes out of his pocket. "Here. Go get yourself a decent meal. You come back here this afternoon when you hear the five o'clock whistle blow. And stay away from that bridge!"

Tommy pocketed the change and wandered off. It took him a minute to get his bearings, then he started down Bay Street and soon arrived at the city market. Saturdays were usually busy there, making it easy to nick something and not get caught. He strolled through the market as inconspicuously as he could, trying to look as if he were shopping like any regular person. When he came to a booth of fresh produce, he walked briskly, grabbed a large potato, slipped it into a pocket of his overalls and kept going. He was just about to break into a run when a large man with an apron wrapped around his belly grabbed him.

"Caught you, ya little bastard! Think you can come stealing potatoes from me, do ya?" The man ripped Tommy's pocket open and retrieved his potato. Tommy took advantage of the moment when the man loosened grip to break away and run. He skittered several blocks without stopping, cutting through alleyways and down little passages between buildings that only a slim and flexible body could maneuver. He was disappointed, but not entirely discouraged. The city market potatoes were the best — large, with a tender peel, they cooked up nice and fluffy. And for just one of the dimes that Butch Warren had given him, he could have bought three of them. But it was much more fun to steal them. And then he could spend the money on something else, like candy or a cigar. He had another source for potato plundering, though.

The shed in the alleyway behind the big church with the funny name was always unattended and full of potatoes. They weren't as big, but they were easy to pilfer. He put three of them deep in the one good pocket he had left, and walked up to the park where the Confederate veterans were beginning to fill the campground. Setting up tents and gathering around campfires, just like old times. He found an old steel can that had once held some beans and rinsed it out as best he could in water dripping from a hand pump. He shoved the potatoes into the can, then rolled it into a fire that some men had built. With a long stick, he kept rolling the can around every few minutes. This constant action helped cook the potatoes, but it also identified the meal as his, should anyone take a mind to grab it. There was so much going on around the campground, nobody took much notice of a kid cooking some potatoes in a campfire. After a while, he used his stick to roll the can out of the fire. Bending the stick in the middle, he used it like a pair of giant tweezers to pick up the can without getting burned. He found a quiet spot away from the bustle of the campground and ate his baked potatoes, an old pocketknife and the stick his only dining utensils.

In the shack near the river, Butch Warren was updating his inventory, noting how many pint bottles of whiskey had been stowed up under the Market Street bridge. Bert Lewis expressed concern about Tommy Whitehead. "I'm worried about that boy knowing our operation. You explained how you done so much to get this to work right, what with paying the man in charge of the bridge and all, but now this little kid could blow the whole damn thing up if he takes a mind to. He might start stealing some of them bottles and going off on his own and selling them."

"Don't you worry about Tommy. I can handle him. He used to hang around some of my construction sites. We just have to keep him busy is all. Remember the secret to my success? You got to get the right people involved and give them a stake in the game. That way, they feel a part of the whole operation, see? That's just what we're gonna do with little Tommy. Except we're going to be able to get some work out of him, and he's going to be loyal to us for that."

"I don't know, boss. Can we trust him?"

"We haven't any choice, Bert. We either make him part of the operation or we kill him. You gonna kill him? No. I didn't think so. As mean and dumb as you are, I don't think you could kill a little kid. Just let me handle him. It'll be all right. He's a right enterprising little bastard. Might be just what we need for our distribution problem." The two men spent the rest of the day working in the river shack, counting pint bottles of whiskey, and staging bridge repair materials in a way to disguise the fact that the barge was carrying contraband. The end of the day sneaked up on them, and a few minutes after the five o'clock whistle blew, Tommy came strolling up to the river shack.

"Tommy, did you get yourself something good to eat?" asked Butch.

"I did OK."

"Do you really want to make yourself some money selling whiskey with us?"

"Yeah, but I want more than two cents a bottle. How 'bout two nickels a bottle?"

"Two nickels a bottle is right steep, kid. Here's my proposition. See, there's still a bit of work to be done before we can sell those bottles of whiskey. I'll pay you two cents a bottle to do the work, then three cents for each bottle you sell. The two cents a bottle is a sure thing, the three cents is what we call incentive pay. The more you sell, the more money you make, see? That's a deal any man would jump at."

"What kind of work?"

"Nothing too difficult. You take each bottle and pull the cork out. Then, use this little medicine dropper to put a little dab of iodine in each bottle, put the cork back in and shake it up good. Then we got these here little strips of paper with writing on them, and you need to slap a little bit of wheat paste on the back, then stick it over the cork. Finally, we got these round labels that need to be pasted on the front of each bottle. So when you're done, all that whiskey will have a nice amber color, a label that says South's Finest Whiskey, and a tax stamp. Every bottle here will look like store-bought, tax-paid whiskey."

"That sounds like an awful lot of work for two pennies."

"We have 20 more cases of whiskey to dress up. Twelve bottles to a case, that's 240 bottles. That comes real close to five dollars. That's as much as any grown working man can make in a day. You don't have to worry about the ones we already stowed. They're already done up right."

"What if I don't want to do it?"

"Well, we might think of another solution to our problem, that problem being you. We might just knock you out, tie you up and throw you in a freight car on a northbound train. Won't nobody find you 'til you get to Richmond."

"All right. I might as well go ahead and get started. You want me to work here?"

"You can start right now and work for a while so I can show how we do it, and I can make sure you can do it right on your own."

Along one wall of the shack was a work bench of sorts. In the middle of it was an old mop sink. Mounted on the wall just above it was an iron water tank that fed into a spigot over the sink. Under the sink, an old bucket stood below the drain to catch refuse water. The two men and the boy started uncorking whiskey bottles. They proceeded to adulterate the appearance of the bottles so that a state liquor inspector might be inclined to approve them as a legitimate tax paid shipment. After an hour, Butch said, “Me and Bert got to get out of here, ’cause we have other things to tend to. You keep on working and you can sleep here tonight. Whatever you get done, I’ll pay you for in the morning when we come back.”

“Yes, sir,” said Tommy. Butch Warren padlocked the door from the outside, and the two men left Tommy to his work disguising the counterfeit containers. Pull the cork. Drop in the iodine. Put the cork back in. Paste the strip of paper over the cork. Paste the label on the front of the bottle. Put the bottle back in the crate. Over and over again. He was working over the sink, so he could run a trickle of water when he needed it to activate the paste for the strip and the label. Tommy tried to speed up the process by working on more than one bottle at a time. It worked with two bottles. Cork, iodine, strip, label. Three bottles at a time was manageable. Four, even better. He tried to lift a new wooden crate with 12 bottles up next to the sink. One hand slipped, the crate tumbled from his grip and all 12 bottles crashed down into the sink and broke. The bottle of iodine fell in among the wreckage as well. Tommy stuck a plug in the drain so all the whiskey wouldn’t run out. The cheap bottles were made of the thinnest, weakest glass and most of it shattered into tiny shards. Tommy picked out as many of the big pieces as he could, cutting his fingers only a couple of times. He looked around the dim wood shack and finally found a box of empty bottles. They weren't like the clear glass bottles that the whiskey was in – they were brown and thick, like medicine bottles. He emptied the water that had gathered in the bucket under the sink, put it back and pulled the plug from the drain. The whiskey eddied down, mixing with some wheat paste, river water, and tiny shards of glass, into the bucket. Using a bottleneck from one of the broken bottles as a funnel, he poured the slop into the brown bottles and corked them up tight. He could get only eight bottles out of the 12 he'd broken. He corked the eight bottles, padded some old rags he'd found around them and stuffed them into a burlap sack. Climbing out through one of the windows, he left. He'd have to find a new place to live, and stay out of sight for a couple of days, or Butch Warren would beat him and put on a train to Richmond for sure.

He found his way back up to the park where the Confederate veterans had set up camp, even though the official start of the reunion was still a few days off. It seemed as good a place as any to bed down for the night. He stowed the burlap sack of bogus whiskey in some bushes behind the gardener's shed in Dignan Park, and started working the area. "Hey," he said to a couple of old men sitting by a fire. "I know where this nigger sells bags of hot roasted peanuts for 10 cents. You want me to run and get y'all a couple bags?" The oldtimers thought on that for a short while and decided the boy running errands for them was a good idea. Each man gave Tommy a dime. He took off like a shot, returning 10 minutes later with the peanuts. He neglected to tell the gentlemen that the peanuts actually cost only a nickel a bag. "You fellers need anything else, you look for me. I'm always around."

"So, what are you? The official camp messenger boy?"

"Yeah, that's right. The messenger boy. I'll run a message anywhere in the park for a nickel. Anywhere Downtown for a dime."

"All right. Here's a nickel. You run up to the headquarters tent and tell that Commander Davidson that he is a son of a bitch." The old men laughed at the prospect of this scrawny little vagrant talking to the important officer like that. Tommy worked the park through the night until he was ready to go to sleep, and he headed for the gardener's shed where he'd hidden the whiskey. He pulled open one of the windows, set the bag of whiskey bottles inside, then slithered in and went to sleep.

Tommy spent Sunday in much the same way, doing whatever he could for a nickel. Then he saw his friend Weasel Jones walking down the sidewalk on the perimeter of Dignan Park, dressed for the occasion in a fine linen suit tailored to fit his slight frame. The tie and kerchief were in a matching yellow, presenting a pleasant contrast to the pale green suit. "Hey, Weasel! What'cha doing?" shouted Tommy as he ran across the park.

"Please, Tommy. When we're out among potential customers, would you kindly refrain from calling me Weasel? Some folks might not understand the fondness with which it is offered and think that it is a descriptive moniker."

"What?"

"Call me William, not Weasel." He straightened his tie and brushed some invisible dust from a sleeve. He usually spent Sundays at the train station in an old brown suit, one that was shiny with wear, with holes starting to develop through the elbows. To further play the righteous beggar there, he carries an old Bible and wears an oversized hat and a pair of very thick spectacles. Almost anything he says to anyone, whether asking directions or querying one's status vis-a-vis the Lord, results in a contribution. Once he got on the train to Lake City and walked from one car to another displaying his Bible and an empty can. By the time he got back to Jacksonville that night, he had more than $50. Today he was dressed in his best clothes, however, surveying the vineyard that lay before him, planning the harvest, looking for all the world like a gentrified squire.

"Oh. OK. So what you been doing?"

"Ah. I am developing a business approach to this opportunity you see unfolding before your very eyes, Tommy. That is what I am doing."

"You going to put your whore barges into action for these old fellers?"

"No, Tommy." He chuckled a little. "I guess there may be a few aspects of the amorous endeavors that you are yet too young to grasp. See, if a man is going to spend a couple of dollars for some tickle time with a woman, he would usually appreciate some level of privacy, perhaps even the pretense of romance. The appeal of the barge is that the park is not often crowded in the evening, and up under the bridge, one can usually find some privacy and perhaps light a candle to add the romance. But now, with the park filling up with these old veterans, it would be a bit of a carnival atmosphere. Lots of gawking and yelling going on. And most of these old men, if they have the money, probably don't have the ability to take satisfaction from a woman anymore. No, I need something a bit more creative than my whore barges."

"Well, I got eight bottles of moonshine right here. Let's sell it to some of these old guys," suggested Tommy eagerly.

"Shhh, boy," responded Weasel, looking all around to make sure no one took note of what Tommy had just said. "Keep some composure about yourself when talking of such things."

"Composure? What's that?"

"Don't go shouting all over the park that you ... well, just keep your voice down until we get somewhere we can discuss business. Follow me, but stay about 20 feet behind." They walked down an alley, behind the grand houses on Phelps Street overlooking the park. Weasel waited for Tommy to catch up and then knocked on a door that opened onto the alley from a garage.

"My friend, Champ, lives here. I am sure he will avail us his premises for a business negotiation." A bearded man with a severely disfigured head cracked open the door. He stared at Weasel as though he had never seen him before. His right eye seemed to continuously water, and only closed completely with some effort. He shifted his head a little so that he could focus on Weasel with his left eye, then brightened a bit with recognition. He did not speak as he let them come in. "Champ, my friend and I need a quiet place to discuss a business proposition without attracting the attention of others. May we?" Then to Tommy, "Don't worry about Champ. We can talk all we want in here. No tale ever leaves this room." Tommy looked around the tiny place, picking up a peculiar odor permeating the area. He looked for the source but was baffled. At one end of the small room were several large, deep shelves that held Champ's collection of junk. It was littered with broken lanterns, bicycle wheels, barrel hoops, nuts and bolts, dried paint brushes, broken tools, mouse traps, and other assorted odds and ends that the apparent recluse hoarded.

"It stinks in here. What happened to his head?" whispered Tommy, trying not to be heard by the curious subject of his inquiry.

"No one really knows. He never talks about it. I think he must have been stepped on by a bull. If you really want to know, you can ask him, but I can't guarantee a civil response. Now, to business matters. What is this talk of whiskey?"

"I got eight bottles right here." He pulled out the amber bottles, showing off. Weasel opened one and sniffed at the neck.

"Smells like whiskey, all right. Where did you get it?"

"I ain't a-telling."

"I like the bottles. Not the usual whiskey bottle. Looks more like a medicine bottle. Hmmm." He poured some into a coffee cup and examined it. It was dark and cloudy, with the effects of the wheat paste, river water and iodine that had mixed with it. "Looks a bit like medicine, doesn't it? Well, eight bottles is hardly worth the time or trouble – or risk – it would take to sell it. If you can't produce more, then I'm not interested."

"Maybe I could get some more, but it would be troublesome. I would have to be well paid," said Tommy mysteriously.

"You will be paid well enough, young man. I'll give you two bucks for the eight bottles of bootleg liquor. I'll be fortunate enough to cover my expenses. If you get any more, come see me, but do not expect such generous terms next time. Now get out of here and leave me to my better business."

Tommy scurried out and Weasel Jones scrutinized the bottles much more closely. Several inchoate ideas formed in his mind, which he shuttled aside for the time being, hoping for some inspiration that would bring one of them to maturity. He returned the bottles to the burlap sack and shoved it way back in the dark recesses of the shelves displaying Champ's collection of junk – which to Champ wasn't junk at all.

Chapter 4

"Grampaw, you're too old!" Susan had lost track of how many times she and her grandfather had had this conversation.

"I'm old, but not too old. And that is exactly the point. This could be the very last chance I have to set something right. Something that desperately needs setting right," the weathered gentleman declared.

"Grampaw, you tell me what needs doing and I will see to it. I promise you. A seventy-one-year-old man has no business traveling alone such a distance."

"What needs doing is no concern of yours. Something only I can do. Now, I will discuss this no more. You can take me to the train station tomorrow, or I will walk. But I am getting on that train to Jacksonville in the morning."

The distraught young lady was right. Train travel from Ashland, Kentucky to Jacksonville, Florida could take a lot out of an old man. But Alden James would not be swayed. The 1914 Confederate Veterans Reunion in Jacksonville might be the last chance he ever had. And he was determined to take it.

"Grampaw, in all these years, you've never had any interest in the reunions. Why now? Why this one?"

"It's nothing I can tell you about. Just something that I have to do." He kept packing clothes and toiletries into a small leather grip.

"I guess I can't stop you, but how I wish I could! You just have to promise me that you'll be careful. Heaven can only tell what kind of trouble is likely to brew. Bunch of old men sitting around, drinking and carrying on, remembering how they were once young, for days on end. I'm so worried that something untoward may happen to you."

"I ain't never touched no liquor in my life. Why would you think I'd go all the way down there and get drunk?"

"I don't know. It's just an awful feelin' that I can't shake. I just wish you wouldn't go."

The old soldier climbed up into the attic and retrieved a beautiful wooden box that he'd made some years back. It was very well constructed, probably among his best work, and that was saying something for a man who had made his living in fine carpentry and furniture-making. Hard maple, dove-tailed joints fit so tight it was probably waterproof. Varnished with linseed oil and turpentine. It had a sturdy hasp and a small lock to secure it. A dark red, plush velvet-and-silk lining comfortably protected and cradled the treasure he kept in it. He carried it with him the next day as his granddaughter and her son took him to the train station and saw him off on his long journey south.

Alden James could not remember the last time he had traveled by train, but he observed that this experience was a vast improvement. It would be all day, overnight and most of the next day before he got to Jacksonville, but the seat was accommodating, and the paper sack stuffed with sandwiches that his granddaughter had fixed could see him halfway around the world. The train car was crowded, but comfortable. He changed trains in Atlanta and found the cars even more spacious. He held out his paper sack and offered a potted meat sandwich to the man in the seat beside him. "My granddaughter made enough for an army. Help yourself if you're hungry."

"Very kind of you, thank you. But I am much more interested in that elegant wooden box that you have in your lap than the bag of sandwiches," said the stranger.

"Oh, that's just a box I made to carry some personal items in when I travel." He unconsciously tightened his grip. The man noticed.

"One rarely sees such elegance in a wooden box. Looks like something made in Europe to carry expensive royal jewels."

"Well, there ain't no jewels in here, if that's what you're wondering. It's just a hobby of mine. I am a carpenter by trade, and I have made some furniture. I just got a little carried away with this one. All the carving and inlay and such was just something to do."

"Well, anyway, it's a very impressive toiletry kit. Where are you headed?"

"Jacksonville."

"Most folks are leaving Jacksonville this time of year, heading back up north."

"I'm going down there for the Confederate Veterans Reunion."

"I didn't know they still did such things."

"They still do 'em. This will be the first one I've ever attended, though. I served in the army of the Confederate States of America, but as soon as the war was over, I went back home and never gave it another thought. Just thought it would be nice to see some old friends once more before we all, uh, move on, you know."

The two men chatted amiably for most of the journey. The box stayed in James' lap. Every so often, he'd move it to the floor, keeping it wedged tightly between his feet. If he felt himself starting to doze off, he would put the box between him and wall of the car so that if anyone even touched it, he'd wake up.

He arrived in Jacksonville at four-thirty on Sunday afternoon, three days before the reunion was to start. He wanted some time to look around the town before the festivities began – and to take care of the task ahead that was foremost on his mind. Perhaps then he could enjoy the reunion, he thought, though try as he might, he could think of only a couple of names and faces that might be familiar from all those years past. And those names and faces brought no pleasant memories. And sleeping in a tent on the ground never appealed to him; he did only it when ordered to during the war. Any man without sense enough to get up off the ground and sleep in a bed when given the opportunity was of questionable judgment, in his mind. And since his judgment was quite sound, he had telegraphed the Phelps Boarding House weeks before and rented a room for a full week. The sixteen dollars and twenty-five cents seemed a princely sum, but he'd have a bed and access to a bathroom with a shower, and breakfast each day, for an extra fifteen cents.

Alden James disembarked from the train and wandered up the concourse to the place where folks claimed their baggage. It took a little longer to loosen his joints than he anticipated, but it felt good to get up and stretch and walk. He kept the paper sack, now only about half-full, under one arm; the all-important box he held tightly with both hands. He'd almost reached the baggage claim area when he felt a tap on his shoulder. He turned to find a well-dressed young man holding what he recognized as the Southern Cross of Honor, an award bestowed upon distinguished Confederate soldiers. "Pardon me, sir. Did you drop this?" asked the fellow politely.

"No, no, I did not. Hey, that's the Southern Cross," exclaimed James, tightening his grip on the box.

"Yes. I recognized it instantly. As soon as I saw it on the ground back there, I started looking around for someone with a military bearing, and look of distinction about them, and I saw you. Naturally, I assumed you must have dropped it. I guess you're here with us for the reunion?"

"I am here for the reunion, yes, but I did not drop that."

"Oh, well. I'm sure someone will be disappointed that they have lost their medal. I don't know an awful lot about these things, but in addition to the personal sense of loss its owner must be suffering, I am guessing such a trinket is right valuable. Will you help me reunite this signal of valor with its proper owner?"

"Well, I'd be happy to help, but however will we find this man?"

"The logical thing to do is to turn it over to the police. But, uh, that may be a bit awkward for me. You see, I am not always in their good graces, and an encounter with the law would result in the assumption that I have stolen it. So, you should take it to a policeman and turn it in. Now, I suspect there will be a reward for it, which should rightly be mine. I would think the owner would sponsor a ten-dollar reward for something this important. I tell you what — you give me five dollars, and ... "

"All right, I've heard enough." A large fellow standing off to the side reached and grabbed the dapper sport holding the medal. "You're under arrest. We'll keep you in jail until all these fine folks coming to the reunion are gone back home." He identified himself to Alden James as a Pinkerton detective working on behalf of the Jacksonville Police Department. He took down James' name and where he was scheduled to stay so that a city detective could drop by and get a statement from him.

James was rattled by the whole experience, and kept a firm grip on the box, shoved it up under his arm and kept on walking. He claimed his suitcase, went out to the street, and asked a redcap what streetcar would get him to the Phelps Boarding House. His only immediate concern was to get to the boarding house so he could safely stow the box. He boarded the 9B streetcar, which seemed to move intolerably slow for the amount of noise and rattling it made. The streetcar stopped at the corner of Phelps and Main streets, and the operator told him Phelps Boarding House was a half-block walk from there. As he walked along, he could see part of Dignan Park, where preparations being made for the big reunion. The whole area was being transformed into a campground, and a very orderly one at that. He was almost beginning to think he might enjoy himself, but not until he returned the treasure that he had taken all those long years past. That it was not his idea to steal, and that he resisted, in no way made him feel less guilty. First thing tomorrow, he would walk to that church and return it. He would never forget the name of the church — Immaculate Conception. Whatever in the heck that meant — Catholics were a strange and mysterious flock, what with their worshipping graven images and all that folderol. But never mind. The chalice was stolen from them and he aimed to see it back where it rightly belonged.

When he got to the Phelps Boarding House door, he felt as though he had only one breath left in him. He went in and rang the palm bell on a desk just inside the front door, then collapsed in fatigue on a divan. A cheerful, attractive woman in her mid-forties bustled out of the kitchen.

"Well, hel-lo! I am Mrs. Brandywine, proprietor of the Phelps Boarding House. Whom do I have the pleasure of addressing?"

"Good afternoon, ma'am. I am Alden James from Ashland, Kentucky. I telegraphed to you some months back, reserving a room for the reunion."

"Oh, yes, indeed. I recall getting your reservation and commenting to my cook how unusual it was for someone to reserve a room so far in advance. You must have really wanted to get to this reunion! No mind; we're happy to have you, Mr. James. Now, I have you booked through Friday night, leaving on Saturday morning. The rate for that amount of time is sixteen dollars and twenty-five cents. You can pay the entire amount right now and just pay for breakfast each day. Or you can pay each day in advance. Your choice."

"I'll pay in full right now."

"Lovely, Mr. James. You can also join us for supper, for fifty cents, if you like. I have reserved you a fine room on the second floor, Room 202. It has a green door. And there are bathrooms at each end of the hall."

"Thank you. I'm right beat from travelling such a distance, I reckon I'll go have a nap right now, but I would be proud to join y'all for supper come sundown," he said.

"Wonderful, Mr. James. We serve at six-thirty this evening.

After supper, I'll show you around the rest of the house."

Alden made his way up the stairs and found his room easily. He unlocked the green door, dropped his grip by the bed, fell on the mattress and took a short nap, fully clothed, the wooden box still in cradled in his arm. He woke abruptly after a half-hour, a bit refreshed. As the gentleman unpacked his few belongings, he found a spot deep in the armoire where he could hide the box. As he did so, he pondered. Why was he always hiding it? No one would be coming into his room. No one would see it. He slowly began to realize that he was hiding it from himself. He didn't want to have to see it and deal with the fact that he had stolen it all those sad years ago. He shrugged off these worries — tomorrow, it would all be over. A nice supper, a good night's sleep, an early breakfast and then he would walk to the church, return the looted item and ask for forgiveness. And who knew? They might thank him for his good deed — and then again, they might send for the police. If they did, he would go willingly. He felt he deserved to be punished.

Alden James joined the other Phelps House guests for a quiet supper. On most Sunday evenings, it was a light meal after a weekend of sumptuous fare. Some cold meats, fried chicken left over from earlier in the day, salad, fresh vegetables, soup and bread. Each weekday, the rooming house opened its doors to the hungry public for the midday meal with a family-style dinner, quite popular with the local population. Supper and breakfast were for rooming house guests only. The dining room was set up with one rather large table that could accommodate a dozen people, and several smaller tables that would seat six or four. The room was easily rearranged for the crowds expected at weekday dinners. Alden James got to the table just in time to participate in the prayer of thanks that was offered, then the plates were passed around. He took small portions; it was his habit to keep his evening meals rather spare. Mrs. Brandywine came and sat at his table.

"Mr. James, I know you only just got here, but how do you find Jacksonville so far?" she asked him brightly, attempting small talk that may be bland, but acceptable at a polite gathering of strangers.

"Well, I am quite fatigued, was accosted by a con man at the train station, and have not had a bath in two days. Perhaps you should ask me that question again tomorrow, when no doubt I will be in better spirits."

"I'm so sorry for your misfortune. Please let any of us know if we can be of any help."

"Indeed. Tomorrow, I will have a great weight lifted from my weary shoulders, and will offer nothing but cheerful observations."

"Well, I purely hope so. Shall I have the kitchen prepare something special for your breakfast? We begin serving bright and early, at seven o'clock."

"I'd be right satisfied to have some coffee and some oatmeal. That would start my day on a positive note."

"We shall have it ready for you sharply at seven, Mr. James."

"And can you tell me how I'd go about gettin' to Immaculate Conception Catholic Church from here?" he asked.

"Well, under most circumstances, I would direct you out the front door, right across the park, then down Ocean Street a few blocks. But the veteran's campground has taken over the park and it might be difficult to navigate. So … go right out to Main Street and catch the street car. The operator will tell you the closest stop."

"Thank you, Mrs. Brandywine."

"If you have finished your supper, sir, now would be a fine time to take a minute and tour the downstairs with me. I usually do that right when a guest checks in, but I could sense that you were anxious to get to your room."

"I would like that very much, thank you."

"We'll start in the entry hall where you came in. The stairs right behind you take you up to the guest rooms, as you've already found. And we have a large storage closet under the stairs if you need to stow anything during the day, you know, if you are going in and out. Now, follow me to the drawing room." As Mrs. Brandywine opened a set of French doors, they entered a large, well-lit room with windows along the front and one side. Several clusters of comfortable-looking furniture were positioned about the room so that groups, large and small, could gather and visit. A large fireplace dominated an interior wall, and several well-stocked bookcases held volumes of general interest. "Guests are welcome in the drawing room any time. Someone from the kitchen will see to it that you have coffee or tea or any other refreshment you might want. Several daily newspapers are available here, as are the most current magazines. I think you will find this quite comfortable. Now, back into the hall and to your right is the parlor." She slid open a set of wooden pocket doors. The parlor also had a fireplace, though much smaller than the grand one in the drawing room. Fewer clusters of furniture, but a large library table held a full service of brandy, sherry and other libations. “We invite our guests to gather in the parlor beginning at five o’clock for an aperitif or just socializing before we start our supper service. And after supper, you are welcome to enjoy either room or the front porch. Just off the parlor is my office. If anything is not up to your expectation, I am usually available here and will do what I can to help. So now you have the full picture of the Phelps House — please make yourself comfortable. We have a large front porch, a verandah really, that wraps around the side of the house. Many folks find relaxing outside quite a lovely way to spend the evening. Have a seat out there and I’ll have someone bring you some iced tea.” Mrs. Brandywine’s assessment of Alden James was that he had seen all of the aspects of the Phelps House that would interest him.

The next morning, Alden James came down to breakfast in the dining room at the Phelps House. He was dressed in his finest suit, with a starched white shirt and a straight, black cotton tie, neatly held in trim with a tie pin. Not knowing what the Catholic clergy expected of their faithful, he took no chances with looking the slouch. James spoke to one of the dining room attendants about the breakfast arrangement he’d made the previous evening, and she was ready to serve him.

Elsewhere in the area, Champ’s morning routine had already started. Around six-thirty, he’d checked all the pipes from the heaters and boilers that provided the house with hot water and steam heat. He stacked firewood in all rooms with a fireplace, the weather still being slightly cool. Mrs. Brandywine wanted it all done early, before any guests were up and about — because of Champ's frighteningly disfigured face and head. As he was going about his chores that Monday morning, he saw the man sitting alone in the dining room. A man whose face was etched in his memory. Even though it had been some fifty years, he was confident this man was indeed one and the same as the man he'd witnessed so many years past. When the gentleman left Phelps House carrying the little wooden box, Champ followed, keeping back a bit so as not to be detected.

Chapter 5

Rudy Harrington was awarded the contract to inventory fire suppression assets for the city. His cousin Tad Ferguson had arranged, just as everyone on the city council had guessed, for him to get paid a hundred dollars to count all the fire plugs in town. It was now Monday, two days before the start of the reunion, and the City Commissioner was failing in his attempt to convey a sense of urgency to his cousin.

"Well, listen here, Tad. It ain't just a-goin' 'round and counting. You want it to be accurate, don't you?" asked Rudy.

"Of course it's got to be accurate, but still, it's taking you a long time. The reunion starts day after tomorrow and the whole idea of this inventory was to help out with the reunion."

"I'm just trying to tell you that in order to properly conduct the inventory, I have to mark each one down on a piece of paper as to its location. Then I got to find that location on a map and put an X there. Then I got to mark the hydrant so I knows it's been counted and don't get counted again. That would throw everything all off and it wouldn't be accurate. To mark it, I've got to take a can of this here black paint and use one of these little brushes and paint a little star on the top valve cover. Then I got to clean the brush. You know, if you don't get that brush right into some turpentine, it'll tighten up on you and then there's nothing to do but throw it away. So you can't rush these things, Cousin. You really can't."

"Good Lord. I set you up with a sweet two-hundred-dollar city contract and you got to go and complicate the dickens out of it. Just count the damn fire plugs, Rudy. I'll buy you more brushes if you need them."

"What two hundred dollars? You only paying me a hunnert."

"I get to keep a little something for going out on a limb for you, Rudy. It's not easy work. Now get to counting!" Ferguson had worked up a powerful sweat getting mad at his cousin, and was dabbing his face with his little satin pillow, trying to keep dry. Rudy left City Hall on his bicycle with his papers and maps, his can of black paint and his brush, and headed to complete the last uncounted section. He spent a good part of the morning on the eastern edge of Downtown counting and marking the devices. Where Liberty Street crossed Hogan's Creek, his map showed a fire plug down in the park, practically under the bridge. He bent down to paint the little black star on the valve cover and saw two feet shod in nice shoes, sticking partly out from under the bridge. "Hey, you!" he called. "You better get up and get on out of here. If the police finds you trying to sleep off a drunk under the bridge, they'll not be kind." No reaction. He went over and kicked at the bottom of the feet. "Hey. Get up and get moving. Here I am trying to put in an honest day's work and I have to put up with the likes of an old sot sleeping under a bridge." He still got no reaction. He finished his counting process of that particular fire plug, and bicycled off. Encountering a policeman, he told his story of the drunk under the bridge. "I tried to wake him up, but couldn't get him to budge." The policeman took his time, but eventually made his way up to the small bridge and, after several unsuccessful attempts to wake the drunk by slapping the bottom of his feet with a truncheon, he grabbed the ankles and pulled, exposing his crushed head.

Chief Luther Wilson summoned his top detective to his office. "Lambert, seldom do we find the stars in such alignment as we do today. It seems one of the Pinkerton men made an arrest of a flim-flam artist at the train depot yesterday, and the intended victim was indeed an elderly veteran here for the reunion. We need to get a statement from him as to the details of the attempted crime. He is staying at Phelps Boarding House, and as fate would have it, I have been awaiting an opportunity to test their cook's mettle. A number of respected individuals in the area, I have been told, visit this establishment with some frequency and regularity. Even elected officials. I suggest that you get a notepad, a sharp pencil and the Cadillac and we shall see how much we are appreciated in this town." Then he added, with an almost evil glee, "I am told she serves short ribs on Monday."

"Yes, sir. I'll meet you right out front." Lambert Van Poole was one of the few men in the Jacksonville Police Department who was properly trained in the safe operation of an automobile. The two men cruised north at the dizzying pace of fifteen miles an hour on Market Street and turned left on Phelps. The city council had adopted that precise speed limit city-wide, to be self-enforced, since the streets – former cattle paths – were so congested, there was no possibility of driving in a stretch long enough for a driver to approach that speed.

Van Poole pulled the car safely off on the side of the road, and he and Chief Wilson headed into Phelps House, straight to the dining room where, it was rumored, for twenty-five cents, a delectable, sumptuous meal could be enjoyed. And, if the woman who runs the place was the least bit civic-minded, the chief and the detective should be able to dine high on the hog for no more than fifteen cents each, that being the generally agreed-upon standard courtesy offered to law enforcement professionals. Chief Wilson was in his uniform, so there would no mistaking him for an ordinary citizen stopping by for dinner.

Mrs. Brandywine greeted the two men as they beelined for a coveted place at a table in the crowded dining room. With an engaging, demure smile, she cooed, “Good afternoon, gentlemen. Please follow me.” She escorted them to a table, and stood nearby, signaling to her dining room staff with hand gestures and facial expressions. “Sara will bring you some iced tea directly.” Although she was talking to both of them, she never took her eyes off Chief Wilson. After they were seated and served their sweet tea, the day’s bounty began to emerge from the kitchen. Bowls of mashed potatoes, rice, yellow squash, pole beans, white acre peas. Platters of sliced tomatoes, glistening with oil and vinegar. Stuffed pork chops. Ham steaks. Fried mullet. The greatly anticipated braised beef short ribs. Baskets of biscuits and pans of cornbread. “You gentlemen just let me know if there is anything else you need.”

“She seems quite friendly, don’t you think, Van Poole?” asked the Chief, trying to sound casual.

“She certainly does. Must be your uniform.”

“Looks like one could make a meal of it,” commented the chief with a wry smile. “Let’s mix a little business with pleasure, shall we?” Van Poole got the hint and waved at Mrs. Brandywine, who quickly bustled to the table. He got out his notebook and pencil, ready to take notes.

"Is everything satisfactory, gentlemen?"

"Why, we haven't even had a chance to serve ourselves yet, ma'am, but everything looks absolutely delightful," said the chief. "Now, Mr. Van Poole here, uh, he's one of my best detectives, has some police business to attend to and we thought while we were enjoying this delectable dinner, we could make some progress in a criminal investigation." The chief was reasoning that if she knew that the two men were involved in fighting crime right then and there, a courtesy regarding the price of their dinner might be more forthcoming, and perhaps even more generous.

"Oh, my goodness," squeaked Mrs. Brandywine, an expression of mild alarm creeping across her face. "I hope this isn't going to be something that's bad for business."

Van Poole responded with his most gentlemanly approach. "Heavens, no, Mrs. Brandywine. We simply need to talk to a man named Alden James, whom we understand to be a guest here. He was accosted by an undesirable element at the train station yesterday, and we want to get his statement. Is he in the house, do you know?"

"No. Mr. James ordered a special breakfast. I was not here when he came down for it, but he must have eaten his oatmeal and gone off to church early. As far as I know, he has not yet returned."

"Gone to church?" asked Van Poole with some surprise. He scribbled in the notebook.

"Yes. Isn't that peculiar? Church on a Monday morning. Last night at supper, he asked directions to Immaculate Conception Catholic Church. I thought it very peculiar. But I don't pry about what my guests do. Particularly when it comes to something like religion. I go to my church every Sunday, and when somebody else wants to tend to their religion, it's no never mind to me. But I did find it a mite peculiar." She gave Chief Wilson her signature single-arched eyebrow, combined with a slight nod that expressed some amount of suspicion, tugging at flirtation.

At just that moment, a uniformed policeman burst into the dining room. When he had found the dead body under the bridge, he'd called into the station from an emergency telephone. The desk commander told him that Chief Wilson and Detective Van Poole were at dinner at Phelps Boarding House, and he might as well walk right up the street to get them. The policeman, unschooled in the art of tact and discretion, stormed clumsily amid the hungry throng. "Chief! Detective! I'm glad y'all are here. We got us a dead man under the bridge, just down here at Liberty Street. I can't say how long he's been dead, but he's still right fresh."

"Oh, my. This won't be good for business," gasped Mrs. Brandywine.

"For heaven's sake, Riley. Hold your voice down," cautioned Wilson. He saw all hope of a courtesy on his dinner bill evaporate before his eyes. "This room is full of people trying to enjoy a pleasant mid-day meal and in you come, hollering about a dead man. Have you no proper breeding at all?"

"Excuse me for forgetting my manners, Chief, but I just seen a man's whole head smashed in like a ripe tomato." Appetites were dropping fast at every table. "The first thing that came to mind was to get the Chief and a detective out here; didn't cross my mind to worry 'bout no one's dinner. You want I should go back down there and swat the flies away from the carcass until y'all have finished eating?" Chief Wilson silently pledged to himself to work harder to identify sarcasm as a character trait among new recruits so they could be eliminated from consideration right off the bat.

"No, Officer Riley. We have not begun to eat yet, so we shall accompany you directly," said the chief. He was gritting his teeth so hard, he reckoned he'd never be able chew solid food again anyway. The men left the boarding house, and headed east toward Liberty Street. Officer Riley rode his bicycle while the chief and Van Poole got in the car. "Well, Van Poole, we may never know now."

"What might we never know, Chief?"

"What caliber of short ribs Mrs. Brandywine's kitchen is capable of producing and whether or not she is truly a civic-minded businesswoman. You know, as far as maintaining a well-fed police force."

"Don't despair, Chief. You and I will come back after the reunion is over and done, and all these distractions are gone. Right now, let's go see if this dead man can tell us who killed him."

When they reached the bridge, Officer Riley was standing over the corpse. He'd had sense enough to pull the man's coat off and cover the skull – it was so gruesome a sight, it would move gawkers to comment more than would be helpful. There was already a small crowd of four or five men and boys gathered on the sidewalk part of the bridge, leaning over the concrete balustrade, offering their thoughts. Officer Riley grew weary of their musings. He scowled up at them and said, "What happened was, he was leaning over the railing just like all y'all are, and a car come by too fast and startled him and he fell forward and smashed his head on this here concrete embankment. And that is exactly what is going to happen to all y'all if you don't move along off that bridge." Unlikely as the scenario was to actually happen, they slowly realized that it was nevertheless possible. Cars had been known to bounce across that bridge well in excess of the posted speed limit of fifteen miles an hour. At such a rapid pace, a driver could easily lose control, with disastrous consequences. One by one, they all decided that more important business awaited them elsewhere, and they drifted off.

Chief Wilson and Detective Van Poole joined Officer Riley to inspect the corpse. Van Poole pulled the coat off the man's head and examined the mortal wound, then checked through the pockets, looking for anything that might reveal the identity of the victim. "Well, it appears that robbery would be our motive. He has been cleaned out. No wallet, no business cards, no engraved pocket watch. No embroidered handkerchief. No name tags sewn in the coat's lining. Stripped clean. The blow struck the right side of his head. Somebody with substantial upper-body strength and a stout weapon. Maybe a baseball bat or piece of lumber or something." Van Poole was scribbling details in his notebook. Mundane stuff. *Victim: White male, appears to be in his sixties or older. Position of the body: Parallel to Hogan's Creek, head toward the east, feet toward the west.*

"Or maybe Officer Riley is right and he fell from the bridge," chirped Chief Wilson optimistically. "What a perfect outcome that would be. I wouldn't be faced with a murder investigation during the reunion, and we could possibly get back to Phelps House and finish dinner. Riley! Ride down the street there and get Judge Travis up here to rule this an accidental death. I think she serves dinner until two. This might work, if we can get the judge here fast enough."

Van Poole mused. "No, I don't think so, Chief. I mean, I guess we need to get Travis up here to begin preparing the death certificate, but this was no accident. First of all, I don't see any evidence of where he might have landed if he had fallen from the bridge. I should think he would have made quite the mess. No, I think this man was struck intentionally and then robbed." Van Poole bent over and walked under the bridge where it separated from grade level. There was a dry spot easily fifteen feet deep, running from the grade separation to the creek bank, with nearly five feet of vertical clearance. After several minutes he came back out, ducking his head and carrying all manner of detritus. He stood up straight, arranged the items on the grass, turned to the Chief and spread his arms, as if offering homage. Van Poole said grandly, "Evidence of a crime, sir." The detective had placed a scrap of plush red velvet material, a small brass handle like what might be found on a lady's jewelry box, several buttons, a pair of crushed reading glasses, and a page of old newspaper with blood dripped all over it. He began entering descriptions of the objects in his notebook, with a notation as to where each was found in reference to the body. Small brass handle: Three feet due east of the left foot, twenty-two inches from the concrete bulkhead. Such details were mind-numbing, but would come in handy as the investigation progressed.

"Excuse me, Van Poole, but this is merely a pile of refuse the likes of which we might find in any place where vagrants tend to congregate. I'm beginning to like the accidental death explanation more and more."

"I beg your pardon, Chief – it is anything but. This velvet material is the kind that is the first choice among jewelers for displaying their wares, but your typical vagrant has little use for such. I would say the same for this little brass handle. Far too fine a piece to have been left by a vagrant. Buttons, reading glasses – these are not things that our typical class of bridge-dwelling tramp has falling from his pocket. Finally, this piece of old newspaper. Several months old by the date; I will admit that this was probably at one time used as a blanket by a hobo. But the copious amounts of freshly spilled blood on it is what I am interested in as pertains to this investigation. And one more thing, sir." Van Poole reached into a pocket. "Here is his tie pin. Engraved with the initials 'A.J.' I think this is the man whose statement we aimed to collect. Furthermore, if you would accompany me, you will see clear evidence of the victim being dragged under here, perhaps already dead. There are footprints and blood everywhere. An awful lot of blood, as a matter of fact. The evidence seems to suggest that he was dragged under the bridge from the other side." Van Poole was making notes of all these things as he was telling them to the chief.

"Well. This adds no delight to my day. I'll take the car and go back to get Mrs. Brandywine and see if she can identify him. You wait here for the judge. And I am not clambering about under any bridge. See if you can get a photographer under there to get pictures. Won't be easy, dark as it is under there, but Pete Dooley can probably manage something."

Officer Riley rode his bicycle a few blocks north to a small brick building at the corner of Third and Liberty, where the aforementioned judge kept his courtroom, resolving neighborhood disputes, settling small claims, conducting weddings, and carrying on the business of jurisprudence in Justice District 5. The unassuming building housed a cobbler's shop, a small sundries store and the even smaller office of the Honorable Sandberg Travis, Justice of the Peace, District 5, which covered a quiet residential area with very little opportunity for people to start, much less finish, any trouble. The result was a disquieting dearth of incidents for which a Justice of the Peace might be called to rule upon. He helped several people collect debts, and got to run the occasional auction of goods or livestock, when a loan went delinquent. He performed more weddings than any other official function, and once convinced his wife that they should try to capitalize on that and offer a package deal, with her doing the catering for the reception. After three or four weddings, word of the sawdust consistency of her cakes got around the neighborhood, and most smitten young couples fled Downtown to one of the churches or the courthouse for their nuptials, holding their receptions at the Odd Fellows Hall or one of the hotels. Mrs. Travis accepted the fact that her baking skills were not celebrated, and set out to study the legal trade as practiced by Justices of the Peace so she and her husband could make a decent living. Officer Riley found the Judge rearranging the three plaques on the wall behind his desk, the better an impact to create. "Got a dead body for you, Judge. Chief Wilson and Detective Van Poole are waiting down by the bridge for you."

"A dead ... a what? A dead body? My goodness. What a terrible thing," the portly judge exclaimed. "Whatever will become of us? I, uh, what? Do I need to issue a death certificate? My goodness. What will come of this earthly existence?" Judge Travis, while perhaps bored with the interior décor of his small office, wished fervently for such activity as settling a small claim or insisting that a man keep his horse shitting on his own property. Such is how a Justice of the Peace earns an honest living. But the state saw fit to invest its Justices of the Peace with the responsibility of viewing the mortal remains of any person who expired unnaturally within his district. If necessary, he must convene a jury and conduct an inquest to determine the cause of such death and issue a death certificate so stating. "Well, let's get on with it. I'll take my car. You tell me where to meet them."

"Right down where Liberty Street crosses Hogan's Creek. Found him up under the bridge with his head bashed in."

"Head bashed in? Oh, my goodness. Whatever is to become of us? If his head is bashed in, it would seem quite reasonable that his death was unnatural. Why in heaven's name do you need me?"

"I'm just carrying out the chief's order, Judge. He said go get Judge Travis, so here I am a-gettin' you."

"Certainly, Officer. Carrying out orders. I'll meet you down there. Liberty Street. At the bridge. Ohh, God help us all. Head bashed in, my goodness."

While Riley had gone in search of Judge Travis, Chief Wilson had driven to the Phelps House and collected Mrs. Brandywine.

Apparently, Chief Wilson was unwilling to let Mrs. Brandywine find out about his discomfort with automobiles, otherwise he would never have driven the Cadillac the three long blocks back to Phelps House. When he returned with Mrs. Brandywine, he tried to prepare her for what she was about to see. "It is a grisly sight, I'll grant you, but you may be the only person who can identify him. Please get a firm grip of yourself. Van Poole, reveal the body."

Van Poole pulled Alden James' coat down, exhibiting the man's crushed head and face.

"Ohhh." Mrs. Brandywine gave a shallow yelp, almost a polite scream. She turned quite pale; Chief Wilson was afraid she would faint, so he stood by her side and supported her. "That's horrible. Who would do something so cruel? I think that is Mr. James, but it is hard to tell. The face is terribly, well, you can see." She stopped for a minute, gulped and got her breath. "Yes, I am sure that is the gentleman from Kentucky."

Officer Riley showed back up and, a few minutes later, Judge Travis could be seen tooling slowly down Liberty Street in a 1908 Oldsmobile. It sat him up quite high above the road, and he wanted to stay in the car and holler down to Chief Wilson and Detective Van Poole. He tried to ask them to describe the dead man to him, but they couldn't hear him over the snuffling, rumbling and backfiring of the tired old engine. When hand gestures and hollering proved a futile medium of communication, he shut off the engine and walked down the slight incline from the street to the area where the dead body now reclined, just next to the bridge.

Although he had great respect for the legal system in general,

Chief Wilson found little use for the role that a Justice of the Peace played in a murder investigation. Some of them, at least, seemed to take an interest in the proceedings. He wasn't sure which was worse. A Justice of the Peace who tried to take over the whole investigation or one who was so squeamish as to disregard the process entirely.

"Oh, heavens to Betsy. What a ... oh, well, I never." The judge kept trying to examine the body while averting his eyes from the calamity at the same time. "Any idea who he is? Oh, that's terrible." He took a handkerchief from his pocket, covering his nose and mouth.

"We think we've got him identified, your honor. An out-of-town visitor, here for the Confederate reunion. We just need your determination of the cause of death. In accordance with the law, of course," said the chief.

"The cause of death is ... well, you can see for yourself. His head is smashed in."

"Yes, your honor. Do you suppose it was accidental or the dastardly work of someone else?"

"Well, how am I supposed to know that?"

Detective Van Poole, while rather enjoying the sport of watching his chief set a judge's head spinning, decided that he could entertain no more such tomfoolery. "I have a suggestion, Your Honor. We shall have this body removed to the morgue and have a doctor conduct a post-mortem examination. Then I will begin my initial inquiries and, in a few days, will be able to present you with my preliminary findings. At that time, you can indicate a cause of death and issue the death certificate and we will have all done our part in maintaining an orderly society. How does that sound?"

"That sounds like a very studied approach to the situation, Detective. You call on me in my chambers at your convenience and I will be happy to execute my judicial duties. Thank you, gentlemen." And the judge scampered up the slight incline faster than most present thought a man of his bulk could scramble, got into his Oldsmobile and spun off.

"Well, Van Poole, looks like you have a murder to investigate. I have a police department to run. That's not something a man can do on an empty stomach. I shall take Mrs. Brandywine back to her boarding house and perhaps see to a bit of dinner. You and Riley here get on with it and I'll come back by for you in about an hour." The possibility of braised short ribs bolstered Wilson's gallantry and helped him overcome his hesitancy about operating the automobile a second time.

"Yessir." Van Poole put the scant evidence he had collected into the back of the Cadillac and told the chief he would log it into the evidence room later. "Riley, go call the station and tell them to have the hospital send the morgue cart around here. Then ask around and see if you can learn who may frequent this bridge."

When the morgue cart finally came on the scene, Van Poole helped the attendants load the dead body. With the corpse now gone, Van Poole was able to wander further afield from the scene of the crime. He began asking questions, trying to find witnesses and more evidence.

Liberty Street crossed Hogan's Creek in a north-to-south direction, demarcating the eastern edge of Downtown and the chain of beautiful parks that flanked the creek. Beyond Liberty Street, the city's maintenance of the banks and floodplain as parkland ceased and Hogan's Creek took on the characteristics of an industrial waterfront. Van Poole crossed Liberty Street and found the unmistakable signs of a struggle in the dirt. The banks at that spot were low and usually soft, if not muddy, and it was difficult for anyone at the site to not leave a sign of having been there. He could make out several sets of footprints, which may or may not indicate much – there was generally considerable foot traffic in the area on the path to a particularly productive fishing spot. But the evidence of a struggle was hard to miss. A fight had clearly started here, and continued under the bridge. And under the bridge, the soft, muddy ground gave up the clue that a body had been dragged and left where they'd found Alden James.

Van Poole walked back to Phelps Rooming House, where he noticed that the Police Department Cadillac had been parked all the way around in the back. Entering the front door, he found Chief Wilson sitting on a divan in the corner of the front parlor, comforting Mrs. Brandywine, who was quietly sobbing on his shoulder. When the chief caught sight of the detective, he extricated himself from the distressed woman and crossed the parlor. In a hushed tone, he murmured, "Martha, uh, that is, Miz Brandywine has been through a most upsetting experience. Having one of her boarders murdered is not a common occurrence. Well, you can see she is most distraught. Here is the key to Mr. James' room. Second floor, Room 202. Green door. See if you can find anything useful to the investigation. Understood?"

"Certainly, Chief. And you seem to be just the rock of solace that a young widow needs just now."

The chief's eyebrows arched noticeably. "Widow? Yes, indeed. Oh, by the way, I drove the Cadillac all the way around to the rear of the building so Miz Brandywine could come in through the kitchen. I'm not quite sure how we are going to get it out."

"It has a reverse gear, Chief. I'll take care of it after I go through his room."

"Good thinking. With any luck, I'll be in the dining room by then," said the Chief, rubbing his hands together, his face holding a lustful grin.

Van Poole entered Mr. James' room, haunted by the idea that he was some kind of morbid voyeur, a feeling he could never quite shake. Even though the man was dead, Van Poole felt that going through his personal things seemed to violate some principal of civility. The feeling was only partially allayed by the fact that he found nothing of a questionable or prurient nature. Several sets of clean underwear and socks, a few changes of clothes, and a bag of overripe sandwiches that needed to be removed to the kitchen garbage pail. A letter folded up and stuffed into the inner pocket of a coat hanging in the closet was the only thing that he found that shed some light. It was typed on the stationery of Jacksonville's Immaculate Conception Catholic Church. Van Poole sat on the side of the bed and read it.

March 23, 1914

Dear Mr. James:

Thank you for making inquiries about Immaculate Conception Catholic

Church. You are correct that Union Forces looted and burned the Church building during the War Between the States. That was a bit before my time here, so I have no firsthand knowledge of the events. The Church was rebuilt after the war, then again destroyed by fire in 1901, along with the rest of Downtown Jacksonville. However, the Church endures and we rebuilt again, opening our current sanctuary in 1910. I invite you to stop by and visit while you are in town for the veterans' reunion. You expressed an interest in making an offering which will be most enthusiastically welcomed.

Yours in Christ,

The Reverend James Donal

Van Poole came downstairs to find Chief Wilson pacing by the front door. "Come on, Van Poole. You've got to get me back to the station."

"What happened? Did you get dinner? Why the rush all of a sudden?"

"Let's go, shall we?"

Van Poole knew the signals. No more questions. The two men walked down the driveway to the car, and Van Poole noticed a series of scrapes on the front left fender that matched a similar pattern of marring on the brick pier that supported the back corner of the house. The two men got in and Van Poole started the engine. He tried to explain to his superior officer how to engage the reverse gear.

"See, this gearstick has to go all the way back, and even with the engine disengaged, you can find that it bounces and grinds a bit. Then you slowly engage the engine and ... "

"Oh, for God's sake, Lambert, I haven't got time for instruction in operating an automobile right now. Get me to the station!"

"Of course, Chief," he replied, holding out the folded letter.

"Read this while I drive."

Wilson took the letter and read it. "Ahh, so this explains the 'going to church' remark. I wonder what kind of offering he had in mind. You said he was stripped clean, so our perpetrators are probably flush with cash. Cash that was meant as an offering for a church. Let the patrol squad know what to look for. Take me to the station and then you can go talk to this priest. See what he knows."

"Don't you want to go with me?"

"No, I do not. That Brandywine woman hoodwinked me into taking her to the Confederate Ball tomorrow night. I have a lot of work to do yet, and will need time to prepare, make sure I have proper attire and so forth. Probably need a haircut. I will need you to drive us, by the way. And to think I never even got dinner out of the deal! What a lousy way to start the week."

After Van Poole dropped the chief off, he took a moment to make some entries in his notebook. A lifetime as a detective had led him to develop the habit of recording every minute detail he encountered. A description of a stolen watch: *Gold with Roman numerals, scratched crystal.* Or the hat worn by a pickpocket: *Brown felt, no hatband, heavy sweat stains.* Sometimes, for reasons that he could not even grasp, he recorded observations about people unrelated to the particular crime under investigation.

The innkeeper at Phelps House seems smitten with the chief. Wants him to take her to Confederate Ball. He seems flummoxed about it.

Judge Travis skittish about dead body. An excitable fellow. If it comes to an inquest, should be very interesting.

Chapter 6

As soon as Chief Wilson and Detective Van Poole rounded the corner from Phelps Street onto Market, Mrs. Brandywine signaled to Sara, one of dining room attendants. Sara ran up the hidden back stairway where Council President Jimmie Calton and Finance Commissioner Tad Ferguson had finished with their special fourth-floor luncheon which they arranged a couple of times each week. It was not on the menu; an unadvertised special. She tapped lightly at two of the doors, first one, then the other, and delivered in a loud whisper, "All clear, sir."

Jimmie Calton had already gotten dressed and took an extra few minutes to apply some face powder to keep his natural look before emerging into the hallway. Ferguson called for some extra towels. The two men came down the back stairway and emerged on the back porch with the laundry equipment. They casually strolled into the kitchen, then to the dining room and, eventually, to the front parlor where they paid for their lunch. Ten dollars each.

"That was a close call. I hope he is not going to make a habit of coming here," said Ferguson.

"Don't you worry about Chief Wilson. He'll never suspect a thing. In fact, the more he frequents this establishment, the less likely he is to suspect that anything is happening upstairs. We just need to keep telling him what a great job he's doing," said Calton.

From the front porch, the two men looked out over Dignan Park. "Well, it's all coming together rather nicely, Jimmie, wouldn't you say?" observed Ferguson.

"Yes, it is, Tad. Better than we could have imagined. Look at all those tents pitched in perfect straight lines. You could almost believe you were in a Confederate Army camp, couldn't you? I just hope we can get through this week with no trouble. Don't like trouble."

"Don't think about it too much. We've got what we want. Thousands of people coming into town. Money in their pockets, liquor on their minds. We got over two-thousand pint bottles of still whiskey out there that men are willing to pay two bucks a pop. Everybody gets what they want. Especially us."

"There's going to be a flock of state tax inspectors on hand, you know. I hope we have taken all the necessary precautions to keep them otherwise occupied so they won't be drawn to our activities."

"There won't be any questions, Jimmie. Trust me on this."

"You're sure?"

"I'm sure. I'm sure. Don't worry about it. Even if they found a bottle of it somewhere, I don't think they are going to hold any suspicions."

"I wish I were as confident as you, Tad."

"Look. Every bottle out there has a tax stamp on it. Even if a state inspector picked up a bottle and poured himself a drink from it, he would have no way of knowing that it was not legally produced, legally transported, and legally sold. Trust me on this one, Jimmie. And as long as we keep the big shots well entertained upstairs, they won't say a thing."

They stood on the porch a few more minutes, admiring the military precision with which Dignan Park was being transformed into a campground. Neat hand-painted signs directed newcomers to sections of the park designated for different outfits, to the mess tent, to the auditorium tent, and even to the latrines. The park itself had become the object of attraction for locals who had not seen the military gather like this since the Spanish-American War in 1898, when they took over Dignan Park as a staging area before their departure for Cuba. Traffic began to back up where Main Street crossed Hogan's Creek as locals drove by to have a look. It was a pleasant, festive atmosphere.

"Well, I have some work left to do in my office. Mrs. Calton and I must be in the receiving line at the Confederate Ball tomorrow evening. I trust we will see you and Mrs. Ferguson there?"

"Of course we will be there. Wouldn't miss it for all the cotton in Georgia."

Father Robert Donal, just back from having lunch with the Board of the Children's Relief Society, was dressing for an afternoon of golf at the Hampton Club. He played several times a week at the open invitation of Mr. Drew Goshell, whose wife chaired the Relief Society. As he was getting ready, his housekeeper knocked tentatively at the door of his dressing chamber. "Yes, Mrs. Trent. What is it?"

Through the door she whispered, "I beg your pardon, Father, but there is a man insisting upon seeing you. I know this is your afternoon for golf, but he is a policeman and is quite insistent."

Father Donal opened the door, "A policeman is he, now?" The priest pondered a moment, hoping his afternoon was not about to be put to ruin. "Well, let us render to Caesar, shall we? Have him wait in the parlor ten minutes, then show him into the library." He went to his closet and took out one of his best cassocks. Black as ink, with deep red piping and red buttons down the front. Fifty-three of them. One for each Hail Mary of the Rosary. He tied a bright red satin cincture around his waist, selected a biretta with a red ball on the top, then went downstairs through a private staircase that came out into his library through a narrow door between two bookcases. He was ensconced at his desk with a stack of books in front of him, appearing deep in thought, when Mrs. Trent gently knocked twice and showed in Detective Lambert Van Poole.

Father Donal stood, all six-and-a-half-feet of his ruddy red Irishness, and placed his biretta snugly on his large head, where it tried to tame his wavy reddish brown locks, to no avail. He slowly walked around the desk and stretched out his arm to shake hands. "Bob Donal, and indeed 'tis a pleasure to welcome you." He signaled to a chair in front of his desk, inviting Van Poole to sit. Rather than returning to the high-backed, leather-upholstered chair, he perched himself on a corner of his large desk. "How might I be of assistance to the police?" He found that the strategic combination of the regalia of office juxtaposed with the casual use of his first name disarmed many people who came to see him. It had effectively put many a sinner at ease, and was particularly useful with non-Catholics.

"I'm very pleased to meet you, uh, sir." Van Poole was now unsure about what to call him, even though vaguely aware of certain Catholic customs and behavior, owing to a short and unfruitful relationship with a young lady many years back. "I am Detective Lambert Van Poole of the Jacksonville Police Department and I am hopeful you may be able to help us."

"I would love to be able to help. And you can call me Bob. But some people prefer Father. You may do as you please."

"Thank you, Father." He sounded relieved as he unfolded the letter and handed it to him. "This letter was found among the belongings of a man we found murdered this morning."

Father Donal removed the biretta, walked around the desk, returned to his chair and retrieved a set of spectacles. "Murdered? Dear Lord in Heaven." He closed his eyes and leaned back in his chair facing toward the heavens, his lips moving slightly but quickly with the remotest auditory hint of whispering. Van Poole assumed he was offering a silent prayer for the departed. After a minute, he read the letter. He leaned forward with what seemed to be enthusiasm. "Oh, yes, I remember this. This fella wrote to me, oh, sometime back in March, I think it was. Wanting to know all about the damage done to the Church during the Civil War. He said he was coming to the reunion and would like to stop by and see the Church and perhaps make an offering. Well, you can see what I wrote in response. I forgot all about it until just now. I don't know what kind of offering he had in mind. Sometimes people just say that because they are at a lack for words. The suggestion of an offering is just that – a suggestion. But, of course, if he had made an offering, it would have fed many hungry children. We have an orphanage here on the grounds, you know. A school as well. By the grace of God and the hard work of the good Sisters, we manage to feed and clothe quite a pack of wayward youngsters. Offerings are always welcome." Father Donal was an animated speaker. The words came from his mouth, helped along with every muscle in his face and accented with both hands.

"So, this Alden James never came to see you?" Van Poole scribbled in his notebook. *Talkative. Sincere. Gets off subject easily.*

"No. As I said, I had completely forgotten about the man. Wasn't expecting him, you see. Have you any ideas about the killer?"

"Nothing yet, but we have just begun the investigation. What about the letter he sent you? Did you save it?"

"Oh, I suppose it must be here somewhere. Mrs. Trent is quite busy, and I have an engagement for the afternoon. I will have her find the letter and you can come by tomorrow morning for it. Say about ten o'clock?"

"That would be fine, Father."

Father Donal walked Van Poole to the library door, held it open for him and called his housekeeper. "Mrs. Trent? Would you show the good policeman the way out? And he'll be back tomorrow morning. Perhaps we will have some coffee to offer him?"

"Yes, Father," said Mrs. Trent. "And I believe Sister Mary Finbar wants a moment of your time."

"Oh, for heaven's sake. Show her in."

Father Donal waited in his library a few minutes then heard an abrupt knock at the door. In came Sister Mary Finbar who, like Father Donal, had left Ireland in the aftermath of the potato famine and never again took a bite to eat for granted. She had Tommy Whitehead in tow, with a rope tied around him restraining his arms, the rope terminating in the good sister's hands, as though she were leading a sheep to shearing. "Look who can't keep his hands out of our potatoes." The convent, the rectory, and the orphanage shared a valuable food source. A devoutly religious potato farmer from the mission territory in Bayard deposited half his harvest every month in a shed behind the Church, he'd built it just for storing potatoes. It had a raised floor, was properly screened and secured so that air could circulate, letting the harvest last a good long time. Of course, with the number of mouths fed from this bounty, regular replenishment was necessary.

"I caught him red-handed, I did, Father. Come back just once too many times, didn't ya? I saw him out the back window of the convent on Saturday, but we were getting ready for our afternoon prayers, and I could not engage in pursuit. So I hid up in the rafters of the shed and when this little thief came along today, I dropped the rope and tied him up. Now, I think you should sentence him to a bit of painting and sprucing up around here and to putting his little behind back into a school desk where it belongs."

"Sister, I don't sentence people. I give them a penance through which they can be absolved of their sins, if they make a confession. Now untie the boy and you can get back to whatever it is that you need to do."

"Yes, Father." She slipped the knot and released the snare, freeing the boy. Then she coiled up the rope with the skill of a Florida cowboy, and slung it over her shoulder, creating a strange contrast to her black habit, veil and starched white wimple. As she left the room, Tommy started toward the big leather chair to sit.

"What have you to say for yourself?" asked Father Donal as he removed the red cincture and began slipping the cassock up over his head.

"Golly, I ain't never seen a priest in regular clothes before."

Father Donal carefully draped the cassock over the back of his chair, knowing that Mrs. Trent or one of the sisters would tend to it, smooth out the wrinkles and return it to his closet. "Come wi' me, lad." They went toward the back of the house. They got to a storage room and Father Donal pointed a bag of golf clubs. "Pick that up and follow me."

Little Tommy struggled to lift the heavy golf bag. It nearly pulled him over onto this back when he stood straight up. "Dang, this thing is heavy, Father. Wha'cha got in here, a bunch of hammers?"

"Ha! May as well be, for all the good they been doing me lately." They walked out into the alleyway behind the rectory, where a garage just next to the potato shed housed Father Donal's 1910 Liberty-Brush Runabout. It was a cheap automobile, merely utilitarian transportation, and he was only slightly embarrassed to be seen driving it to the Hampton Club.

"Where are we going, anyway?" asked Tommy.

"We're going to see what kind of an afternoon's work you are capable of. You will be my caddy today. You carry that bag of hammers, as you so unkindly called it, and give me the one I need when I ask for it. When I give it back, you wipe the mud from it and put it back in the bag. I hope that walking a few miles carrying that golf bag will discourage you from stealing potatoes again. And so why are you stealing my potatoes, anyway?"

"I like potatoes. They's easy to cook and eat. I stole one from the city market the other day and got caught. Had to make a run for it. So I come back to stealing yours. Ain't hardly anybody ever watching the place. The ones at the market are bigger, but yours is easier to get. And the smaller ones is easier to get cooked all the way."

"Young man, you've got to realize what you're doing. Those potatoes are to feed the poor, and the children in the orphanage."

"Well, I'm poor enough, Father. And I am just a child. So it ain't hardly like I'm stealing at all, is it? They was put there for me, the way I see it."

"Oh, but you have to come to school and learn your letters and numbers and whatnot like that, if you aim to eat potatoes honestly. Sister Finbar could likely make a decent sort of you if she had a chance."

"That crazy old battleaxe? She would as likely tie me up and beat me just for the pure fun of it afore she would learn me anything. Anyway, I don't ever have nothing I have to read. And I know enough of numbers to know when I'm coming out all right and when I been took on a deal."

"Oh? What kinds of deals does a young fellow like you get into?"

"Well, I do stuff for folks and they give me money for it. Usually nickels, but nickels is pretty good money."

"What kind of 'stuff'?"

"Oh, uh, nothing you would be interested in, Father. Just things like this and that, fetching stuff, you know. Nothing that takes any reading, that's for sure."

They rode on to the Hampton Club and Father Donal told Mr. Goshell, his golfing partner, that he had a young fellow who had to work off a penance by carrying both of their golf bags. It was seven o'clock that evening before young Tommy had finished cleaning the clubs and washing Father Donal's car. He could barely stay awake another minute when Father Donal ordered him into the kitchen and sat him down at a plate of pork chops, mashed potatoes, pole beans and cornbread. His eyes grew wide as he tucked into the meal with abandon. "I ain't et a supper like this since last year, I reckon," he said with a full mouth.

"The sisters cook me a supper like this every night. You can eat like this most evenings if you start coming to school every day, and then spend your afternoons doing some odd jobs around here. That is, if your mother and father will let you." Father Donal was quite sure that the young lad had no parents to speak of, but he wanted to let the boy get to that fact himself.

"Oh, my ma and pa is probably took off somewhere. But that's OK. They weren't all that much fun to be around, anyway. No, Father. I live on my own and like it that way. But I could stop by for a supper like this now and then. I wouldn't complain one bit."

"Where does a young lad like yourself live on his own?"

"I probably ought not to tell you. You likely to get the police after me, then I'd be sent to one of them reform schools and never be heard of again. That's what Butch Warren said."

"Who is this Butch Warren fellow?"

"He's the man fixing all the bridges up in the park on account of the old soldiers camping out there. He was afraid one a them would collapse under the weight so he shored it up from underneath."

"And why would he be calling the police on you?"

"I think he was just trying to run me out from under the bridge he was fixin'."

"Oh, so you're living up under a bridge now, are ya?" asked the priest.

"Well, I was living there until he run me off."

"You know, lad, we have an orphanage here. I don't know if there's any room in it right now, but we could probably do something to accommodate you."

"An orphanage? I ain't staying in no orphanage. That's a place for babies who got no ma and pa and can't get along on their own. Not for a smart 'un like me."

"You don't seem to get along too well, if you don't mind my saying so. I mean, stealing potatoes and living under a bridge is not exactly 'getting along'."

"I get along just fine. And ol' Butch don't scare me. I just decided to move out and give him some room to work."

"You sound like you could use a little scaring, young lad."

"Nothing much scares me."

"An eternity in the burning fires of hell? That doesn't scare you? That's what you'll have if you don't change your ways, lad. An endless fire. Torture. For all eternity. That ought to scare you right onto the straight path and narrow gate." The young man had no response. As though none of it meant a thing to him. Father Donal stood up to take the boy's plate after he ate everything on it. He took on a gentler tone. "I tell you what, lad. There is a bit of this supper left over. I'll keep it in the larder and you come back around nine o'clock tomorrow morning, do a few chores around here, and you can have the rest of it for your noon-time meal. How's that sound?"

"That sounds great. I'll be here at nine." He got up and ran out the back door before Father Donal could finish washing the plate. Tommy was headed toward the park, where he was assured of finding fun or trouble. Either one would suit him fine.

Monday evening, Weasel Jones returned to the garage on the alley behind the Phelps House to get the whiskey he'd stored there. An opportunity awaited him if only he could figure out the best way to capitalize on it. He knew that the old veterans would spend Tuesday evening at the Confederate Ball being flattered, flirted with, and celebrated. Most would be well on their way to a drunken stupor by the time they returned to camp. And that was the best time for a con man to strike — when the old folks were in a haze. When he arrived at the garage, he was still unsure how he would make a profit from eight bottles of moonshine whiskey, but trusted that something would occur to him. It always did. Perversely, he enjoyed talking through problems with Champ. It gave him a chance to vocalize his thoughts, and he never really had to worry about Champ talking back or disagreeing with him. Weasel paced around the cramped little room, Champ perched on the edge of his cot, trying to follow him with his left eye.

"Eight bottles of whiskey and thousands of men simply does not bring to mind a profitable activity."

"Aah," was Champ's usual reply.

"I need a way to make the hooch more valuable to more people. Kind of a loaves-and-fishes approach, don'cha see?"

"Aah."

Weasel reached into the shelves where he had hidden his whiskey — something new caught his eye that hadn't been there two days ago. A wooden box; its top was shattered. He pulled it out in the light. When he opened it, he found a shiny gold chalice covered with jewels; blood-red rubies, sparkling diamonds, clear green emeralds. "Well, this is something new," said Weasel.

"Aat's mine. Put it back," protested Champ.

"This was not here yesterday. You've been busy."

"Put it back. Mine."

"Yours? You mean you found it somewhere."

"It's mine. Always been mine."

"I'll buy it from you, Champ. Fifty dollars."

"Not for sale."

Weasel held the chalice up to the light, admiring the way it gleamed and sparkled, the jewels refracting the light into a rainbow of colors. He noticed one empty setting where a diamond should be, judging from the pattern. As he looked at the chalice, one of those ideas filed away in his head began to take shape.

"Champ, hear me out. I would like to rent this from you. I will give you five dollars right now, and return it to you by Wednesday with another five dollars."

Champ sat silent for a minute, then said, "Let me hold your watch until I get it back."

"That seems reasonable." He pulled his watch from his pocket, unhooked it from his vest button and handed it over. He took the bottles of whiskey and the chalice and headed back to his apartment on Walnut Street to put the finishing touches on his plan. He got only halfway down the alley when young Tommy Whitehead came toward him, looking like he was loaded for bear.

"Hey, Weasel. Are you going to go sell that moonshine to all the old soldiers? There's a bunch of them over there in the park."

"No. That won't do, Tommy. Do you remember that I said some of these men are so old that it's not worth their money trying take satisfaction in a woman?"

"Yeah."

"Well, I'm going to sell them the chance to believe that they could."

"I don't get it," said Tommy.

"No, I don't expect you would. As I said, your years are yet too tender to understand the urges that will come to you in time. What do you say … on your sixteenth birthday, I treat you to a lesson? Howzat sound?"

"I still don't get it."

"I am going to convince these old men reeling around out there that I have a tonic that will restore their youth. If you want to know more, you come up to the veterans' campground tomorrow night after the ball. Keep your eyes open for something you have never before seen. Watch closely, but do not interfere."

"What if I find a watch or a ring or something? Will you buy it from me?"

"If you find something worthwhile, you just leave it there with Champ and I'll pay you the next time I see you."

Chapter 7

“You takin’ Miz Brandywine to the ball tomorrow night? How did this come about, Chief?” asked one of the detectives. Late afternoons were when the detectives spent time in the squad room at the police station, catching up on the paperwork that inevitably accompanies the work of a detective. Chief Wilson had made the mistake of wandering into the detective squad room to get an update from Van Poole regarding his meeting with the priest earlier that afternoon.

“It is something with which none of you need concern yourselves, except for Van Poole, who will be my driver for the evening. Now get some reports written and show me some activity and then get up to Dignan Park or the train station and keep an eye out for somebody throwing money around. He may be our killer. But don’t sit around here!”

“Chief, did you ever get dinner today?” teased another detective.

“No. The day fell apart soon after we found the dead man, and Miz Brandywine completely lost interest in my need for nourishment. One thing lead to another and before I’d even realized it, I was committed to be her escort for the ball. I had to settle for a fried bologna sandwich from Stan’s. Van Poole! Please come to my office where we can discuss this investigation without further distraction.”

“Yessir,” answered Van Poole, with a derisive glance at his fellow law enforcement officers. The other detectives were enjoying a laugh at the chief’s expense.

“Can’t you just picture him all dressed up, his hair slickered down with pomade? Smelling all of lilacs? See him waltzin’ all over that auditorium? I might just try to have a peek in the window and witness such a sight for myself.” The detectives were carrying on and laughing as Van Poole scribbled furiously. *Men having some fun at Chief's expense. Harmless.*

Van Poole sat in the chief's office and they talked about all the obvious possibilities. A random street robbery? Possible. Perhaps a swindle gone bad. Maybe just a drunken brawl? Always a possibility. Some of these old men get liquored up and start fighting, they may not stop until one of them can't move a muscle. But so early in the morning? Anything is possible.

"I had Riley ask around the park some. A couple of old fellows who were camping down that way think they may have seen a couple of men around the bridge early in the morning," said Van Poole.

"They think? Either they saw someone or they did not."

"Well, the sun was just barely up, so they could not see very clearly. Plus, they were a good distance off. They figured it was some other guys camping who might not have known where the latrine was and went under the bridge to relieve themselves."

Then, Van Poole told the chief about Father Donal's reaction to the letter. "I told him that the letter that Mr. James wrote to him might contain a useful clue. He's going to look for it; he told me to return tomorrow morning to get it."

"Let's hope it does hold something useful so we can get this cleared up. Word gets around that one of these veterans has been killed and this entire event could suffer under a black cloud. We cannot allow that."

"Yes, sir," answered Van Poole.

"In the meantime, you get up to Dignan Park this evening and see what else you can turn up. Men have been coming in setting up camp for days now. Find Commander Davidson. I'm sure he has an official headquarters tent or something. He's probably sleeping there. They may have a list of expected attendees. See what you can find out about this Alden James. Maybe he had an enemy within the ranks. And find out who we need to notify. Next of kin, you know."

"Yes, sir," he replied again. He made notes of the newly assigned tasks that Chief Wilson imagined only he had considered.

"You spend the rest of today and tomorrow working on this case and let's get it cleared. Get some photographs of the scene. Then you pick me up in the Cadillac at my house at seven o'clock tomorrow night, and we shall get Miz Martha and go to the ball. You can certainly decide if you want Lily to accompany you, or you can make yourself useful patrolling the perimeter and making short work of any nefarious characters who wish to prey upon attendees." *Photographs*, he wrote in his notebook.

"I think Lily will still be busy with setting up the hospital tent tomorrow night, so I will be on my own." As much as Van Poole enjoyed Chief Wilson's company, he did not think that socializing with him at the ball would do either of them any good.

"As you wish."

About four o'clock that afternoon, Van Poole met Pete Dooley at the Liberty Street bridge over Hogan's Creek. Pete owned a small photography studio and freelanced his services to newspapers, magazines and the police department.

"I hope this will not involve too much of my time, Officer Lambert. I am the official photographer for the reunion and I was planning to make as much money during the course of this week as I usually make over the entire winter tourist season," protested the photographer, showing some frustration.

"This won't interfere too much, Pete. I'll help you with your equipment, you snap a couple of photographs, I'll pick them up tomorrow and that's that," explained the detective.

"You have no idea what goes into photography, do you?"

"No, I must confess — it seems like some sort of wicked science to me. Nevertheless, let's get to work, shall we? The chief wants photographs, and photographs he shall have." The two men set forth, lugging the tripod, the camera and the large wooden case holding all the accessories. They climbed down under the bridge, walking on small islands of silt built up along the edge of the waterway and around the bridge abutments. Pete went in first, and Lambert handed him each item as he requested it.

"It's awfully dark down here. That will make it challenging," mused the photographer.

"Just take some pictures that the chief can look at," Van Poole spat out, clearly frustrated with the entire endeavor.

"I'll do my best. I need you to hold this carbide lamp for me, since I'm going to have to stand knee-deep in the water here." The photographer affixed the carbide miner's lamp to a long wooden stake and handed it to Van Poole to illuminate the area under the bridge well enough to be photographed. After an hour or so of wrestling equipment in and out of the dark, cramped space, the photographer said he'd done all he could do. "I'll get these developed and drop them by the station sometime tomorrow."

"All right. Thanks, Pete," said Van Poole, with some relief.

They loaded all of the equipment back into Pete's automobile. Then the detective went back down under the bridge. He'd brought an oil lamp that he'd bought from an old railroad man. Pete said it wouldn't produce the kind of light to help with the photography, but it made enough light for Van Poole to find his way around. He clambered up onto the dry land under the bridge, looking for any evidence that he might have missed earlier. He found a stick and poked around to scare off any animals that may have been down there. Suddenly, he hit a wall and the contact noise was a very distinct hollow thump. Crawling closer, he found that several pieces of new lumber had been installed and concealed with a sheet of mud-covered canvas. He removed the canvas and lumber and revealed four wooden crates containing pint bottles — moonshine whiskey, no doubt. Peculiar — they all had what appeared to be tax stamps over the corks. He hauled the crates, one at a time, up to the street and put them in the police department Cadillac. When he got to the police station, he unloaded the crates, carefully placing them in the evidence room. He made entries in his notebook, wrote a report about his find, and went in search of Chief Wilson.

"Anybody seen the chief?" he asked of everyone who was standing around. They all seemed to have an unusually keen interest in his find. He made sure to count the bottles again, out loud and in front of everybody.

"I think he's down at the train station," said the desk commander. "Probably trying to keep an eye on the Pinkerton Men. What are you doing with all of this? These all have tax stamps. Look legal to me.

You going to get us all in trouble, Van Poole."

"If you want to pretend that those tax stamps are legitimate, then we can just record this as abandoned property. I think if you examine them closely, you, too, will judge them counterfeit."

Van Poole drove to the train depot, and found it busier than he could ever recall. He walked around the bustling station, surprised at the crowds of veterans pouring in. Men who saw each other only once every couple of years wasted no time getting to one of the many saloons in the railroad station and renewing old memories. He finally found Chief Wilson in Steel Rail Saloon, seated at a table with several men who were, without a doubt, Pinkerton agents. Something about their natty appearance gave them away. A casual observer wouldn't notice, if there were only one of them — but in a group, it was easy to see what they were.

"Ahh! Lambert! Come and join our revelry," shouted the chief. "Here, meet some friends of mine. These men are all Pinkerton agents. This is Ralph, George, Cedric and — I'm sorry, what was your name again?"

"Rex," answered the man whose name had been forgotten.

"Rex. That's right. Anyway, Ralph was with me at the Citadel, and small world that it is, George used to be a foreman at one of my father's textile mills. And Rex — ol' Rex here was a railroad detective I met some years ago. Cedric, I've never seen before. Sit down. Have a drink. Or a cup of coffee."

Van Poole was surprised that the chief was sitting there, drinking with four private detectives who were being paid to provide security services during the reunion, while hundreds of veterans were streaming through the station. "I'll be right back, Chief. I just saw some daring young ladies of the Ward Street persuasion over here extending invitations to some of our guests. As soon as I escort them off the premises, I'll come back and join your little get-together." He was certain that such sarcasm might incite the chief's displeasure, but the chief responded heartily.

"Yes, go ahead. We'll be right here." The gregarious chief continued carrying on with his friends while Van Poole ran the offending prostitutes out of the depot.

"You know your territory, girls. Don't be up here accosting all manner of folks, some of whom may not wish to know of your profession," Van Poole admonished them.

"Oh, come on, Lambert," cooed one of the girls, batting her eyelashes with enough velocity to cause a storm. "We're just letting them know where to find us when they need us."

"They'll find you, all right. Now get out of here!" demanded the detective. He found his way back to the bar where it was readily apparent that the chief and his friends had been in the Steel Rail Saloon for quite some time before they decided to have coffee, in some vain attempt to restore sound judgment. The group had now thinned to just the chief and his friend, Rex — who was such a close friend Chief Wilson could barely remember his name. "Chief. I have something pressing to take up with you. Do you want to ride back to the station with me?"

"I suppose I better do something to earn the valiant riches with which this city had agreed to shower me. Rex, do stay in touch, now." As they walked out to the car, Chief Wilson seemed to be unable to claim full control of his balancing faculties. He tried to stay close to any solid wall along the way. As they drove down Bay Street, the chief said, "For God's sake, Lambert. Slow down. This machine is incredibly dangerous at high speed. Now, what did you need to talk to me about?"

"I recovered four cases of moonshine whiskey from up under that bridge where we found Alden James' body this morning," said Van Poole.

"I knew it!" shouted the chief, loud enough to startle pedestrians on the sidewalk. "I knew moonshine whiskey was at the root of all this. I'll bet Alden James was killed because he happened upon a stash of illicit liquor."

"Chief, that doesn't make sense. What would possess a man to go scurrying about underneath a bridge when he was supposed to be on his way to church? I don't think it's got a thing to do with him being killed. I'm just telling you because apparently we have some moonshiners hiding whiskey up there. I'll bet they've stashed moonshine whiskey under every bridge all though the park. First thing in the morning, we need to get a bunch of the reserve men up there to search under each bridge and throughout the entire park and confiscate whatever contraband we find."

"Good idea, Van Poole. You confiscate everything you can, bring it back to the station and I'll get the whole City Council, the mayor and the City Commission down there and we'll take sledge hammers and destroy every bottle. Make sure we have somebody from the newspaper there. Oh, this will be a delight! Lambert, why don't you take me on home? I am suddenly quite fatigued."

Van Poole let Chief Wilson out at his small East Third Street house. He wrote in his notebook:

Chief drinking with Pinkerton Detectives. Judgment a little cloudy. These may or may not be related.

The coffee that Chief Wilson poured down his throat did not have the desired sobering affect, and he still suffered some impairment in judgment. It was in this impaired state that he called the mayor on the telephone. The mayor's wife answered and said she'd call the mayor to the phone directly.

"Hello?" the mayor spoke into the receiver.

"Mayor Langen, Luther Wilson here. You will be proud to know that we have found a stash of illicit whiskey hidden up under the Liberty Street Bridge across Hogan's Creek. No doubt it was put there in anticipation of the reunion. We have seized it, and tomorrow we will search the entire campground, under every bridge and in every hedge and shrub. There's bound to be more. We will seize it, and then with the appropriate notification of the newspapers, I thought we could all stand in front of City Hall and destroy every bottle. What a statement that will make! Don't you agree?"

"Oh. Moonshine, huh? Great work, Chief. That's great. Yes. You let me know when you get it. You say you going out looking for it in the morning?"

"Yes, sir. First thing. I will muster my reserve forces and search every park in the city."

"OK. Well, you let me know when you find it. We'll destroy every last bottle." The mayor hung up the phone. "Victoria, I have to go out for a while," he shouted to his wife. The mayor got into his car and drove directly to Phelps House. His runabout automobile was going on two years old, but still ran more quietly than most any other car on the road, a welcome feature as he drove down the alley and parked in the back. He started up the back steps — his destination, the attic rooms, was four flights up.

Most people understood that the attic bedrooms on the fourth floor of Phelps Rooming House were for staff accommodations. But for those select few men who were invited to visit, the attic was much more. Mrs. Brandywine and her mother took advantage of the building boom right after the fire in Jacksonville and had the roof raised on the Phelps House, added a third floor of guest rooms and built a spacious attic. She worked very closely with the architect, who boarded with them while he worked on other big building projects. He had developed a close relationship with the city's new army of building inspectors and managed to design and build the most perfect brothel in the city, without constant interference from officials who were always rejecting building plans for the most absurd reasons. Often they were legitimate concerns with engineering and building code issues, but just as frequently they were concerning the contents of little brown envelopes that were submitted along with the plans for the building permit. Somehow he managed to finish the project without a single building inspector ever questioning any aspect of the construction.

Through a utility closet in the laundry room, one ascended to a most heavenly perch atop the Phelps House. An elegantly appointed salon anchored the operation of seven bedrooms, each with its own small private toilet. The salon was paneled in oak with heavy red draperies over the windows. A small but well-stocked bar was there for the pleasure of the patrons. Mrs. Brandywine made sure that her girls could mix any cocktail any client fancied. And she always told them, "If you don't know, just act like you do and start pouring with confidence." She and the architect made sure to build the attic in such a way that any noise, from the faintest steps to the most raucous chases, would be undetected by rooming house guests on the floor below.

"Who have you got tonight?" one of the girls asked another.

"The drip. I hope we got enough clean towels."

"Oh, heavens. I've done that. It's like being in bed with a salamander."

"I know. Well, I'll try to keep talking for as long as I can and hold any actual contact to a minimum. But Miss B said it's real important to keep him happy right now. With the reunion coming up, he can help us out. If things go really well, I might get a couple of nights off."

"That helps a little, but still ..." The young lady shivered in disgust at the memory of being in bed with Tad Ferguson. "One time she gave me a night off."

"Yeah?"

"Yeah. A couple of years ago. Some old banker. I got him talking all about money and stuff, and he let it slip that he was about to foreclose on a bunch of little shanties over by La Villa. Miss B. swooped in and bought them for next to nothing."

"Wish I understood how all that stuff worked. Wouldn't it be nice to earn a living doing something other than this?"

"Hey, this ain't so bad. You got a bed with sheets. A shower when you want it. Good food. Try making a living on one of Weasel Jones' barges floating up and down a drainage ditch. You best be thankful for what you got here."

"I guess you're right." Finished with her lipstick, she sighed, "I guess I better get out there and get this over with. Will you help me change my sheets later?"

"Sure, hon."

Candy was her nickname on the fourth floor. Short for Catherine, but mostly because her fine red hair brought to mind cotton candy. She left her room and walked, unwillingly, down the central hallway to the salon.

"Why, Mr. Ferguson, what a lovely surprise. I'm so glad to see you again."

"Oh, Candy, my little cotton candy. I am just tickled to be back," gushed the large, sweaty man.

"Hey, I learned a new drink. It's called a Tugboat. Would you like me to make you one?"

"Oh, I can't wait. What's in it?"

"If I tell you that, you might just stay home and mix drinks for you and Mrs. Ferguson and never come back to see me." She feigned a look of sadness and fluttered her eyelashes flirtatiously.

"No worry about that happening — but you can keep your little secret if you want."

Candy went behind the bar and started pouring dashes of this and that into a glass. Bourbon, apple bitters, a slug of grapefruit juice, a twist of lemon peel. She added some ice and stirred, then strained it into a small stemmed glass, topping it off with a slice of orange. "Oh, we got some really big cigars in today. Would like me to light one up for you?"

"Oh, lovely, my dear, lovely."

She clipped off the end of a cigar, inserted it deeply into her mouth, twirled it a few times, and removed it from her mouth slowly, with her lips still wrapped tightly around it. Then, she licked the entire length of it very slowly and suggestively as he watched — and drooled. She explained sweetly, "That keeps it from burning too fast."

"Yeah." He began sweating even more heavily.

She brought the lit stogie and the carelessly concocted liquor over to him, swaying slowly to emphasize her charms. None of the other ladies had appointments, so the City Finance Commissioner and the strumpet had the whole salon to themselves. She wore a very sheer, slinky dress that stopped just below her dimpled knees and showcased her ample cleavage. As she sat next to him, she demonstrated how limber she was by tucking one leg under her bottom. This move caused her dress to creep up near the top of her stocking, making it very simple for the lascivious city official to imagine a garter belt. Such thoughts caused a cascade of sweat to pour down Ferguson's face, which in turn motivated Candy to keep up the conversational part of the hour for as long as possible.

"Have you made any special plans for the big Civil War reunion?" she asked.

"Oh, boy, do I have plans. Of course, because of my position of importance with the city, I play a major role overseeing all of the committees that are working on it. And, being Finance Commissioner, I have a special fiduciary responsibility to the state, to our taxpayers and to all of the business interests that have become involved."

"Fadoosherary?" The girl giggled a little salaciously as she rolled the new word on her tongue. "That's a funny-sounding word. What's it mean?"

"Well, it simply means that I have to make sure all the money gets looked after right and proper."

"That sounds terribly important … but boring. What I mean is, do you have any plans for fun? Big, fancy parties, and like that. How's that drink, by the way?"

"Oh, delicious, but look. It's all gone," pouted Ferguson. Candy popped right up, snatched his glass and sashayed to the bar to mix him another drink.

"You were going to tell me about fun stuff."

"Oh, yes. Well, there's going to be a big fancy ball tomorrow night. Everybody will be there. They even invited all the veterans and they've arranged to have a cadre of young ladies all dressed up to dance with them."

"I would say I wish I could go, but I get more money undressing than dressing up."

"Oh, Cotton Candy, you don't want to go to that ball. You'd have to get all wrapped up in a corset and spend the whole evening dancing with old geezers."

"Just dance? Is that all the poor old men get? A dance?"

"They'll get plenty of everything they want and need. I have seen to that. And, of course, all through the reunion, I will probably be called upon to make speeches and presentations and such as that. All part of the job of civic leadership, little Candy."

"I heard tell some of them old soldiers will be camping practically right outside our front door."

"Yes, right over there in Dignan Park. Thousands of old veterans camping. But you won't have to worry none. I don't think any of them are of the of clientele that Miz Martha wants here in Phelps House. They mostly going to be drinkin' cheap whiskey, and gamblin', and tellin' stories and such all. Probably be a lot of horseshoe-pitching and like that. We'll make sure they have everything they need. I don't think the police force is going to let any ladies work the campgrounds, but be assured if a man wants to know where he can find something, somebody will tell him how to get to Ward Street."

"Oh, too bad. I was hoping to stay busy through the reunion."

"You'll have plenty of extra business, just not from those men camped in the park. I'm sure I'll have some important visitors who might enjoy an evening here. Some of them might even stop in for an afternoon."

"And we will be happy to have them stop in … I just want to make sure that I keep some time for you, Mr. Ferguson." She sat close to him and curled a damp lock of his thin hair that was hanging down on his forehead. "Now, why don't you go on down to room number three, I'll tidy up out here and join you in a minute. And may I make you another drink?"

"Y-y-y-y, OK," and stammered as he headed down the hall.

Candy made a final amalgamation, then threw the nasty cigar in a bucket of water under the sink as though she were discarding a dead, rotting rodent. Finding no other chores to stall her rendezvous with the politician, she finally joined him in the room.

"Have anything particular in mind tonight, Mr. Ferguson?"

"Y-y-y-you know what you did to that cigar?"

Mrs. Brandywine stopped Mayor Langen on the first landing. "Oh, Mr. Mayor. We weren't expecting you this evening. I'm afraid that Marcy is occupied for quite a little while yet."

"Don't care about Marcy. I need to find Ferguson."

"He and Candy are in their usual room, but I would not think it opportune to disturb them at this particular moment."

"What is opportune is not my consideration right now." The mayor continued up the stairs to the attic level, walked to Candy's room, knocked twice and declared a little too loudly, "Tad, in five seconds, I'm coming in this room." He counted down, out loud, and slowly as he thought was appropriate to avoid any embarrassment, then forced the door open. Candy pulled a blanket up to cover her bare breasts as Ferguson tied a bathrobe around his damp girth. "Wilson found the whiskey under the Liberty Street Bridge. At daybreak, he intends to search all the bridges and every nook and cranny of the campground. Get your boys busy right now and move it somewhere safe."

"But, Avery, they got whiskey under every bridge clear up to Eighth Street."

"Well, then, there's no time to waste, is there? You get it moved or you and me are going to be at City Hall in the morning, with sledgehammers and axes, busting up moonshine that we paid good money for."

"Where are we going to put it all?"

"I don't care. Just get it out of those hiding places."

The mayor looked at Candy, who was still holding a blanket over her breasts. "Ha! What are you hiding from me, you little whore? It ain't like I haven't seen your tits a hundred times or more."

"Mr. Ferguson paid the five dollars for this hour, so only he gets to see anything. Show me your money, I'll show you my tits."

The mayor reached into his pocket, found a nickel and flipped it to her. "Here. I saw your foot sticking out from under the blanket when I came in."

Butch Warren roused Bert Lewis out of bed and the two of them worked all night. They poled the barge up to Eighth Street and worked downstream. The nearer they got to Main Street, the harder it became. There were more people around and there was more whiskey to deal with. Even though it was getting onto four o'clock in the morning, plenty of the old veterans had stayed up drinking and carrying on. Some of them were even practicing for the annual Rebel Yell contest. They had their recovery process down to a rhythm: Bert would hand the cases down to Butch, who would stack them and cover them with canvas. If anybody asked what they were doing, they said they were inspecting the bridges by lamplight because that made it easier to see cracks.

"Well, that don't even make sense," said Bert.

"Do you think anything is going to make sense to a bunch of old drunks this time of morning?" snarled Butch, losing his patience.

"Why are we moving the product that we just worked so hard to get up here, Butch?" Butch had cautioned Bert about speaking the word whiskey out loud when they had a barge full of moonshine. Always refer to it as product.

"I told you. Some of our competitors have found about our advantage and decided to let the police in on the secret. Those coppers are going to be searching this area in the morning, so we just have to move it down to the river shed for the little while. We'll probably be able to put it back and resume operations by late afternoon tomorrow."

"Well, I got to tell you, Butch, I have done honest work before and it ain't this damn hard. It may not pay quite so good, but it ain't half as hard."

"Oh, stop your carping. I'll talk to the partners and try to sweeten the pot a little, since we've had to move it around."

The two men secured the barge at the river shed just as the sun was rising. Butch unlocked the padlock and pushed open the door. He lit an oil lamp so they could see better. "Why, that little birdshit troublemaker!" Butch yelled to no one in particular. "Wait until I get my hands on him. Look at this. Four cases of whiskey left to be stamped and sealed and it looks like he dropped some. Look! Broken glass everywhere. You know, it wouldn't surprise me one bit if he's the one who squealed. If I lose out on this opportunity, I'll wring his neck and leave him here for the alligators to fight over." Bert and Butch spent the next several hours unloading the whiskey and cleaning up the mess Tommy had made.

"All right, Bert, we got to find that little turd and teach him some lessons. We've just been under every bridge on the creek, so we know he's not there. I think we ought to split up. You check all down Bay Street and the docks and see if you can find him. I have some meetings at City Hall, then I'll go up to the reunion campground and scout around there."

"What do I do if I find him?"

"Grab him and bring him back down here and tie him up good and tight. We may yet have to find that freight train to Richmond."

Chapter 8

Chief Luther Wilson was angry on Tuesday morning. He was angry for being hungover and angry that his men couldn't find any moonshine. He barked at the day shift commander and Van Poole, "Are you certain they conducted a thorough enough search?"

"I was right there with them the whole time, sir," said Van Poole. "It was a very thorough search."

"And you checked under all the bridges?"

"All the way up to Eighth Street, sir."

"What could have happened?"

"Well, you know, Chief, a lot of tramps and undesirables hang out under those bridges. It could be that some of them just helped themselves to it and got to selling it to the veterans and whoever else was interested. Or it could be possible that there were no more bottles to be found."

"There must be more," said the chief. "And we are going to find them. Let's reverse our approach. Instead of searching everywhere for moonshine, tell the men to be on the look-out for empty pint bottles. That will lead us to the whiskey."

"Yes, sir. I'll alert the men to look for empty bottles while they watch for profligate spenders. Though I don't think you'd find them in the same places."

Chief Wilson ignored Van Poole's churlish remark. "Well, this is going to be embarrassing. I promised the mayor that we would make a big show of busting up all those crates of whiskey right out in front of City Hall. Newspaper photographers and the whole works. He's going to be very disappointed. And with the ball tonight, and the official start of the reunion tomorrow, it would have made quite the statement about law and order in Jacksonville."

When Chief Wilson finished expressing his disappointment with the morning's events, Van Poole ducked out and headed for the rectory of Immaculate Conception Church, where Father Donal invited him in for coffee. Mrs. Trent served it in the library. The priest and the detective passed a few minutes in idle chit-chat until Mrs. Trent retrieved Alden James' letter for them. "You will return that, won't you? We try to keep a meticulous archive of letters and such."

"Of course, Father. I ask that you let me keep it long enough to have one of our records clerks copy the contents for our investigation, then the original will be returned." He looked at it again before folding it back up, putting it in his pocket. "Doesn't seem to reveal much, does it?"

"No, it wouldn't seem so," said the priest. "Clearly a decent Christian man. One with a strong conscience. The world could use a few more like him, eh?"

"I'm sure of that, Father." The two men heard the back door slam and the sound of someone inelegantly tramping through the building. Father Donal recognized it as the way Tommy Whitehead usually entered. Right on time.

"Detective, there is someone else that perhaps you should talk to about the dead man."

"Oh? Who would that be, Father?"

Father Donal quietly moved toward the door and, in one swift movement, pulled the knob with one hand and grabbed Tommy by the collar with the other, yanking him into the room. “This young laddie boy here. He’s currently making his home up under a bridge in the park there. You found Mr. James murdered under a bridge. I thought there might be a connection.”

“You no-good snitchin’ rat of a priest! You turning me over to the police? I thought you had some chores for me to do. I *was* going to tell you where you could get some pretty good whiskey for cheap, but not now. What do the police want with me? I ain’t done nothing. I don’t know nothing. It’s for sure you ain’t turning me in on account of stealing potatoes? I thought we was even on that score! They gonna send me to that reform school and I’ll never get back! I ... ” Father Donal slapped the top of Tommy’s head. Not hard enough to hurt him, just to get his attention and shut him up.

“Hold your tongue, you little urchin. The police aren’t taking you anywhere. You’ll not be going to any reform school. But you will sit here and talk to this man.” Father Donal held Tommy by the scruff of his neck as he marched him across the room to Van Poole. “Detective, he’s all yours.”

Van Poole was a bit flummoxed by the turn of events. But, things like this often happen when people with no knowledge of criminal investigation get even the least bit involved in one. They make leaps in judgment that would prove any man a fool. Why would a priest think he knows about criminal investigation? Van Poole was investigating a murder and the priest hands him a notorious truant and potato thief to interrogate. Well, probably best to humor a priest, given the chance. He was only trying to help.

“What’s this you’re telling Father Bob about whiskey? Cheap

whiskey? Is that what you're doing up there? Selling whiskey to the war veterans?"

"I ain't doing no such thing."

"Don't lie to me, boy. I saw you running around up there at the park last night, didn't I? And now you're talking to the Father here about getting some whiskey real cheap. You were up there selling moonshine, weren't you?"

"Was not. I was just helpin' out, you know. Running errands, delivering messages. They call me their messenger up there."

"You little scamp. You're really not a very good liar," scolded the detective.

"I can see it in your eyes. Right across your face. It says 'I'm lying,'" accused Father Donal. Van Poole shot Father Donal a certain look that the good priest could have interpreted as "I'll do the interrogating," a polite but firm dissuasion.

"I ain't lying. You can go ask them ladies to the hospital tent. I was helping them out, too," said the boy. Van Poole chuckled to himself; he knew he had the kid in a lie now.

"I personally know all of the nurses at the medical tent. In fact, I'm married to a nurse there. I'll find out from her what kind of lies you're telling. For now, though, you will tell me everything you know about moonshine whiskey."

Tommy sat, silent as a mouse, not making eye contact with either of the adults. "Come on, lad. Do yourself a favor. Answer the detective's questions. If you're selling moonshine, that's as much a sin as stealing potatoes, you know," said Father Dolan.

"Let's get to the moonshine later. Father Bob here says you have been living under a bridge. Which bridge?"

"I don't live under a bridge no more. And I ain't a-tellin' you where I live no-how."

"I am looking for a murderer, a cold-blooded killer who beat a man to death right up under one of those bridges yesterday. It seems that the Father is right. If you won't tell me which bridge is yours, I have to assume that you live under the bridge where we found him, the bridge that's now a murder scene. I can easily make a case against you for murder on that fact alone."

"I ain't killed nobody. I was just up there runnin' errands and such for money, so I won't have to steal so much. Father Donal taught me all about how stealin' is wrong, and I'm just tryin' not to commit too many sins." Tommy's rendition of the poor pitiful waif was back on center stage, but Van Poole wasn't buying it.

"Father Donal, may I use your telephone? I need to call the station and have them send the prison cart here to transport this young man to our jail for a few days. Living among the poles and beams covered in barnacles and brine is the lap of luxury compared to the city jail. And he won't go to the reform school. For murder, he'll likely be hanged or, if he gets a sympathetic judge, he'll spend the rest of his life in the turpentine camps. I'd rather be swung on a rope myself — I've seen those work camps — but I don't have to worry about that, since I haven't killed anybody."

"Certainly, detective. The phone is right over there, on the desk. I'll talk to the boy about making his sacraments and getting right with the Lord in preparation for whatever punishment awaits. He's being a bit thick in the head about the whole thing, isn't he?"

Van Poole picked up the phone and jiggled the hook, but then held it down as he dialed numbers, so no call actually went through. "Captain? Van Poole here. We caught our murderer. Little fella about twelve years old. What? One moment, please, Captain." Van Poole turned toward the boy. "How old are you?"

"I'm twelve."

"When's your birthday?"

"Sometime in June."

Van Poole spoke back into the phone, "No problem, Captain. He'll be thirteen before this ever gets to trial. Have the prison cart meet me in the alley behind Immaculate Conception Church. What? Snakes? The cells are infested with snakes again? Well, this kid lives under a bridge, so I don't reckon snakes will bother him all that much. Oh, cottonmouths. Poisonous. Well, no matter. We've got to get him locked up. Yes, I'll tell him. Finish all his crying before he gets there 'cause some of the other prisoners might think he's a little baby if he comes in crying. And you know what they do to little crying kids. Yep. Yessir, we'll be waiting."

Tommy started to whimper, trying to hide his fear. All pretense of bravado had vanished. "You're just tryin' to scare me and I don't scare so easy. Snakes don't bother me none." The tears began to roll down his cheeks. "Besides, you can't put me in jail, I'm just a little kid." He dashed desperately for the door, his only hope of escape. As he flung it open, he smacked headlong into Sister Finbar.

"Oh, and just look at big tough Tommy Whitehead," exclaimed Sister Finbar, "crying like a little girl who lost her dolly. What's the matter, you get caught nicking potatoes again? I ought to tie you up in the rafters of that shed and let the rats have at you."

"Now, Sister, Sister, that's no way to talk to a repentant sinner. You are about to repent, aren't you, Tommy?"

"I ain't done nothing wrong," he whimpered.

Van Poole was in the middle of the strangest circumstance of his career. Here he was with a priest, a nun, and a juvenile delinquent. The priest was convinced that the kid was involved in a homicide, the nun was after him for stealing potatoes. The detective spoke up. "Tommy, we have a few minutes before the jail wagon gets here. We might be able to go easy on you if you help us. Now, tell me who else hangs out under those bridges. If you can't give me an idea of another person who might have done this, I'll have to keep building my case against you. And right now, that doesn't look like it'll be too hard."

"All I know is the guys who been fixin' the bridges have been up under there doing a lot of repair-like work. And that crazy Weasel Jones? He rents barges and puts whores on them to run the river and go up under the bridges sometimes." Sister Finbar winced at the use of the distasteful word, especially from the mouth of someone so young. "He's got some moonshine, too."

"Where did he get this moonshine?"

"I ain't got no idea."

"You're lying again. That's not going to help your cause. He got it from you, didn't he?"

"No!"

"How do you know he has any moonshine?"

Tommy, who, despite thinking of himself as street-tough, was not very sophisticated when it came to didactics. "Well, come to think of it, I guess he did get it from me."

"And where did you get it?" pressed Van Poole.

"Uh, I found it. It was in this burlap sack that I found in some bushes there in the park. I didn't even know what it was, honest. I showed it to Weasel and he give me two dollars for it. Two dollars — that's a lot of nickels."

"I think I better find the guy who's been repairing the bridges and learn what he knows about moonshine. What's his name?"

"Don't remember his name. But he done finished all the work and last I heard he was heading up to Brunswick." Falsehoods rolled off Tommy's tongue instinctively — a survival skill he learned early in life.

"How much moonshine did Weasel buy from you?"

"Eight bottles."

"I don't believe you just found it. Tell me where and who you got it from."

"I done tol' you. I ain't helpin' the police no more. Quickest way I know to a life of sorrow is helpin' the police."

"I can assure you of a right quicker way to a life of sorrow and that's by not helping us. And it'll be a short life of sorrow at that," growled the detective.

Tommy sat silently, stoically, holding back tears of regret, sorrow and fear, a right salty flow.

"Maybe Tommy needs some time to think things over before he has to go away to jail, Detective," suggested Father Bob. "Sister Finbar, have you some chores that might help the lad take his mind off his troubles?"

"Sure and I certainly do, Father. I certainly do."

"Why don't you try to keep him busy for the next couple of days? And, Sister, have you got your rope handy?"

"Of course I do, Father." She left the library and stepped down the hall to the back porch. Grabbing her coiled-up lasso from the hook where she hung it, she slung it over her shoulder. When she returned to the library, she had the looped end of the lasso twirling inches from the polished floor.

"Now, you know, Tommy, if you try to run, Sister Finbar can lasso you from as far away as fifteen yards."

"Yessir. I have done experienced that firsthand."

The nun and little juvenile delinquent started to leave, then Sister Finbar stopped. "Wait. Just for safety's sake, let's make sure temptation never crosses his mind." She expanded the lasso's circumference, slipped it down over his torso, and pulled it tightly, pinning his elbows to his sides. "Keep walking, young man," They went out to the potato shed. Sister Finbar had already unlocked it, and propped open the doors. In front of it were four wheelbarrows. Inside the shed, potatoes were piled up in mounds, some higher than Tommy was tall. "Now, you are going to sort through the potatoes and put the small ones in the first wheelbarrow, the mediums in the next, and the large potatoes in the third barrow."

"What's that fourth one for?"

"That's for the spuds gone rotten."

"How do I know they's rotten?'

"Oh, you'll know. You go to pick it up and it'll squish in your hand like a fresh cow cake. Only it won't smell nearly as nice."

Only once did Tommy think he could make a run for it. Sister Finbar was steering away a wheelbarrow full of small potatoes, on her way to finding an empty one to put in its place. Tommy tried to walk casually toward the alley, figuring he could move some distance down it before she knew he was making a break for it. He'd be out of range before she could crank up and sling that lasso. He was wrong. She threw the lasso, caught him and tightened it around his ankles — had him hogtied fast enough to have won a blue ribbon at a rodeo.

Sister Finbar dragged Tommy Whitehead down the alley, the rope snugly around his ankles. Each time he sat up to reach for the rope to untie it, she gave it a jerk. "It's lucky for you we don't keep that mule tethered up out here like we used to. I'd tie you to his harness, I would, and have him drag you up and down the alley. Just to teach you some manners." Tommy reached for a rock, though he was not sure what he was going to do with it. "You touch that rock and you'll be sorry." The good nun pulled him right up to her and stood firmly on his right wrist with one foot, loosening the lasso and sliding it up around his mid-section. She yanked it tight again. "Get up," she ordered. After a couple of lame attempts, he finally got to his feet, standing upright a bit unsteadily.

She steered to him to a wooden table under a tree in the convent's backyard, and loosened the rope so he could free his hands. "Sit down," she ordered. He sat at the table, the rope still tight around his waist; she tied it to one of the legs of the table. She strode over to a hand pump and filled a bucket with water, then grabbed a bar of soap and a towel from the bottom step of the back porch. "Wash," she commanded. He washed his hands and face. It felt so good he almost dunked his whole head in the bucket of cool water. "Here." She threw him the towel. Another nun came out the back door, carrying a pitcher of lemonade, some tin mugs and a plate of raisin cookies. She silently placed them on the table and went back inside. "Figuring you were trying to run away because you needed something to eat, I am willing to offer you some refreshment. Sister Renee made these raisin cookies. They're not very good, but they'll keep you alive until dinnertime."

"Well, you're right about me being hungry. But I wasn't crying 'cause of that. It was you dragging me down the alley. Ain't no fun being dragged across oyster shells."

"Oh, and I surely do miss the day when a young man served his penance without whimpering and crying like a little girl, and set about doing the work the good Lord gave him to help him reflect on his sinful behavior."

"Stealing a potato when you got nothin' else to eat ain't a sin, Sister, it's survival."

"Rubbish like this I never heard. Not even the worthless rakes in Mallow would peddle such. If you're going to steal, admit that you're a thief, repent of your sins, and take your licks. A young fellow like you has choices. You can go do honest work, or you can continue to steal. If that's the choice you make, you must prepare to live — and die — with the consequences. Or you could come to school, and live in the orphanage, and do good works. I can assure you enough to eat."

"I don't think livin' in a orphanage suits me. A bunch of babies crying for their mommas alla time? That don't sound like the kind of place I would like. I'd rather take my chances, even if I have to steal a potato now and then. I surely won't be messing with yours anymore, though. You can believe that."

"Well, if you're sitting here telling me that you have full intent of stealing potatoes again, you very clearly have learned no lesson and your penance must be extended. So, as soon as we finish sorting the potatoes, we'll see about getting a new coat of paint on the eaves. Ever climbed a ladder with a rope around your ankles? Hard for you but easier for me, though. You have to fall two stories before you can start running."

"Well, you was wrong about one thing, Sister."

"Oh? And what was that?"

"These raisin cookies. They're real good. Can I have another?" He surreptitiously stuck a few in the bib pocket of his overalls, in case he needed something to eat later.

"It's MAY I have another. One more, then back to work with you!" smiled Sister Finbar.

Tommy was in front of the shed sorting the potatoes, the end of his rope still tied to the picnic table. Sister Finbar came out of another shed, wearing a canvas apron over her habit. She threw a drop cloth over the wooden table and pried open a paint can, began to condition a large paint brush with turpentine, then used the liquid, a few drops at a time, to thin the paint. When Tommy was through sorting the potatoes, she said to him, "Take a deep breath of these turpentine fumes. I reckon a young fellow with a mean streak such as yours ought to get used to it, since it seems you are destined to spend your life distilling it. That's what they do with prisoners, you know? Send them out in the woods to work the turpentine mills. Not a pleasant way to spend all your days, but I suppose you think it's better than the rigors of learning to read and write. Some of the sisters here have a prison ministry, and go to visit those poor souls there occasionally. So at least you'll get a raisin cookie now and then, anyway."

Sister Finbar rigged the rope into a safety harness for Tommy and sent him up the ladder. A large pulley was mounted on the eave at the end of the house. "Put the end of the rope through that pulley and feed it down to me," she instructed. She pulled the rope's end through a large pulley anchored in the ground. "Now, if you take a notion to jump from the ladder and run, I'll have you dangling thirty feet above the ground. I hope you're not scared of heights." Tommy started painting the eaves. He painted for what seemed like hours, a constant stream of orders from the ground making sure he didn't miss a spot. "Don't spill any. That paint is very dear, you know." "Get way back in them corners." "Don't put it on too thick!" Finally, when he'd painted half the eaves on one side of the house, she let him climb down. He washed up and sat at the picnic table. Out of the back door came a glass of water and a bologna sandwich borne carefully in the hands of another nun. "I like them raisin cookies and lemonade better'n this," he grumbled.

"Well, you can't do a day's work on lemonade and cookies. Now eat your sandwich, then we'll go into the chapel, say the Angelus and get back to work."

Tommy Whitehead had never felt out of place anywhere in his short life, until he found himself in a chapel with eighteen nuns intoning prayers, kneeling down, standing up, chanting, singing. Whatever they were doing, it seemed serious enough that any tactics of disruption would lead straight to the fires of hell. Immediately. So he mumbled along when they were praying, he knelt when they knelt, stood when they stood. Twenty minutes later, the nuns floated into a dining hall and Tommy was sent to the kitchen to scrub pots and pans. "These ladies sure pray a lot," he thought to himself as one of them announced that they'd offer a prayer of thanks after the meal. Sister Finbar came into the kitchen and inspected the pots and pans that Tommy had been scouring. "I guess that'll do. Well, outside with ya!" she barked. "Go over there and sit in the shade of that pecan tree. Rest for a few minutes."

"Ain't you gonna tie me up?"

"Do you aim to run away?"

"I don't rightly know. What's for supper?"

"Potato soup. There might be a piece of cold mutton."

"Potato soup? Ain't never had nothing like that. And I don't even know what mutton is. Reckon I'll stay around just to try it." Tommy settled down under the tree and was asleep in minutes.

She let him have a thirty-minute nap. Any more than that would have been the sin of sloth. Sister Finbar started poking him with a rake handle. "Get up, sinner. Time to resume your penance. Get up, I tell you. Get that brush back in the paint before it's drawn tight and ruined."

The now-industrious kid painted for the rest of the day. That evening, he got his first taste of cold mutton. Sister Finbar allowed him to sit at the kitchen table in the convent. The potato soup was good, but a little watery and not very filling. He would have preferred a couple of potatoes cooked his way — in an old bean can, rolling around in the fire. The cold mutton was tough, stringy, and tasted like no meat he had ever eaten. He chewed it until his jaw muscles ached.

Spending the day working at the convent kept Tommy far away from any chance encounter with Butch Warren and Bert Lewis, for which he was thankful. But now it was beginning to get dark outside, and Tommy thought he could manage to avoid his new enemies in the darkness of the city. He tip-toed to the back screen door. Knowing how badly the hinges squeaked, he took some of the cold mutton fat and lubricated every moving part on the door. He opened it silently, closed it behind him and was off to Dignan Park. Maybe he could find more fun tonight. Of course, Tommy's idea of fun did not usually comport with that of other boys his age.

He entered the park from Market Street and happened upon a couple of old veterans playing checkers. He walked right up to them and said,

"Hey y'all. Who's winning?"

"I am," said one old man. "I've got four games to his three."

"Y'all got any money riding on this?"

"No, sonny. We don't gamble."

"That ain't no kind of fun. How about I play the winner for fifty cents?"

"Hell, kid, you ain't got the fifty cents to bet with."

"Well, I reckon you're right about that. How 'bout we play for a swaller of whiskey?"

"Now listen hear, you. I don't want no snot-nosed little kid coming 'round here trying to drink and gamble with me. Get your skinny ass on out of here, boy."

Tommy took off and the two men looked at each other with faces of exasperation. "Young'uns today show no respect."

"No respect a-tall. Coming up here wanting to drink and gamble. Can you imagine? Your move." The men continued rearranging their game tokens at lightning speed. The one getting beat finally said, "Where is that bag of beef jerky? I'm hungry." They searched the campsite high and low, but came up empty-handed.

Tommy kept on through the campground, eating the stolen beef jerky. He also had a stack of black wooden checkers that one of the men had captured from the other. He giggled when he thought of them trying to start their next game with only half the checkers they needed. He wondered if he could sell them. When he was tired of tearing at the beef jerky, he threw it on a trash heap. Several mongrel dogs that had found comfort in the discarded leftovers started fighting over the abandoned treasure. An old man in what resembled a military uniform, bedecked with an abundance of pins and medals, stopped Tommy. He pointed to a sign indicating that no unescorted visitors were allowed in this part of the camp and hollered, "Hey! Cain't you read?"

"Well, not really. What's it say?" asked Tommy. He actually could read a little of the sign. The first word was "NO," but the rest of it was beyond his comprehension.

"It says you better get the hell out of here before someone decides you need a whipping."

Tommy walked on right past him and said, "Take it easy, old man, I'm just passin' through." Then he crossed Main Street into the section of the park where the public and the veterans were welcome to mingle all they wanted. Booths and tents and all manner of entertainment were there for folks to enjoy. Tommy saw a bunch of kids lined up two-deep. The biggest of them stood at the front of the line shouldering a long stick like a rifle. Behind him, one kid had a cheap bugle, and another had a little toy drum, then followed several more with ersatz rifles. Tommy walked up to the littlest kid at the back of the line, grabbed the souvenir Confederate cap off the boy's head and put it on himself.

"What the hell kind of an outfit is this?" he asked. The little kid whose hat he'd taken immediately started crying and grabbing to get his cap back. The leader with the long stick confronted Tommy.

"We are the Jacksonville Youth Volunteer Corps. Identify yourself," he demanded with an air of self-importance.

"Hah! You're nothing but a bunch of stupid kids trying to play soldiers."

"Well, we are going to march through the grounds like a real army unit. Now give my brother his hat so we can get goin'. You may join us if you like, but you'll have to go buy your own cap."

"I don't need to. I'll just keep his."

The child cried louder. The drummer started pounding on his drum and the bugler started blowing.

"That sounds like a damn goat caught in a bear trap. I ain't gonna march with a bunch of little kids like you." And he put the swiped cap back on the wailing kid's head and shoved him down, all in one motion. The child started hollering and screaming. All the boys turned and drew their sticks. The leader started barking commands.

"Line up, men! Sticks at the ready!" Before they could charge at Tommy, he took off at a good run, laughing and hollering, heading for the safety of the gardener's shed.

Van Poole had gone back to police headquarters after turning Tommy over to the custody of the diligent Sister Finbar.

He strode into his boss' office. "Chief, you should read this letter, then we need to have it copied so I can take it back to Father Bob. He says he needs it for church records. After you read it, I'll tell you what else I learned that may help us clear this whole mess up rather quickly."

Dear sir:

I am Alden James and I served in Jacksonville during the Civil War. What unit I was with is not important as I got separated from them around Milledgeville, Georgia, but caught up with other Confederate soldiers and made our way to Jacksonville 'cause we heared they needed our help, and we went to running night raids on Union hideouts wherever we could. I have some slight memories of the awful times and it seems to me that you all had a right beautiful church that the Yankees defiled. I am not an adherent of the Roman church, but do not take well to anybody carrying on such vile blaspheme. I am hoping to find that your church has been restored right and proper. I aim to come to the Confederates reunion later this year, and would be much beholden if you could extend me an opportunity to visit the church. Perhaps I will find myself able to make an offering of some sort. I hope you won't find this too much of an imposition, and I hope I can count on your tolerance to grant forgiveness to a sinner.

Yours most humbly,

Alden James

Chief Wilson summoned Harriet into his office and gave her instructions to copy the letter, first by hand and then word for word using the typewriter.

"Why do I need to copy it by hand first?"

"What if you lose the typed copy? We'd have nothing to go back to."

"Why don't I just type two copies of the letter?"

Exasperated, the chief sputtered, "Harriet, I am accustomed to giving orders and having them carried out. This is how I have successfully concluded a large number of military campaigns. If this does not suit you, please find other employment, so I can make room for someone who will act accordingly."

"I'll be glad to do it any way you want it, Chief. But if it seems stupid, I'm going to say so."

"Would you please get about doing it, then?" he said. He turned back to Van Poole, shaking his head in frustration. "All right, now. What do you make of it, Van Poole?"

"Well, it's hard to make much of it, Chief. He makes mention of an offering. But he specifically makes the point that he is not an adherent of the faith. Why would he make an offering to a church he doesn't know?"

"Who knows? Perhaps it eases the memory of seeing the church defiled. Maybe the man became successful and philanthropic and wants to dispose of his earthly treasure. But it reinforces the notion to me that robbery is the motive here. The man likely had a big bundle of cash."

"I don't know, Chief. I think it unlikely that he would travel by train from Kentucky with a large amount of cash. That seems rather unwise."

"We are investigating a murder, Van Poole. We don't know if the victim was wise or unwise. We know he intended to make an offering. He was found with nothing on him to offer. Ergo, robbery. Simple facts and logic, Van Poole. Now, any other developments?"

"Well, I spoke to little Tommy Whitehead. He's been living up under one of the bridges in the park there. One of the nuns caught him stealing potatoes out of their shed at the rectory. Father Bob up there at the church is trying real hard to set that wayward little troublemaker on the right path. Anyway, the kid says he found some moonshine and sold it to Weasel Jones."

"Ahh. Is it part of the same batch of whiskey that you found?"

"It could be. But the bridge where Tommy's been living is not the same bridge where the moonshine was hidden. He said he knew Weasel had some moonshine that he was selling and I pressed him on that a little. All he would say was that he found some bottles of whiskey and sold them to Weasel."

Chief Wilson leaned back in his chair, staring at the ceiling. It was a frequent pose of his – the men called it "counting cracks" because it looked for all the world as if he were counting the cracks in the plaster ceiling above him, not solving major crimes. It was the pose he struck when he was inspired to speak, but to no one in particular. "Tommy Whitehead. God, I wish his folks would've taken him with them when they skipped out. They slid out from a warrant, but I would have let them go if they woulda taken that little hellion. And Weasel Jones. Did I not make myself perfectly clear, Van Poole, that prostitutes and moonshine are to get our highest attention? Let's make sure all the men know to watch for Weasel and to bring him in on the slightest provocation. And do not forget. The Ball is tonight."

Lily Van Poole, née Worthen, did such a good job running the medical clinic at the train station, executives at the Jacksonville Railroad Terminal Company volunteered her services as head of the medical clinic in the campground, in exchange for sponsorship rights. The company took the opportunity to seek some participation from every company that did business with them. By the time all the sponsorship signs were constructed, one could be forgiven for mistaking the medical tent for a convention of railroad companies, ticket agencies and freight forwarders.

She'd been at it since Sunday, supervising the set-up of the tent. Her efforts resulted in a clinic even the most discriminating medical school would envy. She had an army of volunteers, vendors, ladies auxiliaries and Daughters of the Confederacy to order around, and she delegated with glee, then inspected without mercy.

"This cabinet is for gauze and bandages. Disinfectant goes over there."

"Yes, ma'am."

"Don't you know to keep topical treatments and oral medications separate? Take everything out of there and start over."

"Yes, ma'am."

"These may be nothing but a bunch of old veterans, but they will lie on clean linens and in properly made beds."

"Yes, ma'am."

"We are here to treat disease, not to spread it. I want one hand-washing station for each ward of four beds."

"Yes, ma'am."

When the tent was first constructed, she saw that it had a dirt floor, and refused to enter. She told them emphatically that no medical attention would be given on a dirt floor. She persuaded a team of carpenters from the terminal to hastily assemble a raised wooden floor. And the she complained about the uneven areas.

"If I administered medical care the way you hammer boards, hardly a veteran would survive the week. Now find a plane or a spokeshave and even out those boards. If I tripped on an unexpected bump while carrying a suture tray, the consequences would indeed be drastic – maybe even life-threatening."

"Yes, ma'am."

Lambert could always manage to take a break from a busy day of detective work to have lunch with Lily, at the train station or wherever she happened to be. He had no problem finding her among the many distractions and general mayhem at the medical tent. Her stunning beauty stood out against the backdrop of potential misery like a beacon of hope.

"Looks like y'all are off to a busy start," said Lambert. He noticed several veterans slumping in chairs along the wall of the clinic. Some were sick, some simply exhausted from travel. A few had injuries they'd incurred while setting up tents — rope-burned palms, thumbs smashed. And a few were there just because they thrived on the attention of pretty young nurses.

"You don't know the half of it. Honestly, I could take care of all the veterans myself, but I have been burdened with an army of volunteers who apparently thought that nursing consisted of sitting around, primping, gossiping and avoiding anything that might result in a spot on your whites. I spend most of my time thinking of useless errands to send these girls on so that Janie and I can get some work done. But I'm glad you're here now. I'm so hungry I was considering asking the mess tent to send something over."

"Well, I got here just in time, didn't I? And with a surprise for lunch. I have the Cadillac parked right over there. Let's go for a ride." They walked across the park to the automobile, and Lambert opened the door for her. She slid in and he handed her a light blanket, in case she got chilled from the ride. They drove away from the hustle and bustle of Downtown and the reunion, to a small park near the river. "I had Mrs. Boggs fix us a picnic. It might be several days before we can dine together again." Mrs. Boggs owned the rooming house where Lambert Van Poole had lived for twenty years before his marriage to Lily. Mrs. Boggs was happy for them, but the rejection and anger that she felt with Lambert's moving out had never quite subsided. "Twenty years you lived here and I never went up on your rent. And it was a discounted rent at that. This is the thanks I get? You're getting married and moving out?" In spite of such enmity – real or imagined – no one could pack a picnic lunch like Mrs. Boggs. Lambert went by to pick it up, and she jumped on the chance to again complain about his abandoning her, a topic she really enjoyed. "Of course she's a lovely girl. I've always said that. But I never thought you would move out. You! My most trusted and loyal tenant. I don't know what the two of you are paying where you live now, but I bet it's more than three dollars a week. And by the look of the ink stains all over your shirt, she's not a very good laundress. I'd be happy to do your laundry for you if you still lived here. A woman who can't get ink stains out a shirt … I just don't know." That newlyweds might not want to live in a rooming house never crossed her mind. Van Poole paid her a dollar and a half for the picnic lunch. Fifty cents more than her asking price. Maybe the extra money would help her cope.

Lily and Lambert strolled a short distance to a picnic table. Lambert pulled back the towel covering their lunch and revealed fried chicken, potato salad and a variety of pickled vegetables. He smiled with pleasure and an anxious appetite until he saw the cornbread. Three large squares. "Do you think she did this to torment me for moving out?"

"What in the world are you talking about, Lambert?" asked Lily.

"Look. Three pieces of cornbread."

"So?"

"So? There are two of us. She knew this was a picnic for two people and she puts in three pieces of cornbread. What was she thinking?"

"She was probably thinking that you would eat two pieces, and I would enjoy the one, if that."

"Well, of course that's how it will most likely work out, but could there not be at least some acknowledgment of symmetry? Four small pieces instead of three large. That would be the reasonable way to pack a lunch for two." Lambert's obsessive attention to symmetry and even numbers had bubbled to the surface. Lily knew that this must be from the stress of work and dealing with the reunion. Such things tended to bring out this strange eccentricity for all to gawk at. She ignored his petty concerns as they started lunch. Lily's faint feeling was thwarted and her strength restored. Lambert pried the tops off two bottles of Coco-phosphate soda to help wash down the meal.

"Well, we've had our share of excitement. Just yesterday alone, we found a dead body and a load of moonshine. Man's head was smashed in. A veteran here for the reunion. Found his body up under a bridge with a fair quantity of moonshine liquor right nearby."

"Mmm. That's interesting. We hardly got the tent set up properly before patients started coming in for medical attention. And the reunion hasn't even started. I had to get a team of carpenters in here from the terminal to build a proper floor. Can you imagine someone thinking I am going to run a medical clinic in a tent with a dirt floor? And then, I had to get them to come back and do it right. Even out the boards so no one would trip and twist an ankle or worse. Doc Otwell is there in his white coat, but I am sure, or at least I hope, that everyone perceives that as purely honorary. Trusting someone that old and shaky with medical instruments is a situation fraught with danger."

"Well, I can't imagine he can do much damage. I mean, what's the worst thing that could happen? A man pulverize a finger driving a tent stake? I'm sure you will be fully capable of handling whatever comes up. But this man that we found murdered, I think ..."

"What do you mean by that, Lambert?" Her eyes fixed upon him, nearly burning straight through him. Lambert averted his gaze before her stare blinded him. "The primary reason they even have these annual reunions is to provide the opportunity for these old veterans to be examined by medical staff. I'm sure it is the only medical attention most of them get all year." Lily was surprised that Lambert seemed to have forgotten how important proper medical care was to her.

They continued to eat their lunch. Lambert wondered how he could possibly make fighting crime seem at least as important as tending to the sick and injured. After a few minutes, he tried to bring the conversation back to his law enforcement work. "Well, at least we confiscated that moonshine. I uncovered a whole stash under the bridge where we found the dead man. Went back with a photographer to get some photos of the crime scene for the chief to study and, as I was looking around for more evidence, I made the discovery."

"Oh, is that so?" asked Lily, sounding as disinterested in his accomplishments as she could.

"Yes. Then we sent out a squad of reserves this morning to check all the other bridges in the park, figuring there must be more 'shine somewhere, but they came up empty."

"How disappointing."

"Yes. And you know that little ruffian kid, Tommy Whitehead? I think he is involved with it somehow. I am sure I saw him running around up at the park last night. And he let it slip that he found some bottles of moonshine and sold them to Weasel Jones. He says he was in the park just running errands and delivering messages. He even tried to say that he was helping out at the medical tent." Lambert paused for a moment. "He wasn't, was he?"

"Of course not. I would not have a dirty little urchin like that anywhere near the medical tent. The boy has not seen a bar of soap in a month. Have you even the slightest idea of the calamity that befalls a medical setting when unsanitary practices are introduced?"

"That's what I thought. I think he knows a lot more than he is telling. I may not be able to get too much information from him, but I think Sister Finbar can loosen him up a little. He'll be talking by this afternoon, I warrant. Well, if your strength has been restored, my dear, suppose I take you back to your patients who no doubt are pining for your attentions at the very moment." Lily did not get Lambert's sarcasm.

Van Poole drove slowly back to the park. They valued every second together, because they knew that the instant they got back, Lily would spend the next several days tending to sick people, and Lambert would be similarly absorbed, chasing moonshiners, con-men and prostitutes – and a murderer. He recorded some observations in his notebook:

Lily appears under some degree of stress, no doubt owing to the incompetence of others. She had no helpful thoughts regarding the murder.

The Masonic Temple Auditorium was in fine form for the Annual Confederate Ball by Tuesday evening. The Daughters of the Confederacy had spent weeks creating the decorations and no one was disappointed. Multicolored bunting hung from the ceiling and draped the walls. The streamers were alternately red, white and blue, and the blue ones were bedecked with white stars, so that the patriotic nod to the Union was ever so slightly tempered by a reminder of the Confederacy. Three large refreshment tables were laden near to the point of collapse with sandwiches, cookies, candies, cakes, and other refreshments that made a ball a ball. The terrace outside had its own brand of refreshment where the veterans could buy a glass of beer for a nickel. In an attempt to control excess alcohol consumption, the glasses for the beer were very small, and each patron was limited to two glasses. Enforcement of the limit was accomplished by having a young lady tie a red ribbon and a blue ribbon around the wrist of each veteran as they entered the auditorium. The young ladies serving the beer cut one off each time the men got a beer. If a veteran had no ribbon on his wrist, he got no beer. Non-drinkers profited handsomely by selling their beer to others at an inflated price. Within thirty minutes of the start of the ball, a sophisticated black market in red and blue ribbons had developed, with a number of rather creative ways to make a cut ribbon look whole just long enough to get another beer.

And entertainment was as plentiful as the fare. The Windsor

Hotel Orchestra performed lively waltzes, and the Kirby-Smith Camp of the Sons of Confederate Veterans provided a band to play traditional old tunes that many of the veterans remembered from their younger days. Some of the more spritely fellows got up into a spontaneous round of buck dancing when the appropriate tunes came around. The two ensembles traded the stage through the evening, the hotel orchestra playing for an hour, then the Confederate band playing for a half-hour. Each played its own version of "Dixie" more than once, and with every rendition, the crowds stood in respect.

Luther Wilson, for the ninth time that evening, complimented Martha Brandywine on how ravishing she looked. He realized that once they had discussed the weather, he had absolutely no words to say that a beautiful young widow would want to hear. Surely she was not interested in how sharp his pocketknife was, and how he could get a knife sharper than any man he knew, if he put a mind to it. Of course, had he told her this, she might have invited him to come sharpen all the knives in her kitchen, then rewarded him with a decent meal. But that was an opportunity lost that neither of them ever knew was ever there. And she would have no interest in hearing about the Cadillac that had been donated to the Police Department. Beyond the weather and her stunning appearance, he could not think of a thing to say. So he got them each a glass of punch and a plate of cookies and they sat at a table to rest after a less-than-vigorous waltz.

"Luther, I'm sorry I'm not better company tonight, but I cannot get poor Mr. James out of my mind."

"Yes. Truly a tragic circumstance. Your dour mood is understandable."

"Well, I hope I am not actually so unpleasant as to be dour," she said, surprised at his observation.

"No, no. I was merely agreeing that ... uh, well – nonsense, you are perfectly wonderful company, and I would not want to be here with anyone else." They both smiled politely, and several awkward minutes passed.

"I just find the whole thing rather curious, you see," began Mrs. Brandywine.

"Curious. What is curious about it?"

"Mr. James' asking directions to that church. I told him that under normal circumstances, if I was going to walk from my house to Immaculate Conception, not that I would, not being a Catholic, but if I was, I would cross Dignan Park and walk down Ocean Street. But the park, being turned into a campground, might be difficult to navigate. So I suggested that he walk out to Main Street and catch the street car Downtown. But you found him all the way down at Liberty Street. That's the complete opposite direction. Why would he be all the way down there?"

Chief Wilson leaned back, peered upward as was his habit and paused as though he were contemplating one of life's deep mysteries. Then he spoke. "Well, that is where we found a stash of moonshine whiskey. I suspect that he was lured there somehow. Yes. Some conman lured him to the bridge, to sell him whiskey or swindle him somehow, and then resorted to violence rather than the customary guile. Perhaps Mr. James was of moral fiber stronger than the villain could anticipate. One must have a bit of larceny in one's own heart for a con-man's game to work."

"And then he said the most peculiar thing."

"Oh? And what was that?"

"He said that after he went to the church, he would have a great weight lifted from his shoulders."

"Well, you know, Catholics and their confession mumbo-jumbo. Maybe there's something to it, you think? Whatever the reason, I have my best detective on it. I'm sure we will have the guilty party in custody very soon."

"That would please me no end, Luther."

"Shall we dance again, Martha?"

Van Poole kept a close eye on things around the Masonic Temple. He checked with the uniformed men to see that all was well, and told them to keep a lookout for any big spenders. It could be that the man or men who had killed Alden James might have stolen a lot of cash from him. He also had to keep running kids away from the Cadillac that he'd parked right out in front of the building. Occasionally, a drunk would have to be escorted out, or a fight would start over the honors of dancing with one of the young ladies, but all in all, the attendees comported themselves commendably.

At about nine-thirty, Van Poole noticed a steady stream of old veterans leaving the ball and heading north to their campground. Several had automobiles, but a good many were walking or taking the horse-drawn carriages that were deployed for the event under the sponsorship of various civic-minded companies. As Chief Wilson and Mrs. Brandywine came outside, the chief signaled to Van Poole.

"Breaking up kind of early, isn't it, Chief? And good evening,

Miz Brandywine." Mrs. Brandywine reacted with only a demure smile.

"Yes. Apparently one of the younger crowd found some spools of red and blue ribbon in a closet which, if properly deployed, would result in an unending supply of nickel beer. This did not suit the Daughters, so they closed the beer concession and, not so remarkably, a majority of attendees lost their enthusiasm for dance. Now off they all go to their camps where no one, even those with the best of intentions, will spoil their fun. Let us see Mrs. Brandywine home, shall we?"

Getting Mrs. Brandywine home was more than a notion. Absent the reunion, Phelps Boarding House was easily accessible and pleasant lodging for traveling businessmen. It was close to the streetcar line, so one could be in any of the commercial areas of town in minutes. Upon one's return to the house, a pleasant and expansive city park was right across the street. One might even be invited to visit the attic bedrooms, if Mrs. Brandywine's discernment placed one in the category of game.

But now, there were thousands of Confederate war veterans camping in the pleasant park. They were serviced by two mess tents and a hospital tent. The constant flow of automobiles, horse-drawn buggies, and veterans on foot created a congestion that slowed traffic to a crawl at ten o'clock at night, when ordinarily not a soul would be seen upon the street. In usual circumstances, this residential neighborhood that overlooked a beautiful city park would be the very picture of peace and quiet. But now, the night before the Confederate Veterans Reunion was to begin, it was filled with drunken revelers, whooping their Rebel yells, singing and dancing and generally carrying on more than polite folk thought was necessary.

"I will see Miz Brandywine safely into her house, and perhaps sit and visit for a minute. Why don't you walk across the street and stroll through part of the campground and give me a report on things a little later. Come back in, say, about a half-hour?" suggested Chief Wilson.

"Certainly, Chief," said Van Poole as he hopped out and opened the door for the Chief and Mrs. Brandywine. He headed across the street and observed a campground teeming with activity. Groups of old men standing around talking, some of them at makeshift tables they'd set up to play cards or checkers. The place had the chaotic energy of an ant hill that had been kicked, except all the ants were very old. The youngest Confederate veteran would have been in his late sixties. Van Poole's assessment of the situation was that all appeared for the moment to be harmlessly raucous. What could come of a bunch of old veterans enjoying themselves? He returned to Phelps House, collected Chief Wilson and headed home.

A group of three grizzled soldiers were gathered around a campfire, drinking homemade muscadine wine. There was evidence that checkers and cards had lost their entertainment appeal and the old men had resorted to regaling one another with stories. An occasional hunting yarn, the best way to sharpen a knife, then tales of further military service out West, once they were allowed to serve in the U.S. Army again. But eventually the stories all ended up where they always do among men — the conquest of sex.

"Them women in San Francisco will teach you a thing or two, I can tell you that," said one of the men. Then the next one, "I got a job one year on a cattle run into Kansas City. I'll tell you, a week or so in KC with a hunnerd dollars will make up for a season on the cattle trail. Went back the next year and the next. But it's all changed now."

"Yeah, and you have, too. You probably couldn't raise a boner if I paid for the whore." Their raucous laughter was awkward enough as to give away the truth.

As the stories got more and more outrageous and the insults more and more damaging, a man with very dark skin and a bushy black beard approached them. He held his head up high and moved along the ground with seemingly no movement of his feet, which were hidden under his sparkling white robe with gold-braided patterns up and down the front. He wore a red fez with from which a long golden tassel dangled. He stood silently for a moment. Tommy Whitehead was hiding in some darkened bushes, watching the scene play out.

"What the hell are you? Some kind of a wizard?" asked one of the men, as the other two chuckled loudly. The robed man made no comment, and stood there staring at the three men. Finally, he spoke.

"Gentlemen, welcome to our city. We are honored to have such heroes of the great Confederacy among us." The man had a slight but unidentifiable accent. He found an old wooden crate, uprighted it, and sat down without invitation. He addressed the gentleman seated right next to him. "You, sir, look old and weary. I will guess that you are well into your seventh decade and afflicted by rheumatism and catarrh. And from what I have overheard, you are all afflicted with some weakness of vital potency."

"Yup," came the reply. "And I ask again, are you some kind of a wizard?"

"I find the term wizard pejorative. I am Doctor Redobam Mehmed Damascus Al-hazza."

"Hm. Sounds foreign."

"You are very observant, my friend. I am from the family of Al-hazza-al-kim in the northern province of the ancient Persian Kingdom. I have an elixir here," he pulled a dark amber bottle from under his cloak, "developed in the Orient, that will dry your sinuses, make supple your joints, and restore your vigor. It will replenish the physical prowess that you once had, that time has taken from you. The secret is in how the dose is administered." He stood and reached under his cloak and pulled out a golden chalice encrusted with jewels. The three men gasped deeply. "The cure is not only the elixir itself, but it must be taken from this glorious cup in a series of tiny sips, almost continuous, while I recite the ancient chant that summons the healing qualities of the potion." The wizard began to move among the three men, talking to them face-to-face, very close, holding the chalice in one hand while using the other to direct all attention toward it. The array of jewels made it difficult to ignore the cup, as the light from the campfire danced and reflected off the shiny gold and sparkling jewels. "Indeed, some think this is silly Eastern magic. But the scientific proof is that the formula actually absorbs tiny molecules of gold and these mix with the compounds in the elixir to create a cure-all of electrolytes and proteins when broken down by the digestive system. The chant, well, that is a bit of Eastern meditation that, if you listen and concentrate, prepares the body to receive the healing virtues of the medicine. And therein, gentlemen, lies the secret of the cure. For a mere two dollars, I will pour the proper dose into this vessel and administer it. Now what, kind sir, is your weight?"

"About a hunnerd and thirty pound."

"One hundred thirty pounds." He carefully poured about two ounces from the bottle into the bejeweled chalice. To the moonshine, tainted with river water and wheat paste, Weasel had added a good bit of a patent medicine laxative, several bottles of which he had salvaged from mule-drawn cart that had gotten stuck in a mud bog several years before. He had been certain that it would serve him some purpose someday, and that day had arrived. Weasel examined it carefully, tilting the chalice this way and that. "Here, sir, is your ticket to health and no doubt another twenty years of sumptuous living. I would caution that young ladies in the vicinity should put up their guard. Now, sir, your two dollars?"

The old man dug around in his pocket, found two dollar coins and tossed them to the ersatz doctor. "Gimme that." He grabbed at the chalice, but the man in the robe pulled it away. "It smells a little like whiskey," the old soldier said.

"Indeed, there is a component of medicinal alcohol in the tonic, so your olfactory organ serves you well. But heed, sir, I cannot hand the cup over to you. It works only in the hands of one trained in the intricacies of Eastern medicine. Lean your mouth to the cup and drink it in tiny sips, one after another, as I tilt the cup toward you. That's the way."

The old man sipped at the whiskey from the chalice as Weasel turned his head skyward and started a chant. "Al-kazzim, al-hazza! Al-kazzim, el-rabat! Al-Kazzim, al pasha!" He repeated the gibberish several times, each time slightly louder, until the cup was empty. The old man looked at his friends, closed his eyes, and shook his head back and forth. Looked at his friends again. "Well, you two don't look one bit better. But, say, you know I do feel a bit sturdier already."

"Just wait until tomorrow morning. You will awaken to see a bright new world and the world will welcome a bright new inhabitant. Now, gentlemen. Which of you wants another twenty years of vitality?"

Chapter 9

In the months leading up to the Confederate Veterans Reunion, Jacksonville's second-largest newspaper by circulation, **The Jacksonville Evening Metropolis**, did its readers the service of reminding them that the largest newspaper in town, **The Florida Union-Beacon**, had established itself as a Unionist newspaper in the earliest days of the Civil War. The **Beacon** had recently been trying to extricate itself from this awkward and hostile history with the Confederacy, so that the reunion would be a pleasant time for all. The newspaper, once known as **The Florida Daily Beacon,** came under new ownership in early 1860. When the Florida Legislature passed the Ordinance of Secession in 1861, the new owner of the newspaper, in an effort to shout his loyalty to the Union, renamed the paper, adding the word "Union" so that no one would have any doubt as to his and his newspaper's allegiance. Now the owner's descendants were trying to figure out if and how far they should distance themselves from that decision and those who made it.

"Gentlemen, I just don't see how we can undo what was done some fifty years ago. It might be nice to wish that it had never happened. It might be nice to apologize and change the name back. But I truly don't think it will make a tinker's damn bit of a difference." George Wilton, the publisher of the Union-Beacon, was speaking to the managers and editors of his newspaper. "And furthermore, I don't think a single solitary person who advertises in or buys our newspaper will give it a second thought."

"Well, you can think what you want, George, but come down to the sales department with me and try to sell some advertising," said

Pete Tucker, the head of the sales department. "I agree that it is admirable to declare and hold one's position on moral and political issues, but such an admirable act begins to tarnish when it interferes with sales. Why, Prudence Jones over at Grove Bakery told me she wouldn't buy advertising in a nigger-loving Yankee newspaper. And she's been advertising with us since before I had this job. I think it's a great time to drop 'Union' from our name. Hell, we could make a big story out of it, timed to run the week of the reunion. I could double our sales quota if you give me something like that to work with."

"Well, it's not going to happen. My grandfather did what he thought was right and I am not going to undo it for the sake of selling a few ads."

"What if people stop reading? Would that inspire you to take action?" questioned City Editor Al Tiner.

"Al, nobody is going to stop reading this newspaper because of the word 'Union' in the name. If they do, then they're going to miss out on reading the best newspaper in the city. Pete, you and your men do the best you can selling ads. Al, send your reporters out and get the best stories you can. We will cover the reunion, and all the news leading up to it. Good and bad. If sales falter a bit, so be it. We can weather a storm. We've done so in the past and will do so in the future, I have no doubt. Within a few weeks after the reunion, I guarantee you no one will question the loyalties or the quality of **The Florida Union-Beacon."**

"How about we run a story about our friends over at the Metropolis? Surely somebody can come up with something. I know for a fact that is no bunch of angels over there," suggested the editor.

"You're the editor, Al. We report the news. Digging up mud on our competition is only news if we make it the news. I would rather you concentrate on getting news out of the reunion, not plotting revenge."

Such were the orders that young reporter Louis Housend was following when, in the early morning hours of the first day of the reunion, he brought in a story about something happening in the campground at Dignan Park. Like most front page stories, it was given a series of headlines.

DYSENTERY OUTBREAK IN DIGNAN PARK?

Thousands Could Be Affected

City, State Health Officials to Conduct Investigation

Festivities not yet started and disaster falls

The story did not have to wait until long for publication, because the **Union-Beacon**, like all the other local newspapers, ran special editions several times each day during events like the Confederate Veterans Reunion. Special editions were such a dandy way to sell more advertising that some advertisers were getting right tired of so many special events. Nevertheless, by eight o'clock that morning, newsboys were out on the street corners, hollering "Dysentery among the veterans! Special news story! Hot off the presses! Dysentery outbreak!"

The details of the story were that several men had turned up at the medical clinic during the night reporting episodes of vomiting and diarrhea. If that continued, it could certainly indicate a dysentery outbreak among the veterans, the story noted. The intrepid young reporter got quotations from state health officials. The reporter had asked the question, "What efforts would be taken if there were an outbreak of disease in Dignan Park during the reunion?" The response was, "Naturally, our first priority is to treat the stricken veterans. Then we will devote all of our resources to investigating the source of the outbreak. Whether it is sanitary conditions at the mess tents, or a problem with the latrine situation, that is where we will focus our efforts." That answer made it into the story, out of context, but not the question.

Housend was prowling the campground to get more details and quotes. He asked several veterans if they had heard of the dysentery outbreak. "I heared of some men getting sick, but nobody said nothing 'bout the dysentery. If that's what it is, I'm heading to the train station," said one of them. "It's the coloreds working at the mess tents. They musta put something in the food. Matter of fact, I'm not feeling so good myself," said another. A third man offered a lengthy diatribe, "I ain't et nor drank nothing that I didn't bring with me. I had a bout of that dysintury during the war and have never et nor drank nothin' since then that I didn't prepare myself. I'll take water from a well, but I dissolve these here iodine pills in it to make it fair to drink. And I won't go near a privy. I deal with my business in my own way. When I run out of my own food, I'm a-goin' back home to Arkinsaw."

Lily Worthen allowed as how it was true that quite a number of men had turned up throughout the night with symptoms of vomiting and diarrhea. They were all under medication and were resting quietly and the doctor had asked they not be disturbed. The reporter asked the nurse if she thought there was an outbreak of dysentery in the campground.

"I don't have any idea on what's going on in the campground. I have administered medication as I was ordered to by the doctor. Whether it is dysentery or typhoid or diphtheria makes no difference to me. I will tend to the patients in whatever manner the physicians direct to the staff."

The newspaper article reported:

> "Officials at the hospital tent in Dignan Park are unsure whether the disease spreading through the campground is dysentery, typhoid or diphtheria, but were inclined to think the former, based on the cases that have presented so far."

The Jacksonville Evening Metropolis stuck to the high ground of the Confederacy and did not report on an unsubstantiated rumor about any dysentery outbreak. They did, however, print and distribute throughout the campground a special Confederate Reunion edition of their newspaper, containing all the daily news of the reunion. Among the other items, there was a report on the unfortunate robbery and brutal murder of one of the Confederate veterans attending the reunion. The newspaper went on to note that the remains of Alden James had been found, beaten savagely, head nearly unrecognizable as to human form. His body was then hidden underneath a bridge at the eastern end of the very park where some reunion attendees were beginning to make camp. This was the story that George Townsend read. It interested him much more than a possible outbreak of dysentery.

Mayor Avery Langen was displeased. Very displeased. It was just after eight o'clock on Wednesday morning and he was reading the special morning edition of the **Union-Beacon**. The first official day of the reunion with parades, speeches and welcomings and the newspaper goes and reports a dysentery outbreak. He called his secretary on his brand-new voice-tube communicating device. "Miz Patricia," he said as politely as words can be uttered through clenched teeth, "would you gather those gentlemen whose livelihoods depend on my happiness in my office in the next thirty minutes, please? Tell them to be prompt. Then please bring me some coffee." He rocked back in his large leather chair and swiveled around to look out the window of his third-floor office. He filled his pipe with some too-moist Turkish-Perique blend that he'd spread out on his windowsill to dry. It took five matches to get it burning right, but it was well worth the effort, as the thick, aromatic purplish smoke rose from the bowl and hung in the air, encircling his head. The mayor was an easy-going man as long as things were easily going his way. He was neatly groomed, soft-spoken and always wore a pleasant, half-smile on his face. He was never happier than when he was in control. But, as control slipped away, so did his easy-going nature. The smile became a mere slit of the lips, behind which teeth clenched visibly.

His secretary brought in a full coffee service and he impatiently waved her away, then poured himself a cup. He alternately sipped the brew and drew on his pipe, thinking about what he would say when his staff arrived. Mayor Langen had extraordinary power in Jacksonville, only partially because of his office. As mayor, he chaired the City Commission, which must act in concert for any individual commissioner to execute almost anything but the most routine ministerial operations of his office. He also had direct control over the police department, the fire department, and the building inspector's office, among others.

But his real power was derived not from his official title, but from his ability to select and support candidates for other offices in such a way as they understood that they held office only because of him and his considerable clout, and they owed their full and devoted allegiance to him. He allowed them to make most minor decisions on their own, just so that they could maintain a semblance of independence for a good rapport with the voters. They were even allowed, on occasion, to not vote with him on issues when it would not have an effect on the desired outcome. If, however, a measure came before the City Commission in which some fraction of the public treasury was to be disposed of in some way, no wavering from prescribed behavior was tolerated. Thus did Mayor Langen and Council President Jimmie Calton compete for political power in Jacksonville.

The first man to arrive was Police Chief Luther Wilson. Langen could see him standing in the anteroom. "I hope he was not a mistake," thought Mayor Langen. The mayor had done a good bit of business over the years with Wilson Textile Mills in South Carolina. Sold them a lot of machinery. Brokered railroad and shipping deals. He thought that young Luther would be the right man for the job of police chief, and an easy sell to his fellow commissioners and the City Council. He'd impressed everyone with his Citadel education and his military service. A college-educated man running the police department. Jacksonville could very well be the only such Southern city so graced. And the fellow was smart. So smart, Langen was convinced, that you could put him in charge of an operation and get away with dang near anything right under his nose, as long as you kept telling him what a good job he was doing. At least, that had been Langen's experience upon which he relied, until Wilson had found the moonshine whiskey in the park. But maybe that was just dumb luck. "Oh, let my judgment be sound this time!" he prayed.

"Luther! Come on in. I'm just waiting on everybody else. Everything is well with you, I trust?"

"Everything is absolutely delightful, Mr. Mayor. I once again sincerely apologize for not being able to come through on my end regarding the moonshine. It would have made a great piece for the paper. I can't imagine that the paltry amount Van Poole found under the one bridge is all there is. I'm sure there's more, and I'm sure we'll find it. And when we do, you, sir, will be the first to know."

"Thank you, Chief. That's very thoughtful of you. Was that Widow Brandywine I saw you with at the Confederate Ball last night?"

"Yes. Lovely lady. After we found Mr. James murdered – you

know he was a guest at her house – she was very distraught, and it seemed like a nice gesture to accompany her," said Wilson.

"Oh. Well, that's very gallant of you, Chief." The two men chatted pleasantly. *How's your Dad doing?*

Quite well, thank you. He sends his best.

Did that deal with the mattress company work out?

Oh, quite profitably.

Things going well with the Pinkerton Men?

Oh, no harm done yet.

The rest of those summoned drifted in, one at a time. Finance Commissioner, Health and Sanitation Commissioner. Hank Clark, Roads and Bridges Commissioner, never attended such meetings. He could always be relied upon to do what the mayor wanted, but refused to acknowledge any tribute. This angered Langen personally, but it never fouled any plans, so he'd let it go. The other member of the City Commission was the Utilities Commissioner, who managed to get himself elected and re-elected without any mayoral influence. He'd created his own very cozy world with the gas, water and electric utility companies to such an extent that Mayor Langen was unnecessary for his election and re-election. The man had even managed to get coal and ice companies to bow to his authority and cooperate with price regulation. There was no symbiosis in the relationship, so his presence was not required. Council President Calton had to duck into the men's room to powder his face before he could walk into the mayor's office. He was quite tricky to corral for a meeting like this, but the two men knew just enough about each other's activity that they could learn to share power or learn to share a prison cell. And then there was Cyrus Tippington, the municipal judge who tried to avoid the strenuous work of sentencing drunks and vagrants to jail terms, but did love the camaraderie of a meeting, and he was pleasant enough to have around if he'd had his morning brandy.

The mayor had arranged chairs in a semicircle in front of his desk. The full coffee service was on the desk's corner, and he continued to enjoy his brew, but didn't offer any to the men gathered in the room. When everyone had taken a seat, he began. "Gentlemen, we all know how important it is that this Confederate Veterans Reunion is successful. I needn't go through all the reasons, need I? Good. I didn't think so. Now, I would hope that no one here needs to be told in any explicit terms that these three days are not the time to be making a fuss about things that need not be fussed about. The corollary to that is that neither should anyone be turning their heads to, or away, from something simply because of an oversight of some unspoken courtesy."

Chief Wilson interrupted. "I'm sorry, Mayor. I'm not following any of this at all."

"None of this is directed at you, Chief. This is a discussion of some technical issues that some of these other city officials have to deal with managing municipal government. You'll catch on," said the Mayor. "Heaven knows the other three-hundred and sixty-two days of the years we are all presented with ample opportunity to connect in that special way with our various constituencies. Now that we are all clear on that, we can discuss the misperception reported in one of our daily newspapers that there is an outbreak of disease in the reunion campground. I am going to ask a question, and starting at my extreme left, you will each attempt to answer it. If you have no answer, so indicate and we will move on, but I will not have my time wasted by excuses and explanations of what may or may not be. Everybody understand?" There were nods of assent all around. "Now, is there an outbreak of dysentery in the veterans' campground? The appropriate answer, if you know it, would be 'yes' or 'no'." He pointed to his left. Jimmie Calton was the unfortunate first lamb to slaughter. He silently waved his hand indicating he had no answer. This was not his first ride in the mayor's office. Langen moved down the line and some of the men tried to get out a "Well, you see, sir ... " A sharp slap on the desk and the glare of Mayor Langen silenced each who tried and failed. He came to Judge Tippington. "Dysentery. Now that's an unpleasant experience. I recall once when ... "

"Thank you, Judge. No time for stories, though," the mayor barked. Then he looked at Chief Wilson. "Yes," came the answer from the highest cop in the city.

"That was a mighty sure sounding 'yes,' when nobody else could even utter a cogent syllable, Chief. What makes you so sure?"

"Well, of course, I have no actual medical training, but I have a rather extensive military background. Served in the Philippines ten years ago. Spent a few years on the Mexican border. The symptoms reported certainly seem consistent with the types of diseases that can spread quickly through a camp. Thousands of men in close quarters. Using the same crude latrines. No running water. Conditions are perfect for something like this. Imagine just one of them arriving here with the early signs of some undiagnosed malady. Pass around a canteen a couple of times, share swigs from a whiskey bottle, maybe offer someone a piece of jerky or a corn dodger. It would spread like wildfire."

The room of men sat in stunned silence as they all realized that Chief Wilson was accurately describing exactly what they all feared. The confidence with which the Chief had spoken had as much impact as the words he'd said.

"Well, what do you think we should do about it?" asked the mayor. "We can't have something like this ruining the whole reunion, and our city's reputation to boot."

"Do as we would in a military operation. A cross-functional task force. I suggest that you assign some men with decision-making authority from the appropriate city bureaus, health and sanitation and so on. Put them at the disposal of the state health inspector. Act quickly and decisively to remedy the conditions. Treat the latrines with lime. Drop iodine pills in the water supply. Inspect mess tent kitchens. Do it immediately and limit the damage."

"Good thinking, Chief. I will have each commissioner send someone over immediately. Have you anything else to report to us, Chief?"

"Yes, since you asked. I am grieved to report to you that an out-of-town visitor has been brutally murdered. We found him Monday, under the Liberty Street bridge at Hogan's Creek. I suspect you all have read that in the papers by now. In addition, it seems someone is trying to smuggle untaxed whiskey into the park for the reunion. We uncovered quite a stash under the same bridge where the dead body was found. Whether or not there's any connection, we cannot yet confirm."

"Well, yes, that's great work, Chief. You stay on top of this for us now, y'hear?"

Weasel Jones got to be one of Jacksonville's most successful con-men by adhering to a few simple concepts. The most important of these was variety. Something might be working like a charm, but that's no reason to keep doing it. Every day he woke up thinking of new ways to separate people from their money; some were legal, others not. So, having made a few hundred dollars in one night — more than a month's wages for most skilled tradesmen — by selling sips of a life-prolonging elixir, which was nothing more than some cheap whiskey mixed with a laxative, he decided to spend the next day doing something different, and possibly even legal.

When not dealing directly with the public, Weasel spent his time in a small suite of rented rooms on the second floor of a building on Walnut Street, which housed a hardware and dry goods store on the ground floor. When his schemes were successful, he had to find places to hide his money. He'd loosened as many floorboards as he thought safe, and was now prying baseboards loose and concealing bundles of money behind those. The business of providing female companionship to gentlemen who had no natural ability to attract it resulted in rent money and day-to-day walkin'-around money, which occasionally had to be supplemented by various cons. The big cash schemes, like selling sips of cheap whiskey for two dollars, brought in money that he'd set aside for the future. He was a very conscientious shyster.

On this, the first full day of the Confederate Veterans Reunion, he opted for an activity with an air of respectability — selling commemorative badges, rings, belt buckles, neckerchief slides and tie pins. He bought the necessary license to peddle these legally, so that he wouldn't be harassed by the officials. Weasel had designed and built a wooden case that folded up like a traveling valise, but concealed a spring-loaded wooden stand that opened to make an attractive display table for his wares. Selling the souvenirs would not make him a lot of money — he knew that from the start. But life for Weasel was always about creating opportunity. The portable souvenir table created opportunity for other, more profitable endeavors.

Before he set out for the day, he wrapped the chalice in some old cotton cloth and put it into a bag. The gold, jewel-encrusted chalice was missing one stone. Weasel could see the empty mount that once held it in the base. He wondered if Champ had pried it off and sold it. He approached Phelps House from the service alley and knocked twice on the garage door. The sound of bolt locks being slid was followed by the door being opened a few inches. The old man let him in. The room was hot, still, and uncomfortable. Clearly the space of a man who worked hard and bathed infrequently. The bearded man sat down on the edge of a cot and looked up at Weasel. "Well?" he asked.

"Here," said Jones as he handed over the bundle of cotton rags.

The man unwrapped the chalice and found a tight bundle of one-dollar bills, five of them, wrapped up and tied with twine, stuffed into the cup. He glanced up at Weasel with a look of approval. "'Bout time you got here. Got a full day's work ahead of me. Can't waste time waitin' 'round for the likes o' you." Champ's speech was very slow and slightly impaired, the result of a broken jaw and several missing teeth. The facial injuries were said to have happened many years before and medical attention was never rendered.

"Look, Champ, I gave you five dollars yesterday and another five today, just like I promised. That's probably more than you make in a month working here."

"Don't want Miz Brandywine come out and catch you here. Supposed to be fissin' the boiler for the lawndwy today. She get mad at you hangin' 'round. Wouldn't do neither of us no good."

"She's doing fine with her business in the attic. I don't know why she worries about me."

"I don't know nothing, but she'll fire me if she come out here and I ain't started on that boiler yet."

"Well, you can get on about your work then."

"Hey! Don't tell nobody 'bout this thing," hissed Champ, referring to the chalice. He picked up a well-worn, solid oak newel post and indicated its effectiveness as a weapon.

"Champ, who do you think you're talking to? I know enough not to kill the goose that lays golden egg. All the same, if you decide you need to pry any more of them jewels off to sell, you let me know, 'cause I can get you a better deal than anybody in town."

"Get out of here. Got work to do."

Weasel left the old man in his shabby little room. To avoid the possibility of being seen by anyone in Phelps House, he circled the block and came out into Dignan Park by another way. He thought that it looked suspiciously quiet and almost deserted. Then he remembered that the opening parade for the reunion was being held that morning. It seemed like it might be a good time to pillage through some of the tents and see what kind of valuables might have been left behind. But he changed his mind when he saw that each camp had left behind two sentries — fully armed, uniformed guards on vigilant patrol. Weasel smiled and waved at each one he saw as he passed through Dignan Park on his way Downtown to watch the parade.

Chief Wilson had managed, after a series of debates that went from the self-deprecating to the "I'm too important," to be excused from riding in the parade. But since the police department Cadillac was the finest automobile in the entire city fleet — the best of the eight — it was determined that Lambert Van Poole and the chief would chauffeur the mayor and the city council president from City Hall to the reviewing stand, where they could see the entire parade but, more important, where everyone could see them. It was timed so that they'd arrive at the reviewing stand with just minutes to spare before the parade began several blocks away. Van Poole started out from City Hall with the mayor and council president in the back seat, the top folded and buckled down, and the chief up front next to him.

"Slow down, for heaven's sake, Lambert," said the chief, in fear for the safety of the occupants and the people lined up along the sidewalks.

"Yes, please," echoed the mayor. "You go by so fast, nobody is able to see who we are. This automobile is more important than anything in the entire parade. There are a lot of citizens standing around here who want to wave to me and I intend to wave back. And I want them to know it is me."

The council president agreed with the mayor and gave further instructions. "Now, when we get out, you two make a quick exit. That's when you can speed up, Detective. But don't go too far. The second the last car or band or whatever passes the review stand, I want to see this car right out front, ready for you can take us back to City Hall."

Van Poole stopped in the middle of Laura Street, where the reviewing stand had been erected along the east side of Hemming Park. The mayor and council president stood up in the back of the car, removed their hats and started waving to the adoring crowd. Pointing and waving, smiling and clapping, holding their hats over their hearts, they descended from the confines of the automobile and shook just a few hands before making their way to the VIP box. The mayor lingered a bit among the crowd, shaking hands, hugging women, poking young boys in the ribs, air-kissing drooling babies. Like a game of chicken, he wanted to see how close the lead parade car could get before he breathlessly made it to his seat.

"Good God, but you are a show-off, aren't you, Avery?" stage-whispered Jimmie Calton.

"Oh, hell. They expect that. It's a great balancing act. Let them know that the parade is important, but so is greeting my constituents. I do it every chance I get. So who did they finally get to marshal this parade? I missed the lead car. Was talking to some voters. I hope they found somebody other than Davidson. He's so involved in the event that it wouldn't seem right to put him in the lead car of the parade."

"They got the chairman of the County Commission."

"Frank Saunders? What in the hell has the county done to help with this thing? When does the county ever get involved in city affairs?"

Van Poole pulled the car around the corner and up on the sidewalk. Since it had Jacksonville Police Department stenciled on the side, he felt secure knowing no one would harass him about it. He and Chief Wilson found an arrangement of tables set up behind the reviewing stand for volunteers and otherwise unoccupied city officials to sit. A young lady in period costume brought them coffee in tin mugs. Chief Wilson took a sip and disapprovingly asked, "Good God. Is this left over from the war?"

"No, they actually think coffee tastes like this."

"Well, this is absolutely undrinkable." He signaled to the girl and asked for a glass of lemonade. Van Poole made do with the coffee. "Well, Lambert, who is our murderer? Is it Weasel Jones or Tommy Whitehead?"

"I don't think it's either. Tommy gives the impression of a delinquent full a brass and vinegar, but I think it's an act. He's actually a rather fragile little kid. Don't you think he could get away from that old nun if he really wanted to? He's all talk. And Weasel, troublesome though he is, is not a man to resort to violence. He can get what he wants from people by sleight of hand and his gift of gab. No reason to stain his hands with blood. And, from what Tommy was saying, Weasel has some moonshine. But selling cheap whiskey is an activity I'm sure Weasel perceives to be beneath his station."

"Well, let's make sure we clear up something soon. With what appears to be a dysentery outbreak, everybody is anxious for something positive. Busting up bottles of illicit whiskey would have been nice, but that didn't come to fruition as we had hoped. So let's try to make an arrest for something, all right?"

"Sure, Chief. I'll get something for you. Do you really think we have a dysentery epidemic on our hands?"

"Don't know for sure, but it certainly cannot be ruled out. Look at the conditions. How many thousand men are shoved into campgrounds with less than ideal sanitary facilities? Many of them sharing food, canteens, eating utensils. It would be no great surprise if some type of traveling infection should break out. The key at this point is to act decisively and not panic. I shared as much with the mayor and some others this morning. Dysentery or not, why sit around and wonder about it? Take action."

"I guess they're unaccustomed to someone so disposed to action as you, Chief."

"You know, we were planning on six thousand people for this reunion? Well, the count as of last night was more than thirty thousand. And more are coming in today. They had to open up sections of the park for camping that they hadn't anticipated. The whole park up to Sixth Street is now a campground. And I understand some men are camping in the woods along the railroad track out west of town and jumping the morning freight to get here."

"It's certainly much more of a crowd than we thought it would be. But dysentery? Kind of makes me want to keep my distance from the campground. Maybe it's a good thing we got the Pinkerton Men. Let them handle the park."

"Now, Lambert. There will no duty-shirking by Jacksonville Police. Just be mindful about any person with whom you make physical contact. Wash your hands every chance you get. A bit of common sense, vigilance and personal hygiene goes a long way in such circumstances."

"Shouldn't this parade be nearing the end by now? I thought it was supposed to last only a half-hour," asked Van Poole, clearly impatient with the whole thing.

They walked around to the front of the reviewing stand and saw Laura Street filled with slow-moving marching bands, horse-drawn wagons, and automobiles packed with men waving the Confederate flag and holding signs identifying their various camps. The final official part of the parade, the large, impressive military band called The Stonewall Brass from a Virginia military academy, had passed. Now, renegade participants, few of whom were part of the official parade, had gridlocked the street. Several cars kept circling Downtown blocks at random, honking horns, firing guns with blank cartridges, and generally causing a scene which was a disturbance to some, but quite entertaining to most.

Mayor Langen leaned over the side of the VIP box where he and the council president were effectively trapped and shouted down to the chief, "Wilson! Do something! Get us out of here!" Chief Wilson found a ladder stowed by the workmen who'd assembled the bleachers, and propped it up alongside the box. The two politicians clambered down and got into the car. Van Poole couldn't get out into the street because of the gridlock caused by a midget on a Shetland pony, carrying a sign identifying him as the mascot for the Missouri Short Rifles. So, he put the car in gear and drove across Hemming Park, missing tables, booths and pedestrians by mere inches, and pulled into a street unaffected by the circus atmosphere.

Hemming Park remained full of people after the parade. Veterans and their families were walking around, enjoying the complimentary refreshments, and looking at the games and booths that had been set up. It was, for all the world, just like a carnival or a small version of a county fair. Vendors were selling souvenirs, and there were games that could be played, the winners getting a cheap stuffed animal. One air-rifle game had panels that popped up, showing a Union regiment or a Confederate outfit. If you knocked down all the Union placards, you won. This game was popular enough that no prizes were awarded. Winning was its own reward. In the middle of a row of vendors was Weasel Jones, with his pop-up display table full of trinkets commemorating the reunion. He could spot potential purchasers he thought would be interested in some of his more special items not on display. A couple of old veterans were casually inspecting his wares. Weasel grandly addressed them, "Gentlemen, I never had the privilege of defending the Confederacy, so let me express my gratitude to you for your valiant service."

"Why, thank ye, young man," would be the expected response, but one of the men, back bent with age and care, told him, "Don't feel too bad, sonny. You didn't miss a thing."

"I'll bet that a couple of brave men like you found an ample harvest of souvenirs on the battlefield. Am I right? Some Union belt buckles, hat badges, maybe a sidearm? Such things have become quite collectible."

"Uh, well, no. I actually never did get anything worth keeping. You see, I was mostly in the supply group, so we, uh, never, you know."

"Oh, yes, I see. My grandfather came home with quite a trove of Union trinkets. I have no real use for them and if you gentlemen have any interest in acquiring anything, I can make you a friendly deal. Special reunion discount." After several conversations like this, he had lassoed quite a number of men expressing an interest in purchasing some of this battlefield memorabilia. He gave them directions to a tavern on East Monroe Street where he would be dining at ten o'clock that evening, with his full collection of battle memorabilia that, regrettably, he had to liquidate in order to care for his aging widowed grandmother. The veterans would find themselves looking at cheap imitations in a dimly lit bar, with drinks flowing freely.

After those two left, another group of codgers stopped by his table. "Good day, gentlemen," said Weasel. "What parts of the great Confederacy are y'all from?"

Two of them said Birmingham, but the third responded, "Vicksburg, Mississippi."

"Vicksburg?" responded Weasel. "What a coincidence. I wonder if you know my friend Stan Cartwell, owner of Standard Diamonds & Jewelry?"

"I don't know him personally, but everyone in Vicksburg knows that jewelry store. He's a right prominent man in town."

"And a fine, honest businessman. I have done my share of business with him over the years. Always felt very good about dealing with him."

"Yessir, that is his reputation."

"You know, I just thought of something. Maybe you could do us a favor. I have been corresponding with Stan about a very valuable watch taken from a Union officer who was captured in a battle up near Chickamauga. I feel uneasy about putting that thing in a box and trusting it to a freight company. Maybe you could take it with you and deliver it to him for me."

"I don't know any reason why not."

"See, he wrote me in his last letter that he had a collector willing to pay one hundred dollars for that watch. We agreed that he would pay me fifty for it, that way he could pay the shipping costs and still make a tidy little profit. But if you're willing to help us out, you could pay me twenty-five for the watch, and then sell it to Stan for fifty when you get there. That way you make some money, I make some money, Stan makes money. And nobody has to worry about it getting broken or stolen in transit. I can't see a disadvantage to anybody."

"Why, you make it sound downright tempting. All right, sir. I'll do it."

When he had finished making arrangements to get the watch to the man and collect the payment, Lambert Van Poole stepped up to the table.

"Well, as I live and breathe. Weasel Jones engaged in a

legitimate business enterprise. Where is a photographer when you need one?"

"Good afternoon, Detective. Isn't this reunion wonderful? Such a festive atmosphere and folks are so willing to spend their money."

"Where did you get all your merchandise, Weasel?"

"I bought it all legal and proper. From the companies that are licensed to make it. I have my permit right here, Detective." He handed the permit to the detective, who took it and put it in his pocket without even looking at it.

"Well, it looks like you had to dig them out of a coal mine or something. Your hands are so filthy, they're almost black," the detective observed drolly.

"You know, Detective, even a successful businessman such as myself has to put in some manual labor when sales are slow. I have been working with my hands. Uh, I was up at the gas plant helping them clean the soot from the smokestacks. That's what all that is."

"You used to be a better liar, Weasel. I don't know what you've been up to, but I intend to find out." The detective waved to two uniformed men standing a post nearby. One of them must have been part of the reserve force; he seemed very anxious to help. "Hold this man in custody. He is under arrest." Van Poole took down the display table, walked to the corner and called the station on the emergency phone, asking for the jail wagon to be sent. Then he left the prisoner with the two officers and drove to the station with Weasel's display case.

Van Poole put Weasel Jones alone in an interrogation room for a spell, to let his nerves and imagination become quite anxious. The detective finally strode in with authority, tersely directing the prisoner, "Weasel, let's cut right to the bone of this whole mess. I have testimony from a very reliable informant that you have been selling homemade, untaxed whiskey to some of our distinguished guests during this celebration."

"I have no idea what you're talking about, Detective."

"Don't interrupt. I haven't even gotten to the good part yet. Don't you want to hear everything that you're going to confess to? So, my source says that you're selling whiskey. That's number one. Then we find a man murdered and stuffed up under the Liberty Street bridge. That's number two. Then, what do you think I find back behind the dead body but a whole load of moonshine? So, I've got you selling whiskey, a cache of whiskey hidden away, and a dead body. I am sure an intelligent man like you can guess the conclusion I reached. You found somebody messing with your stash and killed him."

"Detective Van Poole, that is preposterous!"

"I know it is. A fellow like you is not schooled in violent interactions, otherwise you wouldn't have left the body and the moonshine right there for me to find. The whole thing is so preposterous that it leaves no doubt — you are the guilty party."

"I don't know anything about a dead man or a stash of moonshine. Little Tommy Whitehead is who you want to talk to about moonshine. OK, I bought a couple of bottles of the stuff from him, but he didn't tell me about any more. You go find that little bastard if you want to know about moonshine. Otherwise, I insist that you release me, as I have several important business engagements to attend to this evening."

"Oh, you won't be making it to any business engagements tonight. I'm arresting you for peddling without a permit."

"I showed you my permit. I paid one dollar and fifty cents for it just like everybody else selling stuff at Hemming Park."

"Permit? What permit? I never saw a permit," replied the glib detective. Van Poole sent Jones back to his cell, then inventoried the contents of the sales kit and placed it all the evidence room at the police station. It was not very well organized. Neckerchief slides and belt buckles all thrown together into one compartment. Hat badges and ribbons all mixed up. After separating the disparate goods, he counted everything again, and if there was an even number of any one particular item, he left them altogether in one compartment. If there was an odd number, he took out the last one and placed in a compartment by itself. That would make it so much easier to inventory the next time. Van Poole was amazed that some people could manage at all without a system as logical as his. He made a few entries in his notebook.

Arrested Weasel Jones for peddling. Claims to know nothing about moonshine or the dead body. His sales kit was in complete disarray.

He walked out of the station on his way to get the Cadillac so he could take the chief up to Springfield Park for the opening speeches and celebrations. A bicycle patrolman stopped him before he reached the car, saying, "Hey, Lambert. Did you forget your rosary this morning or something?"

"What in the hell are you talking about?" he answered, annoyed at yet another delay.

"That sister up there at the Catholic Church asked me to tell you to come see her. What else could it be?"

"Very funny. Where is she?"

"She came out to the sidewalk on Ocean Street to flag me down, but she said for you to come to the rectory and they will send for her there."

"Thanks."

Lambert continued to the car in the alley behind the police station and found Chief Wilson waiting for him. Impatiently waiting for him. "Let's get a move on, Lambert. A lot of important people are expected at the opening ceremony, and they expect to see me there. Not that I care anything about it, but it just goes with the territory of responsible leadership, you know?"

"Yessir. I'll get you there as quickly as I can, and drop you off. One of the nuns at Immaculate Conception Church has sent word that she wants to talk to me. I suppose it must about Tommy Whitehead. As soon as I find out, I'll come back and meet you at the VIP tent. Is that acceptable, sir?"

"Well. I certainly would not want you to keep a nun waiting. But do not abandon me, Lambert. You know how uncomfortable I get around all these politicians and rainmakers. I just want to be seen long enough so that they can say I was there. Then I want to get back to work."

"Yes, sir. You can count on me, Chief."

Early Wednesday morning, before the sun was even up, Tommy was awakened by the ear-splitting sound of a drunken Confederate bugler who may have, at one time, been capable of blowing something recognizable. He sneaked out of the gardener's shed and walked to the alley behind the convent. He crawled quietly to a darkened corner of the back porch and went to sleep.

At six, Sister Finbar started poking him with a mop handle. Tommy jumped up with a start, apparently in the middle of an unpleasant dream. "No! I ain't done nothin'. I don't want to go. Let me go!" And then he realized where he was. Sister Finbar could see tears welling up in his eyes.

"It must be an awful batch of sins to cause you such agony through the night. Can you not see that you must confess? Lay your burdens at the feet of Christ and get an honest night's sleep, lad."

"I don't know what you're talking about."

"I'm talking about you and your sinful ways. I guess you haven't done enough penance. But that's all right. We have plenty of penitential work to be done around this place. What made you decide to come back?"

"What are you talking about? I slept here all night. I's 'fraid if I ran away, you'd come with your lasso and drag me back here."

"Lying to a nun, eh? Is that the way you plan to go through life? I heard you leave last night. I came out here at five o'clock to get some potatoes for breakfast and you were nowhere to be seen. So now you have a whole new basket of sins for which you must atone. Come eat breakfast, then hew some firewood. Then we'll paint some more. Maybe some window-washing after that."

The formal opening of the 24th annual United Confederate

Veterans Reunion took place in the Kirby-Smith Auditorium tent, which had been set up in the middle of Springfield Park. After the official and unofficial parade through Downtown that Wednesday morning, all gathered met at the cavernous structure which had taken three days to assemble and erect. It had a capacity that far exceeded any other meeting space in Jacksonville, and even still, the sides of the huge tent had to be rolled up so that seating outside could accommodate the overflow crowd. Chief Wilson made his way through the crowds, shaking hands when necessary, speaking when unavoidable, trying to get to the auditorium tent and to his assigned seat before the formal introductions began. Not being an elected official or an actual Confederate veteran, but still an important figure, he was relegated to a second-tier VIP section. He got there just in time for his assigned section to stand and be recognized — not quite as prestigious as being introduced individually, but significant nonetheless. He scanned the crowd, mostly trying to see if his men were at their assigned posts. Then he turned his attention to making sure the mayor, the City Council president, and other important folks saw that he was there. Park Trammell, the governor of Florida himself, was in attendance to welcome the Confederate veterans on behalf of all Floridians.

Then flowed the remarks from the mayor, the chairman of the County Commission, the president of the City Council, and Commander Davidson of R. E. Lee Camp, the host camp for the reunion. He alluded to the business agenda of the meeting, election of officers, by-law amendments, treasurer's report, all of which would be conducted at committee level, which was good, because not a living soul there cared one fig about such nonsense. These men wanted to know about the band competitions, the horseshoe toss championships, the rope climbing contests and, most important, the Rebel Yell contest, the single event in which it is a proven fact that the drunker you are, the better you yell. Up to a point, anyway. After the formalities, the presiding officer announced a half-hour recess, after which he would discuss more business involving joint activities being undertaken with the Confederate Memorial Society and the Sons of Confederate Veterans. No one returned after the recess.

Chief Wilson found his way to where the mayor and council president were standing. "Prescient remarks, Mr. Mayor," he said as he joined them, shaking the hands of everyone within arm's reach.

"It was just a welcome to Jacksonville, Luther."

"All the same, they were delivered with fervor that befits the occasion, sir."

"Let's go the hospitality tent and see if we can find a little something worth nibbling."

"Excellent thought, sir." They headed for the hospitality tent, stopping to shake hands and talk about nothing at the slightest provocation. They finally arrived at the hospitality tent and sat, sipping coffee, waiting for the volunteer who'd agreed to assemble plates for them.

"How close are you to arresting that murderer, Luther? I hope we can expect something soon."

"What? Oh, uh, yes sir. Detective Van Poole is on top of the situation, sir. My most capable man, you know. He will have it all sorted out soon, I assure you. Tomorrow, perhaps."

"Yes. Van Poole. Very capable. Very smart, that man," muttered the mayor.

"Between you and me, sir, I am surprised that you didn't make him the chief of police instead of bringing me in from the outside." Chief Wilson was testing his self-deprecating rhetorical skills to see what level of reassurance he might get.

"Nonsense, Luther." The mayor began to chuckle, a little nervously. "You are exactly the man we need for the job. Van Poole is smart and a very capable detective, but you are the man we need to lead this police department. Don't sell yourself short, Chief." The mayor shuddered as he thought about the financial devastation that most elected officials would suffer should Lambert Van Poole ever be elevated to such lofty heights.

The magnificent edifice that was Immaculate Conception Catholic Church stood at the corner of Duval and Ocean streets. Next to it was a courtyard containing a small shrine to the Virgin Mary, and beyond that was the rectory which housed the church offices and the living quarters for the priest. Behind the church and the rectory was an alleyway, across which was the convent, the orphanage and parish school. These three buildings shared a common backyard, with the potato shed and other utility buildings. In this backyard area was young Tommy Whitehead, chopping firewood under the watchful eye of Sister Finbar. Van Poole followed the instructions he had been given and asked for her at the rectory. He was seated at a table in the large kitchen and served iced tea while the sister was summoned. She came in, washed her hands and filled a glass of water from the tap. “Oh, thank you for coming, Detective. I have a broken heart for little Tommy, but of course I can’t let him see that. The poor fellow has been sorting potatoes, painting eaves and chopping wood for a day-and-a-half now. I think he’s give up any notion of running away. I don’t even keep the rope on him now.”

“Well, it seems you have been able to inspire some productive behavior in him. You are to be congratulated.”

“Oh, pish-posh. That’s not what I’m getting at. He is working himself so hard in order to keep from facing something. And not just his sins. He is scared. He won’t show it, but he’s scared. He must be mixed up in some awful stuff. I left him untied for a bit yesterday and he didn’t run off until after supper. Then he came back this morning. Fell asleep on the back porch. When I woke him, he came up with a start, screaming, ‘Let me go, I ain’t done nothing’ and on and on like that. I don’t know what it all means, but he’s right frightened of something or someone. Why else would he come back? I don’t know a thing about police procedures, but I am well-versed in the ways of the sinner. And that little boy out there is just dying to tell someone something. He won’t confess to a priest, but he may tell all to a policeman. This might be a good time for you to go and talk to him.”

“I know a bit about the ways of the sinful myself, Sister. I think you’re right. This would be a good time to have a chat with the boy.” Van Poole rose from the table, looked out the back window and saw Tommy stacking firewood. He walked out the back door of the rectory and across the alley toward Tommy. As soon as the boy saw the detective, he dropped an armload of firewood and ran, through the narrow space that separated the convent from the orphanage, emerging out on Church Street. Tommy knew the honeycomb of alleyways and shortcuts like the back of his hand. He turned between buildings instinctively, without having to look to see if there was an exit through to the other side. He moved quickly, reaching to topple stacks of firewood and other obstructions behind him to slow down his pursuer. Down an alley behind a building, he saw a man making a coal delivery, and he crawled under the chute that went from the truck to the below-ground coal storage area. Van Poole never saw him. He kept on running, looking for Tommy, then gave up when he reached Dignan Park.

Sweating and winded, Van Poole walked back to Immaculate Conception Church. Sister Finbar was waiting for him in the alley.

"Well, did you get anything out of him?" she asked, handing him a fresh glass of iced tea.

"No. He had nothing useful to say. But I will want to talk to him again, once we gather a little more evidence. You try to get a little more work out of him and maybe he'll be ready to talk tomorrow." Lying to a nun? The by-the-book detective could not believe his own audacity. But telling a harmless white lie was better than admitting that the little bastard gave him the slip.

"Oh. I see. Yes, a little more work, you say? And where is the laddie now?"

"I told him he could go up to the park and watch the men practice for the horseshoe pitching contest. He seemed right keen on it. I'm sure he'll be back before too long." Van Poole jotted down some observations in his notebook:

Sister Finbar seems to have a deep and abiding concern for Tommy Whitehead.

He made no mention of his failure to catch the delinquent. Now he was hiding the truth from two people.

Detective Lambert Van Poole drove the Cadillac back to Springfield Park where he had dropped the chief earlier, maneuvering toward the VIP mess tent where he expected his boss to be impatiently waiting for a ride back to the station. Even parking the automobile as close as he possibly could, it still took him a full ten minutes to get to his destination. The park was crowded. Each camp or local chapter had a tent or table set up on the main area of the grounds where their members could check in. Most camps had some kind of display, banner or gimmick that made them stand out. For a lot of them, it was a brass band, several of which were practicing for the band competition, resulting in a din of dissonant notes that was not altogether unpleasant. There were also tables set up selling anything one could possibly need to survive such a festive event as the Confederate Veterans Reunion. If you came up short of rope needed to keep a tent in trim, you could buy a length of rope. Maybe you needed a leather belt, suspenders or a holster. You could buy a cap, and then at the tent of your own home camp, buy a pin to put on it, so there would be no mistaking which camp you represented. One of the camps from Alabama had cleared an area, marked it off with rocks and ropes, and were performing some quite entertaining tricks on horseback. It was part circus, part carnival, part convention.

When he finally got to the VIP tent, he found Chief Wilson, instead of reluctantly tolerating the fragile egos of the officials in his presence, trying his best to ingratiate himself to a crowd of dignitaries that had grown and now included several members of the Legislative Delegation, the governor, and one member of the U.S. Congress. He was trying to catch the chief's attention and motioned that he had the car and was ready to go, and got close enough to overhear parts of the conversation. The mayor was speaking to an important-looking man. "Yes, there were some early reports of a dysentery-like infection spreading through the camps, but we acted quickly. Took the advice of our Police Chief Luther Wilson and put together a team. You can see some of them working around the area now. Inspecting water supplies and latrines. And you know what? I think we nipped it. Not a single new case since this morning." Chief Wilson's face was beaming, as if he were about to receive an award of some kind. "Yessir, Chief Wilson here has proven his mettle. I think we'll keep him around." Laughter bellowed from all corners of the group. The chief saw Van Poole and waved him off. Communicating in hand signals, he indicated that he would be ready in an hour.

Van Poole walked to the headquarters tent and asked for Commander Davidson, and was shown into his private quarters at the back of the tent.

"Detective, come in, come in. Are you in need of any refreshment?"

"No, thank you, Commander."

"Well, you won't mind if I have a little drop of something? Aids the digestion, you know." The commander had a small glass and large bottle of dark rum on his desk.

"Not at all, sir. I was hoping we could talk about a serious situation, though."

"Serious? By all means. I can be very serious."

"This man found murdered Monday morning. It is a sure bet he was here for the reunion. We know that from some of the correspondence we found in his room."

"Oh, yes, the man who was killed. Beat to death and left under a bridge. All through the camp, everybody's talking about it. Half the camp is blaming it on some Yankees, the other half think it's the darkies. I don't know who did it, but I hope you can clear it up shortly."

"I'm sure we will, Commander. I was wondering if you have any information on your attendees that may be of some help to us. We know he came here from Kentucky, but that may not mean much. We would like to find out all we can about him."

"Detective, we have thousands men registered, and more pouring in every hour. I can't keep information on all of them. Membership in the Veterans is through local camps, and I rely on the local camp commanders to keep up with their membership. I would venture to say at this point that you know more about him than I. But give me his name and his hometown, and I will see what I can find out." Van Poole wrote down the information and left it with the Commander's assistant, harboring little hope that any new or useful information would be forthcoming in twenty-four hours.

He realized that he was quite close to the medical facilities, and he thought it unforgivable not to drop in on Lily at the clinic tent. He found her very busy. In addition to the usual activities of a clinic tending to thousands of geriatric men, she was handling what was widely assumed to be an outbreak of dysentery. "Can you give me the real story about this dysentery outbreak?" asked Lambert.

"I don't know if there is a dysentery outbreak. It's something, but I don't know if it's dysentery." She was very short with him, as she had been set to a sour mood by the appearance of the mystery disease, compounded by the newspaper report that she was certain had singled her out as an incompetent medical professional. "Besides, what difference does it make? There is nothing you can do but keep fluids going in at least as fast as they're coming out. Honestly, the things these newspapers will print. The shameful thing is, if there really were a dysentery outbreak, they would probably cover it up for fear of bad publicity. Well, over a hundred men came to the tent during the night complaining of terrible stomach pains, and quite a bit of vomiting. A good bit of blood was expelled as well. From both ends, mind you. I don't know if any of them had a fever, but several of them seemed to be hallucinating. That's often a sign of fever. I thought maybe something that they might have eaten at the ball had made them sick. But there were an awful lot of men at the ball who reported no symptoms. So then I thought maybe somebody brought some spoiled food and had passed it around. That seems most likely. But the newspaper entirely misquoted me. That is the last time I will ever speak to a reporter."

"You just have to know how to handle them. They will certainly take advantage of anyone not accustomed to responding to their questions. Remember, they're not there to do anything but sell newspapers. And if that means misquoting a nurse, then so be it."

"Just the same, it's a mistake I will not make again." They stood just outside the tent while Lily took in a breath of clean air, and two men walked by, carrying a stretcher on which lay a body covered with a white sheet. Two more men on stretchers were carried past and placed in a motorized ambulance. Lily held back tears. When she had full composure, she asked one of the nurses, "Janie, what happened?"

"Oh, it's terrible. These men's symptoms, after subsiding this morning, became quite pronounced just a while ago. I sent for Dr. Otwell immediately, but it became apparent that whatever this is, it's far beyond our ability to treat here in this tent. So he and I decided that they should be evacuated to the hospital, and one poor man died before we could get him ready to go."

"What did Dr. Otwell say?"

"He's blaming the Yankees, of course. Says they have come south to poison the food and try to kill off everybody they couldn't get during the war. He's sitting down at the back of the tent trying to calm himself. He got right worked up."

"Oh, for heaven's sake. We have got to get a real doctor out here. This is getting entirely too serious for someone like him. Send one of our volunteer girls over to the command tent and see if Mr. Davidson can find an actual doctor."

Van Poole was finally able to get the chief away from all the people whom he continued to insist he held in utter disdain. They returned to the station to find Pete Dooley waiting with photographs of the area under the bridge for them to examine. Chief Wilson grabbed at the photos, but Dooley was protective of his handiwork. "Please, Chief. Try to handle them only at the edges."

Chief Wilson sat at his desk and the photographer passed him the pictures one by one. Wilson respected the photographer's request, and kept his fingers to the edges. He moved through them quickly, impatiently. "Well, nothing here I can see that we didn't know already. But I am sure you made a valiant effort."

Things rarely look the same in a photograph as they do in reality, thought Van Poole, as he peered over the chief's shoulder. The image of the abutment under the bridge didn't look like the same place he had stood when he found the stash of moonshine. It looked more pleasant and inviting in some of the shots, darker and more foreboding in others.

"I can certainly see clear evidence of a struggle right here. And there seems to be quite a lot of blood. Just as you had said, Van Poole." The chief was pointing to disturbed areas of soil and weeds. "Oh, well. At least I didn't have to go scampering about down there like a wharf rat." When he realized that what he said could be taken as a personal affront by the one who had scampered about like a wharf rat, he acquired an apologetic expression. He approved the photographer's invoice and handed it back to him. "Here. Take this to the City Clerk's office and they will make payment. Van Poole, take these pictures and keep them with the case file. And handle them only by the edges!"

When the two men got out of Chief Wilson's earshot, Van Poole explained to Dooley, "Chief Wilson is not well-versed in the matters of our bursar. They will not pay that invoice without a voucher."

"Huh. So how do I get a voucher?"

"You go the Clerk's Office like he said, show them the invoice; they will issue a voucher that you have to take to the City Treasurer's Office to approve. Then bring it back here and we'll get the chief to sign it the next time he's available. Then you can take that to the City Clerk's office and they will add it to payables resolution to be approved at the next Council meeting."

"Oh, the hell with that. I'm losing too much money not being up at the reunion taking portraits. Count this as a favor that I hope will remembered, should I need it." The photographer left in a hurry, displaying his annoyance with inane city government bureaucracy.

Van Poole took the photos to his desk. He did not see what use they could be, and thus was not overly worried about Pete Dooley's invoice for a dollar seventy-five. Van Poole's notebook entry regarding this matter: *$1.75 on useless photographs.*

He quickly thumbed through the photos. When he reached the last of them, something made him flip through the stack again. He realized that something was different in a couple of them. Even though each was shot from a slightly different angle, something nagged at him. He examined them a third time, very slowly and carefully. He laid them all out, next to one another, and there it was. In one of the eight photographs, there was a bright white spot in the lower right-hand corner. He scratched through his notebook entry about the useless photographs, then ran out of the station and grabbed Pete Dooley before he'd even walked a block away.

"I haven't got time, Lambert. You already stiffed me on my invoice — can't you let me go try to make a living?"

"Just one minute, Pete. That's all I want. I have to ask you something." Dooley reluctantly accompanied the detective back to the squad room. Van Poole showed him the photo. "See this? Right down here in the corner? That bright white spot. Is that an imperfection on the photograph?"

"There are no imperfections in my photographs, Detective," Dooley said as he put on spectacles. "Hmmm. Probably the light from the carbide lamp reflecting off a piece of broken glass or something shiny. I don't know. Now can I get back to work?"

"Certainly, Pete. Give me that invoice, and I'll get it approved for you."

Van Poole left the office and hopped on a street car. As prestigious as it was to be one of the only men authorized to drive the Cadillac, when in a hurry, nothing beat taking the streetcar. He had the picture with the white spot wrapped up in some old newspaper and stowed in a large envelope to keep it from getting damaged. He got off the streetcar at the Liberty Street Bridge and clambered down underneath the roadway decking. It was still light enough outside so that he could see most of what he needed to. He held up the picture until he was certain he had the orientation right, and looked at the white spot. Then he felt around where he thought that spot would be and, after sifting the dirt gently for a few minutes, came up with a large, flat-cut diamond. He put the diamond in his pocket and made another entry in his notebook, keeping track of the date, time, location, then: *Large diamond, must be worth hundreds. Dropped by the victim, or perhaps the assailant? Was this the offering that A. James was going to make at IC?*

Then he looked and felt around some more, but found no other treasure.

On the way back to the police station, Van Poole stopped at a pawn shop owned by an old friend. A pawnbroker who cooperates with police was not easy to find, and this one had helped Van Poole several times, as well as giving him a great deal on an engagement ring and wedding band when he married Lily. And he was a man who knew stones. He asked the pawnbroker for his professional opinion about the diamond, making clear that it was evidence in a criminal investigation and not something he was offering for sale.

"Ahh, Van Poole. You rascal. Tell me you want to sell this. I make you good deal."

"No. It's not for sale, but you just told me what I need to know. It is real, not glass?"

"Is real. And very good. From Europe, probably Switzerland."

"Thank you, sir. What do you suppose it's worth?"

"If you not sell, what difference it make?" asked his friend.

"Just a bit curious, that's all. This might be evidence of a murder, and I just want to be diligent."

"It worth money more than you will ever make as policeman."

"Thank you. I will buy you lunch one day next week."

"Lunch? Ha! You should feed my whole family for week."

Back at the police station, Van Poole put the jewel in a heavy brown envelope, sealed it shut and wrote on the outside, "EVIDENCE." He put it in a drawer in the evidence room and made a similarly cryptic entry in the evidence log book. He was not sure why he was being so secretive about it. If a person wanted to hide something from policemen, the evidence room was a good place to do it. And although it was his practice to keep Chief Wilson up to date on every aspect of high-profile cases, he thought that disclosure of this development could wait a little while. He wasn't sure what it meant, and he was less sure what Wilson's reaction would be to his finding a diamond of this quality under a bridge where a man had been brutally murdered and illicit whiskey had been stored.

He returned to his small desk and made several entries in his notebook, then began to straighten up his area in the squad room before he left for the evening. He left nothing on the desk. He always kept the ink bottle and blotting paper locked in his desk drawer. It didn't take him long to learn that a bottle of ink was not something to be left unattended in the company of idle detectives. The temptation to tinker with it was irresistible. His neat desk was a source of pride to him, but one of aggravation to the other detectives, whose work areas were unsightly heaps of paper, unrecorded evidence, empty coffee mugs and ashtrays overflowing with smelly cigar stubs. One desk looked more like a shoeshine stand than a work station. Detective Jim-Toe Henry (no one was sure about the name Jim-Toe and no one ever asked him to explain it) spent most of the day shining his shoes. He was constantly applying or rubbing off boot black. Every time he was asked to help with something or hurry to get one of his reports finished, he always had a ready excuse. "I got to go wash this boot black off my hands before I can do anything." The only cleanser abrasive enough to make him presentable was the kind used by printers, a coarse powder of volcanic pumice and borax. He'd walk a block to a small printing company, take a half-hour to get his hands scrubbed clean, walk back to the station, by which time somebody else would have done all the work. His shoes always looked tip-top, though.

Just as Lambert finished securing his desk, Chief Wilson came in. "Van Poole! I know you've got your hands full with the murder investigation, but I need to see some activity." Van Poole knew that by 'activity,' his boss really meant 'reports.' Chief Wilson dearly loved stacks of reports. Perhaps it was his military background. "Word is, there are miscreants all over town. Get one of the Pinkerton Men and go put a dent in some of this stuff." The duty roster that was posted told Van Poole that the campground area was sufficiently policed for the evening, so to satisfy the chief's demand for activity, he asked one of the Pinkerton Agents to go to the train station with him, where there would be abundant opportunities for correcting misbehavior, thus plenty of activity for a couple of detectives.

The narrow streets around the train station were packed with bars, small hotels, restaurants, billiard parlors and bowling alleys. One very popular spot was Marty's Walk-up. Each morning, Marty Hendrix unlocked a set of folding doors and pushed them back in to a recess in the wall. Behind those doors was a bar with twelve stools tucked up underneath. If you pulled the stool out, you were sitting at the bar, but also on the sidewalk, and Marty would pour you a beer or a glass of whiskey. It was quite a fuss when he first opened, with preachers and temperance societies complaining that he was blocking the sidewalk. The idea that he was serving alcohol right on city property caused a legal ruckus that had been going on for years and showed no signs of letting up during the reunion. City councilmen and commissioners frequently showed up to conduct their own investigations and could often be seen sitting at the bar, with a folding ruler stretched out to the edge of street, trying to determine if he was on public or private property. You had to calculate in the setback requirements, right-of-way boundaries and all manner of technical considerations. Marty welcomed the inquisitive public officials with free drinks and, inevitably, the ruler would break or get lost, which would remind someone of a story, and then all decorum was lost to a night of friendly drinking. One city councilman had calculated that a drink, sitting on the bar, was on Marty's property. He reached this conclusion based on a survey map that he had seen in the city records, but which now no one could find. Only when a man brought the drink past the edge of the bar did it enter upon public property, thus becoming an offense. Men at Marty's would lean in over the bar to sip at their drinks when there was a policeman nearby, unless that policeman happened to be the sort of fellow who would join them for a drink. And they all leaned in over the bar if there was a clergyman in sight, unless it was Father Donal. It was this leaning over the bar, which men did in order to remain compliant with city ordinance, that left them so vulnerable to pickpockets. Van Poole often wondered if Marty was aware of this, and took a cut from the pickpockets at the end of the night.

Van Poole and Rex Tarrant from Pinkerton Agency determined that pickpockets at the train station would be their focus for the evening. Travelers tended to be an absent-minded bunch, stuffing wads of cash, billfolds, and other valuables carelessly into their pockets. Fatigued from their travels, excited by their arrival, they become distracted by the beautiful sights of the train station. In such a state, a delicate hand could penetrate and lighten the pocket without being detected.

Rex was excited by the prospect. "Great idea, sir. I have made some modifications to my latest security invention and this will give me a chance to test it out."

"What kind of invention?"

From his locker at the station, the Pinkerton Agent took a long brown coat and held it up by the collar. "This, sir, is the Tarrant Pickpocket Trap Coat. I have used it to great success at the terminal in Atlanta, and will be happy to deploy it here for further testing. I will be submitting paperwork for a patent soon, so don't go getting any ideas. You see these big, brown, baggy pockets? That is the secret. I will come up the ramp like an arriving passenger wearing this coat. I will behave in a manner that will let everyone know I am a tourist who has just arrived. I will use this large leather billfold, which is stuffed full of paper, by the way, except for the dollar bill I will remove from it. I'll make a big show of buying something — a cigar, a bag of peanuts, whatever. Then I put the oversized, overstuffed billfold back into the coat pocket." Rex unfolded the pocket of the coat and showed the internal workings to Van Poole. "As I push it in, it arms this spring clamp, see? It works rather like a conventional mouse trap. As soon as some pickpocket applies the slightest pressure to grasp the billfold, the stop releases and his fingers get creased with a bar applying about a hundred pounds of pressure. The mechanism is stitched into the pocket so the thief cannot run away. It is designed to inflict minimal injury, but the effect is to immobilize the hand of the perpetrator, and I simply apply the handcuffs."

"Why, that's quite clever. Even ingenious, I might say. But it's only for good for one catch, right? I would think that the kind of commotion that this would create would send a signal to all the other pickpockets around."

"I thought that as well, but if these folks were that smart, they wouldn't be pickpockets. The inside pockets of the coat have various disguise elements. Look. Fake mustache, glasses, hat. I just create a different look, come up the ramp again and catch another one. These big pockets and that fat billfold are simply too great a temptation for a pickpocket to resist." Rex stood up and put the coat on and carefully pushed the billfold into the pocket. They headed out the door of the squad room and into the main area of the police station, just as Chief Wilson was leaving his office.

"Ah, gentlemen, off to stamp out crime? What miscreants are your quarry tonight?"

"Pickpockets, sir," said Van Poole. "Going to the train station."

"Excellent. I'm sure you will find it a satisfying outing." Wilson saw the big leather billfold protruding from the big pocket of Rex's coat and thought he would teach his subordinates a quick lesson about pickpocketry. He let them walk past, then turned quickly and grabbed the billfold. His scream was enough to startle the horses at the police stable across the alley.

Chapter 10

Thursday morning, Van Poole took the streetcar out to the hospital to see if the autopsy on Alden James had revealed anything he didn't already know. He walked into the exam room and found Doc Otwell standing over the cold, naked remains of the unfortunate man. Otwell had been a medical officer for the Confederate Army and never really accepted that the South had lost the war for independence. He had been on a steady drunk since the war ended. There were usually a few hours each day that he remained sober, and he would sometimes be found at the Soldiers & Sailors Home, tending to veterans who needed a peaceful place to die. He had been working in the medical tent at the reunion, but everyone knew that it was merely an honorary duty.

"Doc Otwell! I didn't expect to find you here. Thought you would be down at the reunion."

"Yankees come in there trying to poison everybody. Got all the doctors busy, so they asked me to do the post-mortem on this guy that got his head caved in," said the doctor. Van Poole knew that Doc Otwell was old, addled and had a vivid imagination that was enhanced by his regular intake of alcohol. Only Doc Otwell would see a Yankee conspiracy in the illness that had struck at the veterans' campground. "I have seen this before. But only once. It's a very distinctive wound."

"What do you mean you've seen this before? Is there another murder case I don't know about?"

"No. Back during the war. Saw this exact same thing, once. I don't remember if the man lived, but I would be doubtful."

"How can you remember a man's head wound from that long ago? Most days, you can't remember where the hospital is." Van Poole had been friends with Doc Otwell long enough that he could speak so casually and personally to him. Then the doctor became surprisingly lucid, and appeared almost unimpaired by the whiskey he kept swigging from the cobalt-blue bottle in his pocket.

"This was not one to forget. It was just after the Union troops evacuated in '63. Set fire to the whole town. Destroyed everything they could. 'Bout the time they all got on their boats, we came in under Finegan's command to try to reclaim the city, and got most of the fires under control. There were a lot of injured civilians around, so I set up a makeshift hospital. We set out to find the injured we thought we could save and do what we could for them. I found a man, a Yankee soldier, lying in a building that had been partially burnt, but was still standing. He had been stripped pretty good. His belt buckle was gone. His hat was gone. His gun, if he'd ever had one, was gone. I suspect some locals had helped themselves to whatever they could get, presuming he were dead. Them Yankees took outta here so quick, they left one of their own to die. Just like Yankees. That's why you can't trust them. Damn Yankees.

"Now you look at this man here. You see the damage to the side of his head and his face? It is the indentation of a perfect right angle. Just like I saw back then. And the results of the attack are the same. That fellow back then had the same thing. The bone structure around the eye has been completely obliterated, and the jaw bone is fractured beyond any ability to repair. Cheekbone gone. Hardly a tooth left in his mouth. I found him lying there, alive but unconscious. Didn't think there was much I could do for him. And, as he was a Yankee soldier, I didn't have much interest in helping him, but I am sworn to heal, if I can. Even if it's a Yankee. I figured they would take him prisoner anyway, and he would get medical treatment under those circumstances. I found a half-bottle of whiskey on its side near him and figured at least I could use the alcohol to disinfect the wound. Was tempted to drink it, but instead I poured what was left on his face, dabbed it with some cotton rags, and left him for Finegan's men to deal with. Ooh, he screamed when I did that. I don't ever remember seeing him again, so I figured he must have died. Even if he had lived, he would be blind in that one eye, and have difficulty talking and eating the rest of his life."

"Could you guess what might have been the weapon that would have wrought such destruction?"

"Well, the building we were in was an old rooming house with a tavern on the bottom floor. He was on the floor near the bottom of the staircase. The thing I remember noticing at the time, even though the building was in a shambles, was that the newel post at the bottom of the banister was missing. I thought if it was a heavy oak newel post, maybe turned on a lathe for a part of it, but left square at the top, it would make a dandy weapon, and would surely leave an indentation like that."

"I see. Well, what about this poor fellow? What will your report say? I have to get something to Judge Travis for the death certificate."

"Well, it's right clear he didn't die from the dysentery. What the hell would you think killed him?"

"Come on, Doc. You know I'm just talking paperwork here.

Judge Travis is none too keen about holding an inquest. I'm just trying to get him what he needs to issue the death certificate."

"Travis? How in the hell we ever got a lily-livered notary public as a judge, I'll never know. Tell him the man was mortally wounded by means of a blunt, heavy object coming into contact with his head at a velocity capable of landing his brains over in the Suwannee River. If he can't figure it out from there, then he needs to go back to honest work for a living."

Van Poole left the hospital and caught the streetcar again, getting off at the stop that he calculated would be closest to Commander Davidson's tent. He found the commander valiantly fighting off dysentery infection by the internal use of store-bought alcohol. "Van Poole! Come on in. I deeply regret that your father is not here to see this glorious assemblage of Confederate loyalty." All that Lambert could think was that the alcohol was destroying more brain cells than dysentery germs. The commander apparently had no knowledge of Arlen Van Poole's participation in the war. Lambert's father was prevented from serving due to very poor vision and a disabling injury from a construction accident. But he was a skilled engineer, and helped rebuild Jacksonville after the war. Unfortunately, the occupying Union forces paid him in scraps of paper that were ultimately worthless. So, Arlen Van Poole was left broke and drunk, bitter toward both sides, ultimately drinking himself to death.

"I'm sure he would be pleased," said Lambert, deftly avoiding that discussion. "Have you unearthed any useful information regarding the unfortunate Mr. James?"

Commander Davidson paused for a minute, as though he had no knowledge what Van Poole meant. "Oh, yes, yes. Mr. James. Private Alden James. I have assembled a file on him right here." He motioned to a thin pile of papers on his desk. Then he slowly walked around the desk and sat down, looking at the Alden file as if daring Van Poole to reach over and touch it. "It's not much information, but given the short notice, I think you will find it more than you would have gotten anywhere else. Original muster point, current camp affiliation, sketchy information on his service record. Oh, and next of kin. I suspect you will want to send a telegram or something."

"Excellent. Sounds quite complete." Van Poole thought the Commander might pick up the file and hand it to him. Instead, he laid his right hand in the middle of it, as if he were taking an oath on the Bible.

"Well, actually, it is not terribly complete. You see, Mr. James was what we would refer to as an indifferent soldier."

"An indifferent soldier? That's an interesting description." Van Poole held his hand out for the file, a questioning look on his face. Commander Davidson kept his hand firmly on top of the file folder, and stared up at Van Poole. He eventually put the entire file into an oversized brown envelope.

"Not that it makes any difference now, but Mr. James' heart was not in the conflict," said the Commander.

"I see. Thank you, Commander. The chief will be very pleased," said Van Poole. He tried to remove the envelope from Davidson's grasp, but the commander was reluctant to let go, and pulled back.

"What I mean to be saying is, the service record you find in there is quite factual in nature, but sometimes there are things about a soldier that can only be derived by an experienced commander drawing the whole truth from the facts. But it's all right in here. Facts. If that's what you want. You can take this file with you, and return it when you're finished. The service record is rather spotty, though." It was now clear to Van Poole that Commander Davidson had something to say, and was going to say it. Van Poole could take it in little doses of incomplete sentences, or he could sit down, share the Commander's rum and get the whole ugly story as Commander Davidson wanted it told. Van Poole found a small glass that was about as clean as could be expected under the circumstances and put it on the desktop. He pointed to the bottle of rum and raised his eyebrows at the commander. "May I have just a taste of your rum, sir?" he asked politely. The commander enthusiastically poured him two fingers of dark rum, then freshened his own drink.

"I appreciate you taking the time to assemble this file, and am quite anxious to read it. But I may miss some subtle nuance, not being a military man myself. Supposing you tell me what in this file is really important." Van Poole sat and took out his notebook and pen.

"All right. I would be delighted to." Davidson first reached into a box for a cheroot. He had spent the previous day wrapping several dozen. He offered one to Van Poole, who politely declined. Davidson lit one, puffing and causing the match to flare wildly, nearly burning off one of his eyebrows. "Mmmm. Good Virginia tobacco. Nothing quite like it." He contemplated the smoke for a minute. “Alden James. As I said, he was an indifferent soldier. I might describe him as reluctant, based on what little I know of him. He did what he was ordered to do, but no more. No heroics. It almost appears that he had no real love for the Confederacy. Did what was asked of him, though. Strange man. And this is the first reunion he has ever attended. Not at all active in his local camp. In fact, it appears he just joined so he could come to this reunion. The reason the service record is spotty is because his detachment took enemy fire and split up very soon after he joined up. And make no mistake, he joined because the alternative was quite unpleasant. But he did his duty. That’s almost the only thing that can be said about the man. Until he wound up here.”

“So, he served in Jacksonville? Maybe that is why he unexpectedly joined with the veterans’ group — to come see Jacksonville, where he served. Does that make sense?”

“I don’t know. You see, he wound up here, more than served here. Every time his unit would get into a battle or a skirmish, they would get split up. James always did the right thing and found his way to another Confederate unit and reported to the commanding officer. He could have deserted, but we would have found him and shot him. Instead, he always found another unit. Always did the right thing, but never did anything great. He wound up just outside of town during the federal occupation. He was with a ragtag group of men from different outfits that had been scattered about. They were loosely under Finegan’s command. He was out west of town waiting for reinforcements so they could take Jacksonville back from the Union. Of course, the Union Army burned the town and evacuated.

Everybody knows the story by now. Well, the only thing in Alden James' service record of anything the least bit remarkable is his bravery in confronting three Union soldiers and the recovery of looted religious items from them. He was nominated for a distinguished service medal, but never accepted it. A man who refuses to accept an award for which he is nominated occupies the highest level of suspicion in my book."

"Well, that certainly is an interesting story, Commander. I look forward to reading the entire file."

"If you reach any alternative conclusion, please let me know. I would like to have some men plan a little bit of a memorial service for him during the reunion, if appropriate."

"Yessir. We will keep you informed."

Van Poole left Springfield Park and went back to the police station. He had an awful lot of work to do. The hardest task ahead of him was to inform Chief Wilson of everything. The diamond, the background on Alden James, Doc Otwell's comments. And he had to organize it all to present to Judge Travis for a death certificate and finding of unnatural death before they proceeded much further. The problem with Chief Wilson, Van Poole had come to realize, is that he always over-reacted. Too eager to please. Desperate to convince everyone how indispensable he was. Show him that fancy diamond and he would parade it around the park. "Look what I found. This will surely crack the case." And now with the added burden of the chief getting his left hand caught in Rex Tarrant's pickpocket trap, he would no doubt be in a sour mood.

The detective dived head-first into the paperwork required by the half-dozen pickpocket arrests that he and Rex had made the previous evening. This could take a good portion of what remained of the day. Each arrest would require a written report, and an affidavit that would have to be notarized and taken to the city solicitor so he could begin filing the case. If one were careful, one could spend the entire day shuffling paper around the police station. Van Poole used to chuckle when a new man got transferred to the detective squad and discovered how easy it was to appear diligent. The earnest looks on their faces as they carried folders full of affidavits and arrest reports from office to office was comical, and almost endearing. Eventually, they learned that they were fooling nobody when Chief Wilson started assigning them real work. “Since there are no crimes for you to solve, maybe you could put all of these suspect cards in alphabetical order, then cross reference them to their last arrest. After that I think the banisters could use a coat of wax.” So they reverted to goofing off elsewhere instead of hanging around the station.

Late that afternoon as Van Poole was just finishing up the last of the paperwork, Chief Wilson found him at his desk in the squad room.

“Lambert! I’m glad you’re here,” exclaimed the chief. “Been looking all over for you. I need you to drive me to Phelps House. I promised Miz Martha I would join her in a glass of sherry at five-thirty. No telling what sort of an evening might await me. Do you suppose she serves a nice roast beef for supper? Oh! Maybe a leg of lamb. Wouldn’t that be wonderful?”

"Yes, sir. I was just coming to see you to discuss the James case."

"Hah. That can wait until tomorrow. Go get the Cadillac!" The chief waited in front of the police station while Van Poole fired up the Cadillac and drove around to pick him up.

When he got in, Van Poole asked about his boss' hand.

"My hand is just fine, thank you." He showed him his fingers which were only slightly swollen and bluish. "That is quite an ingenious trap he's devised, but as far as anyone is to know, an inmate slammed a cell door on my hand when I was doing a surprise inspection. Feel free to embellish the condition of the inmate."

They traveled north on Market Street, with the chief laying out the rest of the evening for them. "Now after you drop me off, you better go and get yourself something to eat, and then maybe patrol around the park. Later, I would say about eight o'clock, sort of nonchalantly walk up the front steps and just make it look like you are keeping an eye on things. By that time, I will either have already eaten or at least have an idea of what the chances for a late supper may look like. I'll see you and, well, we will communicate in some manner. Sound good?"

"Yes, sir." So Van Poole was off the hook for discussing the case for the day, and could focus on organizing all the parts of stories floating around in his mind.

Chief Wilson walked through the door of the front parlor of Phelps House and found it to be as pleasant and inviting as any fine men's club he could remember. Green-flocked wallpaper, leather upholstered furniture, two elegant writing desks for guests to use, a stack of newspapers for guests to read, and a sideboard covered with a full afternoon cordial service. Many of the guests were standing, holding conversations, enjoying one another's company. Most had been military officers and were obviously there for the reunion, resplendent in full dress uniforms. Mrs. Brandywine greeted the policeman and poured him a glass of sherry. "Luther, so lovely that you could join us." She introduced him to several of the guests that were in the parlor, and conversation was pleasant and meaningless — mostly about how wonderful the reunion was and how soon it would be before the local race tracks reopened.

Among the legion of notable folks, Chief Wilson spied Mayor Langen mingling with a small group. The mayor waved him over and introduced him to the group. "And, gentlemen, it was the quick thinking and decisive action recommended by Chief Wilson that snuffed out an intestinal infection that could have spread through the camps and ruined the entire reunion."

"Ahh."

"Good work."

"Tell us more, Mayor."

"Well," began the mayor, "at the first sight of what we all presumed to be an outbreak of dysentery, Wilson recommended a military approach. What did you call it? A cross-functional task force, that's it. That's it. I knew it was a military term of some sort. We put a team of men at the disposal of the state health inspector and they went to work. Put a prison crew out cleaning the latrines. Sterilized the drinking water, inspected the kitchens. Even put up signs discouraging the folks from sharing eating utensils. Must have worked. Not one new case reported." Handshakes all around, nods of approval and congratulations were murmured.

Mrs. Brandywine gently pulled Wilson over to a corner and cooed, "Maybe we can get away from all these people and I can have a drink with the local hero in my private parlor." Wilson readily agreed and soon found himself ushered into a room that the proprietor used as an office as well as an area to entertain special guests.

"Martha, I must apologize that I could not make it here for dinner earlier today." Luther had not even planned to take his midday meal at Phelps House. He just thought it would be a good way to make sure Mrs. Brandywine knew that he, too, could be counted among the important people in town. "Had to go and eat at the VIP tent in Springfield Park, you know, with the mayor and all the other politicians. I really haven't much use for these people whose self-perception is one of such importance that the world must revolve around them."

"Yes, I know what you mean, Luther. But that's how some people are. It's the same thing here. I have to mingle with my guests for a few minutes every afternoon. There are several important visitors among us tonight, but I'm sure the dining room can manage the rest of the evening without me."

"Well, it certainly seems to be an agreeable crowd. Tell me, is their evening meal already paid for with their rooms or do you charge extra for that?"

"Oh, they pay extra for that. Head count is complete by mid-morning. The easiest way to lose money in this business is to throw away food. The kitchen prepared just enough for the guests tonight. My staff is quite good with such details."

"Oh. And what will these lucky guests be served?"

"Cook's presenting her prime roast of beef tonight."

"Really?"

"Yes. A fish soup to start. Then a salad course. And I think she has an escalloped oyster pie to serve with the beef."

"Really? Oyster pie?" Wilson's mouth was watering so much, he hoped he wasn't visibly drooling.

"Well, that's what she calls it. Yorkshire pudding baked with oysters in it is what it really is. Just talking about it makes me hungry. Let's have another glass of sherry and let the guests settle in the dining room and perhaps you and I could go out for a little something?"

"Lovely idea," said the chief as she refilled their glasses. "So tell me, Martha, how did you end up running Phelps House?"

"Oh, that's a long story. I'm not sure I have enough sherry here for all that, but I'll give it a try. My parents lived here during the war. Oddly enough, they were Unionists. I wasn't born until several years after, but I heard the stories all my life. They owned several small boarding establishments in town, catering to Northerners who would come down in winter. They were evacuated on some Union ships in '63, I think it was. The federals did not want to leave any Union sympathizers behind for fear of what might happen to them. But my father didn't want to get too far away from his investments, so he bribed the captain of the boat to let him and my mother off the transport north of town. Down river, at an area called New Berlin.

He owned an old fishing lodge out there somewhere. They waited out the war there, putting up travelers who showed up from time to time. Never asking any questions. Then, shortly after the war, they moved back into town, and my father convinced several friends of his from up North to come down and help him invest in real estate and such."

"Ah, a carpetbag enabler. I never would have suspected."

"Call it what you will, they did a lot to rebuild Jacksonville. Well, then the yellow fever epidemic in the 1880s took Father. Mother and I continued to run rooming houses, then the Great Fire in 1901 took all that. But we had one thing no one else had. Cash. Father had always kept money in a Yankee bank. Well, the fire never crossed Hogan's Creek, so Phelps House was spared. It was slightly damaged from some flying ashes, and we bought it at a rock-bottom price. Everybody who came to rebuild after the fire stayed with us. Eventually we added another wing and the third floor and expanded the kitchen. Converted the carriage house to a garage with rooms above it, and that's what you see today."

"Running boarding houses seems a great deal of work for two women. I suppose there was a Mister Brandywine to help at some point?"

"There was, but he wasn't much help. Had neither the skills nor the inclination to hard work. But there was an old man my father befriended. A Yankee soldier, but I never really knew the whole story. His head is terribly disfigured — I assume from a war injury. But he is inclined to hard work. Very handy with tools. My father gave him chores and allowed him to live somewhere on the property.

He lives out in the garage now."

"Oh. So he is still with you?"

"Yes. But he keeps very much to himself. Frankly, he always avoided contact with people other than my father, something I assumed was self-consciousness about his disfigurement. To this day, he's reluctant to come in the house. In fact, I rarely see him outside the garage unless he's fixing something. As a little girl, I was frightened of him. Then as I grew up, I realized he was really quite a gentle person. Some loss of mental abilities, apparently from his war injury, but really quite gentle."

"He must be gettin' up there in age by now."

"Yes. He's very old, but after all he had done to help us over the years, I could not abandon him. He has made a bit of workshop out there. As I said, he can fix most anything. Keeps to himself. I pay him four dollars a week and don't know what he could possibly spend it on."

"And what became of Mr. Brandywine?"

"Mr. Brandywine was a man of weak constitution. The travails of daily life necessitated an enormous amount of alcohol. More than a man ought to consume in his first thirty-five years."

"I am very sorry."

"Don't be, Luther. I'm too hungry for sympathy."

"By all means, then, let us go eat."

A few blocks north of Phelps Street on Main Street was a diner that stayed open until ten o'clock. It was more crowded than usual due to the reunion, but they managed to get a table. Luther ordered a pork chop that could have made a quite utilitarian pair of work boots, and tried not to think about the prime roast of beef and oyster pie that was being served a few blocks away.

Just as they were finishing and getting ready to pay the tab, Van Poole came in. “Good evening, Miz Brandywine, Chief. They told me at the boarding house that you two went out for a bite to eat. I figured you might be here. Hard to beat one of Frank’s pork chops when you have a serious appetite. Just checking to see if you needed a ride.”

“Perfect timing, Van Poole. We were just about to stroll back. You can drive us and I’ll see Miss Martha to her door.” They inched their way through the heavy traffic and carnival atmosphere and finally made it to the front steps of Phelps House. Luther escorted Martha safely inside.

As soon as she was sure that Van Poole and Chief Wilson were well out of sight, she strode through the kitchen to the back door and met Mayor Langen and several other gentlemen. “Now, Martha, I’d like for you to meet some very influential and important men from Tallahassee.” He introduced everybody, then pulled Miss Brandywine aside. “Martha, it is very important that these men enjoy themselves tonight. And I mean a very memorable evening. When they get back to Tallahassee, I want them to have pleasant memories about Jacksonville. I would not want their thoughts wandering to things like tax audits and health code violations. Just pleasant memories, you savvy?”

“No need to worry, Mayor. Marcy is ready to blend cocktails and she has several very lovely friends in the house. Very game for anything and everything.”

"So pleased to be able to count on you, Martha."

"Gentlemen, this way, if you will," she invited them as she opened the door to the stairway up to the memorable fourth floor.

Chapter 11

As the coal delivery wagon pulled away, Tommy Whitehead slid down the chute into the basement, now full of coal. His street smarts had taught him that if you come out too soon, the police are waiting right there. If you wait long enough, they will eventually get either too hungry or too horny, and give up the pursuit of one punk to go satisfy other needs. It was well on toward dusk, so after he crawled out, he quickly scooted toward Dignan Park, which he reckoned was the safest place to hide. There were plenty of coppers there, but there were also so many other people, it would be easy for a kid to get lost in the crowds.

Because he'd lived under bridges, in caves and corncribs and tents made from cast-off clothing, Tommy had never established the habit of observing his appearance in a mirror. So he was unaware that he was covered in coal dust from head to toe. This saved him from one batch of trouble but dumped him right into another. As he entered the park, he got within one foot of Butch Warren, looked him right in the face, and started running. Butch took no notice, figuring he was just another of the little colored boys who'd been coming to the park to entertain the white folks with tap dance routines for pennies or carry footlockers and luggage for nickels. But if a colored boy was running through the park, it was a sure bet he'd stolen something. The hue and cry rose quickly.

"Colored boy on the run! Check your pockets!"

"You see that pickaninny? Wonder what he stole?"

"Where is a policeman? Somebody get a policeman."

Tommy didn't realize that he was the cause of all the

commotion; he tried to slip unseen into the gardener's shed where he'd slept the night before, but a couple of camp sentries grabbed him. As they did, he caught sight of his black face reflected in the window — it dawned on him that he was the pickaninny folks were hollering about.

"What do you think you're running from, Leroy?"

"I ain't a-runnin' nowhere, Mister. I's a jus' warming up to do my dance for you gentlemens." He hopped up on a large wooden crate and started dancing. He had no idea how to perform, but he'd watched enough colored boys at the train station to fake the general routine. And he knew that the secret to success in almost any endeavor was distraction. "Why'nt you gentlemens pour yo' a drink o' dat whiskey and I show y'all how us darkies dance jus' to entertain us-selves." He spun around and jumped and kept his feet moving, slapping his shoes as he brought first his right, then his left leg up.

Within a few minutes, one of the old veterans tuned up a fiddle. "Let's see ya dance to this one, darkie." And he started playing the fiddle. Tommy found the rhythm and kept dancing. "What's a'matter, little nigger? Can't ya sing while ya dance?"

Tommy started singing, "Jump down, spin around, pick a bale o' cotton. Jump down, spin around, pick a bale o' hay." His singing didn't quite match the tune the old fella was playing, so he tried another song he had heard colored boys singing. "Little bee work the blossom, big bee get the honey. Colored man pick the cotton, white man get the money." That effort wasn't much better, but nobody took notice as long as he kept dancing. Tommy was working up quite a sweat, and as he wiped his brow with his sleeve, he felt the black coal sludge dripping from his face. As he wiped, one of the veterans saw Tommy's forehead was now as white as anyone watching him.

"Hey! That ain't no nigger boy. He's white!" As soon as Tommy heard that, he grabbed all the nickels and pennies that had been thrown his way and ran. He headed out of the park and up the driveway next to Phelps House, darting to the alley garage where Weasel's friend lived. He banged on the door as loudly as he could, hoping to be let in to hide. A window opened upstairs, and a lady shouted down.

"What is all that noise? Who is out there?"

"I'm looking for the ol' man that lives in here," shouted Tommy.

"Leave that old man alone. Now get out of here before I get a policeman after you!"

Tommy took off running again, sticking close to the dark shadows of the tall buildings, and trying to rub coal soot from his clothes back on his face. He headed to the convent, where he knew he could crawl under the back porch and stay safe for the night. As he moved quietly down the alley toward the hiding place, he heard Sister Finbar speak from a rocking chair on the porch.

"Lad! Every time you run away, you come back in a finer mess than before. What a slow learner you must be." Tommy was caught quite by surprise.

"I don't know what you're talking about."

"You're covered hide and hair in coal soot. I can't wait to hear this story."

"I was hauling buckets of coal up to the campground for the old soldiers. I just got a little dirty doing that." He took note of a stack of neatly folded clothes and towels by her feet. Next to that, a bucket with a sponge and a cake of soap.

"Over behind the potato shed is a tub of warm water. Take this bucket and soap and towels, and go scrub yourself clean and put on these clean clothes. If you come back not as clean as I think you should be, I'll bathe you again myself. I'll break out my favorite wire brush if need be! I intend to get you clean, inside and out."

Over the tub, a kerosene lantern suspended from a rope lit the spot brightly so he could see what he was doing. Tommy pulled off the greasy, grimy clothes he'd been wearing the better part of a month. When he'd bathed in the past, it was usually in a creek, and never involved soap. One time, he washed up in a fountain in a city park near one of the nicer neighborhoods. That water was clear and clean, not like creek water, but it was cold. So, sitting in a tub of clean, warm water with a cake of soap was a treat he'd never known and had not expected to enjoy as much as he did. He soaped up and rinsed off several times. He stood up in the tub, stark naked, not even caring if anyone could see, took the bucket, filled it with water, and poured it over his head. After his final rinse, he stepped out of the tub and toweled off. He dressed in the clothes that Sister Finbar had laid out. They weren't brand-new store-bought duds, but they weren't worn and torn like his. The denim trousers were a bit loose, but a pair of well-made canvas suspenders that buttoned in front and stitched up in the back held the pants up. The shirt was comfortable and was probably the first one he'd ever worn without permanent stains or holes. There was even a pair of socks and leather shoes that fit him better than the beat-up shoes he'd stolen years ago. He walked to the back porch where Sister Finbar rocked, reading prayers from a leather-bound book.

"Well, don't you seem a brand new sight?" asked the nun.

"How did you know?"

"Know what?"

"That all my clothes would be ruint and that I would need a bath?"

"What do you think, I sit here and pray the rosary all day? You don't think I'm knowing what's going on with ye?" She stared at him and let the concept of her omnipotence sink in. "Where do you intend to sleep the night?"

"I was going to crawl up under your back porch."

"Not in those clean clothes you aren't. There's a spare bed in the orphanage, but you'll have to put on this nightgown to sleep in it. There's a canvas hammock strung up in the potato shed if you'd rather. The choice is yours. Oatmeal at six o'clock tomorrow morning." She stood and glided inside. "Too bad you missed supper. Ham and sweet potatoes."

Van Poole took the diamond from the station evidence room and went to call on Father Donal at Immaculate Conception. He encountered Mrs. Trent at the front door.

"Oh, hello again, Detective. Wait here in the front parlor, and I'll see if Father is busy." Van Poole stood patiently until Mrs. Trent returned. She escorted him to the library, where he found Father

Donal, relaxing with a large snifter of brandy.

"Detective Van Poole! How grand to see you again. Would you have a spot of brandy with me?"

"It's a bit early for that, don't you think, Father?" Van Poole pulled his watch from his waistcoat pocket and saw that it was a little after three.

"Nonsense. I'm sure the Holy Father doesn't wait for some appointed hour to have a wee dram. Besides, I am told that this particular brandy is distilled from the finest altar wine in all of France. So it's like receiving the sacrament. What could be wrong with that, I ask you?"

"You have made me a believer. I will join you."

"What an evangelist I am," He chuckled as he poured a bit of brandy into a fine glass snifter and handed it to Van Poole. "Well, now, to what do I owe this visit? Have you caught a murderer? I would be happy to visit the poor soul in jail and offer what counseling I can."

"No, Father, we have no one in custody, yet. But I think I'm getting close. I wonder if I could show you something? Get your reaction?"

"Indeed. Yes. What is it?" The priest swallowed a slug of brandy that was more than what most people would imbibe in polite company. Van Poole took the envelope from his pocket, opened it and slid the diamond out into the palm of his hand, and showed it to the priest. Father Donal took the jewel and stared at it, and gasped. He walked to his desk and sat down, adjusting the light for maximum effect. "'Tis beautiful, it is."

"Have you ever seen anything like this before?"

"I have read about such jewels. Look … if you hold it just right, so that the light strikes it at just the correct angle, you can see the Christian cross in it. It is a rare diamond indeed. This looks like a chalice mount. 'Tis a sad history to be sure, but some priests and bishops, God forgive them their vanity, for they did it all in Thy Holy Name, would have specially cut diamonds, rubies and emeralds mounted on their chalices. I have seen some that have so many jewels that they look like barnacles on a boat hull. So many empty bellies could be filled with a stone as grand as this. My chalice is very plain. Sterling silver, sure it is, but no jewels or engraving. It holds the blood of Our Lord Jesus Christ just as well, though." He took another long gulp of brandy, stood and went to the side table, where he poured some more. "Where did you find such a treasure?"

"Where I found it may not be important just now. Do I understand that you recognize it as a diamond that would probably have had some significance in a religious setting or to a religious personality?"

"I am no expert, but yes, you could say that this diamond was most likely cut and polished specifically at the commission of an influential religious personage. Such a jeweled chalice, I have been told, was used by this very church many, many years ago. There are stories about it, but no one alive today remembers what might have come of it."

"Thank you, Father," said Van Poole. He was doing his best not to reveal his confusion.

"Oh, say, have you gotten any useful information out of that ragamuffin Tommy Whitehead?"

"Nothing yet, Father. But I think if Sister Finbar keeps him working for a few more days, he'll confess to anything." Van Poole made a cryptic entry in his notebook: *A diamond. A jeweled chalice?*

Tommy Whitehead went to the potato shed. The hammock looked comfortable enough and there was even a blanket. It would be a nice, new place to sleep, but he wasn't ready for bed — not just yet. He waited quite a while for all the lights to go out in the convent, then headed up to Dignan Park. He was hungry. How could Sister Finbar just plain send him to bed with no supper after all the dang work he'd done? If that didn't prove that deep down she was just as mean as the devil himself, he didn't know what did. Maybe he could nick a bologna sandwich from the mess tent or find an old soldier making some stew he might be willing to share.

He crossed Main Street into Springfield Park, and worked his way up to the mess tent, which he knew was designated for members of the United Confederate Veterans only. The staff inside was instructed to serve only veterans wearing their local camp pin. Any meal for five cents. They tried to keep to this rigor at first, but so many of the veterans came along in the chow line and asked for a sandwich for their son who was traveling with them, or an old friend who'd fallen behind on his dues and didn't have a current camp membership badge — or some similar story. The rule was mostly ignored and, eventually, almost anybody who came through the line could have something to eat. A little ruffian like Tommy coming through by himself would send up a red flag, though. He conned a reunion attendee into getting him a sandwich and bowl of soup.

"I was spozed to meet my great-grandpa here. He said he'd show me how real soldiers eat in a mess tent. But I ain't found him yet. Reckon he coulda got lost, though. He's right old and forgetful. And now he ain't here and I'm hungry. He was goin' to buy my dinner. He told me the Brunswick stew was the best he ever had. Gots real squirrel brains in it and everything." The lad was a smooth liar, his "poor lost child" routine convincing.

"All right. Quit your bellyachin' and come with me. I'll get you some vittles. When you find your grandpa, tell him he owes me a nickel." Tommy thanked the man and tore into a bologna sandwich on stale bread — it was filling but unappetizing. It may have been out in the elements most of the day. But the Brunswick stew was even better than Tommy's fictitious grandpa made it out to be.

"First, we hid the stuff up under the bridges. Then we unhid it and took it all back down here. Now you want to go and hide it up under the bridges again? Land sakes, man, make up yer mind!"

"Bert, I don't blame you for not understanding business concepts like inventory control and product distribution. They are complex and can be confusing at times to the apprentice. But that is why you have me, the master, in charge of such things. Yes, we will have to work a little harder, but the important thing for you is to pay attention and learn. Now let's get as much of this as we dare load onto that barge and floated upstream."

"I'm getting tired of that whiskey and I ain't even had a nip. And I thought you said we could do this stuff only after dark, when won't nobody be seein' us."

"We can't wait that long. It'll be near dusk by the time we get up to the park, and we need to get the product staged so that we can take advantage of the sales opportunities for tonight. Now less talk, more work."

The two men put the crates of whiskey back onto the barge, covered them with sheets of canvas, then loaded on a few stacks of lumber, and set out. They poled the barge upstream and the first bridge they came to was Liberty Street. That was where the first load had been confiscated. "Keep going, Bert. I don't want to put any here."

"Why not? They's lots of thirsty fellers camping nearby."

"Call me superstitious if you want. I think that when a man gets killed and liquor gets confiscated in the same place, said place has a dangerous curse upon it. Keep going."

They got to the next bridge, the one where Tommy Whitehead used to live, and unloaded several crates. At the next bridge, they did the same. The third bridge they poled to was at Main Street, which they passed under. The space was so bound up with water mains, sewer pipes, gas lines, and such, there was no clear access to the dead space where they could store anything. Over the next three hours, they stored whiskey crates at every bridge clear up to Sixth Street, which was as far as Butch wanted to go with it. Since he never developed the sophisticated distribution system, he would have to be retrieving the product himself, and he wanted it kept as close as possible. They moored the barge back under the bridge at Main Street and shimmied out from the structure at a dark shadowy space. Butch unzipped his dirty coveralls, and stepped out of them, resplendent in his starched collar, silk necktie and light woolen suit. "Now, let's split up and let the old gentlemen know that we have a spot where they can buy some high-quality whiskey right cheap."

As Tommy sat at one of the tables outside the mess tent finishing his supper, he saw a man walking along the promenade beside the creek who looked a lot like Butch Warren. It was dark, but the promenade was illuminated with new electricity powered lights that had been strung just for the reunion, and it sure looked like Butch. It was hard to tell, though, since the park was, at this point, resembling a small county fair, with gaming booths, cotton candy stands, and hawkers keeping up a steady come-on for bags of popcorn for three cents, two bags for a nickel. Instead of running from his fellow thief, Tommy decided to confront him.

He made his way through the crowds, tempted more than once to stop and roll some dice with some of the stooped veterans, maybe pocket a couple of nickels or dimes. Instead, he moved furtively but quickly, assuming that if he saw Butch Warren, Bert Lewis was likely not far away. He'd rather deal with Butch. At least Butch was smart enough to know when to talk and when to beat. Bert was just plain stupid. No reasoning with him at all. Tommy saw Butch stop and peer over the decorative concrete balustrade that separated the promenade from the creek bed. He was very near a small pedestrian bridge across the creek. Tommy circled past Butch, jumped the balustrade and went under the footbridge, standing on a little sand bar near the creek's edge. He peeked out from underneath and called to the man in a slightly raised voice. He wanted Butch to hear him, but didn't want to attract any additional attention ... like from the cops patrolling the campgrounds.

"Butch! Hey, Butch!" hollered Tommy. The man heard his name and gaped, swiveling his head to discover the source.

"Down here. Under the bridge," hissed Tommy.

Butch looked down and saw the kid lurking in the shadows. He walked a little closer to the bridge and responded, trying to keep his voice low.

"What're you doin' down there? We been looking all over for you. We have some business to discuss." Butch clipped his words to be certain the kid could understand, without upping his volume.

"I know. I can explain everything. I jes' don't want you to put me on a train to Richmond."

"You come out from under that bridge, and we'll set down at one of these here picnic tables and have a nice little chat."

Tommy agreed and went out of sight, then under the bridge, then up the other side and sitting at the picnic table before Butch could amble over. When Butch got settled, Tommy started to talk, the words rushing out in fear and falsehood, all at once.

"Mr. Butch, I'm right sorry I spilled some of your moonshine, Mr. Butch, sir, but ..."

Butch held up his open palm. "Hush, boy. Don't say 'moonshine.' People will hear you and start talking. We will refer to it as 'juice'."

"Juice. Yessir. Anyway, I'm sorry I spilled a bit, but it really wasn't that much. I sopped it up and drained it out into some other bottles and sold it to Weasel."

"Don't pull that innocent act with me, you raggedy pipsqueak. You went and told the cops about the whole operation, didn't you? Well, you can't pull that shit on me, young fellow. I got wind of it and moved all the moon ... uh ... juice before they could find it."

"I didn't tell a soul, Mr. Butch. I wouldn't do a thing like that. 'Specially since you allowed me such generous terms for helping you to sell it."

"Well, then, how is it that as soon as you disappear, we start getting word to move all the juice before the police find it? How about that, sir? Where have you been the last couple of days, anyway?"

"Aw, that crazy old nun over to the convent caught me stealing potatoes out of her shed and she's had me tied up — for real, tied up! — and working for her for two days. She gave me these real snappy clothes, but I had to sneak out to get up here tonight. If I'm gone too long, she'll get the police out looking for me."

"I've got to admit, son, I wish I had your talent for lying. You're a smooth one, you are."

"I'm not lyin', Mr. Butch. First that priest made me carry his golfing clubs, then that nun lassoed me like a dang cowboy and put me to work. I been through hell, I'm tellin' you."

Butch pondered for a moment and figured that there must be some truth to the story. The kid was street-smart, but he couldn't make up the part about carrying the priest's golf clubs. "What do you mean, you sold some to Weasel? It ain't yours to sell."

"I dropped a whole crate of them bottles into the sink and they shattered. But I caught all the whisk ... uh ... juice in a bucket and then poured it into some empty bottles that was layin' around. I figgered you and Bert would put me on a freight train to Richmond, so I got scared and took off. Before I ran, though, I sold them eight bottles to Weasel Jones."

"Well, somebody blew the whistle on the whole operation and we had to move the juice before the police showed up. We've just now finished restaging the product for quick access and distribution. So we may yet be able to sell a fair amount of it. We could use you tonight, if you want to make some money."

"I like making money, but that nun will call the police again if she goes out to check on me and I'm not there."

"AGAIN? She already called the police on you?"

"Yeah. For some reason, she and the Father think I know somethin' about some old man who got himself kilt up under one of them bridges. Not the one I was living under ... that'd give me the heebie-jeebies. They keep trying to get me to talk to that detective about it. They was about to put me in jail and charge me with murder."

"Dead man under the bridge, you say? That could explain why we had to move all the juice. And if you sold Weasel some of my fine product, you certainly owe me some money. How many bottles did you sell him and what did you get for them?"

"He gave me two bucks for the whole bunch. So I figure I probably owe you a dollar to make up for all the trouble I been through. Are you gonna tie me up and throw me on a train? I don't wanna go to Richmond!" The frantic boy suddenly seemed younger than his years, his demeanor far more fearful than his usual bravado.

"Simmer down. Listen, with dead men under bridges, and that nun on the prowl, we just need to keep you out of action for a while, until all this trouble passes."

Tommy didn't like the sound of "out of action." It sounded a lot like being tied up somewhere, something he wanted no more of. He started to get up from the table when he felt a strong hand on his shoulder push him back down. It was Bert Lewis.

"Whatcha want me to do with him, boss?"

"Let's all just get up calmly. Bert, you keep your hand on the back of his neck. Tommy, you just walk along like you're enjoying spending time with your two favorite uncles at the veterans reunion. We will all walk calmly to Main Street, take the steps down to the creek and get on the barge. We will pole our merry way downstream and when we get to the river shed, we'll work out the details. OK? Now, nice and easy and nobody's going to get hurt. We're all friends here, right?" They all quietly nodded and walked through the park, leisurely like they were on a … well, like a walk in the park.

Just before they got to Main Street, they saw there was an opening in the balustrade through which one could walk to narrow concrete steps leading down to where small boats could be tied up. Right where the weight-bearing pilings were, silt and sand had built up, forming a small area of dry land around each. As the three boarded the barge and pushed off, Tommy made a neat, easy jump over the side — as only the young can do — landing on the islet around the bridge abutment. One wide, striding leap got him to the concrete wall that contained the waterway. He scrambled up and took off.

Tommy tore through the park, and sneaked quietly back to the garage behind Phelps House. The window was too high for him to see through, so he found an old bucket, turned it over and stood on it. Now he could see what was going on inside the shack. He saw Champ, Weasel's friend, sitting at a table, trying to eat some cornmeal mush and having a tough go at it. The boy tapped gently on the window. Champ heard, and stopped for a moment, but could not discern where it was coming from. He continued to struggle to feed himself. Tommy tapped again, this time tapping until Champ finally looked up at the window and saw him. Champ's face quickly changed to a look of fierce anger. The deformed man rose and walked with an uncertain gait toward the door. Tommy watched him open the door and move back. He didn't venture outside, but stood in his room, holding his oak newel post in one hand. Tommy hopped down from the bucket and went to the door.

"Mister Champ, 'member me? I'm a friend of Weasel's. Can I come in?"

Champ said nothing, but went back to his table and his ineffective efforts to finish the bowl of gruel. He kept the sturdy post handy.

"Wha' you wan'?" barked the bearded old man.

"I'm tryin' to find Weasel. Ain't seen him in a day or two." Tommy's troubled, short life had conditioned him to lie instinctively, even when it wasn't necessary. Instead of saying he was running for his life from two men who wanted to kill him, he said he was just looking for a friend.

"I hear he in jail," grunted the handyman.

"In jail? What happened? What's he in jail for?" Tommy kept asking questions until he realized that trying to answer them was more than a simple challenge for Champ. Tommy stood up and said, "I'm sorry to bother you, Mr. Champ. I sure would like to talk to Weasel. There's things going on that I don't understand, but I can't go near the police station." The old man just stared at him, one eye only half-open, shining with permanent rage. "Hey, Champ? What happened to your head, anyway?"

Champ just stared at Tommy. He picked up the heavy post and held it next to his head. "See? Man hit me with this. Left me for dead. Goddam Rebel. Now get outta here!" He raised the newel post as if to swing it at the child's head. As he swiveled to avoid the blow, Tommy noticed a golden, jewel-encrusted chalice, filled with hot coffee.

Lambert Van Poole sat at his tiny desk in the detective squad room. He had finally found peace and quiet, with no interference from the other detectives or from Chief Wilson. He began listing everything he knew about the death of Alden James. Once he had all the facts in front of him, he'd write an official investigation report, detailing each piece of the evidence and see what led to a suspect. Then he would prepare all the proper affidavits to take to Judge Travis and see if he was willing to issue the cause of death decision or if he would have to hold an inquest. But first, he'd find out what Weasel Jones knew about fine jewelry. He had the prisoner brought to an interrogation room.

"All right, Weasel. Here's what you're looking at. I got you for peddling without a license, and ..."

"I had a license. Official. You took it from me and I guess you tore it up. But I got witnesses. There's bound to be a record at the City Clerk's office."

"Even if you did and even if there is a record, it doesn't help you. I have also charged you with violating special ordinance 14-1, which the City Council just passed, outlawing the sale of any unauthorized memorabilia during the reunion. All that junk you had in your case was just that — junk. In addition to being a disorganized mess, it was not properly sanctioned by the Confederate Veterans Reunion Committee, so that puts a ten-dollar fine on your ass along with a 30-day jail sentence. In addition, I am going to see the judge tomorrow about the murder of Alden James and I'm naming you as the prime suspect. After all, he was found dead right next to a stash of illegal moonshine which, I have no doubt, can be attributed to you. I don't think you're enjoying the reunion festivities near as much as I am."

"Listen, Van Poole, you can't prove any of this."

"Do you know Judge Travis? I've never seen a man so nervous by the prospect of holding a coroner's inquest. He'll go along with anything I present to him. He just wants to get the investigation over and done with so he can go back to what he's good at — collecting bad debts and marrying folks. I just can't figure that you have much of a way out of this, Weasel, I really don't."

Jones became uncharacteristically quiet and introspective. His glib confidence and his brazenness, always his stock in trade, seemed to have failed him for the first time in his life.

Van Poole waited a moment, then spoke quietly — Weasel had to lean in a little to hear him. "And this small object just might be the piece of evidence that seals your fate." He placed the large, sparkling rectangular diamond on the table.

"Where did you find that? I mean, what is that?" sputtered Weasel, after a gasp at the sight of the precious stone.

"Oh, boy, what a giveaway that was! A day or two in jail and you start to lose all your quick wit."

"Aren't I supposed to have a lawyer here? I mean … uh … I'm not guilty of any of this stuff you're saying. Except maybe the counterfeit goods. But I want to have a lawyer here to help me because you're going to twist everything I say into something to make me seem like I'm guilty, when I really am not guilty of anything but trying to make an honest living. I might skate a little close to the edge sometimes, but I could never kill anybody." Weasel started talking faster and faster, losing the swagger that had eased him through many a tangle. He was getting close to the edge, all right — the edge of a complete nervous breakdown. "And why are you shoving that big shiny diamond at me? I don't know nothing about that."

"You just keep talking — and digging yourself deeper and deeper into this, Weasel. You knew what that diamond was the instant I put it in front of you." Now came the test of the detective's real talent — concocting a story to convince the suspect he knew more than he did about what happened. He only hoped that what he assumed to be the story was right. "It's what you intended to swindle off that old man, but you ended up having to fight him for it. In the scuffle, it got lost under that bridge. I happen to know he was taking that diamond to give to the Catholic Church as an offering. So now we can add attempted robbery, compounded by stupidity, to your rap sheet."

"I don't know what you are talking about, and I'm saying not a word more until my lawyer is here."

"Good. You have just sealed the case shut for me, Weasel. Because we all know that only the guilty need lawyers. Whoo boy, Judge Travis is going to love this. He likes easy cases. I tell you what. I got a lot of work to do to get this case ready for him in the morning. As soon as I'm finished, I'll get word to that lawyer Vern Piggott to sober up and come by to pay you a visit." Van Poole had Weasel Jones hauled back to his cell and then wrote in his notebook: *Weasel was rattled when I showed him the diamond. He might not have killed the man, but I can probably pin it on him if nothing else comes along.*

First thing the next morning, Van Poole was in Judge Travis' office. As promised, he brought Doc Otwell's report of post-mortem examination and all of his investigative notes, and a nicely completed finding of unnatural death certificate with all of the blanks filled in. All it needed was the Judge's signature. Judge Travis was not particularly agreeable to this meeting, but graciously invited Van Poole into his chambers.

"My heavens, Detective, what is it that you want from me regarding this man's death?" Judge Travis was so nervous, he fidgeted with everything within reach. The items he intended to pick up, he fumbled with, dropping several. He knocked over a bottle of ink, spreading the coal-black liquid across his desk. Trying to clean it up and stop it from oozing resulted in ink-stained fingers that left black smudges across his face each time he rubbed his nose or scratched his cheek. It looked like a fluttershow. Van Poole felt a certain sympathy for him at this moment, as well as no small amount of amusement.

"Well, your honor, he died in your district, and from all appearances by an act of violence at the hands of another."

"I am aware of all that, but what does that have to do with the Justice of the Peace?"

"You act as coroner for all unexplained deaths in your district. Says so right in the state statutes. You have to determine the cause of death. Hold an inquest if you see it necessary."

"Coroner? No one ever told me that. The governor appointed me to fill out the term of Judge Weldon when he died. 'Easy work, Sandy' he told me. Impoundments, auctions, collections, peace bonds, arrest warrants. 'If you work well with your constable you'll both make a good living.' Not to mention the weddings. No one ever mentioned this part of the job. Death certificates, sure. But never any mention of inquests. Oh, my heavens. What am I to do?"

"Take it easy, Judge. I will make this as simple as possible for you. I have Doc Otwell's post-mortem examination report, and my investigative notes, and a list of physical evidence that we have gathered. If you would just take a minute and look it all over, then you can with good conscience sign these papers that I brought."

"Sign? Oh, my God in heaven. You expect me to sign some papers? What kind of papers are you trying to get me to sign? I only sign papers Mrs. Travis has prepared for me. That's how this office operates."

"Sir, it's just a cause of death finding. It states that the death was unnatural and unattended by a physician, brought on by blunt force administered by an unknown assailant. As such, it requires further investigation by the appropriate investigative body. That, sir, unless you want to convene a coroner's jury, will be the Jacksonville Police Department. So you see? It's really quite simple."

Judge Travis took the papers from Van Poole's hand and struggled with a set of now-ink-smeared spectacles so he could read. They heard an outer door slam and Judge Travis called out, "Genevieve? Is that you? Come in here!"

"Yes, it's me. I'm coming, dear."

To Van Poole, the judge said, "Now we'll see what's what. Mrs. Travis checks over everything that comes out of this office. She may not be able to bake a wedding cake, but she knows a thing or two about legal documents."

A tall, handsome woman blew into the room with an air of dignity and importance. "Yes, Sandy, darling, what is ... " Then she noticed Van Poole. "Oh. I did not know you had an appointment this morning, Judge Travis. How may I help?"

"Genevieve, this is Detective Lambert Van Poole. He says I am supposed to act like a coroner or something. You know anything about this? And he wants me to sign these papers." He handed them to her.

"How do you do, Detective?" she politely asked as she took the papers and sat down. She started reading through each page.

"Very well, ma'am, thank you. Everything is in proper order, I assure you. I guess this may be the first time Judge Travis has had to deal with such a situation, but it's quite routine for us in the JPD. I think you'll find that all the papers there are in order."

"Yes. It certainly seems that everything is properly drawn," she murmured. Then she turned to her husband, instructing him, "I think you should sign these papers where indicated, Judge Travis."

"Do we get paid for doing any of this?" asked the judge.

"I will file the finding of unnatural death certificate with the Clerk's Office, and we get a dollar and twenty cents for that. The death certificate will bring us three dollars."

"Well, then, give me the dang papers." It was clear to Van Poole that Sandberg Travis and his wife Genevieve had decided to make the Office of Justice of the Peace a family business, with Genevieve in charge of the whole process.

Tommy Whitehead finished his breakfast, sitting alone on the convent's back porch. He didn't much care for oatmeal, but he allowed as how it was filling. And with a handful of raisins tossed in, even more so. Sister Finbar came out.

"Up with you, sinner. It's quite a wagonload of penance awaits you, it is. Firewood needs to be chopped. Coal scuttles need filling. Potatoes need to be gathered. Then I think we'll see what you can do about fixing a roof."

"Firewood and coal? Can't you just use one or the other? Why do you need both?"

"Shows what you know about running a house. Living under a bridge like a reptile. Coal is for heating and wood is for cooking. Now, never you mind about that and just do as you're told."

After the wood, coal and potatoes were seen to, Sister Finbar explained the next phase of his penance. "Some of the wood shingles on the roof are rotten. You pull them up, smear some of this pine tar on the bad spots, then nail down new ones."

"How am I supposed to get up on that roof? Shimmy up the downspout?"

"Of course not, ya ninny. Come with me." They climbed three flights of stairs to the attic where Tommy noticed several small windows strategically placed about the walls. Sister Finbar pointed to them. "That's how you get to the roof. First, we put this harness on you and secure you with an angel rope."

"Angel rope?"

"Yes. You get out there on the roof, and the devil will try to pull you down to him. The angel rope will keep you up here. Unless, that is, your sins are too much an unholy burden for the rope. Then the devil wins."

Sister Finbar tied the harness and rope around Tommy and sent him out the window with a stack of cedar shingles, a hammer, a bag of nails and a bucket of pine tar. Through the propped-up window, Sister Finbar directed the repairs. Tommy looked up the steeply pitched roof and saw Sister Finbar's angry, wrinkled face in the tiny window, barking orders at him. "How could hell itself be any worse than this?" he mused. Though he had difficulty staying upright on the roof, he finally replaced all the rotten shingles. When he was safely back inside the attic, Sister Finbar gave him a look of disapproval. “That must be some terrible passel of sins you’re carrying around. The devil was tugging mightily at you the whole time you were out there. And the clever fellow nearly got you more than once.”

“Got scairt enough once that he could have had me, no problem. I wouldn’t of cared.”

“Well, it must be some sort of sign that you’re back in here safe and sound. It means you’re on the path to a righteous life. But your biggest penance is yet to be served. After lunch, then.”

On the way back to the police station, Detective Van Poole met Chief Wilson for a late breakfast at Bay Street Diner. Fried ham, corn cakes and coffee. Van Poole explained his experience with Judge Travis and his wife, and both men had a good laugh. “Well, I guess we could do worse. I suppose that if you’re trying to limit the damage of patronage by restricting it to minor positions, the Justice of the Peace is not a bad place to put political supporters,” reasoned the chief.

“Yes, I agree. Still, sometimes you wish you could count on them to know what to do. Oh, listen. Don’t eat too much, you’ll spoil your appetite. I think Thursday is chicken fricassee day at Phelps House.”

“Chicken fricassee? Aaah. Fricassee. Not an easy thing to do properly. I can’t think of the last decent fricassee I had. Thank you, Lambert.” He pushed his plate away, the breakfast half-eaten. Van

Poole finished it for him and left a quarter on the table as they left. The Bay Street diner was known to have very friendly attitudes toward policemen. "I might need some sort of pretext for showing up there right at dinnertime. Since I accompanied her to the ball, I don't want her thinking that I'm going to be calling on her socially, but then again, it might seem awkward to arrive for dinner having already engaged with her socially. An awful lot of work for chicken fricassee."

"Chief, I think you're complicating it unnecessarily. Just go and sit down and they'll serve you."

"Ah, Van Poole. You may be the best detective in these parts, but an unsophisticated lout you are, when it comes to the understanding the fairer sex. No, I think I must develop a pretext. Have we recovered all of Mr. James' belongings from his room?"

"Yessir, we have and she has already let out the room to someone else. Why can't you just stop in and see how things are going? You know, with the crowds from the reunion and the noise and so on."

"That just might work, Van Poole. It just might work." They reached the door of the police station. "Now prove to me why you're the best detective in these parts and clear up this goddamn murder case."

Van Poole took the exhortation to mean that the chief had finished the conversation, and that Van Poole had free rein from here on. Which was a good thing, as Van Poole had previously arranged through Sister Finbar another "chance" meeting with Tommy Whitehead. He had a plan he didn't think the Chief would appreciate.

Chapter 12

At a quarter to twelve Thursday morning, Van Poole dropped Chief Wilson off at Phelps House. Every seat in the large dining room was taken, and the front parlor was near capacity with guests waiting for a spot to open. The family-style service reminded one of poorly organized chaos. But no one who showed up to dine seemed put off by that. Every couple of minutes, a young lady working the dining room would step into the parlor and call for hungry diners. "I got two open at the far end of table four. Next two who want to eat, follow me."

Wilson noticed Mayor Langen and Jimmie Calton dining together at the end of a long, crowded table. He hoped that a seat would open up near them so that he could sit with the city's movers and shakers. They were both clearly enjoying the company of the others at their table, and no one appeared to be finishing up their meal — a fresh pan of fricasseed chicken was placed on the table and the men dug in heartily. One of the group was the state legislator who had been among the notables milling about the day before, at the VIP tent. Wilson picked up a newspaper and plopped down in an upholstered chair by the front window and pretended to read the broadsheet. Martha Brandywine peeked over the pages and said, at first playfully, "Well, it's Chief Luther Wilson!" Then, seeing his injury, exclaimed with unrecognized false concern, "Oh, dear! What happened to your hand?"

"Oh, that? Just the rigors of being chief of police. A cell door slammed on my fingers during a surprise inspection of the prison quarters. It's nothing. Goes with the territory."

"Well, you should probably soak it in some epsom salts or something. Seems like every time you show up here for dinner, trouble breaks out nearby. What'll it be today, I wonder? A stolen bicycle?" Their conversation was interrupted by a loud boom, then one of the kitchen maids let go with an ear-splitting scream.

Wilson ran into the kitchen, followed closely by Miz Martha. The kitchen and the dining room were rapidly filling up with up with a combination of steam and smoke, and several people on the kitchen staff were covering their faces with wet towels. Some pointed to a door in the rear of the room, indicating that was the source of the disturbance. It was the laundry area, which housed two large-capacity water heaters to meet the demand of the guests and the laundry workers. It looked like one was spewing forth the brimstone of hell. As Chief Wilson assessed the situation, he kept everyone calm. He went into the laundry area and spied an old, bearded man with a badly misshapen head — someone he didn't recognize. The man was clumsily working on a set of valves, trying to stop the flow of water to the ruptured tank. A small fire was burning, spreading to some fresh-washed sheets that had been hung on an inside clothesline to dry. Wilson looked around for the regulation-required canvas firehose, saw it and quickly connected it. He opened the valve and in no time at all had the small fires reduced to a wet smolder. The mysterious man slunk out of the boiler room by another door and loped to the garage.

Tommy sat alone in the convent dining room, eating his lunch. That he was allowed in that hallowed room should have been a giveaway to him that something was up. He never ate in the dining room — always the back porch. Once in the kitchen. He was slurping some watery chicken soup and eating a piece of fatty ham when Lambert Van Poole walked in, carrying a lunch tray of his own. The door shut behind Van Poole and Tommy heard an extra click. Locked in. An awkward silence lasted well over two minutes as the detective offloaded his bowl of soup and his plate of ham onto the table, then sat and began to eat.

"Soup's good," said Van Poole.

"Yeah," said Tommy.

"A bit thin."

"I reckon."

"Ham is pretty salty."

"You sure complain a lot."

"You can't run away from me this time, Tommy."

"Can't run away from Sister Finbar any time."

"I can get you out of here for a while, maybe for good, if you'll come with me and agree not to take off. I could use your help to find that murderer."

"How am I gonna help find a murderer? I don't even know where to look."

"I'll tell you where to look and what to look for."

"I reckon. But if I see Mr. Warren or Bert Lewis, I'm goin' to run. They want to put me out of circulation."

"Why would they want to put you out of circulation?"

"They think I squealed about something. That's what I mean by a life of sorrow if you talk to the police."

"Well, I might like to talk to them. I can attest that you have not squealed about anything, otherwise I would have a lot more information than I do about moonshine and murder."

"I'll tell you like I told them. I don't know nothin'."

Lambert Van Poole got his guarantee from Tommy to not to run away, and they began to build a relationship of sorts. They complained to each other about the lousy lunch. Van Poole started to talk about Sister Finbar's cruel personality, but Tommy stopped him cold.

"I'll warrant she's mean as the devil. But I think she means well. She just don't know any other way to be."

Lambert agreed and congratulated Tommy on his perceptiveness. He thought that they had a couple of things in common ... from an abandonment perspective. Tommy had been abandoned by his parents, as had Van Poole. Admittedly, the circumstances were different, but Van Poole thought that if he could connect with the boy on some level, they could begin to build some trust. Maybe he could turn the kid from a life of crime. At the very least, maybe he could solve a murder. They finished eating and cleaned up the dishes, then went into the alley and climbed into the Cadillac.

"You ain't takin' me to no jail, are ya?"

"No, Tommy, I'm not taking you to jail. At least not this time. But if you don't start living right, I can't promise that you won't end up there some time in the future."

"This car is a lot nicer than Father Donal's. His makes a lot of rattlin' noises and has hard, wooden seats."

"When have you ever ridden in Father Donal's car?"

"I had to carry his golfing clubs for him one day, and he drove me out to the golf course."

"Well, even an old car like his is better than no car at all, wouldn't you say?"

"I reckon."

"What about Weasel Jones? Ever been in is car?"

"Weasel ain't got no car."

"You're good friends with Weasel, aren't you?"

"Yeah. He helps me a lot."

"Think for a minute about all the people you know. Who has an automobile and who does not?"

Tommy thought for a minute. "What're you gettin' at?"

"Isn't it a bit curious that of all the folks you know, a policeman and a priest have automobiles. The thieves and con-men don't."

"I reckon. So where are we going, anyway?" Van Poole saw immediately that motivation and positive reinforcement would be of little value in counseling this delinquent.

"You know where Weasel lives, don't you?"

"Yeah. Over there on Walnut Street."

"Have you ever been in his apartment?"

"Once. He was s'pozed to give me some money for some work I done for him but he didn't, so I went up there to try to get it."

"And did you get it?"

"No. Said he didn't have none. But I know he was lying. He always has money. So after he left, I clumbed up a tree and in through a winder and tried to find it."

"Did you?"

"No. Found about everything but, though. So I took an old pocket-watch and sold it at the train station for a dollar. I figured that about evened us up. I heered you got Weasel in jail. What for?"

"Right now, it looks like we will be charging him with murder, among other various crimes."

"I don't think Weasel would kill nobody."

"Well, unless you or he can give me something else to go on, he's going to hang. The judge has practically signed off on it — it's just about a done deal. If there's anything of yours at Weasel's apartment or anything he owes you, we might as well go get it, because I don't think he's going to be coming back."

"Once he said he had a whore for me, but I would have to wait until I was sixteen. He probably got some other stuff of mine, too. Things that I find around, you know, like a ring or pocket-watch or somethin'. He always tells me to bring the stuff to him and he'll sell it for me and give me the money. He never has the money, though, so I reckon he never sells nothin'. He must have a pile of my stuff in there."

"Now, how do you manage to find rings and watches and such?"

"Well, see, he taught me how to play this game at the train station. He gives me a cheap ring and tells me to go up to a fancy-dressed tourist lady and tell her I found a ring on the ground, and ask her if it belongs to her. And she says, 'Oh, no, little boy, I have my ring right here on my finger.' Real sweet like." Tommy raised the pitch of his voice to imitate a lady. "And I say, 'Let me see it.' And she holds out her hand to show it to me, and I say, 'That looks just like the one I found. Let me show you. And I take the ring out of my pocket to show it to her, and quick as a wink, I pull the ring off her finger and take off. It won't work with a big fat lady, though. You can't get their rings off their fingers. But sometimes I can talk one into taking it off and giving it to me to look at real close. I'll just say, 'Take that ring off your finger and let me look at it side by side with this one.' And she'll take it off and I look at it and while she ain't watching, I switch it with the ring that Weasel gave me. And then I'm gone like a flash. I'll take that ring to Weasel and he says he'll sell it and give me a dollar. Or if you see a lady who don't have a ring at all, you say you found it, and somebody might as well have it, and they'll offer to buy it from you for two dollars or something. There's all sorts of games Weasel taught me. Sometimes you can do the same thing with a pocket-watch, but you got to look for just the right kind of fella. Find one who's eager to dangle an expensive pocket watch in front of your face just to show off how rich he is. I just grab it and run like hell."

"Do you realize that you're stealing? You know what you're doing is against the law?"

"Well, I'm just doing what Weasel tells me to. He says it's OK because those people have so much money anyway that it don't matter. So it ain't really stealin' if they don't really need it. I figure Weasel must owe me 'bout twenty-five dollars by now."

"We'll just go and see if we can get you your twenty-five dollars, or at the very least, some of those items you 'found.'"

They parked about a block from the building where Weasel lived. The second floor window to Weasel's apartment overlooked the alley. Tommy scampered up a camphor tree growing close against the building, leaned over and slid open the window. On the ground floor, Van Poole entered the small general store that had a little bit of everything. Some hardware, some groceries, some dry goods and notions. He kept the proprietor busy looking for a set of buckets of a particular size in the front of the store so that any noises that Tommy might make moving around upstairs wouldn't be heard. "No, that bucket is too big. Fill that with coal and my wife can't lift it. I need a smaller one that she can handle." After he calculated that Tommy would have had enough time rummaging around Weasel's place, he feigned anger and disgust with the inept merchant and left. He started up the car and pulled it into the alley just as Tommy was jumping from the lowest limb of the camphor tree.

"Did you find anything of yours?"

"I found lots of stuff. That whole place is full of watches and rings, and fancy clothes, even ladies' clothes. Tools, crates of wine, boxes of cigars and all sorts of gear. I snagged two rings that I knew were ones I'd gotten for him that he never paid me for." He dug the jewelry from his pocket and showed them to the detective.

"You just hang onto them for right now. You didn't happen to see a big fancy cup, made out of gold and covered with rubies and diamonds and like that, did you?"

"Not in there. But Champ's got a cup like that."

"Champ? Who is Champ?"

"He's another friend of Weasel's. Lives in a garage by Phelps House, near the park where the old soldiers are camped out."

"Well, let's go pay Champ a visit. I am very curious to see his fancy cup."

"That Champ!" hissed Martha Brandywine, from the back of the kitchen. "Maybe he's getting too old to keep working as much. I've been after him for a week to repair those boilers. They start knocking the pipes around and you just know something's going to blow." She paused and sighed. "I guess we have to shut down dinner service. Can't have those girls working in a smoky kitchen. And with only one boiler, I'll have to put all the girls on laundry duty."

Chief Wilson made his way to the dining room just in time to observe the mayor scraping the last helping of chicken fricassee onto his plate, as Mrs. Brandywine stood in the parlor apologizing, and explaining to anxious customers that, regrettably, the dinner service had been interrupted by a small fire. Wilson went out to the garage to try to get some information from the odd-looking man he'd seen during all the excitement. He quickly walked once around the garage, then again quite slowly, noting the placement of windows, doors or any other possible escape. After a few minutes, he saw Van Poole driving the Cadillac down the alley. Motioning for his detective to pull into the Phelps House backyard, past the garage, the chief was trying to get the vehicle in position for a quick exit. As he did so, Van Poole said to Tommy, "Remember our bargain. You run away now and I'll find you — and the next stop is jail."

"Van Poole! Once again, perfect timing. There has been a slight mishap here at Phelps House — or perhaps mischief. A boiler overheated and the expansion tank blew up. Damage was minimal, but further inquiry is in order. Miz Brandywine's maintenance man lives in the garage, here. I saw him working inside with the pipes just after the explosion, then he ran out here. I want to check the scene, make sure he's uninjured, and ask him if he can explain anything about what happened. I have checked the perimeters. There's a set of stairs on the other side leading up to an apartment, but I saw him go inside through this first floor entrance. You cover the other side for me. I'll signal when I'm in." Then the Chief looked at Tommy. "What the blazes is he doing here with you?"

"He's just tagging along with me for a bit today." The detective, mindful of another person's feelings and always aware of police procedure, indicated for the chief to step away to where the boy wouldn't overhear them. "I think he knows a lot of details that could prove rather useful. He thinks of himself as a serious street tough, one who's not going to give anything up to the police. But he doesn't know what's important and what isn't so I have to try to trick it out of him. Finagle the facts, as it were." After telling Tommy to stay put, Van Poole darted around to the other side of the garage, and Chief Wilson started knocking on the door.

"Open up in there. This is the Jacksonville police. Open up or the door comes down."

Champ opened the door a few inches — just enough for the chief to see the gray, frizzled beard that partially hid his scarred face, and to see full-on the eye that never quite completely closed. He could see the permanent tobacco stain that ran through his beard from the corner of his mouth to his chin, the result of a jaw fracture not healing correctly, which kept the man from being able to close his mouth all the way. The frightful sight was compounded by an equally frightful odor. Sweaty clothes, stale food, alcohol, eucalyptus and other medicinals hit the chief's nostrils full force.

"Wha' you wan'?" asked the man.

"Mostly I want to check on your condition. Make sure you weren't injured in the explosion."

"I'm fine. 'hank you for stoppin' by," said the man as he tried to close the door. The chief let out a whistle and a call to Van Poole to come around to the door.

"Not so fast." The chief stuck his foot in the jamb and leaned inside. "I want to come in and make sure everything is all right, and find out what you know about what happened in the laundry room."

Van Poole now stood right behind the chief, and Champ relented when he realized he was up against two of Jacksonville's finest. The door swung open wide as Champ moved quickly toward his bed, nearly obscured in a dark corner of the room.

"I din' do nut'n wrong. Lemme 'lone." Champ's usual difficulty in speaking was aggravated when he was nervous.

"I intend to find out what caused that explosion. We will need a report of property damage so Miss Martha can file a claim with her insurance agent," said Chief Wilson.

"The etspansion tank walief valve stuck. Tank too small anyway. Boiler too hot. Boom," explained the maintenance man.

"Miz Brandywine said you were given orders to fix that boiler last week. Why wasn't it repaired?"

"Can't fix. Too small. She too cheap to buy new one. All her money coul' heat the whole damn town."

"Such critical remarks of one's employer may not be in one's best interest. So you knew what was wrong with it and you reckoned it would blow at any time?"

"Yeah."

"That's how you happened to know just what tool to bring and just what to do when you heard the explosion?"

"Yeah." Both Champ and Van Poole were wondering what method of police investigation the chief was conducting.

"You didn't rig that tank to explode right at dinner time on one of Miz Brandywine's busiest days? You knew there'd be a big crowd — her chicken fricassee is particularly sought after."

"No."

Van Poole joined in on the questioning, before Chief Wilson demonstrated his complete ineptness regarding interrogation. "Hey, Champ, have you been frequenting the park for the veterans reunion?"

Champ stared at Van Poole for nearly a full minute before answering with a barely audible, "How you know my name?"

"I know a lot about you, Champ. And you look old enough to be a Civil War veteran yourself."

"Well, I'm no'. Not 'federate anyway."

"Oh, I see. A Yankee."

"So what if I'm a Yankee? Nothin' wrong with that," barked the old man.

"Nothing much right about it, either." There was a pause in the conversation as Van Poole walked around the room for a minute. "What happened to your head?"

"Ol' war injury," said Champ.

"Confederate cannon ball? That would have taken your entire head off."

"Long time ago. Got hit with somethin'."

"Stand up. I want to see how tall you are," ordered Van Poole.

"I'm five foo' ten."

"I don't take anybody's word for anything. Stand up." Van Poole reached to help him up, and as he did, something that Champ had been struggling to conceal under his pillow rolled onto the floor. A golden chalice, mounted with several gleaming jewels, came to rest at their feet. "Well, now, that is one mighty fancy drinking cup. Where did you get that?"

"Not mine. Belong to a frien'."

"What are you doing with it?"

"Keeping it for him."

"Is he coming back for it?"

"Said he would."

"What's your friend's name?"

"Don't wemember."

"Ah, I'll bet you have so many friends that it's tough to keep track of all them."

"It was a long time ago."

"Yes, I'll bet it was a long time ago. Maybe fifty years or so?" The detective walked to the cluttered shelves at the end of the room where Champ's trash-collecting harvest was displayed. Among the scrap items were the shattered remains of a wooden box with tight dovetail joints, what was left of brass hinges and hasp, and velvet cloth and padding glued to the inside. With great anticipation pumping through him, the detective set the chalice in the space — it fit perfectly. Then he noticed something just a ways up under

Champ's small cot — an oak newel post. He kicked it out into the open, then bent to pick it up. "Chief, here's your murder weapon. And this chalice here was the offering that the late Alden James was going to make to the Immaculate Conception Catholic Church. So it would seem that we also have our murderer."

"What the devil are you talking about, Van Poole? This man is no murderer. He is Miz Brandywine's maintenance man. Why, she has known him all of her life and will attest to his gentle nature."

"Chief, here is all the evidence. It's staring you in the face."

"Did you not hear what he said, Van Poole? The cup belongs to a friend who's coming back for it. That man is the murderer. And my bet is that it's Weasel Jones. Why, Champ here is nothing more than a stooge. An unwitting accomplice at worst." Then he took the heavy piece of oak. "And look at this. This is no murder weapon." He pointed to gouges and marks in the flat surfaces. "This is an all-purpose tool. You can see where it has been used as a hammer, a pry bar, and who knows what else."

"There's bloodstains on it, Chief. I bet it matches the fatal wound on Alden James' head." Van Poole looked at Champ, thinking. The facts in Commander Davidson's report and Dr. Otwell's words were finally coming together, beginning to make sense where there had been none.

Chief Luther Wilson drew himself up to his full height, not consciously trying to control the situation, but achieving that anyway. "That could very well be red paint. Now take all this to the evidence room and then confront Weasel Jones with the facts and the evidence and get a confession. Let's leave this man to get on with his work."

Wilson returned to the dining room to make sure all was in order. His irrepressible need to be seen as the indispensable leader, if not the hero, of the hour had yet to be satisfied. The big room was empty, and not a morsel of chicken fricassee was left there or in the kitchen. The staff was stacking dishes to be taken outside and washed in tubs being filled from a cauldron boiling over a fire. Wilson asked Mrs. Brandywine why the help was using the old-fashioned method of washing dishes.

"With only one boiler operating, Luther, there won't be enough hot water for everything. I would rather the guests not be inconvenienced, so we'll do the dishes and the laundry out in the yard. Just like Mama did in the old days, when I was a little girl."

Wilson went into the parlor and noticed that Mayor Langen and his entourage were still lingering. Their conversational tone changed abruptly as he approached. "There he is, gentlemen. Our very own Police Chief Luther Wilson. The man who runs toward trouble while the rest of us are running away." Jimmie Calton joined the group, rushing in as if he'd been there the whole time. He'd been applying new foundation to his face since the excessive steam and all the hubbub had caused a good bit of it to run.

"Ah. Thank you, Mayor Langen. I trust these unfortunate circumstances did not prevent you from enjoying a proper dinner?"

"Oh, we managed to take in some sustenance before the billowing clouds of smoke and steam dampened the mood. But we truly thank you for your quick response. Could easily have gotten tragically out of hand but for your presence."

"Well, one does what one is called upon to do."

Chapter 13

Van Poole took Tommy back to the convent and put him in the custody of Sister Finbar, then drove to the police station, angry at Chief Wilson for being so irrational in his interrogation of Champ. Worse than that was his cavalier refusal to see the obvious grounds for an arrest. The Chief constantly hounded his detectives for activity. Of all the activity possible, clearing a case was by far the most highly rewarded. Of all the ways to clear a case, making an arrest was by far the most celebrated — and the most final. Here was a chance right in the chief's hands to clear a murder by arrest, and he was blind to it. It did not really matter in the long run. A fellow as old and infirm as Champ had little chance of running away. Van Poole could go back and arrest him if he needed to. He just felt a tinge of resentment, not real anger. He checked the newel post and the chalice into the evidence room and requested that Weasel Jones be brought up to an interrogation cell.

"I thought I would be meetin' my lawyer. I'm not talking until I see my lawyer. Vernon Piggot. You were supposed to get him for me."

"Nonsense. You don't need a lawyer for this conversation. Tell me about Champ. The unfortunate fellow who lives in the garage at Phelps House. Tell me everything you know about him."

Weasel thought for a minute. Something big was going on and he had to figure out how to get a strategic advantage. "Well, there ain't much to know. Like you said, he's the old man who lives in the garage at Phelps. I think he does some odd jobs for Miss Martha. I can't imagine he does enough to earn his keep. I hardly ever see him outside the garage."

"I just paid him a little visit. He was trying to hide something up under his pillow, but when he got up, it fell to the floor. A gold chalice. Jewels all over it. Missing only one that I could see. The empty setting looks just right to hold the flat diamond that I found under the bridge where the man was murdered on Monday. You know, the one I showed you which you recognized. He also had an oak newel post that I'm willing to wager will match the wound on the deceased's skull. Both of these items I have confiscated and logged in as evidence."

"Congratulations, Detective. You have solved the murder. With Champ being in possession of the evidence, and trying to conceal it from you at that, it seems ironclad that he's your man. I presume I'll be released now. Have them bring my clothes in here, would you? Oh, and my sales case. I might yet be able to make a few dollars."

"Not so fast, Weasel. Champ said that chalice belonged to a friend who was coming back for it. I think that if you gave him that chalice to keep, it stands to reason that you'd hide the murder weapon there as well. It seems that there are a few chapters of the whole story that have been left out. So let's talk."

"When Piggott gets here."

"Piggott knows you have been detained and he will get here at his convenience. If he hasn't been drinking too heavily, he may even have some useful legal advice. But I am certain that he would advise any client of his to divulge anything they know about someone else committing a crime. That can only help in the defense."

"Really? You think so?" Jones was sounding a bit nervous.

"Believe me, he would be disappointed if you didn't."

"I don't know if I should trust you."

"I speak from years of experience, Weasel."

"Well, all right then. I'll tell you what I know, but I suspect it won't be very useful."

"You just talk. I'll decide what's useful," ordered Van Poole, acknowledging to himself that Weasel could be among the most talented liars in the human race.

"All right. I don't know exactly where Champ came from. I've been here most of my life and he has been around about as long as I can remember. He's right good at fixing things, but beyond that, he's not very smart. And by that I suppose I mean not very sophisticated. He's easy to trick, but he's got a temper. He can be mean if he finds out that he's not been treated fairly. He's always got a knife or a blade on him. And he's quick to use it. He also carries that oak stair post with him most all the time. He may be thin and wiry, but he is powerful strong."

"So far you have not shared much that I find interesting or useful, Weasel. And nothing comports with what some very reputable character witnesses would say about him."

"Well, Detective, you need only examine the secret book of clients that his employer keeps. They will say anything she tells them to. I am sure she's convinced most Jacksonville civic leaders that Champ is a poor circus freak only to be pitied. If they question her position on anything, they and their dalliances will end up being raked over the coals in every ladies' bridge club in town. Of course they hold Champ in only the highest regard."

"What about the chalice?"

"Well, Champ goes out most nights, very late. Goes scavenging. He sifts through garbage piles, goes to unattended work sites, and takes what trinkets and treasures he can carry. I don't know what drives this behavior. He very clearly is not possessed of the mental faculties that most of us are. But sometimes he comes up with some useful stuff. I stop by every couple of days to see what he has and he often picks up something worth buying. Quite a few good tools make their way through the community owing to his nighttime prowls. He's come back with bicycles that he swears he found abandoned. So, a few days ago, there in his room, I saw the golden chalice in a nice wooden box. Well, it once was a nice wooden box. It had been busted up, and part of the top was missing, some of the lining ripped out. I took an interest in it and wanted to buy it and he got angry. Not for sale, he said. I kept on trying to buy it from him and he got angrier. I offered that man fifty dollars and he nearly took that banister post to me. I thought he would run me out of his little garage there. I came back after a while and proposed my renting it from him. I would give him five dollars up front, and another five when I returned in a couple of days. He finally agreed, but made me give him a gold pocket-watch to hold until I brought the chalice back."

"Where did he say he got the chalice?"

"Says he found it in a smashed-up trunk by the railroad track. Must have fallen off one of the freight cars, was what he thought."

"So why did you want the chalice? What did you do with it?"

Van Poole stared at Weasel Jones, silently. He was almost

winning — he picked up on a slight twitch around Weasel's left eye that was growing more noticeable. Van Poole knew that if he could hold Weasel in a stare, that twitch would get worse and worse until even Weasel knew that his lying was exposed. It was Van Poole's favorite part of an interrogation. But it was not to be this time. A knock at the door and several loud voices interrupted the contest. The door flew open and in strode Vernon Piggott wreathed in his ever-present aura of alcohol. He was in that middle-of-the-day haze, somewhere between the hair of the dog and drunk as a skunk but still, apparently, able to grasp certain legal concepts.

"You will release this man into my custody immediately!" shouted the attorney.

"We are holding him in a murder investigation," Van Poole calmly replied.

"Well, let's all investigate together, Detective. Just make sure I am here to advise my client in his defense."

"Naturally, Mr. Piggott. I would never think otherwise. In fact, I was telling your client just a while ago how I am sure you would advise him to tell us who did it, if he knows. He refused to. Now, wouldn't you think that if a man has information that is crucial to his own defense, it would be best to share it?"

Piggott was temporarily speechless, confronted with a dialectic dilemma. "Don't try to confuse me, Van Poole. If you have charges, let's get on with it. We'll make bail and go work on our defenses in a more suitable setting. But don't try to ... well, just let's get on with this. What have you got on him?"

"What we've got down tight is selling untaxed whiskey and

peddling without a permit."

"Now that's more like it. Now we can move on. Shouldn't need a bond hearing on the peddling, we'll just pay the fine. Have you scheduled the first appearance on the untaxed ... ." He paused and then turned toward his client and lowered his voice. "Untaxed whiskey? How much?" Weasel communicated by facial expression, but may as well have shouted at the top of his lungs, 'Shut up, you stupid idiot. If you want some cheap whiskey, negotiating for it with your client in an interrogation room at police headquarters is not the clearest path to success.' The learned attorney realized his faux pas and went back to pleading on behalf of his client. "If you have scheduled the first appearance, I would ask you to release him into my custody, pending that action, and we can all go about our business."

Van Poole hated to release the suspect, if only because of the entertainment value of watching Vernon Piggott struggle with impending sobriety. But he realized that he had held Weasel Jones for about as long as he dared under the circumstances. He would release him and put a Pinkerton's man on them to look out for any incriminating behavior.

"And how was your afternoon of penance with the detective?" asked Sister Finbar.

"It was all right. He's not such a bad guy. 'Bout half the time I don't understand what he's talkin' about."

"I'm surprised he brought you back. Thought he might have wanted to take you to jail."

"Nah, he said he wasn't taking me to jail. We rode around in his nice car for a while. Talked about Weasel Jones. The detective don't think too highly of him. Said they probably be going to hang him for murder."

"The Fifth Commandment is Thou Shalt Not Kill. And two wrongs don't make a right."

"I don't know what all you mean by that, but I don't think Weasel killed nobody."

"Whether he did or didn't, the Lord will have the last judgment. Just as He will with you. Don't you see the wicked path you tread?"

"Not really. But the detective was sure keen to see Mr. Champ's fancy golden cup. So we went over there and there was a big fuss going on. Don't know what it was all about. That's when things got real confusing. He thought that meant that Mr. Champ killed the man under the bridge."

"What tale are you spinning now? What golden cup?"

"Weasel's friend, Champ. He's got this big fancy golden drinking cup. Gots jewels all over it. He was trying to drink some coffee out of it first time I seen it. It ain't easy for him 'cause he got his skull bashed in by a Rebel is what he told me. Can't hardly talk nor shut his mouth all the way. Don't know why he would want such a fancy cup when he can't hardly use it. He tries to slurp from it and it just dribbles all down into his beard. Anyway, the detective thought that Champ killed the guy, but the chief kept saying it had to of been Weasel. They kept fussing at each other about it and that's when he brought me back here."

"You get into that kitchen and start mopping those floors. Keep your mind on your work, lad, and forget all about your friends and golden cups, and such fanciful things."

Chapter 14

"Well, Van Poole, we have made it to Friday. A few hours and this reunion and all of its distractions will be over and we can get back to restoring order in this town. And I hope the first order of business will be to prepare an indictment against Weasel Jones for murder." The two men were having their usual Friday morning discussion in Chief Luther Wilson's office.

"It will be nice to get back to normal around here, but I wouldn't set my heart so unwaveringly on Weasel Jones as the murderer of the unfortunate Mr. James."

"I don't know why you won't accept the facts staring you right in the face, Lambert. For now, though, let's focus on getting this reunion over and done, with no more major crimes to investigate. I believe the city has invited veterans to stay on a few days, camping in the park, so we still have a weekend to get through. We can suggest in polite but strong terms that they should all be packing up by early Sunday."

"That directive would seem to rest in the hands of other city departments, don't you think?"

"Indeed, but we can provide some assistance. Perhaps some encouragement by means of a bit more vigilance about public drinking, noise-making and such. If the old guys realize that a night in jail is not the way to end the reunion, they'll be encouraged to leave."

"That would certainly seem to help some of them make up their minds. What events remain?"

"They have the final official business session this afternoon at four. That's when they will approve the resolutions, swear in officers for next year and whatever else it is they do. Presumably some of them have stayed sober and cogent enough over the past three days to have accomplished something. Then, the big finale starts after supper tonight, with the brass band contests, a fiddling contest of all things, and then the Rebel yell contest. So it will be a late night. Now tell me, Lambert, why don't you think Weasel Jones is our man?"

"I'm working on another theory, Chief. It may take the rest of today and most of the weekend to flesh it out completely. By the way, I assigned one of the Pinkerton detectives to tail Weasel and his attorney. I think any information gleaned from that detail may help me finalize my theory."

"Don't let him skip town, Lambert. If he does, it may well be your job."

"I won't."

Cedric Platt, a fifteen-year veteran of the Pinkerton organization, had his standard kit of disguises that Pinkerton Agents relied upon for tailing jobs. And, in case he needed them, he selected a handful of medals and camp badges from the loot that had already been confiscated and gathered at the police station. Decked out in his best suit, black bowler, fake beard and mustache, he started out after Jones and Piggott. He watched them go up to Vern Piggott's office on Forsyth Street and followed up the stairs of the building. Piggott's office occupied one small corner of the second floor, the remainder taken up by the Jacksonville office of Southern Mutual

Life & Accident Insurance Company. Platt was from Atlanta, where Southern Mutual was headquartered, so he was familiar with the company.

"Good morning," he said to the young lady at the reception desk. "I presume you are expecting me. Cedric Platt from the home office. Bring the files I am to examine to this front office." He pointed to an office that would have a window right next to Vernon Piggott's window, telling the woman, "I'll stay out of everyone's way."

"I beg your pardon, sir. I don't know what you're talking about."

"A telegram should have arrived here yesterday, identifying three files that are to be examined. I am here to conduct that examination. Now, the standard procedure is that I select the office in which I wish to work, you bring me the files, I examine them, then I go back to Atlanta. It was not easy to arrange this trip with this Confederate business going on, but the insurance industry cannot yield to the frivolities of others." He walked toward the office he'd chosen.

"I don't think we ever received your telegram, sir."

"It was not my telegram. It was from Broderick Nelson, president and founder of our company. He will not be happy to hear that I was met with such obstruction. Now please get the files."

"Which files did you want, sir?"

"I don't know. Mr. Nelson selected them. Just pick three commercial accounts at random." He went into the office and ordered its two occupants to vacate. When he was alone, he closed and locked the door and opened a large valise. From this he extracted three lengths of small brass organ-pipe with threaded ends.

One had a large cone at one end. He connected them and pushed the pipe along the ledge outside the window until it was just at the edge of the open window of Vernon Piggott's office. He listened to a conversation there, already in progress.

"Weasel, all the times that I have helped you out of your troubles, I would hope that you would think a kind thought of me. I have to learn from the police that you've got a stash of unlicensed whiskey? Couldn't you have thought to set aside a bottle or two for your old lawyer pal?"

"Listen, Vern, this rotgut is not any whiskey you'd be interested in. It's some old moonshine and God knows what-all. I'm not even sure where it came from in the first place."

"Weasel, that moonshine is the best stuff you can get. Store-bought whiskey is aged and colored, and all the kick is drawn right out of it. Whiskey from a moonshiner, that's the best. It ain't easy to come by. They been crackin' down on it for years. I can't think when I last had a good bottle. We can begin working on your defense as soon as you get me a couple bottles."

"Sure, Vern, sure. I only got two bottles left. It'll take me about an hour to go fetch them."

"Good. I'll start gathering what paperwork we need, you go get me some moonshine. And don't get tempted to stop off on the way. I tell you what: You leave that sales case of yours here, and when I have some whiskey in my hand, you get it back."

Cedric Platt quickly disassembled his listening device and put it back into his case. He left the office and went to the reception area. Puffing out his chest like the corporate bigwig he was pretending to be, he announced, "Mr. Nelson is going to be very displeased with this whole situation. I will send him a telegram and wait at my hotel for his response." He stormed out of the office, moving quickly down the sidewalk. As he passed each commercial establishment, he glanced in to see if any had installed a telephone he could use. Once he realized that he could be back at the station before he could find one he strode on, running the last two blocks.

"Van Poole! I heard them talking about moonshine. That lawyer wants two bottles of moonshine before he'll even begin to start work on the case. The Jones fellow said he only had two bottles left — he's gonna go get them. Told Piggott he'd be back in an hour. I thought it best to report that immediately to you rather than keep tailing him. We know he's coming back to the lawyer's office, so we can watch for him there."

"Good work, Cedric. Why don't you get yourself some lunch and keep an eye on that lawyer's office? Let me know if anything else happens." Van Poole was not quite sure how to handle a private detective on a tailing assignment. He just wanted the man to keep a low profile — preferably none at all. Platt hurried back to Forsyth Street, and spied an empty table right by a window in the Wisteria Diner, just across the street from the building where Vernon Piggot practiced his particular method of law. The view from the table would allow him to see when Weasel Jones returned. He ordered a plate of fried chicken gizzards and settled easily into the surveillance assignment. An hour later, he observed Weasel double-timing on the Forsyth Street sidewalk and bolting up the stairs, two at a time, to Piggott's office. Cedric could not chance the same pretense with the insurance company, so he just waited and watched as Van Poole had directed. He ordered more fried gizzards.

"Here," Weasel said as he thrust the illegal contraband at the barrister. "Two bottles of rotgut whiskey. Now get me out of this goddam mess."

"Patience, my friend. Patience. It's Friday afternoon. Nothing in the world we do now is going to make a difference. No sense getting too far ahead of ourselves. Let's relax and have a drink. You never know — what if the courthouse burns down over the weekend? We would have done a lot of work for naught." The two heavy, amber-colored bottles sat on his desk, speaking in tones that only Vernon could hear. *'Hurry up. Where's your glass?'*

But he couldn't find a glass. He usually kept one or two around or in his desk, but glasses from which one frequently drinks whiskey have a way of not being where you expect them to be. "I'll pour us each a slug as soon as I find two glasses," he said.

"None for me," said Weasel. "Never touch the stuff. Lose my edge, you know."

"Well, in that case ..." and Vernon Piggott yanked the cork out of the first bottle and took a long slow gulp. "My God, you were right! That is some kind of rotgut whiskey. Oh, but I bet it'll do the job. Whereas it might cause you to lose your edge, I find that whiskey sharpens my faculties." He took another long pull and wiped his lips with his sleeve. "I wonder what they put in this to get that unusual flavor. Sorghum, maybe?" His third drink was even longer, the fourth emptied the first bottle. He reached for the second.

"So what am I charged with, exactly?" asked Weasel.

"What are you charged with? Hell, who really knows? At this point, who cares? I reckon they got that jail full of 'federate veterans, pickpockets, whores and thieves. They ain't gonna concern themselves with you. I think they got you for gambling or something."

"I thought it was peddling without a license."

"That's right. Peddling. Peddling. What the hell were you peddling, anyway? No, no, don't answer that. We'll just build a defense based on the extenuating circumstances of the reunion."

"What about the murder?"

Piggott began to diminish the contents of the second bottle. "Murder? Did you kill somebody, Weasel? Can they prove it?" Another swig. "My fee may have to go up some considerable amount if I have to defend a moonshiner on a murder charge. Whoa, neighbor, I don't feel so good." He stood up and moved toward an open window, but didn't make it. He collapsed and lay prostrate on the floor, heaving and moaning. Weasel Jones rose wearily and left the office. He stopped in the first floor café and told the proprietor that just as he'd left the insurance office, he'd heard a man in the next office moaning and carrying on something terrible, and perhaps someone would check on the situation.

Ernest was one of the best all-around young boys at Immaculate Conception School. Made perfect grades, excelled at sports, was the leader of the altar boys, and had perfect attendance. That stellar comportment is why Sister Finbar selected him to deliver a very important message. She wrote out the message, put it in an envelope and gave it to Ernest. She instructed him to ride his brand-new bicycle, the envy of every Western-Union messenger in town, to the police station as quickly as possible to immediately deliver the missive. Ernest did this, with all the gravity that Sister Finbar had instilled in him. He parked his bicycle at the rack in front of the station, and locked it with a chain. He entered the police station, approached the duty desk and asked the sergeant if he could speak to Detective Lambert Van Poole. When the detective walked into the lobby, Ernest said, "Good afternoon, sir. I have an urgent message for you from Sister Finbar at Immaculate Conception Catholic Church." He handed the detective the envelope. Van Poole tore it open and read the note.

Dear Detective Van Poole,
I know you have had difficulty getting any useful information from Tommy Whitehead, regarding instances of sinful behavior in our city. I may have some historical knowledge that could be helpful. Please indicate the approximate time I might expect you and send word back with the young man who delivers this message.

Yours in Christ,
Sister Mary Finbar

Van Poole read the message and chuckled a bit. It was as if she were sending notes home to the parents of wayward children and thought to drop him a note similar in tone. He asked the patient but eager Ernest, "How long will it take you to get this back to Sister Finbar?"

"About ten minutes, sir."

"Good." He turned the note over and took a pencil from his pocket to write a reply. He thought better of it and went to his desk, retrieving his pen and a bottle of ink. Carefully dipping the pen and struggling to put down the letters in his best possible penmanship, he wrote on the back of the note that he would be at the convent fifteen minutes after the boy delivered the message. There were one or two splotches, but he would have to let the imperfections stay. He gave the note back to Ernest, who acted as though he were entrusted with the message that would save the life of a pope. Van Poole spent a few minutes tying up loose ends at the police station and then started out toward Immaculate Conception. Upon arriving, he knocked at the rectory door. Mrs. Trent showed him into the kitchen, where Sister Finbar was waiting.

"Did you and Tommy have a productive visit, Detective?"

"We accomplished several things, Sister. Most of all, I think I may have established a level of trust that was absent earlier."

"Sounds to me like you didn't get anything out of him and you're just trying it make it seem like it was not a waste of time." Sister Finbar had a way of making Van Poole feel like a schoolboy who had misbehaved. He half-expected a ruler to come crashing down on his knuckles. He unobtrusively eased his hands into his coat pockets.

"Well, actually, I did get some very useful information."

"So he told you what he knows of all the mischief about?" asked the nun.

"He shared some things that will be useful in my investigation," said Van Poole.

"What about the golden cup?"

"What? What golden cup?"

"He said that a man named Champ has a golden cup. With jewels mounted on it. That's what golden cup, Detective. If it is a bejeweled gold chalice, it likely belongs to this church."

"Well, that may be so, but right now it's in the evidence room at the police station. Can you prove it belongs to the church?"

"There is proof enough."

"I may need more than just your say so, Sister."

"I arrived here in 1902. The year after the fire that destroyed everything. You remember that?"

"I remember it well, indeed, Sister."

"Well, then. We were teaching school in tents. The convent was about half-built. We helped out as we could. Sister Margaret — God rest her soul — and I were trying to salvage what we could of the church records. Marriages, baptisms, census counts, bequeaths, whatever we could manage to find amid the burned rubble. All the important papers were stored in the rectory in cabinets and cupboards. Of course, the rectory and every other building was destroyed in the blaze. So there was not much to work with. Scraps of paper here and there. Mostly ashes, but a few usable bits and pieces survived. I found some pencil drawings. Rough sketches, you know. They appeared to be a study for a portrait. I presumed that the priest serving at the time suffered from the type of vanity that would make someone want to have their portrait painted. In this case, perhaps his vanity will be of some use to us. Some of these drawings had been colored in with ink or watercolors. One of the sketches shows the priest at the altar, lifting a golden chalice covered with jewels. There are more sketches of the chalice alone. A thing like that doesn't pop up every day, does it now, Detective? Sure and if someone has it, I aim to secure it back where it belongs."

"Father Donal had told me that there had been some talk of such a chalice but that no one could remember any details."

"Father Donal would take no notice of it unless it was put in front of him with brandy in it," she snorted.

The detective was taken aback but hid his surprise at her blatant disrespect. "Sister, where are these pictures now?"

"I have no idea. The focus in those years was rebuilding, not gathering up bits of burned paper. I'm not aware what may have become of them."

"Do you think you could try to find them?"

"I'll do my best. We have had several priests and nuns come through here over many years, each one certain to know more than the last about conserving archives. Who knows where they all might have ended up?"

Activity at the auditorium tent was slowly ramping up as veterans who had been fulfilling official duties — chairing committees, drafting by-law changes, and promoting the proper curriculum of American history in public schools — began to show up, sheafs of paper in hand, motions for approval ready. Charles F. Davidson called to order the final plenary session of the official business of the 1914 United Confederate Veterans Reunion. He droned through several announcements that he hoped would be of general interest before the serious discussion began.

The mess tents close for good at nine o'clock.

The medical clinics stay open until midnight. Anyone needing medical attention after that will have to go to the hospital.

Veterans whose membership in their local camp is in good standing are welcome to stay camping in the park until sun-up on Monday, after which local ordinances against camping in public parks will be enforced.

All vendors must cease operations at nine o'clock.

The brass band contest finales will begin at seven this evening on the field by the walking bridge at Hogan Street.

The fiddling contest, which is not an official activity of the reunion, it having no significant historical relevance, but is carried on because of its enormous popularity, will also be at seven o'clock, on the commons of Dignan Park.

At nine, the most awaited activity — Rebel Yell demonstrations — will begin, also in Dignan Park.

The Commander managed to bore enough people into leaving so that the dozen or so actual committee chairmen could huddle in the corner and do what they needed to in order to adjourn for another year.

Chief Wilson stuck his head in the door of the detective squad room. He'd learned not to go any further than that. Any deeper penetration only led to an erosion of respect in both directions. "Van Poole! My office. Right away."

"Yessir, Chief." He looked around the room at his fellow detectives, wondering if any man there had a clue what the chief was riled up about. Nothing but blank faces. He headed toward the chief's office.

"Well, Lambert, this might be the night." His boss using his first name was disarming. The previous chief called him Lambert only when he was angry or impatient with him. Luther Wilson used it to signal that less-than-formal terms were appropriate for the moment.

"What do you mean, Chief?"

"I mean, I finally got Miz Brandywine to invite me for supper. It will be a small group, I am lead to believe. Several gentlemen registered at Phelps House have made last minute meal plans, so I have earned a place at the finest table in Jacksonville. Leg of lamb. Can you believe my luck? Leg of lamb!"

"Looks like things with the lady are certainly going your way, Chief. Congratulations."

"Thank you. Now, I would like you to drive me up there about seven-thirty this evening. I believe she will serve dinner around eight. No, let's plan to get me there about seven. I recall that her stock of sherry is worth an extra half-hour of my time. Is there anything you need to tell me about the murder and mayhem?"

"The Alden James murder gets more and more complicated with each new clue, sir. That nun, Sister Finbar, thinks that the gold cup we found in Champ's room belongs to Immaculate Conception Church. You seem to think that it is somehow attributable to Weasel Jones, who maintains that he got it from Champ, who found it in a box of salvage materials that fell off a train. Of all those characters, I am inclined to believe only the nun. But she has no proof at the moment. Another item that I have not had the time keep you informed of is the loose diamond."

"Loose diamond?" The chief was incredulous. He arched his eyebrows an impossible distance. Of course it was impossible for his men to keep him entirely up to date on every little development, but a loose diamond is a significant development in any case.

"Yes, sir. I picked it up under the bridge where we found Mr. James' body. I have had it looked at by a couple of people who know about these things, and it is a diamond of the highest quality. My first thought was that the diamond was the offering that Mr. James was going to make to the church. That makes a lot more sense than traveling with a big bundle of cash money. And Weasel Jones, as I have found out from Tommy Whitehead, specializes in swindling jewelry from innocent people. My initial theory was that it was a swindle gone bad, Weasel had to get violent, and in the ensuing struggle, lost the diamond in the dirt under the bridge."

"Now, you see how easy it is when you start putting facts together, Van Poole?" He had reverted to using the surname, a signal that they were back to business. "That is an intriguing theory, completely supported by the facts as we know them, and it comports with the behaviors of the individuals we know to be involved. Good work, Van Poole. Wrap it all up on Monday, now. That's a good man."

"Not so fast, Chief. There may be a few more details that need careful attention."

"Of course there are always details. We'll deal with them

Monday. Right now I need you to drive me home so I can prepare for dinner tonight. I don't think I'll wear my dress uniform. My dark blue suit will be perfect. Leg of lamb!"

Lily and her volunteers were in the process of closing down the medical tent, packing up medical supplies, putting medicine bottles into portable wooden cabinets, packing bandaging supplies in leather cases. They had no patients in the tent and the demand for their services was dwindling. "Wrapping things up here?" asked Van Poole, smiling at his wife. He had taken the chief to Phelps House and had a few hours on his hands.

"Yes. By midnight tonight, it will all be over. Everything back to normal. Of course, I'll be back at the depot clinic tomorrow."

"All in all, not a bad couple of days, I guess. Once you got past the dysentery thing."

"Well, speaking of that, one more case has been reported. But it is no concern of ours. Has nothing to do with the reunion. Janie told me that she heard from a friend at the hospital that a man came in with the same symptoms. Except that he was not hallucinating. All of our men kept wailing about a Persian wizard."

"Oh, the chief is not going to like to hear that."

"Why not?"

"The mayor had been bragging to all the visiting dignitaries how the chief came up with the idea to snuff it out. I'm sure he thought he would get an award from the city or the veterans or something."

"Well, according to Janie's friend, it is not snuffed out."

"But the patient isn't not a veteran, you say?"

"No, some local person. A lawyer named Vernon Piggott."

"What?" sputtered Lambert.

"Vernon Piggott. Janie said he's a lawyer and someone brought him in this afternoon with the same symptoms we saw here on Wednesday."

"Yes, but what was that you said about hallucinating?"

"Oh, some of the men who took sick here were carrying on about a wizard. One of them said a Persian doctor was going to make him young again. It all sounded so unbelievable, I took it to be fever-induced."

"Hmm. Well, dearest, I have some things to do. If I am unencumbered later, I'll come back and assist you."

"Where are you going?"

"To visit a sick friend."

Van Poole was certain visiting hours were over, but he knew how to get hospital nurses to bend the rules. That was, after all, how he'd met his wife — cajoling with blandishments and finesse, or what he thought was finesse. When he got to the hospital, the head nurse told him visiting hours were over and besides, she added, "Mr. Piggott may very well have a communicable disease of some sort, and visitors are not allowed in his room anyway." This news was delivered with an attitude of haughty contempt that would rival French revolutionaries sending an aristocrat to the guillotine. This head nurse was one medical professional no amount of blandishment could move. It was his incredible luck that Doc Otwell was making some notes at the nurses' station. As he started to walk away, Van Poole caught him and said, in hushed tones, "Doc, when was the last time you got your hands on some good Irish whiskey?"

"Oh, that's been a long time, my boy."

"Well, sir, I can bring you a bottle of the finest, if you'll persuade that nurse in charge over there to let me in to visit a patient."

"What patient?"

"He was brought in earlier, and I think there might be some thought that he has the same dysentery that was going around the campground."

"Oh, that fellow. It's not dysentery. Don't rightly know what's wrong with him, but it is not dysentery."

"I know that, Doc. That's why you have got to let me talk to him."

"Nurse! Let this man in to visit that patient who came in this afternoon."

"Doctor, you said he was to have no visitors. And it is getting very late."

"I said, let him in. You want me to write it on the chart?"

The nurse reluctantly escorted Van Poole to Piggott's room. The patient was pale and clammy, in a semi-conscious state, rolling around in the narrow bed as much as space would allow. "Piggott!" Van Poole intoned lightly. "Piggott, wake up."

The lawyer struggled to open his eyes. When he saw Van Poole, he wasn't sure if he'd gone to heaven or hell, but neither suited him at the moment. He opened his mouth and some wheezes and noises came out, but nothing coherent. He kept trying. "Detective ... dete ...

wha' happened? Where am I? Weasel. Wease ...."

"Did you drink some of Weasel's whiskey?"

"Yeah. Somethin' 's not right. Somethin's bad wrong." Then he vomited a bloody mess into a bucket at his bedside.

"Chin up, Piggott. Maybe you'll survive. Then again, who knows?" Van Poole left the room and headed back to Dignan Park.

Chapter 15

Chief Wilson's thoughts of the Phelps House's fine sherry were immediately banished when he noticed a large cut-glass canister of amber liquid. He opened it, sniffed, and his nose was pinched by the spicy fragrance of good rye whiskey. He poured himself a generous portion and added just a splash of water. Martha, clucking around like a mother hen, introduced him to some of the other guests who would be having supper with them.

"These fine folks are Captain and Mrs. Abner Winters of Lexington, North Carolina. And I am sure you know Commander Davidson. This is his lovely wife, Nora."

"Very pleased to meet all of you," drawled Wilson. They stood in the parlor, enjoying their drinks and making meaningless small talk. "I do hope you folks have enjoyed the reunion."

"Why, this has been one of the best reunions I can remember," gushed Captain Winters.

"I guess we have Commander Davidson to thank for that." Chief Wilson stood next to the uniformed dignitary and raised his glass. "To Commander Davidson. Thank you for your hard work." Everyone in the room took his cue and raised their glasses as well, accompanied by a few huzzahs and good shows, and several other unintelligible remarks that were no doubt congratulatory.

"Mrs. Davidson, however did you get the Commander to abandon his post and join us for supper?"

"This is the final night of the reunion, and he's going to be out there till heaven only knows when. I convinced him that a shower and shave and a nice relaxing meal would serve him well."

"Ladies and gentlemen, I believe that Marcie would like us to proceed into the dining room," announced Martha Brandywine.

The sumptuous meal began with a robust crab soup. It was a recipe that Martha's mother had learned from some fishermen back in the days just after the war, when they lived north of town and food supplies were scarce. Any conversation that was not about the soup was barely given notice. A sweet white wine made from local muscadine grapes was a perfect accompaniment. Between the soup and the salad course, each diner was served a tiny scoop of lime sherbet. The salad earned rave reviews as well. Fresh hearts of palm, pickled okra and wedges of local tomato were served with lettuce and dressed with peanut puree dressing. Few words were spoken through the salad course, which was followed by another minute amount of lemon sherbet. Clean plates and wine glasses were brought out and one of the dining room staff poured a rich red wine from Bordeaux, which Wilson knew presaged a fine leg of lamb. His anticipation was rewarded as the dutiful Marcie brought in a platter of roast leg of lamb; two legs, to be precise. The meat was presented with an array of roasted root vegetables. She walked around the table, holding the platter at a level so that all the guests could see the magnificent entrée, then stopped at the sideboard to carve it. Aproned kitchen staff carried the platters piled high with the slabs of lamb, bending low so that the guests could serve themselves in turn. Finally, they were presented with a dessert of orange sherbet atop sponge cake. As the last person savored the last bite of the confection, a large display of cheese, fresh fruit and nuts was placed on the table.

By eight-thirty, the sated diners were rising from the table and Mrs. Brandywine invited any so inclined to linger in the parlor for a glass of Madeira or other digestive of their choice. Commander Davidson approached Chief Wilson and spoke in a slightly hushed tone, not wanting to be overheard, "Chief, that poor fellow who was killed, Alden James."

"Yes," said Wilson.

"Your detective had been over to see me about him earlier in the week and I was able to assemble some information for him."

"Yes, yes. Very helpful, Commander. I am certain Van Poole is close to making an arrest."

"Well, one of the men who was in Jacksonville with him during the war came to see me today. Fella by the name of George Townsend. He tells me that he has remained close friends with James through the years. He is devastated by the news and wants to do something to help. Perhaps he can liaison with the family, do something about returning his belongings, something like that. He's leaving town tomorrow, so I told him I would inquire."

"Very touching. Serve with a comrade through a war and have him die in a senseless street crime. Very sad. And I understand his sentiments more than you know. I will tell Detective Van Poole to meet with him tomorrow at the police station and they can discuss what might be done. Tell him to be there at nine in the morning."

"That's wonderful. I'll pass that on to Townsend." Davidson put down his glass and announced, "I thank you all for the wonderful company, but I must be leaving now. The highlight of the reunion is upon us, and I must be there for the introductions."

"I thought your official duties were concluded, Commander," said Wilson.

"No. The Rebel Yell demonstration is about to start, and I need to be there for that. It's a spectacle not to be missed!"

Even in the parlor, with the door closed, sipping after-dinner drinks, everyone was aware of the Rebel Yell demonstrations going on in Dignan Park.

"Yeeeeee-aaaaaaaa-heeeee-owwww!"

"You wouldn't think these old men would be capable of generating such noise," remarked one of the guests.

"Heeeee-eeeeeee-aaaaaa-yowwwww!"

Commander Davidson introduced each contestant separately, calling out his name and his current camp affiliation. It was really not a contest, but a demonstration. Over the years, however, it had come to be called the Rebel Yell contest, although no one knew how to declare a winner. Volume? Clarity? Crowd reaction? So they called it a contest, with every entrant being declared a winner. And yet there were still men who lost bets on the outcome.

"Yeeeeeee-howwwwww-yaaaaaaa-heeeeeeee!"

A relaxed Chief Wilson was enjoying the evening when the thought occurred to him that this was his first visit to the Phelps House that hadn't ended in disappointment or interruption of one kind or another. The fleeting thought proved false when one yell from the contest was so loud, it rattled the windows on the back side of the house on the fourth floor. Up in the private area, Finance Commissioner Tad Ferguson, mind numbed from too many tugboats, body depleted after a second hour with Candy, rose in a stupor when the blood-curdling scream reached his ears. He wrapped a large towel around his naked body as best he could, ran down the back steps and through the kitchen, screaming "Call the police! Call the police! Something terrible's happenin' out there. Call the police!"

He burst through the kitchen door into the parlor, his large, sweaty body — looking for all the world like a monster-sized oyster out of the shell — barely covered by the towels, the redheaded prostitute in a frou-frou dressing gown scurrying in a few seconds behind him, pleading, "Mr. Ferguson, it's all right. Come back upstairs. Mr. Ferguson?"

"What is all that horrible screaming out there? It sounds like the devil himself come to harvest sinners. Who is ... oh, uh, Chief Wilson. Get over there and find out what in the hell is going on."

"Commissioner Ferguson, what in the hell are you doing here? Did you take a room for the night? A bit early to be turned in for the evening, isn't it?"

"What? Never mind what I'm doing here. What are you doing, sitting here drinking wine, when some sort of mayhem is occurring right outside? Get out there and restore order!"

"There's nothing to get upset over. They're doing the Rebel Yell there. Some people find it quite entertaining. And many attend properly attired for the event," said Wilson, stifling laughter with only moderate success.

Candy stood back behind the kitchen door, with a robe pulled around her naked body. She spoke quietly. "Come on, Commissioner Ferguson. Everything's all right. Let's go mix another drink." He followed her, too befuddled to be embarrassed.

Van Poole came in the front door and headed toward the parlor. As he slid open the door, Mrs. Brandywine and Candy were getting the commissioner calmed down and back upstairs. "Are you ready, Chief?" asked Van Poole.

"Yes, I think I am. Martha, thank you for a delightful meal and stimulating company."

"So glad you enjoyed it, Luther. That will be one dollar and seventy-five cents."

"What?" gasped the astonished police chief.

"One dollar for supper. Fifty cents for the whiskey and twenty five cents for the glass of port," Miz Brandywine ticked off the chief's purchases on her fingers.

"Oh, uh, certainly. Must pay for the privilege. And let me say that it would be a bargain at twice the price." He handed her two dollars and did not wait for change.

On the way to Wilson's house, the chief complained to Van Poole, "I'll tell ya, Detective, I never thought she'd expect me to pay. I came at her invitation. Don't you think that an invitation to dine precludes any remunerative responsibility on the part of the invitee?"

"I would certainly think so, Chief."

"It'll be a cold day in hell before I grace her establishment with my presence again. Oh, by the way, Commander Davidson told me that one of Alden James' compatriots wants to help out somehow. A close friend who fought with him, apparently. I told him to come by and see you at the office tomorrow morning at nine. I know it's Saturday, but the man is scheduled to leave and probably has a train to catch. You won't mind, will you?"

"A day off would have been nice, but Lily is right back on duty at the depot tomorrow morning at seven, so I might as well speak to the man."

They drove on in silence for a few minutes.

"And you missed quite the excitement at Phelps House. It seems that Commissioner Ferguson has taken a room there for the night. The Rebel Yell demonstration woke him up and he came barging in through the kitchen, wrapped in a towel, wondering what manner of mayhem was going on outside. It was quite comical, really. Martha and one of her chambermaids settled him down and got him back to his room."

"Yes, I'll just bet they did," Van Poole laughed.

"They must have a back staircase. He came from that direction, not down the front staircase into the foyer."

"I'm sure it's part of the fire code, that a rooming house must have a back staircase."

"Of course. That must it. A back staircase. I've never noticed a back staircase."

Saturday mornings at police headquarters were usually quiet, after the revelers of a Friday night had been processed and jailed. Only a few civilian employees worked on Saturday. The chief, if he came in at all, was there for a few hours, late in the morning, just enough time so that someone would offer to buy him lunch. So Van Poole was confident he wouldn't be disturbed by much at nine o'clock on a Saturday, when Alden James' friend was expected.

George Townsend was shown into the detective squad room.

"Good morning, sir. My name is George Townsend, I'm from Columbus, Georgia. Commander Davidson suggested that I stop by here this morning," said the old man. He was rough in appearance, with unkempt hair, grown down into bushy sideburns. Townsend smiled, showing a mouth that was severely out of balance concerning teeth. Van Poole had been suspicious from the instant the chief mentioned this man. Where James had been clean and well-groomed, this man was sorely lacking. His left hand was bandaged, with stains of blood showing through.

"Indeed, Mr. Townsend. Come in, come in. Sit down, please," said Van Poole. "Would you care for some coffee? I'm afraid our station-house coffee is not much better than your campground coffee, but it is all I have to offer."

"Some coffee would be right nice," said the man. Van Poole busied himself with the coffee, leaving Townsend seated next to his desk.

"What happened to your hand?"

"Uh, shekking ersters. Had a stubborn one and the blade slipped. Cut myself fair to the bone."

"Eating oysters in May? That can be risky."

"At my age, everything is risky."

"Yes. Well, let me first express my deep sympathies to you. Losing a close friend is very difficult, I know."

"Oh, yes. Thank you, sir. It were quite a shock," said Townsend.

"So you served here in Jacksonville with James, did you?" asked Van Poole.

"We was both here at the same time. Don't know how he got here, but I got sent here with a group from Columbus after we finished fighting up along the Tennessee line. They said some fellers needed help down hereabouts, so some of us volunteered. We did more trouble-making than what you'd-a call fightin', but we was here when them Yankees took out."

"I understand you two had quite an adventure while you were here. Chasing down Yankees who were looting a church."

"Oh, we did indeed, sir. It weren't much really, though. Them Yankees was drunk as coots and we tricked them into thinking a bottle of piss was whiskey. Well, they took to that right quick and while they was trying to figure out what the hell was going on, we grabbed the stuff they'd stole and took off running." The old man was laughing as he told the story, clearly enjoying the memory of it.

"But you weren't able to recover everything they had stolen?"

"Aw, hell. We was lucky to get what we could. If them guys hadn't been so drunk that they couldn't shoot straight, I might not be here today."

"Yes. You were very brave. And the church is very grateful, but the priest and nuns really wish they could have gotten everything back. There's still a chalice missing, several gold crosses, and a lot of other valuables."

"I don't know nothing about that. I just come here to see could I help out any with James' things, you know. I got a train to ride this afternoon." It was beginning to work, Van Poole thought. Townsend was beginning to feel uncomfortable about something.

"So, you and Mr. James kept in close touch over the years since the war?" asked Van Poole.

"You might say that."

"I might say that, but what would you say, Mr. Townsend?"

"We kept in touch."

"You ever go visit him?"

"No. Not much. I think I might have stopped to see him once."

"Up in Ashland, Tennessee?"

"Yeh."

"What about when he lived in Ashland, Kentucky?"

"What? That's what I meant. Ashland, Kentucky. Ha! You're messing with ol' Towney, ain't ya?"

"You two were awarded some kind of medal for recovering the church loot, right?"

"Yessir. I got it right here." Townsend pulled his coat open and showed where he had an assortment of medals and pins affixed to the inside of his jacket. Most were contemporary medals and badges from his United Confederate Veterans camp, but several were original medals presented to him during the war.

"That's very impressive," said Van Poole. "Why wouldn't James come here and accept his medal?"

"I don't know, Detective. I can't speak for him. Now, can we talk about how I might help? I would be right proud to be able to take his possessions back to his family, his wife and daughter. It's a mite out of my way, but I want to do it."

"Certainly, certainly. I'll go get his stuff for you." Van Poole left the squad room and walked across the hall to the property and evidence room, to sign out the suitcase full of Alden James' belongings. He had been in the evidence room earlier that morning and had removed the flat diamond he'd found under the bridge. He left the gem on his desk, not in an obvious place, but where Townsend would surely see it when he sat down. When Van Poole came back, he said, "Here's everything. We were going ship this whole suitcase back. That's what we told Miz James in our telegram, but I know she will be moved by your trouble to take these to her personally. Nothing in here but a bunch of old clothes anyway. Don't know why she was so anxious to get everything back."

"Well, who can figger how a woman thinks, eh, Detective?"

"Most people just decide to leave old clothes with us, and we give them to charity. I tried to suggest that to her, but she would not hear of it. I hear she told the man at the funeral home not to let the police keep anything, because she was afraid we might steal something. She must have thought he had something valuable with him. Nothing here but some old clothes and toiletries."

"Like I said, Detective — no accountin' for what a wife does. Well, if I need to sign something, let's do that so's I can get to the train station and see if I can get this shipped."

"You going to ship it back to her in Asheville?"

"Yessir. Oh. There you go again! Ashland."

"I thought you were going it take it to her yourself."

"Well, yes. I was going to have it shipped to Ashland, then I will have to change my ticket from Columbus to Ashland. But, uh, in case I can't get my ticket changed, at least his suitcase will get there and I can send her a telegram to pick it up."

"That seems quite impersonal, Mr. Townsend. Not the way I

would want to treat the womenfolk of a good friend and war buddy. I could just ship the suitcase to her directly from here and leave you out of it."

"No, no. Don't do that. I tell you what — I will keep the suitcase with me the whole time and deliver it to Miz James personally," said Townsend.

"That's a much better plan." A sharp tap! tap! sounded on the door and a well-dressed man entered. A large badge pinned to his vest indicated he was the Chief Constable of District IV of Duval County, Florida.

"Detective Van Poole?" asked the man. Without waiting for an answer, he began to read from a document he held up in both hands. "I have here a writ for the impoundment of evidence to be considered in the matter of the unnatural death of one Alden James, which took place in Duval County, Florida. All personal belongings of the aforesaid deceased shall be inventoried and held in a secure manner at the Jacksonville Police Station until an inquest into the death of the aforesaid deceased can be convened."

"Oh, my, and just in the nick of time. Constable Anderson, I was just about to release all of these personal belongings of Mr. James to the custody of this man to return to his family. I'm glad you got here when you did."

"Well, it's a good thing you didn't do that. The judge don't like people messing about with evidence of his homicides," said the man with the writ.

"What does this-all mean?" asked Townsend, confused by the events.

"It looks like a judge is going to want to examine these items, so I'm not going to be able to release them into your custody. I'm sure Miz James will understand."

"Well, that don't hardly seem fair, Detective. That little lady ought to be able to have her husband's things back," protested Townsend.

"Nothing to worry about, Mr. Townsend. We will ship it all to her as soon as the judge concludes the inquest."

"Oh, uh, yeah. Well, kin I just look at ol' Alden's stuff once more before I have to leave?"

"Certainly, Mr. Townsend. I'm going to have to do a full inventory of it now anyway, so you can have a look through it with me. I had it entered in the evidence book as 'suitcase full of clothes and personal belongings.' That won't do now that a judge wants them for evidence." The detective popped open the suitcase and started sorting things out. "Let's see, all the shirts, collars and ties over here. Now undershorts over here. Look, he had an extra suit folded up in here. I hope he was ready to pay to get that pressed. I wouldn't be seen outside of my bedroom in such a wrinkled mess. Let's see here, an extra pair of shoes, looks like about five pairs of socks. And here is a very nice wooden box, which I guess has all his shaving equipment. Mighty fancy way to carry an ordinary razor blade and soap around."

"Detective Van Poole, I reckon when the judge is through with all this, Miz James would have no objection to letting y'all donate it to charity. But can I take his shaving kit? I mean, that is something that she might really want, you know, to keep a memory of him."

"Oh, I don't know. The judge said he wants it all as evidence."

"What in the world kind of evidence can a man's razor be?"

"That's why you and I are not judges, Mr. Townsend. There are secrets to administering justice that we could not begin to comprehend." Townsend was thinking of everything he could to try to get the box. He finally left the police station, frustrated and angry.

As soon as he was down the block a bit, Van Poole called the other detectives who were at the station that weekend morning, and they had a laugh at the conniver's expense. "Well, that ought to keep him around town a couple of days, don't you think? And it looks like he pocketed the diamond, to boot."

"Yes, he did. I was peeking through the door and saw him stick it right in his vest pocket," said Jim-Toe Henry. He had just come back from washing his hands and one of the men cautioned him to stay out of the detective squad room, because they had someone in there they were watching. So, he watched, too.

"Good work, Jim-Toe. Anderson, you did a great job reading that writ. Wasn't sure that a Pinkerton man could pull it off. And who did you get to fix that wooden case? It was quite bashed up."

"We got a cabinetmaker who's serving thirty days for disturbing the peace. Had to promise to cut two days off his time. Told him it was a jewelry box that belonged to the judge's wife."

"Well, all in all, a rather productive Saturday morning. Let's all take the rest of the day off. Anderson, why don't you suit up a disguise and tail Townsend for a few hours and see what he does? I'll wager he'll be lurking about."

Lambert Van Poole was now racing against time. It was nearly eleven o'clock and Chief Wilson was likely to walk through the door any minute, and if that happened, the detective would be on the hook to buy him lunch. He was busy making two sets of notes. The set for the official case file regarding his interview with Townsend contained factual statements, dry as tinder: *Subject appeared confused about where the victim had lived. Claimed acquaintance with victim and his wife and daughter. It is known that the victim is widowed and only relative is granddaughter.*

In his private notebook, Van Poole wrote: *Townsend is gullible, easily tricked, a thief and a poor liar. He took the diamond that we left as bait, indicating that he is just a natural thief, or that he knew the significance of it. I will find out which of these is true.*

Then he had to get James' possessions sorted out again and placed back into the property and evidence room. He almost made it out the door — almost.

"Van Poole!" shouted the chief as he strode down the hall toward his office. "Glad you're still here. I have a few minutes of paperwork to get through, then I thought we might take a stroll up to Finley's for a nice Saturday lunch. I'm in the mood for some oysters."

"But, Chief, I was going to get all these items in the evidence room sorted out and ..."

"Good, good. Finish up what you're doing there and I'll be ready in a few minutes."

"Don't you think I ought to go and keep an eye on things up at the campgrounds?"

"Not necessary. After all the festivities last night, I cannot imagine a single soul stirring up any trouble. Thousands of old drunks, screaming and hollering at the top of their lungs — I would be surprised if any of them could even talk this morning. No, it will be a docile day as far as Confederate veterans are concerned. Honestly, based on the behavior I observed in the park last night, you'd think someone got through our impenetrable perimeter with a couple of wagonloads of cheap whiskey."

"Um, yes. Well, just think what might have been had we let our guard down."

"Come on. Let's get going. Finley's oyster supply may be finite."

"Sir, we are well into the month of May. I don't think Finley will have another oyster until the fall. My usual Saturday routine involves meeting Lily at the Golden Horn for lunch. You are welcome to accompany us there."

"The Golden Horn? At the train station? I suppose I could find something appetizing there. Do they offer a courtesy for policemen? Well, that doesn't matter. Bring the Cadillac around front and I'll meet you there in a couple of minutes."

The three of them sat in a booth at the Golden Horn. Lily, as usual, had a bowl of soup that she mysteriously managed to consume without tilting the bowl, slurping the liquid from the rim, or spattering a single drop on her crisp white uniform. Wilson quizzed the waitress as to the origin and preparation method of each item on the menu, but was unimpressed with her knowledge of kitchen operations. Unhappy with all of the answers, he played it safe and ordered a bologna sandwich. Van Poole had sausages and sauerkraut. He let out an exasperated sigh when they brought the dish with three plump sausages. He bisected one of them so that he had exactly one-and-a-half sausages on either side of a large mound of sauerkraut, creating a symmetrical balance that had been sorely lacking from his life the past few days. He started to eat, taking equal-sized portions from alternating sides of the plate, starting on the left. After each even numbered bite, the plate displayed perfect symmetry. Such a comfort.

"Well, Miss Lily," said Chief Wilson, "What can you do to help me convince your husband to act on the facts of a murder case that are staring him right in the face?"

"Oh, he can be stubborn at times, can't he?" she responded playfully, lightly kicking Lambert's shin under the table.

"Perhaps you two would not be so quick to gang up on me if you knew all the facts that I know," Van Poole defended himself.

"Come on, Van Poole. You know me as man of action. When faced with an indisputable set of facts, we must act." He turned his attention slightly toward Lily. "Like the dysentery outbreak. It was clear what needed to be done. I showed the mayor and others the way to act. This is how we get results."

"Speaking of that, did you know we had one more case show up?" asked Van Poole.

"No. When did this happen?"

"It's not even a veteran. Vernon Piggott is in the hospital with the same symptoms as all the sickened soldiers. And it's quite serious, from what I was able to gather. He may not make it," said the detective.

"That doesn't make sense. How would he get the dysentery? He was nowhere near the reunion."

"He got it from the same place as the veterans, but it's not dysentery," said Van Poole.

"I didn't know you were diagnosing patients for the hospital, Van Poole. What a multi-talented man you are. Surely there must be more to this story."

"There is. A lot more. And I do not think that this is the best place to discuss an active police investigation and unpleasant bodily functions. Shall we simply enjoy our lunch and go into this in greater detail back at the station?"

"Well, to the extent that a bologna sandwich can be enjoyed, I will follow your suggestion. Although if you're going to contradict me, I would have preferred that you did it over roasted oysters at Finley's. Lily, how do you put up with this man?"

"Usually I just say, 'Yes, dear' and ignore him — but this time he might be worth listening to."

"Oh, is that a fact? You're in the medical field. How can this man say there was no dysentery? We all saw it. You treated those men."

"It was glass."

"What in the world do you mean, it was glass?"

"Little shards of glass is what tore the insides of the patients to pieces. That's what the post-mortem of the poor man who died showed us. And laboratory examination of samples from the other men bear this out. I have no doubt that tests on Mr. Piggott will show the same."

"Don't you see, Chief? It was the moonshine. It was full of

broken glass. We're going to be able to get Weasel Jones good this time. But not for killing Alden James."

"No? Not a killer? All right. The rest of the story after lunch." He pushed away his plate with half a sandwich left on it. "They better not charge me full price."

"I've got few more things to wrap up this afternoon, Chief, and they won't wait. How about if I take you on home, and then maybe tomorrow we can meet and I will give you a full briefing."

"Take me back to the station. I still have some work to do. I'll take the streetcar home."

After Van Poole deposited Chief Wilson at headquarters, he went to Immaculate Conception Church. He drove slowly down the alley that separated the church and rectory from the convent and school. Sister Finbar had Tommy out painting the potato shed. While she had not restrained him this time, Van Poole noticed she was keeping her lasso close by. "Good afternoon, Detective," said the nun politely.

"Good afternoon, Sister," nodded Van Poole. He looked at her lasso and slightly arched an eyebrow.

"He had that look on his face. Like he was going to make a run for it. But his soul is still suffering."

"I'm glad you can interpret such things. May I interrupt the work for a few minutes? There may be more that he wishes to tell. If he can be persuaded."

"Most certainly. Tommy! Come talk to the detective." The busy child put down the paint brush and walked hesitantly over to them.

“What’d I do now?” he asked, with a ready-to-fight tone.

“Ooh, lad, now that seems like something you should be telling, not asking. Now, you answer the policeman’s questions, and I will go see to some lemonade.” Sister Finbar went inside, walked straight to the tiny chapel and said a decade of the rosary before she started squeezing lemons.

Van Poole strolled over and sat on the picnic table. “I’m surprised you’re still here, Tommy.”

“Where am I goin’ to go? Mister Butch told me they was gonna to fence off that space under the bridge to keep me out. I got to live somewhere and the food here ain’t bad. The work is right hard sometimes, though.”

“How long you think they’ll let you stay here?”

“I don’t know. They keep wanting me to live in the orphanage, but that ain’t for me. I’ll sleep in the shed.”

“I hope you don’t try to run. I’m not as good with a lasso as Sister Finbar is. I’d have to shoot you, or run you down with that fancy automobile if you took off. In a way, that would make it all a lot easier for me.”

“What do you mean?”

“See, if you took off running, I would have to come chasing after you and run you over and probably kill you. Oh, that would be so sad. Three, maybe four people would show up at your funeral. Bury you in an old pine box out at the paupers’ graveyard right by the incinerator. But then, I could take all this crime and mischief that’s been going on all through the reunion and pin it all on you. We got witnesses that put you up in the park every time something bad happened. You'd be dead, so you couldn't deny it. And anybody who knew anything about you would believe it. The chief would be off my back about clearing these cases. That man who was fixing the bridges, he would be glad not to have you in his hair ever again. Weasel Jones, as worthless as he is, would be glad to be rid of you. Hell, I bet even Sister Finbar and Father Donal would be happier without you around stealing potatoes all the time. Now, I know it's not the truth, but I have got to come up with something. Why don't you help me, Tommy?" Van Poole was ready for anything. A kid like Tommy, raised without benefit of much moral parental guidance, learns to live by instinct rather than judgment. It was like cornering an armadillo — very difficult to predict the next move.

Tommy went for the tried-and-true, poor-little-orphan-child, abandoned to his own devices. He started in a loud, halting voice. "How am I s'poze to know the truth? I'm just a little kid. Not even got a mom or dad." The tears came in full flow, now. "I just try to get by the best way I can. I don't know nothin'. Why'nt y'all just leave me alone? All I want is a potato every now and then." Tommy overplayed the hand and Van Poole burst out a laugh.

"Sister Finbar was right. You really got the 'poor little me' act going pretty good. Tommy, let me tell you something. We've all had enough of it. Now you tell me everything about Weasel Jones, moonshine whiskey, Champ and his golden cup, and anything else that comes to mind. Because the free ride is over. Sister Finbar is a saint and this work you've been doing around here is a little slice of heaven compared to the life that awaits you at reform school. You may not have a grasp of how serious all this is, Tommy, but let me tell you, you are up to your neck in murder and foul deeds. You are way beyond stealing rings from tourists. Murder is serious."

"Aw, hell, I don't care what you say. Just do whatever you're gonna do."

"Look, Tommy. You've had a rough go at life so far. I know that. I didn't have it so great, either. But you can turn things around. Stop acting like such a little shit most of the time and you'll get along fine. Your mom and dad were right worthless. Everybody knows that. But they're gone. You have one chance to straighten out your life and it starts with you telling me about Weasel Jones and Champ's magic cup."

The boy hesitated for a long moment. He did all he could to avoid eye contact with the detective. He thought about living under a bridge instead of in a house, with a roof over him. He thought about stealing potatoes instead of eating pork chops. He thought about having clean clothes to put on once in a while. He thought about not having to trick little old ladies out of their jewelry. "Well, Weasel told me that he was goin' to sell the veterans the chance to be young again. I didn't understand what he meant. Still don't, really. But he dressed up in a fancy robe and put on a fake beard and went around the campground telling folks he had a tonic that could make them young again. They give him two bucks and he would pour some of that moonshine I sold him into the big, fancy cup, then they would drink while he whooped and hollered some kind of Indian war chant. I bet he made a couple hunnert dollars doing that, and he only gave me two dollars for the moonshine. So I still say he owes me some money."

"That's good, Tommy. Maybe I can help you get some of that money. But I have to know where you got the moonshine."

"If I tell you, they'll probably come and kill me."

"If you don't, you may have to take the punishment for this all on your own, and they'll get off scot-free."

"It was them two guys fixing the bridges. They were hiding crates of it up under all the bridges, and I saw them, so they allowed as how they'd cut me in on the deal. They had a whole building down the creek full of the stuff. They were going to let me sleep there, but they put me to work first. I had to put a drop of iodine in each bottle, then paste a little slip of paper over the cork, then paste a label on the bottle. They said that would make it look real. Well, I lost my grip on a whole case of it and it fell into the sink and all the bottles busted. I tried to save what I could of it, and drained it into some other bottles. I knew they'd be mad at me, so I left and sold what I had to Weasel. That's what he was selling to the old soldiers."

"Tommy, you have done the right thing by telling me. The bad part of it is, that moonshine was poisoned and full of glass. And it made all those old men sick. One of them died. Now, you are just as responsible for that as Weasel is, but I am going to do everything in my power to keep you out of trouble. You've got to stay here with Sister Finbar and do everything she says. Don't you take a notion of wondering off somewhere. If you do, I can't help you any."

"Yessir," said Tommy, much mollified. Sister Finbar came out with a pitcher of fresh lemonade and some cookies.

"Well, are you two getting along all right?"

"We are indeed, Sister. Tommy was just looking forward to

getting back to work painting the potato shed. Then I think he will be very enthusiastic about the next set of chores you have. Right, Tommy?"

"Yessir."

Sister Finbar handed Van Poole a large envelope. "Here, Detective. The pictures I told you about. You will be very careful with them, won't you? No one knows I took them."

"Yes, Sister. I will be very careful."

Lambert Van Poole slowly drove north on Walnut Street. He spied Weasel walking toward his apartment, so he turned off Walnut and drove down the alley behind the building. He found the camphor tree that Tommy had climbed to get into Weasel's apartment and started up himself. Tree climbing was a dangerous activity for young boys. It was treacherous for grown men. He made it up to the second floor after freezing up a couple of times. He slid open the window and climbed in. He was grateful the tree was a camphor, one of the easier trees to navigate for a primate built for ground travel.

Weasel eased the key into the lock on his door and unlatched it. Then he used a second key to open the lock on the knob. He went into his apartment and was astonished to see Detective Lambert Van Poole dressed in a white robe and red fez. "Howdy, Weasel. How would you like a drink of a magic elixir that will make you feel young again?"

Weasel turned to run, but got only halfway down the stairs when Van Poole dropped a huge coil of stolen chain at his feet just as he hit the landing. The coil weighed about twenty-five pounds and landed right on Weasel's foot, sending him tumbling the rest of the way down the stairs. "You son-of-a-bitch!" he hollered. "What are you doing here?" He made an attempt to get up, but was practically immobilized by the pain of falling down the stairs, and being tangled up in chains designed to keep boats from drifting off to sea.

Van Poole walked slowly down the stairs and stared at Weasel for as long as he could without laughing. "Get up. And pick that chain up before someone comes along and trips on it. Get upstairs. You and I need to have a talk." They made their way back up to Weasel's apartment, Weasel limping and bleeding slightly from a cut over his eyebrow. The interior of the apartment looked like a warehouse for a general merchandise distributor. Clothes were hanging on ropes strung from one wall to another. Rugs were rolled up and standing in the corner. Crates of wine sat stacked up. And more — boxes of cigars, lots of jewelry. Van Poole sat him down in one of the few chairs in the apartment, and put the twenty-five pounds of iron chain in his lap. "Why don't you tell me about your magic potion, Mister Wizard?"

"Oh, for heaven's sake, Van Poole. Is that the best you can come up with? All right. I took some whiskey, cut it with some laxative and sold shots of it to a bunch of old men. Probably gave them a cleaning out that they needed anyway. I am only ashamed at how easy it was."

"Well, let's see. You told them you were a doctor, so I think that's practicing medicine without a license. We add that to the peddling charge, and the selling moonshine, and it gets serious, but the old man who died from drinking it? That makes it murder. And people hang for murder. Especially the murder of a poor old Confederate veteran. That won't set well at all around these parts."

"What are you talking about? I didn't kill nobody."

"Oh, that's right. You were in jail during most of the reunion. You never got the news. All of those old men took deathly ill from your tonic. One of them died."

"How do you know it was from me?"

"Because you gave two bottles to your attorney, who right now is lingering near death in the hospital."

"It was nothing but whiskey and castor oil!"

"And glass. And iodine. And God knows what else."

"You'll never prove I killed anybody. It was that little kid who sold me the moonshine. He's who ought to go to jail."

"I won't have to prove much. In a case like this, where the old man just dies in the clinic tent at the reunion, there will no doubt be a coroner's inquest. You won't stand a chance, Weasel. Don't you leave town, now. Judge Travis is going to want to see you at the inquest." Van Poole knew Weasel would not leave town. There had to be fifty thousand dollars' worth of merchandise stuffed into that tiny apartment. Weasel could not walk off and leave that. Van Poole grabbed a box of cigars on his way out the door.

Detective Van Poole drove back to the police station. The chief had gone home, and the evening shift was a few hours away from their muster. It was a quiet Saturday afternoon. No doubt that would change in a few hours when the sun started to set and the saloons started to fill up. The Confederate veterans still camping in Dignan

Park would be sobering up before long. They had no official activities to occupy them, so they would make their presence known in the whorehouses, bars, billiard halls and bowling alleys. It was sure to be a busy night — but for now, it was a quiet place to work.

Van Poole retrieved the chalice from the property room and compared it to the sketches that Sister Finbar had given him. Some were rough sketches, others more detailed, the lines and shading crisp. Then there were the watercolor renderings. Every detail was exquisitely represented. The red rubies, shaped like little droplets of blood. The dark green emeralds and finally the resplendent diamonds. Except for the one that came loose. It was a definite match.

The Saturday shift commander walked into the squad room. "Hey, Van. One of them Pinkerton men left you a note."

It was difficult to decipher, Pinkerton not requiring penmanship skills as a hiring standard, but apparently George Townsend went to the train station, *chased* or *cashed* in his ticket, depending upon how you interpreted the sloppy handwriting, went to the DeSoto Hotel and took room 207. So he was going to stick around a bit longer. Van Poole hatched a plan. Like most of his plans, he had no idea how it would turn out, but he had a vision for it. He returned the sketches to the envelope and locked it in his desk, then took the chalice back to the evidence room.

Chapter 16

Van Poole nudged the Cadillac slowly down the alley behind Phelps House. He stopped a little way down the alley from the garage where Champ lived. It was getting on toward dusk, which was in his favor, as he didn't want to be noticed. He got out of the Cadillac and took a short reconnaissance walk around. No one in the house was paying any attention to what was happening out back. He knocked abruptly at the door to Champ's living quarters. "Hey! Open up in there. This is the police."

Champ slowly opened the door and peeked out. "Wha' you wan'?"

"I want you to come with me."

"Why? You 'resting me?"

"There's an old friend of yours in town who wants to see you."

"Get outta here."

"Get in the car, Champ. Now."

The old man hobbled out the door, using a long stick to help him balance, since his newel post had been taken. "Never been in a ottymobeel before. Is it safe?"

"Being safe in an automobile is the last thing you need to worry about, Champ." Van Poole took the stick away from the man, removing the possibility of it becoming a weapon. They drove to the Desoto Hotel. "Follow me," ordered Van Poole. They walked through the small lobby, past a man at a check-in window, either getting his room key or hiring the services of a prostitute. He didn't look up, and Van Poole and Champ started up the stairs. Champ moved slowly on each step, but they finally made it to the second floor. The detective tapped on the door of room 207.

"Who's there?" came a question from inside.

"Detective Van Poole. I think I have a way that you can help us."

The door opened to reveal a puzzled George Townsend. He smiled at Van Poole, and said, "Hello, Detective. I, uh decided to stay on an extra day or so ... how did you know I was here?"

"I'm a policeman. I make it my business to know where people are." There was silence. Champ was standing behind Van Poole, but Townsend saw him and a look of combined confusion and fear came across his face. "I think you two know each other. May we come in?" Townsend stepped back and let the two men enter.

"You must be mistaken, Detective. I don't think I've ever seen this man before. It's not a face I would forget."

"Well, I bet if you think back about fifty years, you'll remember it. Try to imagine this man as he was right before you smashed his head to pieces."

Townsend stood silently. He looked at Champ, then at Van Poole. "They was looting a God-danged church! What was I supposed to do?"

"I don't know. I wasn't there. But you came to town looking for that golden chalice, didn't you?"

"I was trying to be helpful. Get his belongings back to his wife."

"You haven't laid eyes on Alden James since the war. He was not active with the veterans group. He doesn't even have a wife. And you don't even know where he lives."

"But this Yankee," he pointed at Champ, "was robbing a church. A church right here in your town. I would think you would be on my side."

"I might be if I didn't think that you were here to do the same. What about the loot you took? Are you here to return that? There are no sides to this, Mr. Townsend. Just right and wrong."

"This here Yankee killed Alden James. Trying to get that stolen chalice back."

"It might have been this Yankee. But it might have been you. Trying to keep him from returning the chalice and telling what he knows about your war loot. How about we put the two of you in jail until we can cipher it all out?"

"Detective, I don't know nothing about war loot. And why would I kill Alden? He and I served together. He was my friend. We looked out for each other. A soldier don't go killing his own kind."

Van Poole moved closer to Townsend. Their faces were two inches apart. Intimidation was part of the plan, but so were logistics. Townsend did not back down, which helped Van Poole, who reached straight to Townsend's vest pocket and pulled out the diamond. "This is why you would kill him. You came to the police station trying to get your hands on that chalice. But you settled for a diamond."

"What? Hey, that's mine. I was going to pawn it to cover my expenses of staying on here a few days to help you out."

"You're not a very good liar, Townsend. And that has earned you a chance to experience Southern hospitality, at taxpayers' expense. Now let's all walk calmly downstairs together and sit in the lobby. Champ, you go first." Van Poole figured Champ would move slowly enough to keep Townsend from trying to run. When they got to the lobby, Van Poole called the station and had the jail wagon sent over.

After the Townsend was removed, Van Poole drove Champ to jail. He did not think it prudent to put the two men in the wagon together. It was possible that they could cook up a plan together. It was more likely that one of them would kill the other. Neither outcome would be particularly useful. "That still my cup," protested Champ.

"No, it's not. And you're going to jail, too. Maybe to a military prison — when I figure out how to do that."

After Van Poole booked Champ into the jail, he drove down Bay Street beyond the eastern edge of Downtown, where Hogan's Creek emptied into the St. Johns River. He crossed the rickety wooden bridge over the creek, looking for the shack that Tommy had described as the place where Butch Warren had stored his moonshine. He turned north into a wooded area that was sparsely developed with warehouses and industrial properties. He followed a dirt road to a small building and dock with a narrow barge moored there. He parked the car and approached the building on foot, hearing the murmur of voices from inside. He took note of the signs all around. No Trespassing. Warren Maritime Construction. It was dark and he could see the bright glow of an oil lamp. That meant he had no hope of peeking in a window without being seen. He got as close as he could to the building to try to listen to the conversation.

"All right, Bert, our sales were not as robust as we might have hoped, but that was no fault of yours, so you won't be penalized too much. The partners have authorized a twenty-five dollar advance on our agreed-upon amount of one hundred dollars."

"When do I get the rest of it?"

"When I report all the details of the operation to the partners, I am sure they will authorize payment of the remainder. I will certainly advocate on your behalf. I would say we should be able to finalize everything by next Friday."

"OK, Mr. Warren. Don't forget about me, now. I done everything you asked me to, so I earned it."

"Don't worry, Bert. I shall give a glowing report on your diligence. Now you get on out of here and let me finish up the books. You come back here next Friday afternoon and we'll settle everything up."

Van Poole moved as quietly as he could back to the car and drove back to the station. He found the four Pinkerton men sitting in the lobby, drinking coffee. "Are you guys still on the clock?" he asked.

"We are under contract through Tuesday at midnight. Then we head back to Atlanta."

"You going to be lazy 'til then?"

"Unless somebody gives us an assignment, yes."

"Everybody get on some dark clothes. We're going on a moonshine bust." Then he turned to the Watch Commander. "Lieutenant, you might want to call the chief and tell him I'm taking all the Pinkerton men on a moonshine bust. If he wants to join us, he better get here quick. Everybody be back here in twenty minutes." Van Poole went to the squad room and retrieved some dark clothes that he kept in a closet for just such occasions.

When he went back to the lobby, the lieutenant said, "Chief says to come by his house and pick him up. He'll be ready."

"Damn. That did not go the way I wanted it to," Van Poole grumbled. He'd hoped the Chief would send word for the raid to go ahead without him.

The four Pinkerton detectives piled into the Cadillac with Van Poole behind the wheel and headed to Chief Wilson's house. Wilson was waiting in a rocking chair on the front porch. A jail wagon followed. The carload of men pulled up and Wilson rose, dressed all in black, but somehow looking as though he might be going to a bank to negotiate a loan, except for the shotgun that rested on his shoulder, the breech open. The men squeezed as much as they could to make room for the chief. Van Poole steered the car down to the waterfront.

They approached the building on foot the same way Van Poole had earlier, the detective signaling to keep as quiet as possible. They crept along when Chief Wilson stood up straight and said, "Van Poole. You've got us in the wrong place altogether. This is the headquarters for the Warren Maritime Construction Company. Look. There's a no trespassing sign."

"I know. Now be quiet, Chief. This is where they've been storing it. This is the center of the whole operation."

"I find that hard to believe. Mr. Warren is a successful engineer. The mayor will not be pleased at us harassing such a respected friend and businessman."

"You can believe what you want, Chief. He's got untaxed liquor in there, and the books detailing the whole operation."

The men walked around the front of the shack that faced the creek. A six-foot-wide dock was all that separated the building from the water. They heard voices from inside. Occasional laughter. Counting money. The detectives were all armed and ready for action. Van Poole directed them to stay to the side of the door as he opened it with a long oak branch. He pushed it ajar slowly and signaled to each man to hold his place.

"Hey, shut that door, will ya, Tad?" came a holler from inside.

Commissioner Tad Ferguson went toward the door. "As I was saying, I don't know how they found out about the liquor, but that little Bert Lewis don't get his hundred dollars 'til the rest of us get our return. Only fair, am I right?"

"You're right. Don't worry about Bert. I'll make it up to him." Chief Wilson turned white as a sheet. As soon as the commissioner reached the door from the inside, Van Poole signaled and the whole team went rushing in, loaded guns pointed.

"Don't anybody move! Don't anybody touch anything. Hands where I can see them!" shouted Van Poole. Chief Wilson came walking in behind him, carrying the shotgun. The look on his face was some mad mix of embarrassment, astonishment and anger. He made a show of closing the shotgun, but kept it at his side.

"Van Poole, cuff 'em. Rex, count the money. Cedric, start taking these crates of whiskey out to the Cadillac. You! Whatever your name is … search the place for any other contraband or stashes of money. Look for any floorboards that are loose or wall panels that could be a hiding place. You know what to do. Get moving.

Commissioner Ferguson, you seem to have worked up quite a sweat."

"I, uh, uh … uh, I … well..." Water was cascading in streams down Ferguson's face.

"Shut up, Tad," said Warren. Then, to Chief Wilson, "You men are making a big mistake. We are simply conducting a final accounting of my work for the city regarding bridge repair." Then he whispered toward Ferguson, "Don't say a thing and we'll have a lawyer straighten this all out in no time."

"No, I don't think you will. Because before you can call an attorney, I am going to call the mayor. I wonder what he will think about a finance commissioner conspiring with an engineer to sell untaxed liquor."

"That may not be a great idea, Chief," said Warren with a big smile. "Let's allow him to enjoy the success of the reunion for a day or two before you get him involved in what you will see is a huge and embarrassing mistake."

"Oh, I think he'll want to know about this right away. Get them out of here!" The chief walked around the shack, barking orders. "Count that money again. I don't want any mistakes. Did you climb up in the rafters? They might be hiding more whiskey up there. Well, what are you waiting for? What about this desk? Did someone search this? You call this a desk? This is nothing but a stack of orange crates and lumber!" He kicked it over and stormed out of the shack.

Van Poole and the Pinkerton Agents finished moving all of the evidence from the river shack to the police station. Butch Warren and Tad Ferguson were booked into custody. The money, the ledger books and the moonshine liquor that wasn't get sold were all placed into evidence. It was late on Saturday night, and Chief Wilson came around to the thought that not alerting the mayor might be the best course of action for the moment. He called Van Poole into his office. Van Poole sat across the desk, a little nervous. Wilson was untested in such circumstances as these, and Van Poole didn't know what to expect. He might crumble under the pressure. He might leap across the desk at Van Poole, attacking him as the nearest threat to his employment and position.

Wilson poked his head out the door and looked up and down the hallway to make sure no one else was close by. He came in and walked slowly around the desk to his chair. He reclined and stared up at the ceiling, counting cracks in the plaster as usual. He was silent for a moment, then, still staring at the ceiling, said, "Van Poole, what in the living hell is going on?"

"Well, sir, you were there. We caught Commissioner Ferguson and Butch Warren counting the money from selling illegal liquor. It's not really very complicated. I don't know if you want to call the mayor in on this or not. That's up to you. Frankly, situations like this are exactly why I don't ever want to be chief of police."

"I'll call him tomorrow. What about the Alden James murder? Is it connected at all?"

"No, not really. But I will allow that we have a big confusing mess. You were right about some things, but dead wrong about others."

"Please enlighten me."

"The murder of Alden James goes all the way back to the war. The way I have this figured, Alden James and two other Confederate soldiers, one of whom was this George Townsend who Commander Davis sent to see me, confronted three Union soldiers who had just looted Immaculate Conception Church. One of the Yankees was Champ, Miz Brandywine's maintenance man. One of the Rebels yanked a newel post from a staircase and used it to give Mr. Champ that distinctive look his head has. Doc Otwell, believe it or not, has clear memories of Champ and his shattered head. When he was doing the post-mortem on Alden James, he said he had seen the same head wound only once before. So, these Confederate soldiers relieved the Yankees of their loot and returned it to the church. But not all of it. They each kept a little something. Souvenirs, you know. Well, Alden James must have felt some tremendous guilt about it all these years and when the reunion was scheduled for Jacksonville, he decided he would attend and return the chalice. This fellow Townsend found out that James was here. How, I don't know. Maybe he checked with James' home camp, figuring he might want to come and see Jacksonville, but somehow he became aware of him coming to the reunion. Champ, working there at Phelps House, must have seen James when he checked in and kept a close eye on him. Since he had stolen the chalice first, he always figured it was his, fair and square, and aimed to get it back. So, when Alden James set out for Immaculate Conception Church on Monday morning, Champ followed with the idea of getting his chalice back. Somehow, he enticed James to the bridge and returned the favor from fifty years ago, by caving his head in with the very same newel post that had been used on him. Then he took the chalice. They must have scuffled over the thing a bit before Champ got violent. The photographs show evidence of that. But also, in the fight, one of the diamonds from the chalice came loose. I spotted it in a photograph and went back to retrieve it. You remember me telling you about the diamond, right, Chief? Well, when George Townsend came to the station this morning, he stole it. Right off my desk. So we got the two of them in jail right now."

Chief Wilson stared at Van Poole. He looked like a drowning man, crying out be saved, his cries unheard. "But, but ... what about Weasel Jones? I thought he was behind all this."

"Weasel is too chicken-shit to do something like this. He borrowed the chalice from Champ, dressed up like a wizard and went through the campgrounds selling shots of that moonshine as a youth-restoring tonic. That led to what everyone assumed was the dysentery outbreak. Killed one of the veterans. Then he gave his last two bottles to Vern Piggott and killed him. So we got him for two murders."

"Stop! All this talk about wizards and moonshine is just too much for this late hour. Take me home. I will talk to the mayor tomorrow afternoon."

"Chief?"

"What?"

"Don't be surprised by anything, OK?"

"What do you mean by that?"

"Do you think all of this moonshine business could be going on without him knowing about it? We need to be careful about who else might be involved."

"Who else could possibly be involved?"

"I don't know, Chief. I need to have some conversation with Mr. Warren and Commissioner Ferguson to find out. I'd like to know where they got the moonshine. And where they got the counterfeit tax seals for them. Tommy Whitehead may be of some use to us still, as well as a man named Bert Lewis, who I understand was helping Mr. Warren."

"Van Poole. You have a vivid imagination. I suppose the next thing you'll be telling me is that the staff dormitory in the attic of Phelps House is actually a brothel."

Van Poole laughed. "Let's get you home, sir. You sound tired."

When Chief Wilson had estimated that the mayor would be through with his Sunday obligations that afternoon, he called him.

"You'll never guess who we found last night celebrating ill-gotten gains."

"What the hell are you talking about, Wilson?"

"Tad Ferguson and Butch Warren. Apparently they were behind the whole moonshine operation. I don't mind confiding in you that this deflates my esteem for the virtue of civic leadership."

"There must be some mistake, Chief."

"No mistake, Mayor. I saw it all with my own eyes. Was not the state beverage commissioner with you at dinner the other day? I'm glad he left town before we discovered all this. What an embarrassment that would have been."

"Indeed it would have been. Listen, do me a favor. Before either of those men gets a lawyer, or is questioned about this, let me come down there and have a little talk with them. Maybe I can shame them a little bit for sullying the good reputation of public servants everywhere."

"I'm not sure that comports with good investigative procedure, but maybe we can bend the rules this time."

"I'm on my way."

What the chief did not know was that Van Poole had already begun his interrogation. He was questioning Butch Warren about the origin of the illicit liquor.

"That is not liquor, Detective. I can see how one might make that mistake, but that is a solvent that I use on creosoted lumber when I am trying to shore up the joints. You have to prime the joint with that solvent before you pack it with oakum. Gives it a nice tight seal. This sloppy police work of yours is not going to end well. Unless you release me and return to me my supply of chemical solvent, I will sue this city for false arrest, illegal imprisonment and anything else I can think of. You call Commissioner Clark, he'll set you straight. He knew what we were doing down there. Shoring up the bridge supports so that they didn't collapse."

"I will make sure to question Mr. Clark. In fact, the chief is on the phone with the mayor right now, so I suspect that the both of them will be here directly."

Bert Lewis might never have been mistaken for a man with an overabundance of intelligence, but he was smart enough not to leave things to chance. While he was working with Butch Warren hiding whiskey, he managed to steal several large of coils of maritime-grade rope and hide it under the bridges on the opposite sides of the creek from the moonshine. It was not easy to do working right along with Butch, but Bert managed it. When he was arrested down at the city docks trying to sell the stolen rope, he was unable to concoct a story to give an account of himself. Van Poole became aware of his arrest and arranged to interview him.

"The last guy we arrested for stealing rope got hung with it. This is that maritime rope. It's got a little give to it, so it does not break your neck immediately, which is good. But it does cut off your breathing, so you suffocate, kind of slow-like. Which is not so good. And it leaves a terrible rope burn all around your neck. The morticians have a hard time with those, you know, making you presentable."

"I ain't stole them ropes," Bert shouted, on the edge of hysteria. "Mr. Warren owes me some money, so I took them in lieu of cash. If he comes up with the rest of my money, I'll give him his rope back."

"We know that's not true. You were caught trying to sell it. So even though you are sitting here lying right to my face, I'm going to give you a chance to escape being hung. You tell me all about Mr. Warren's whiskey operations and you get a one-way train ticket to Athens, Georgia."

Lewis proceeded to tell him about renting the space under the bridges, and that Mr. Warren had some associates who had a load of moonshine to dispose of. Van Poole, acting on a hunch, sent a telegram to the state alcoholic beverage bureau. It responded that yes, two hundred and forty cases of moonshine in pint bottles had been seized in Central Florida and had been sent to the Jacksonville office to be inventoried and stored as evidence, and ultimately be destroyed.

After the Grand Jury indictments, the criminal trials dragged on for months. Butch Warren, respected and successful surveyor, road-builder and bridge engineer, was on trial for possession and distribution of untaxed liquor. He convinced the jury that he was in possession of what he thought was creosote solvent which he had been using on the lumber supports of the bridges as he undertook to ensure the safety of visitors to Jacksonville for the Confederate Veterans Reunion. Tad Ferguson was tried for conspiracy to sell untaxed liquor and a host of other charges that go along with abusing public office. He supported Butch Warren's story about the solvent. He said that he was actually trying to buy some of the solvent from Warren so that the city could use it on other projects when needed, instead of having to pay a high-priced bridge engineer every time a bridge showed some deterioration. Just being a good fiduciary steward of the public's money. That's when the police came barging into Mr. Warren's place of business, thinking they were busting up a moonshine operation. The defense relied heavily on the mistaken identity of the liquor and attacked the veracity of most of the state's witnesses as unreliable, seeing as how they didn't have any advanced training in chemistry.

Mayor Langen expressed anger and disappointment in his fellow public servants to such a degree, that he was never even suspected of being involved. Hank Clark was also on trial, but had the confidence to stand trial without an attorney doing his objecting for him. He treated the proceedings as just another meeting of the city commission, claimed no knowledge of moonshine — and people believed him. Bob Vincent, state beverage commissioner, testified that he had entered into a contract with a man named Bert Lewis to destroy 240 cases of moonshine liquor. Mr. Lewis apparently did not live up to his end of the bargain, and there was now an outstanding warrant for his arrest, if anybody knew his whereabouts.

Judge Sandberg Travis convened a Coroner's Jury and began an inquest into the unexplained death of the veteran in the campground. About two hours into the testimony, Judge Travis had a nervous breakdown from the stress, stood up, took off his robe and ran out of the courtroom. The next day, the governor appointed Travis' wife Genevieve to fill out his unexpired term. She reconvened the inquest, which came to the conclusion that Bert Lewis, whose whereabouts remained a mystery, was responsible for the death of the veteran and Vernon T. Piggott, by putting poisoned moonshine into circulation. Weasel Jones bore some culpability, and should surely have been prosecuted for illegally selling untaxed whiskey. And she found that Weldon Beauchamp, better known around the neighborhood as Champ, was responsible for the brutal death of Alden James and was bound over to circuit court to stand trial. When all was concluded, she filed the death certificates, the transcripts of the inquest and copies of all the subpoenae and got about eighteen dollars for her trouble.

City Councilmembers who had managed not to get indicted worried that the ongoing criminal trials would sully the good reputation of Jacksonville, a real shame after having just hosted such a successful Confederate Veterans Reunion. In order to deflect attention away from the foibles of the few who were caught up in the detective's never-ending quest for justice, they decided to appoint a committee to investigate changing the name of Dignan Park to Confederate Park, and erecting a suitable Confederate memorial commemorating the successful reunion for generations to come. Several citizens' committees were appointed for the purpose of selecting the appropriate adornments for the park once it officially had its new name. A bandshell would be nice. Maybe a couple of statues.

Lambert Van Poole was authorized to take the chalice out of the property and evidence room and return it to Immaculate Conception Church. He had Tommy Whitehead in the car with him when he went to the rectory that day. They were shown into the priest's library where Father Donal and Sister Finbar awaited. The priest, the nun and the detective looked at the chalice and compared it to the sketches that had been made so many years before and had somehow survived a war, a fire and that most destructive force of all, vanity. Tommy sat quietly while they did this, successfully resisting the temptation to steal any of the several shiny objects that lay around the room. Van Poole also had the loose diamond, the one that should have been mounted on the base, which had come loose in the struggle under the bridge. He thought about having a jeweler remount the stone before presenting the chalice to the priest, but the cost of having that done exceeded the wildest notion that Van Poole may have had. As they sat in the library, Father Donal offered coffee to everyone. Van Poole accepted, Sister Finbar had tea and Tommy had a glass of milk. They talked about the events of the past several weeks, trying to focus on the more pleasant moments.

"Well, the first order of business is to get that diamond remounted. I am sure Mr. Goshell knows someone who could do it. He will probably even pay for it. Then what do we do with it? Sister, any ideas?" asked Father Donal.

"Oooh, Father. You should be knowing better than to ask me. When you think of the children we could feed and clothe, the sinners we could save with the money from that, what choice is there? But of course, if you think that it would serve a greater purpose through liturgical use, who am I to argue with such theology?"

"Sister, it may surprise you, but I think the same as you do. We could sell it. That is certainly one choice. I could keep it and we could become known as the church with the jeweled chalice. Can't see what earthly or heavenly purpose that would serve, except possible enhancement of the collection plate. Certainly something to be considered. We could turn it over to the bishop of the diocese. Let him decide what to do with it. I suppose I shall have to pray and meditate for a bit before I come to a decision. Thank you all for your help."

As they all stood, Tommy picked up his small, cheap suitcase. "Tommy and I went shopping. We got him some decent clothes that he can wear to school. And some work clothes, in case you aim to keep him chopping wood, sorting potatoes or painting," said Van Poole.

"Oh, that's lovely, Detective. Every child in the orphanage does something to earn their keep. Of course, we will have to leave him enough time for his studies."

After everyone left, Father Donal sat at his desk. He prayed. He read his daily office. He read Bible passages. He did everything he could think of to help him decide what was to be done with the now-legendary chalice. It was so beautiful, yet had brought such misery. He went to a cabinet in his library and brought out his finest bottle of cognac. Before he would do anything with the chalice, he reasoned, he should check it for leaks. He poured some brandy in it. Swirled it around. Examined the chalice closely. Surely the Lord would allow him a nip of cognac from the beautiful vessel. After all, Tommy Whitehead was moving into the orphanage and the good father would need all the strength he could muster.